The Ivory Seal

Also by Guy Stanley

A Death in Tokyo

GUY STANLEY

THE IVORY SEAL

BANTAM PRESS

LONDON · NEW YORK · TORONTO · SYDNEY · AUCKLAND

TRANSWORLD PUBLISHERS LTD
61–63 Uxbridge Road, London W5 5SA

TRANSWORLD PUBLISHERS (AUSTRALIA) PTY LTD
15–23 Helles Avenue, Moorebank, NSW 2170

TRANSWORLD PUBLISHERS (NZ) LTD
Cnr Moselle and Waipareira Aves,
Henderson, Auckland

Published 1991 by Bantam Press
a division of Transworld Publishers Ltd
Copyright © Guy Stanley 1991

British Library Cataloguing in Publication Data
Stanley, Guy, *1945–*
The ivory seal
I. Title
823.914 [F]

ISBN 0-593-01916-4

Typeset in 11/12pt Century Schoolbook by
Chippendale Type Ltd., Otley, West Yorkshire.
Printed in Great Britain by
Biddles Ltd, Guildford and King's Lynn.

For my friends Kyoko
and Graham

Prologue

Above the crown of the road, where it peaked and curved and began a downward loop to the lake, she could see the mountain's misty, purple cone, with its plateau and slopes covered with snow, except where the sharp ridges of rock protruded through in long, grey lines like scars. Her heart raced, and her breathing was constricted by the high, tight obi which bound the plain, brown kimono to her frail body. She prayed to the gods of her religion for a car, or a helpful hiker or any form of human life except the ever closing voice, urging her to stop, she thought she could hear in her panic. But she pressed on with urgent shuffling steps, her breath emerging in sharp, rapid, cloudy bursts, her age gradually betraying her and panic beginning to confuse her senses. She had to rest at the top of the hill, slipping to her knees and tugging at the obi to ease the pressure on her chest. She looked back, but the long shadows in the fading light confused her. A row of pines on the hillside cast zebra-like stripes across the mountain road and she peered through frightened eyes towards the illusion of a figure which seemed to turn the corner below and merge with the flickering images created by the breeze and the trees. She thought of discarding the slipper-shoes, which flapped loose the more she hurried, but the road was gritty and coarse and slippery from melted snow. Instead, she leaned forward and fell to her knees, her head tucked almost at her waist, her hands clenched into her lap, and began to sob. Then, as if struck by lightning, her back straightened and the nerves in her face tensed. She looked across the road and reached for her handbag.

1

The youngest of the city officials was already swaying listlessly against the backrest of the floor-level seat, his ankles crossed in the well which lay hidden below the low table running across the centre of the room of soft new reed mats. Ten men, six guests with their four hosts, sat across from each other on cushions around the table now heavy with food. Each man contemplated at least eight dishes, from side plates of pickled cucumber and carrot and salads of vinegared sea-weeds to staple bowls of pungent soya bean soup and steaming sticky rice. They had started with transparent slivers of raw globefish, the guests marvelling at the danger they faced in eating this 'fugu' delicacy and the expense it would have entailed. They toasted on sake and moved quickly to follow it with beer, topping up each other as etiquette demanded, even though the glasses had barely been touched. The six Tokyo bureaucrats did not notice the self-restraint of their hosts, or how their glasses were kept filled and the choicest of dishes left for them. It was warm in the room and although early March the windows were drawn apart, and when the conversation ebbed, the diners could hear the rush of the Tone River in the gorge below the inn. They had worked dutifully on the Saturday morning in the ward council building and after three hours in the luxury mini-coach which picked them up they relished the relaxing sulphurs of an outdoor hotspring. All in their fifties, some wore longjohn underwear beneath the comfortable wrap-around kimonos the inn provided and in this style met their hosts, who were similarly dressed, for dinner. They were served by friendly, round-faced country women in kimonos who flattered the guests as instructed, topping up their glasses and describing the preparation of the local dishes.

In front of the inn two men stood smoking and talking in the early evening chill. The older man, his grey, thin hair parted down the middle, kept his hands crossed as he listened to the other, confirming with a nod each statement. Finally, the man from Tokyo, who would not be at the party, withdrew an envelope from the inside pocket of his jacket and handed it to the other on an open palm. No counting, no receipt. Only an exchange of bows, the innkeeper's deep and prolonged.

The fusuma doors opened again, and in practised fashion the team of waitresses shed their slippers with a flick of the heels and stepped up into the room. Most of the guests were already satiated and could only lean back, holding their cigarettes harmlessly in the air and admiring and marvelling at the plates of cold lobster with mayonnaise and skewers of tender breaded pork fillets laid before them. The food was unimportant, a mere part of the gesture, but another round of toasts seemed to revive the visitors. They were flushed and boisterous, speaking through mouthfuls of food and dribbling on to their undershirts which lay exposed as their kimonos loosened. Each in turn was encouraged to introduce himself formally to the hosts, who reciprocated, as their turn at the table came around, with a totally contrived personal history. With one exception, the senior member, the bureaucrats shared a similar background. Graduates of minor, second or third-ranking universities and with careers in one of Tokyo's twenty-three administrative wards, their current posts were in the land and housing planning department where they formed the senior core. The head of the delegation had a more distinguished background, moving between the metropolitan government and progressively senior posts in half a dozen individual wards. He now headed the land planning department of his present appointment.

The party broke up for a few minutes when the guests filed to the toilets and the inn staff cleared the tables. When the group took their places again, a bank of electronic equipment had been wheeled in along with a detachable microphone on a stand beside it in a corner of the room. The lights were dimmed and again the sliding door to the corridor opened. Six women, half the age of the inn's waitresses, entered. Eyes lowered, smiling reverently, one carried a lacquered tray with a pair of bottles of Johnny Walker Black Label whisky. The others brought ice buckets and small bottles of soda water which they placed on the table near the guest to whom they had been assigned. They were dressed in similar colourful western clothes. Short, tight dresses clenched at the waist with a belt and shimmering blouses with long sleeves buttoned modestly half way over their hands. Their hair was uniformly straight, cut across the shoulders and low along their foreheads, above faces which were thin and attractive and lightly tinged with colour. They were in their twenties, aspirant actresses, models and singers in an over-populated peer group where the demand was for a conveyor line of pliant eighteen-year-olds whose useful media life ended at twenty. At twenty-five, when reality dawned as the dreams and ambitions receded, they were left to pursue their fortunes in the floating world of the inns and pleasure houses.

The women sang, accompanied by synthesized music from the machine and the efforts of their enthusiastic but ill-coordinated guests. The songs were maudlin enka folk tunes, accompanied with rhythmic clapping from the visitors, who swayed in reasonable disorder. The oldest of the hostesses was twenty-eight and she was assigned to the department head. She poured him a second whisky and let him create one for her. Don't pressure him to sing, they had told her, or force yourself on him sexually. Let him move at his own pace. Try and sense his feelings

11

and respond accordingly. She knelt by his side, her dress above her knees, half way to her waist, her left hand resting over the fold of his kimono. One of the girls was singing a Japanese song from the Sixties while her designated guest stood next to her, leering proudly. Couples were dancing, the bolder of the men rubbing the buttocks of their partners who seemed to encourage them, at least doing nothing to discourage. One of the hosts refilled the glasses of his guests and slid quietly from the room when two of the civil servants and their appealing companions began a game of scissors, paper and stone. The penalty for losing, it was agreed, was to drink a thimble of warm sake in one gulp, not particularly onerous given the size of each shot but the clear rice wine is deceptively strong and the effects delayed by the euphoria of the moment and the food in the stomach. The men were reckless in their strategy and lost regularly. Giggling, one of the girls suggested that the punishment should be the shedding of a piece of clothing to which the men, emboldened by drink and secure in the dark and noisy womb, agreed. Another of the host group retired discreetly but stayed outside the room, his arms folded across his chest.

The senior bureaucrat sat back, hands inside the sleeves of his kimono, watching his red-faced juniors romping, laughing and relaxing. He drank sparingly, his feeling of comfort rising as the doubts he had felt when he had accepted the invitation receded. The young woman beside him had a ready smile and a bright, intelligent attentiveness that fell well short of the sort of deliberate condescension he found in the normal hostess bars of Tokyo. She drew his attention to the individual indiscretions of his colleagues and they laughed together like caring surrogate parents. He assured himself that the hospitality of his hosts was just another gesture, like all the others his department could expect during the year. Even so, the weekend at the mountain inn was turning into one of the more memorable of their invitations.

12

At the end of the table, in the smoky dimly lit corner there were now three couples playing the forfeit game. The men had little to shed, some losers having lost their watches and the boldest their undershirts, having first wriggled out of the top part of their kimonos. The women seemed to be losing more. Faking embarrassment, one lifted her legs from the well in the floor and turned to remove her tights. Her middle-aged reddened companion shrieked with mirth and leaned over to help. She thanked him, letting him peel the stockings slowly and making no effort to straighten her short, tight skirt which had become bunched beneath her. He held up the coiled fabric like a trophy. In the next round, the youngest of the girls, with large, round eyes and long hair dyed auburn, unbuttoned her blouse with studied laziness, allowing her man to draw it over her shoulders.

'Next round,' she said casually, while the men around her struggled not to stare at the transparent blue, strapless bra and the shallowest of cleavages it created.

The eyes of the general manager were diverted from his hostess to the activity at the end of the table and he laughed. 'My boys have drunk too much,' he said, as another of his employees lost a round and stood up to take off his gown. 'I'll have to put a stop to it.' 'Bucho-san,' the woman next to him said formally. 'Doesn't the general manager like to play sometimes?'

The man only smiled, accepted another whisky, this one more generous than the others. 'Do you like her?' she asked, motioning to the impromptu stage where the tall, thin-faced hostess was warbling a sad love-song with her eyes tightly shut. Her private guest sat slumped below a window, his head rolling languidly as he lapsed into sleep.

'Do you like her breasts?'

The leader of the visitors' group grunted approvingly, watching the singer's full blouse rise and fall with her breathing.

'Like a foreigner's,' he said admiringly.

13

The woman leaned across, letting her hair brush his face as her lips almost touched his ears. 'They're not real you know,' she whispered conspiratorially. 'Mine are.' The chief looked long at the singer, who spread her hands to draw the whole of her small audience into the climax of her song, and then at his companion who was proudly stretching her shoulders backwards to emphasize her charms. Released from society's demands by alcohol, under whose influence all events become pleasurable and acceptable, whatever the excesses, the senior civil servant reached over to touch the woman's neck. She let him trace her jugular with his thick, slightly scuffed fingers. He was not physically attractive but he was not very drunk and he did not have to press and paw to receive exquisite tactile sensations. 'Really?' he said, leaving her in doubt as to which body, hers or the singer, he alluded to. She slapped his arm playfully, letting him assume that he challenged her claim.

'Please be patient for a moment,' she purred, topping up his glass before sliding from the seat.

Outside, in the cold, clear February night, the man with the grey hair lit another cigarette and looked up at the glow along the upper floor of the inn. The music throbbed in the still air and the sudden and frequent outbursts of chortling and impassioned pleading told that the evening was going well and that the money was well spent. A figure approached him from the inn's brightly lit porch.

'Suwano-san?'

'Yes. It's me. Is it going well?'

'I think so,' the woman said.

'But is he drunk?'

She felt the cold through her inadequate party clothes and shivered.

'No,' she said, smiling. 'He's trying to act like a general manager.'

Suwano offered her a cigarette which she declined.

Turning towards the inn, she asked, 'Should I carry it through?'

14

The man removed his glasses and massaged his eye sockets with the tips of his fingers. He looked up, a broad grin on his face.

'All the way,' he said triumphantly.

Another loyal civil servant dropped from the festivities, shifting the backrest of his seat and crashing backwards into oblivion. His companion placed a cushion beneath his head and then joyously joined the forfeit game. There were two of the women left in the round, which was in its final stages. They turned their shoulders dramatically and then thrust the air with their choice. Their screams competed with the throbbing of the music centre. One gave an outburst of delight at the victory of her scissors over the open paper palm of her antagonist who squealed in mock horror at her own defeat. Both wore only brassières above the waist and the discarded skirts on the matting told the players and audience that the forfeits left were limited. The loser, the girl with the auburn hair who earlier had been the first to remove her tights, now pretended shame at the choices available to her and crossed her arms across her chest. She looked at her man for protection, and reached to embrace him, her sweat-moistened body sticking to his as the other two women clapped and chanted in unison as they demanded the penalty. The general manager sat alone, shaking his head indulgently, and watching the sliding door with expectation. His hopes rose when they opened but dropped when one of the older women returned with a tray of drinks. She was oblivious to the debauchery around her and departed with a blank mind. The department head's designated companion returned, her arms wrapped around herself as she complained of the outside temperature. To prove her point she ran a hand beneath his kimono, lightly depressing his flesh with her fingernails. He flinched but did not complain. Her lips were freshly touched in watery pink and a light perfume of flowers flowed from her clothes with each slight movement of her body.

15

'You didn't believe me,' she pouted, nudging her soft upper body into his. 'I want you to know what the truth is.'

The man looked around the room, now heavy with smoke and odours of human bodies in states of warm, sweaty arousal, and saw that to all intents he was alone with his companion. He let his hand be guided to her blouse and the tiny buttons seemed to split aside without much pressure. He kneaded softly and stroked, all the time feeling warm breath on his cheeks and a quiet pleading in his ear. They were all sensations new to him: tactile, sensuous, causing reactions throughout his body he could neither control or try to stop. For the first time in his life he held a full, responsive breast and let it slip through his fingers before retrieving it possessively. His hand traced her body down to her thighs which opened to him as they sat on the reed matting. The professional hostess's left hand drifted beneath the dishevelled kimono of her guest and brushed his underpants. Over his shoulder she saw the door slide open the width of a chopstick and knew that the man from the car park was making his final farewell.

2

Araki watched from his window as the young, fashion-
ably-dressed woman paid the taxi-driver. There was
urgency in her behaviour as she looked around while
the driver found some change and was half way out of the
car when she received it. She wore a brown, open jacket
with padded shoulders over a beige dress held loosely by
a broad belt. He heard her asking for him among the
vegetables arranged on the forecourt below him and
could imagine Teri, the daughter of the greengrocer
Tanaka, his landlord, running her eyes critically over
his attractive visitor.

Araki stepped over his futon, which, as usual, he
had neglected to air over the balcony, and closed
the shoji sliding door which separated his reed-mat
sleeping room from the cramped living room he had
decorated with western-style furniture: a sofa, two
chairs and a bureau with a portable television on its
top shelf. His guest would have to pass across his
tight kitchen, the only other room, apart from the
toilet-bathroom, for which he paid Tanaka seventy
thousand yen a month. He heard the rasp of her
footsteps on the metal stairway which gave access to
his apartment and its mirror image next door where
the landlord's nephew and his new bride lived. There
was an exchange of greetings, watched from below
by the greengrocer's daughter, and Araki motioned
to a pair of slippers and led the woman inside to
the sofa. He took the host's position on a matching
chair across from a low, glass-topped coffee table.

'How did you find me?' he asked with minimal formality, sliding a name-card across the table. He was surprised when the visitor reciprocated with an embossed version of her own which introduced her as Mariko Izumi, fashion consultant, with a business address in Aoyama. She smiled with embarrassment and motioned towards the card.

'I'm in the fashion business and as you can imagine that leads to contacts with the media, television, magazines, that sort of thing. I was talking over my problem with some of my friends and one of them, he's on a weekly magazine . . . '

'Which one?' Araki interrupted.

'Sorry? The friend? Nakao.'

Again Araki broke in.

'The magazine, which one was it?'

The woman had a narrow face with sharp features and mobile, intelligent eyes. She looked up in thought.

'The *Kanto Journal*. That's it. *Kanto Journal*.'

Araki smiled in recognition. He was relieved, or perhaps a little disappointed, that it was not the *Tokyo Weekly*, another of the cheap popular magazines which competed with dozens of similar titles in the Tokyo area for the escapist literary needs of Japan's educated white-collar workers, the salarymen.

Topical, often salacious, the articles varied little from week to week: the affairs of a popular actor; recurring bribery scandals in the governing political party; Japan's spectacular economic triumphs abroad, and a tongue-in-cheek revelation of the latest perversions in the bars and clubs of the floating world.

Three years earlier he had agreed to resign for several breaches of company discipline and for activities which brought the magazine official censure and disturbed the harmony within which was that unwritten code of acceptance and non-involvement amongst the stratified levels of Japanese society. The conspiracy he had exposed gave him a short-lived cult status among the

18

anti-establishment literati and had secured some writing assignments to supplement the royalties from the book he wrote describing the distribution of stimulant drugs and the involvement of legitimate business with the yakuza. He taught English privately to groups of bored housewives, exploiting the fruits of his university major and the year he had spent in London and Berkeley where he had perfected his spoken language. With his financial obligations to his ex-wife and son completed, he lived comfortably above the Tanakas' vegetable and drink shop which prospered in this bustling corner of west central Tokyo. The houses in the row backed on to a vacant lot used as a car park but no doubt destined to accommodate a ten-storey mansion-block when the price was right and the necessary permissions obtained.

'I'm sorry. You were saying how you found me.'

'The friend of mine, on the magazine,' the woman said nervously. 'She remembered the work you did on your own and how you were nearly killed for what you believed in. I'm sorry if I'm embarrassing you,' she said, noticing Araki's twist of the head. 'But she called some newspapers and your former magazine and eventually came up with your address. I hope you don't mind.'

Araki did not. He was quite flattered, as well as impressed by the poise of the youngish woman, late twenties he assumed, in front of him. The tone of her voice was proper without being condescending or overtly feminine and the words were precise and carefully chosen.

'She thought you were a private investigator,' she said, lowering her head as she realized the mistaken assumption.

'She was wrong,' Araki said gently drawing a cigarette from his shirt pocket. He was pleasantly bemused by the smart, confident woman who watched with tolerance as he fumbled with the disposable lighter in an attempt to coax it to life. She smiled and took a thin book of matches from her handbag and struck one for him. Her fingers were long and slim, the bones almost visible, and she

19

wore no rings. With her silky, black, shoulder-length hair cut straight in front, angular, narrow face and little make-up save for a light coat of pale pink lipstick on her heart-shaped mouth, Araki thought she might even be younger than he first guessed. She had telephoned the previous day and although he had been drunk he recalled she had sought his pardon for calling without a formal introduction, saying something about a missing parent. He ran his fingertips through his long but sparse hair as he struggled to recall the conversation.

'You mentioned your father.'

'My mother actually. A month ago, the beginning of March, my mother, Masako, disappeared. She left home in the morning and has never been back or seen again.'

'But surely the police . . . ?' he began, now remembering the media's stampede to report on the disappearance of an important businessman's wife.

She seemed on the edge of tears, making Araki regret his bluntness.

'I'm sorry,' he said, 'I interrupted you.'

'That's all right,' the woman responded, sniffling, her eyes fixed on some spot on the coffee table. 'The police are doing all they can to find her but obviously their resources are limited.'

In the awkward silence they both heard the click as the electric kettle turned itself off in the kitchen. Araki excused himself and returned with a pot and poured the steaming green tea into matching bowls.

'They can't look for her day and night,' she continued.

'Of course not,' Araki agreed, 'but there are special-ized agencies.'

The woman sighed. 'I've looked at those. They check the family backgrounds of new recruits to the big companies and chase after philandering husbands. They aren't very interested in a case the police are still actively looking into. Anyway,' she continued, pausing to sip the bitter tea, 'my father finds such people a little . . . er.'

'Sordid?'

20

Mariko nodded slightly and smiled, reluctantly.

'Is that why he hasn't come with you today? Because you both thought I was a private detective?'

'Partly,' she said, nodding again. 'He's very busy running his company and trying to cope with mother's disappearance.'

'But he didn't mind you coming here?'

'Yes he did,' she confessed. 'He wants the police to conduct the search without us suggesting by our actions that they are incompetent.'

'Not unreasonable,' Araki had to agree. 'But you still came.'

'My younger sister feels the same as I do. We want a little more effort made by someone who will not antagonize the police. On that basis father agreed to my coming.'

Araki realized she was not totally familiar with the events of three years ago when he came close to arrest for obstructing the police, but saw no point in elaborating. 'I'm not sure I can help,' he said. 'Like your father, I'm a bit tied up at the moment.'

Through the rear window a chorus of children's voices were calling Araki's name.

'Excuse me,' he said, shoving aside the futon as he passed through his sleeping room on the way to the balcony. He leaned over the concrete barrier protecting the narrow terrace. A dozen second-grade primary school boys, in jeans and T-shirts and wearing baseball caps, were gathered below his window.

'Araki-san,' they cried in unison. 'Let's play baseball.'

'I can't today. I'm busy.'

The children's voices faded and their faces creased with disappointment. The tallest, a round-faced lad in a Giants cap, stepped forward.

'But it's Saturday. You always catch for us on Saturdays.'

It was true, and he enjoyed coaching the bunch of enthusiastic youngsters on what was little more than a sand-lot.

21

'OK,' he conceded. 'I'll be down in an hour. Why don't you go home and study first.'

They all groaned together. 'We'll stay and practise,' the leader said defiantly. 'Please don't be long.'

Mariko Izumi had joined him on the strip of terracing. She smiled at his discomfort. There was no unpleasantness or sarcasm when she said, 'You really are busy, aren't you?'

They returned to his modest sitting room, stepping around the crumpled mattress and an unemptied ashtray. She opened her handbag and placed a thick, white envelope on the table. It had the name and logo of a prominent bank embossed in green.

'Please hear my proposal, Araki-san. I shall fully understand if you are unable to accept it.'

Araki beckoned to her to continue.

'I, we, would like you to spend a month looking for mother. As an outsider you might find some reason, some motive that we, who are so close to her, can't see or understand. You would have the confidence of the family and full access to my mother's documents and family records and our authority to talk to the police, her friends and business acquaintances. For a month of your services we would give you a small retaining fee.' She gestured towards the envelope. 'Two million yen,' she said, hiding the bluntness of the offer with a prolonged examination of the table-top. 'And, of course, any expenses you incur.'

In a good month, Araki thought rapidly, he could earn less than a tenth of what she was offering. If he took this assignment, he reckoned, he could easily cancel his teaching commitments for the next four weeks and still find time to complete his writing commissions. He had grown used to living with little sleep during his years as a journalist.

'If the police can't trace your mother, I doubt if I can,' he said, offering her an opportunity to withdraw without further loss of dignity.

'As I mentioned, the police are doing all they can.

I'm sure they think she's dead.' She stopped for a moment and, when she resumed, the dejection in her voice had deepened.

'All they can do is wait for her to turn up.' And, in a voice which almost cracked, she added: 'and try to match her with unidentified corpses of elderly ladies.'

'Wasn't there a suggestion in the press,' he said, as gently as accuracy allowed, 'that the lady found in Tokyo Bay about a week ago was your mother?' There was a moment's silence, then the weakest of nods from across the table.

He looked at the clear, black eyes, now shining with moisture, and then at the bulky envelope.

'I'll help you,' he said, and smiled as he saw her shoulders sag with relief. 'Please tell me about your mother.'

The story was tragic, even by the standards of the cases Araki wrote about years earlier for the *Tokyo Weekly*, and when she finished he felt the task was even more desperate than he had first imagined. He had taken several pages of notes and before he had drawn the last stroke the voices of his youthful playmates were rising in supplication.

Mariko smiled indulgently.

'You'd better go before they get violent. Are you free to meet my family tonight for dinner?'

He returned the smile. 'I'll have to be,' he said. 'I'm at your permanent disposal from now on.'

Chris Bingham was late, but Araki was sympathetic to his excuse which was that he had just been told his contract at the language school where he taught English would not be renewed. There had been an argument. Chris's Japanese was good but when he was flustered it emerged disjointed and ungrammatical. Worst of all he lost his composure and along with it his credibility.

'When do you finish?' Araki asked.

Chris scowled.

23

'A week next Monday,' he said. 'But in view of my attitude, and I'm quoting old Akabane now, it would be preferable if I terminate my employment immediately.'

'Compensation?'

Chris's mouth twisted into an ironic grin.

'A month's salary.'

'What will you do? Weren't they your official sponsors for your work permit?'

'I've still got a few private classes,' the young Englishman said unconvincingly. 'And it shouldn't be hard to find another school to sponsor me. The *Japan Times* is full of advertisements for native speakers.'

'While you're looking, I have a proposal that might interest you. By the way, what do you want to drink?'

They were in a dark coffee shop among the restaurants and snack-bars grouped around the level crossings which signalled the entry to Ikenoue station. It was early evening, the swarms of office workers were still in their glass and concrete buildings in Marunouchi and Shinjuku, but it was dark enough for the stacks of neon lights to splash their garish reflections on to the road. They had worked together when Chris's one year's secondment to the Japanese newspaper industry finished with three months on Araki's weekly magazine. They had also left together: Chris to return to London, Araki by mutually agreed resignation. Chris was restless in England, a little guilty Araki thought at abandoning his live-in girlfriend in Tokyo, but he also saw in Japan a relatively unexplored frontier. Within twelve months he was back in Tokyo, teaching English to live while trying to develop a career as a freelance journalist. He was accredited as a stringer for a pair of obscure American newspapers and this gave him access to the facilities of the Foreign Correspondents' Club and their library and bar. His hair was still a straw gold colour, though slightly darker, and parted in the centre. It was thick and wavy, a contrast to the growth of natural curls Araki recalled when Chris had made his first appearance at the *Tokyo*

Weekly three years earlier. He also sported a moustache which curved around his mouth in the style of the ancient Chinese mandarins and added character to an otherwise pale, narrow face.

'I'd like a beer. What the hell are you drinking?' Chris asked, pointing at Araki's coffee and speaking in a low-level Japanese drawl.

'I'm going to dinner with my clients. I'm saving myself.'

Chris slapped the table.

'Are they part of this proposal?'

Araki tapped a cigarette on the Hi-lite packet and pushed the cup away from him.

'Yes,' he said seriously. 'It's the family of the missing woman.'

'What missing woman?' Chris asked.

'The one I want you to help me find,' Araki said, leaning across towards Chris. Chris touched his forehead with the tips of his fingers. He grinned and said: 'OK mate, I'll help you. Just don't forget I can't walk out of this coffee shop without half a dozen kids rushing over and yelling "foreigner" at me. I can't leave the flat without my ID card, and if I do and the police stop me I end up in the station for five hours of interrogation. You know I can't walk around this city inconspicuously.'

Araki smiled. 'I don't want you to follow people around. I'll pay for the use of your brain.'

'I'm with you,' Chris conceded. 'But remember you used to find my race a handicap.' Before Araki could agree with him he said: 'Tell me about the missing woman.'

Araki lit the cigarette.

'Masako Izumi was fifty-eight years old. She left the family home on Friday, 28 February, wearing a dark brown kimono. She visited the bank, withdrew five million yen in cash and was due to go to the Honshinkyo temple in Ueno where she was a senior participant in one of the so-called new religions. She left the bank at eleven-thirty and has not been seen since.'

25

Araki paused to drain his coffee cup and order another. He checked the time.

'Masako's husband is the president of a company, most of which the family owns. It makes bulbs, light covers and other such accessories for the car industry. Masako's married son Ken is being groomed to take over the company. There is a married daughter Shinobu and her older sister, Mariko, who came to my apartment today. I can't tell you any more about the family until I meet them tonight.'

'What do the police think?'

'They think, and I have to concur at this stage with them, that she just wandered off. Women of her age who disappear do so because their children have grown up and got married. Mrs Izumi is only different because she is the wife of a very wealthy husband and in those circumstances she could have been expected to cope.'

'So do they think her case is outside the usual?'

'No, not really,' Araki conceded.

'How can I help?' the Englishman asked.

'I'll have a clearer idea after tonight. Meanwhile, do you still have any connections on the magazine?'

'I can still use their library if that's any use.'

'Great. Who's left from when we were both there?'

Chris sucked in air, too noisily and theatrically for a native Japanese. He tapped a pencil across his knuckles as he recalled in his mind the names of the people he had met those years earlier. He was still welcome at the weekly where he had assisted Araki for three months and he sometimes researched his articles there.

'Of course, the editor Kobayashi retired on health grounds. Not long after you were given the shove, didn't he?'

Araki resented the implication that his alleged irresponsible behaviour had somehow contributed to the editor's premature departure but Chris had not waited for a reply.

'And Kondo went too, but he was already in his mid-sixties. Mochizuki became editor and Maruta runs research. Maruta's very helpful. His son stayed with my parents in London last year but the obligation account is still in my favour.'

Araki drained his coffee and wiped his mouth on the back of his hand.

'Good. Please draw on some of this goodwill and ask him to help you review newspapers and magazines going back to the day Mrs Izumi went missing. Look for headlines which say "Missing wife of company president", "Fears for safety", "Possible kidnap victim", all the usual things. Can you manage the kanji?'

Chris had made a genuine effort towards literacy, a task not achieved by the Japanese child until the early teens, and in three years was confident that he could read two thousand Chinese hieroglyphics, each of whose construction might need between one and more than twenty strokes of the pen. His mastery of the two other simpler phonetic writing systems of only seventy letters each went without saying.

'I think so,' he said modestly.

Traffic was backing up on each side of the level crossing as the rush-hour frequency on the Inokashira-line increased. Waiting at the barrier with its flashing warning light as he accompanied Chris to the station Araki said, 'I thought I saw your old girlfriend in Shibuya the other day.' His thinning hair was swept back, reaching the collar of the sombre suit jacket he was wearing for the occasion, and he ran a splayed hand through it as the cool spring breeze ruffled it. 'What was her name?' he said, mumbling a few candidates.

'Takako.'

'Takako. Right. Do you still see her?'

'I haven't seen her for months. Why do you ask?'

Araki's reply was swamped by the crescendo of noise when a train emerged from between the packed buildings and applied its brakes on the crossing as it prepared to enter the station.

'You've lost her,' he repeated.

27

Chris nodded solemnly. They waited in a short queue for the ticket machine; Araki probed further.

'What's she doing now?'

'She worked for an insurance firm after graduating and now that she's twenty-five her employers have found her a husband.' Araki recognized the tone of bitterness that always affected his friend's speech when he attempted to interpret and evaluate a peculiarly Japanese fact of life which his western mind could not comprehend. 'So she resigned,' Chris was saying, 'and studied flower arrangement and the tea ceremony until the big day.'

'I did try to tell you how it would be.'

'I just didn't believe she could be so callous,' Chris said, reaching the machine and hitting the appropriate button with a frustrated thump. 'She loved me again after I got back to Tokyo.' He saw Araki's knowing look and rephrased his statement.

'OK. We slept together a few times and then said goodbye. Incredible. How could she go to bed with me two weeks before her marriage?'

Araki smiled sympathetically.

'Because the two events are not connected. She could have slept with you the night before she married. It'd be her way of saying thank you and sayonara.'

Chris gave his shorter oriental friend a mock two-handed Sumo push as a gesture of farewell.

'We'll talk tomorrow,' they said, almost together.

He could have seen Chris off from the platform, taking the Inokashira-line on a forty-minute haul, changing in Shibuya to the Shin Tamagawa-line and a final stop at Todoroki, but he preferred the privacy of his car, an emerald-green, second-hand Toyota Corona saloon, and had given himself an hour to reach the estate of high-walled detached houses a kilometre or so from the Tama River on the capital's western edge. Most of the traffic was heading west in the direction of the sprawling suburbs. Araki left the Tamagawa-dori quickly, and

28

turned right on the Number Eight Loop. After twenty minutes, he turned again, this time on to a minor road which flirted with views of the Tama River as the urban landscape changed from the weathered tenements and cramped wooden dwellings to the walled houses in the wealthier suburbs.

With no street names for reference, Araki had to stop twice to consult his map and again to find the location of the block the Izumis shared with similar detached premises separated from each other by uniform, adult-high walls of grey concrete, with additional privacy from cherry trees and evergreens. The news Araki had listened to on the journey had pronounced that the cherry blossoms, three days late this year in Tokyo, were in full bloom over most of the Kanto region, which included metropolitan Tokyo. The television news had shown a map of Japan, with the progress of the cherry-blossom flowering season solemnly plotted on its march from the warmer south to the cooler climes of Hokkaido by a carefully drawn line. This vital annual occurrence, as important to the Japanese as the arrival of the rains in desert countries, inspired an outpouring of unrestrained emotion. The TV film had shown the thick bunches of rich, pink blossoms and the citizenry of Fukuoka and Osaka squatting below them, swaying drunkenly while singing their local folk songs. The buds on the branches overhanging the Izumi house wall were heavy, most of them fully open. Another day, Araki agreed. Perfect beauty. The house itself was an old wooden structure with elegant, overlapping tiles on a sloping roof. The crowded garden was illuminated by spotlights attached to the guttering, and from where Araki stood inside the gateway there seemed to be two separate buildings joined by a corridor, no doubt, he thought, the result of an extension being added to the main house for the eldest son on marriage. The silhouettes of the surrounding buildings were more solid, roofs flatter, clearly concrete structures which their

29

wealthy occupants had built to replace traditional wooden dwellings at the end of their normal forty-year life spans.

Evidence of the old-fashioned, modest expression of wealth greeted him at the door. A housekeeper, in a plain brown kimono covered with an apron, was at least seventy, frail, with a round, pinched face and crinkled, dark-grey hair pulled around her head and tied into a bun. Their eyes never met and, once Araki had slipped his shoes and stepped out of the low-ceilinged entrance hall, the old woman fell to her knees and almost touched the tatami reed mat with her forehead, forcing the guest into an embarrassed nod at the prostrate form. A rather stiff shoji sliding door gave access straight into the main living room, and if the exterior of the house beckoned with its Japaneseness the room where Mariko Izumi waited with two other women was decorated in a completely western manner. The ceiling had been raised and inlaid with a circle of uncovered pearl textured light bulbs. A television, built into a mahogany cabinet with shelves around it for magazines and books, dominated one corner and could be viewed in comfort from the sofa and matching armchairs arranged around the low table whose heavy wooden legs had gouged deeply into the pale-green carpet. A sideboard supported an array of golf trophies and its glass-panelled front exposed a collection of crystal glasses.

'This is my younger sister, Shinobu,' Mariko said politely towards a shorter, slighter plumper version of herself, whose married name was Ohashi. Her hair and clothes were more conventional, as befitted a mother and wife of a junior bureaucrat at the Ministry of Finance.

'And this is my sister-in-law, Reiko.'

Reiko was twenty-two, thin, and if there was shape to her body it was hidden beneath a loose black dress which reached her knees but was not long enough to conceal the bones. She wore no stockings or tights and no make-up to give colour to the pale, listless face which, like her clothes, seemed to Araki to be neglected. In deference to the guest,

30

only her hair appeared to have been groomed with any degree of concern, out of necessity really, for it was long and straight and she had draped it across a shoulder and kept the fingers of one hand almost constantly entwined in it. Whereas her married sister-in-law Shinobu was profuse in her greeting, thanking Araki in advance for his help in searching for her mother and apologizing for causing a disturbance in his life, Reiko leaned forward, her eyes always on Araki's, like the Sumo wrestlers who try to outstare each other in the ritual tachiai before the fight, and simply said, 'Hello. Would you like a drink?'

Araki looked to the woman who had employed him for guidance, and thought he saw for the first time a flash of anger; it was directed at the younger woman whose lack of self-respect she tolerated but obviously despised.

'You've met Mrs Shimazaki,' she said, indicating the housekeeper who now hovered by the rear door with a tray. 'She's been with the family for years. She's one of us.' She noticed Araki looking beyond the old retainer. 'I'm sorry my father and brother are not back from golf yet. They must be caught in the traffic.' She looked fleetingly at her watch for reassurance. 'They should be here soon.'

If Mariko was flustered it was not for long. Her dress, open-necked with a brief line of tiny buttons, was the deep, pink colour of the cherry blossoms. It had flared cuffs and matching white collar and moulded itself to her slender figure, but was just loose enough to be comfortable.

'I think Araki-san would like a proper drink,' the pale woman in the black dress said, rephrasing her question almost into a plea, her own need showing through, as the housekeeper knelt at the table to serve the green tea. Mariko agreed and took the orders.

'Whisky-water please,' Araki said.

'Younger sister?' Mariko said, ignoring the more urgent needs of her sister-in-law. Shinobu Ohashi refused the offer of alcohol, flapping her hand limply across her face.

She shared her older sister's thin downward curving lips but her face was rounder and her eyes less open and her hair was expensively shaped and heavily lacquered, unlike the free-flowing style of Mariko. She wore a plain, cream-coloured blouse with starched cuffs and a brown plaid skirt. From the timid way she scolded the two under-fives who scampered in and out noisily, Araki judged her to be a typical housewife, uncomfortable in company other than family, and relaxed only when alone in a three-room apartment in some company housing complex. What would keep her apart from her peers, Araki remembered, was the family wealth. The children prodded their mother and the elder, a five-year-old boy, asked belligerently why the stranger had long hair and why he wasn't at the office at night like his father. The mother flushed and told them to go and play elsewhere. Araki wondered where the menfolk were and why he had been left alone with the house's women, none of whom had mentioned, except in passing, his missing client, their mother and mother-in-law.

Reiko had despaired of the delay and had brought a bottle of Chivas Regal, an ice bucket and some soda to the table and poured three glasses in the two-handed manner of the bar hostess, kneeling in front of her clients and concentrating on the measures with a studied intensity.

Araki smiled to himself, questions unrelated to the missing housewife massing inside him. Reiko was now more relaxed and after distributing the drinks lit a cigarette. She leaned back in the chair, cupped her cut crystal glass and drank deeply, some colour seeping through into her cheeks as the tension left her body. Barefoot, having discarded somewhere the uniformly cobalt-blue slippers worn by Araki and the others, she crossed her legs, oblivious to the disclaiming looks of disdain from her sisters-in-law.

'Thank you for helping us to look for mother,' the eldest daughter Mariko said. Her relative by marriage was slow in joining with the required bow and when she did it was more of a lurch and the remains of her drink slopped over the rim of her glass.

'I'll do my best,' Araki promised. 'Could I ask you,' he continued gently, spreading his arms to show the question was aimed at all three of them, 'where you think your mother could have gone?'

The younger, married daughter was suddenly overcome with emotion and lowered her head and sniffed, while Reiko, in whom Araki was more interested than the other two, shrugged her shoulders, as if to suggest the answer to the question was obvious and leaned forward to refill her glass and that of her new drinking companion. Mariko touched her sister lightly on the arm and gave her a sad, comforting smile before turning to Araki. 'Mother was not an irrational person,' she said. 'Her character was stronger than her face suggests.'

Araki remembered the photograph she had shown him of the stout, grim-faced matron.

'Unless she's had an accident, or an attack of amnesia, I just can't imagine any reason why she would stay away from home.'

Reiko pushed a very full tumbler towards Araki and seemed to think it natural to break into the conversation once her task had finished.

'Those crazies at the temple got to her,' she scoffed. 'They probably convinced her she wasn't doing enough for them and sent her to wander round Osaki collecting money.' And she returned to her drink and another cigarette as if the whole issue was resolved. Araki looked towards Mariko, the more composed of the two grieving sisters, for an explanation.

'Mother found a great deal of spiritual comfort in religion,' she said, a flash of disapproval aimed towards her sister-in-law.

'Christianity?' Araki offered.

'No. The Honshinkyo. They have that strange, purple building with the golden dome on the other side of Ueno Park.'

33

'I know it,' Araki said. 'Hardly pure Buddhism I'd say.' He was comparing his own family's religious obligations which were entirely conventional in following the most funereal rituals of the older Buddhist sects. Unlike the requirements to practise of continental Buddhism, the Japanese see this imported religion as simply a convenient vehicle to the after-life, should it exist, and even Araki would light a stick of incense and summon the soul of the departed at the butsudan altar which enshrined his father's at the family home in Shimane Prefecture. The newer sects, to one of which the missing woman belonged, were neither traditional or conventional and Araki made a mental note to investigate this particular sect. Meanwhile, Reiko was emphasizing her point.

'She was obsessed with it. It was her passion.'

'Nonsense,' Mariko said, her composure ruffled for the first time, Araki noted. 'She found the companionship she needed. After all, none of us live at home.' Araki wondered why she had ignored the fact that the seemingly least compassionate family member, the missing woman's daughter-in-law, did live in the family house.

Trying to prevent a dispute he said: 'How often did she visit the temple?'

'Five, sometimes six times a week,' Reiko replied confidently, knowing that only she could observe her mother-in-law's daily habits.

Araki was constructing another question when the side of the house shook as the front door was slammed shut. He heard a metallic rattle which he later realized was the sound of golf clubs bouncing around inside a pair of golf bags. The men of the house had returned home.

After a month apart from his life's partner, Araki did not expect the husband to be disconsolate and reclusive in his grief, but neither was he prepared for the guffaw as the two men stashed their shoes and shed jackets in the hallway or the cheerful, excited faces that sagged when they saw their guest and remembered the invitation to him and its primary purpose. Yasuo Izumi was sixty-one,

34

although the thick, black hair, lightly streaked with silver, on a square, boyish face gave him a younger appearance. He was short with a little neck and a broad, fleshy frame. His daughters had inherited his thin, feminine lips and pale complexion. Momentarily embarrassed, he motioned Araki back to his chair and ordered a beer, a command to which only the housekeeper responded, no doubt by established custom. The son was in his mid-thirties, with his father's stocky frame and full face with thin lips which drooped into a permanent leer. His hair was closely cut and permed and his face was wind-blown, the result of regular and recent golf, Araki assumed. Unlike his father he was relaxed and expansive and sitting next to his wife, whom he acknowledged only as a source for a strong whisky and a cigarette; he talked fondly of his missing mother and how he was sure she was alive. Araki listened sympathetically while each expounded his or her theory on the mysterious disappearance to the understanding nods of family and none even came close to suggesting that she might be dead.

The men went off to change, returning as the housekeeper was announcing dinner.

The area given over to dining was along a corridor with squeaky, bare floorboards and behind a simple fusuma which separated two Japanese rooms, one with a low table over a floor well and no other adornments beyond an arrangement of spring flowers in the tokonoma alcove, and another with a rosewood table laid for six at its centre. The first course of pink, oily raw tuna slices, with a garnish of shiso nettle leaves and shredded white radish was laid out on flat willow-patterned dishes alongside the tiny saucers which had already been thoughtfully filled with soya sauce.

'May I ask who saw her last,' Araki asked as he deftly manipulated his chopsticks to wrap a nettle around a sliver of tuna and soak the bundle in soya.

The Izumis looked at each other inquisitively. It had been a month, Araki thought, but it was puzzling that

35

the facts of the disappearance were not etched in their minds from the persistent questioning by the police in the early stages.

'It was me,' the old housekeeper said. She had backed quietly in the room and placed a tray with lacquered bowls of steaming bean paste soup on to the ornate Japanese chest-of-drawers. Shuffling between the table and the sideboard with the bowls she spoke without looking up.

'Izumi-san left as usual around eleven. She helped me with some cleaning and then I laid out her kimono for her.'

'Did she always wear a kimono when she went out?' Araki queried. Apart from ceremonial occasions such as weddings and funerals and the New Year celebrations the restrictive kimono with its bundling obi sash was a rare sight in the capital.

'It was customary at the temple,' the old retainer said casually and retired bowing with her tray before Araki could interrogate her further.

Reiko was toying with her food. She had chewed on a slice of fish but most of it was left in the mixture of soya sauce and green horse-radish in the side dish. Araki wondered what she had meant earlier by 'crazies at the temple'. Was she thinking about them now?

'She's around somewhere,' her husband Ken said a shade too dismissively.

'So where do you think she is?' Araki asked.

'She was forgetful. What's the word for it? When you can't remember who you are or where you've been?'

'Amnesia.'

'Right. Amnesia.' Ken lifted the soup bowl to his lips and, sucking noisily, steered the finely chopped vegetable into his mouth with his chopsticks. Looking around for support from the family he said, 'She's been distracted for some months, forgetting the occasional appointment or what we'd told her about the business. Isn't that right Father?'

36

Izumi senior nodded, breathing audibly to add conviction. His son continued, 'She's probably in a hotel somewhere with the five million yen she drew out for some reason from the bank.'

'Where would she go?' Araki asked.

'We own a number of properties,' the son began but it was his wife whose head jerked up in riposte.

'Your mother owns the property,' she said in a remark which stressed 'mother' and silenced the room. Her husband fixed her with a vicious look but Reiko looked across to her sisters-in-law for support. Araki read the look of hatred in the man's eyes, but it was the face of the father which held him. He had been holding his grand-daughter to him and was feigning interest in a picture she had drawn and brought to him from the next room. Araki could not tell at what point Izumi senior looked towards his family, whether it was something his son had said or what his daughter-in-law had interjected with drink-induced lack of caution he could not tell. What was not in doubt was the warning that flashed amongst them. The son Ken was talking, having ignored his wife's interruption.

'She may have been pulled subconsciously to a place she knew. I guess she's in a hotel near one of the family properties.'

The taciturn housekeeper came back into the room, labouring with a tray of sake pots and beer bottles.

Araki was grateful for the breathing space. There was something disturbing about this family. Instead of being united in grief and desperately using any means, even this former reporter, there were divisions and tensions which suggested a divergence of loyalties. They poured sake for each other, except for Shinobu who drank nothing, and the men also chased the tiny cups of rice wine with cold beer. The married daughter affected extreme politeness when asking Araki about his personal life and while Shimazaki-san, the honorific saying nothing about her status as a widow, wife or spinster, trundled in and out with dishes of grilled salmon fillets garnished with green beans and bowls of boiled, sticky rice, the others joined in with deferential nosiness. Araki knew he could not enjoy any form of confidence if he was unwilling to expose his real self to the scrutiny of those who needed his services enough to pay him two million yen in cash. He told them of his early life in Shimane Prefecture, born the second son of an ordinary rice-growing family. Leaving his three strong brothers to care for his mother, a widow now for twenty years, he was considered bright enough to sit for and pass the entrance examination to Keio University in Tokyo, the prestigious private college.

They all knew that employment by Japan's largest national daily newspaper was a privilege and a guarantee of a working lifetime's security. Yet they were left to imagine what act of gross misconduct or negligence he had committed to have to leave after a decade and enter the frantic world of the popular weekly journals and the often sleazy techniques of investigation they demanded in order to upstage the ubiquitous competition. The son Ken was particularly interested in the anecdotes Araki told about the politicians and their mistresses he tried to trace and he forced a sardonic grin and nodded as if in recognition of the circumstances. In turn Mariko described the Izumis' recent history. They had always been a practical, hardworking family and as a small family concern in pre-war days had supplied the emerging motor industry with electrical parts and lighting equipment. The first years of the post-war period were a struggle, as it was for everyone, but an injection of capital came in time to allow the company to join the great procurement bonanza provided by the conflict on the Korean peninsula. Izumi Seisakusho was one of thousands of small businesses catapulted along the road to growth and prosperity, the end of which is still not in sight. Hard work and sacrifice and no great ostentation of wealth beyond this old, classically Japanese house, hidden modestly behind a concrete wall and a topping of cherry trees, had provided a comfortable childhood and university education for all three children and for that Mariko said they were all grateful. She spoke of their parents' happy marriage, a view Araki appreciated and looked at the embarrassed smile of Shinobu, imagining the bureaucrat husband she would only see at breakfast and bedtime but who honoured her with his commitment. But he could not fathom the marriage of the son and presumed heir to the presidency of the company, to the undernourished, heavy-drinking woman who was once attractive and self-confident, but who now was so audacious and un-Japanese that she openly challenged her husband in front of guests. She could have been a bar hostess but she was too young and lacked the hardness and tact of the women of the floating world who would do nothing to prejudice the cherished finale to lives spent pampering male egos. Their dream was achieved when they married a widower or broke up the marriage of a rich patron in those dangerous years for the Japanese – their fifties, when the children leave and the couple who have not known each other find they still have nothing in common, least of all physical attraction. When the housekeeper had cleared the dishes and replenished the sake pots for the third time and delivered segments of fresh green melon to the table before bowing obsequiously out of the room, Shinobu supplied the last piece of the family puzzle.

'Shimazaki-san is part of the family,' she said gesturing towards the space near the door. 'More than forty years with us. Long before we were born.'

'Really,' Araki said with exaggerated appreciation of the statistic, and while retrieving a wedge of melon from his lap wondered how long a family member must wait before she is allowed to sit at the table and eat with guests.

They took green tea in the living room which had been cleared of glasses and supplied with empty ashtrays. Shinobu went off to check that the children were sleeping

– they were evidently staying with their grandfather, perhaps to give him support, as they were too young to suffer. Araki wanted to return to the son's theory, which had his missing mother lodged in a hotel near some family property waiting for a friend or relative to awaken her from the amnesia the change of life was obviously causing. Her religious fervour was also worth exploring. Yasuo, the father, yawned, signalling the end of the evening but made the offer Araki wanted to hear.

'Come round on Monday and I'll leave my wife's private papers out for you to study. I'm sure it won't be of any use but the fact that you are trying to help is very comforting.' With that they all bowed in appreciation.

Mariko showed him to the door, holding a golf club-shaped horn and watching patiently while her guest preferred to struggle unaided into a dusty pair of shoes. As they exchanged words, promising to contact each other with or without any concrete news, Araki saw a silhouette behind the opaque white paper stretched across the frames of the sliding door behind Mariko. Tying his shoe-laces and straightening up with deliberate slowness he saw the crack widen as the two sides of the screen were eased apart. She said nothing, not even a repeat of her subdued farewell of a little earlier, but the narrow, tired eyes told him she had something to say but, with her sister-in-law nearby, Reiko's message would have to wait.

The elderly housewife, hunched in a thick coat although the April day was mild and free of breeze, had seen the white, foreign car before, or one like it. It looked like a stranded whale among the bicycles that claimed priority in the narrow shopping street with no pavements and an irregular line of telegraph poles to weave around. It advanced, then backed up, and finally pulled into the alley which led to the lane bordering an overgrown plot of land where the house she shared with her crippled husband stood like a lonely trespasser on an otherwise

40

vacant site. She hurried forward, a heavy shopping bag rasping against her leg. Her breathing was laboured and her tired heart thumped in her chest. For two generations they had paid a small but regular rent and enjoyed a warm relationship with the owner. In the last two years, the surrounding early post-war wooden structures had been demolished and cleared as the tenants died or grew old and moved in with their children. The couple, whose name was Ando, had no children, but enjoyed a contented if lonely life in this bustling part of Nakameguro in central Tokyo.

The first visit, three weeks earlier, was meticulously polite. The two gentlemen, whose name-cards identified them as real-estate agents, brought glossy brochures describing apartments and houses for rent in the neighbourhood and select sheltered homes for elderly residents. Her husband had suffered a stroke and although he could understand what was said to him, his mouth was paralysed and as he fought to control the muscles in his neck when he tried to correct the drooping head, he gave the impression either of nodding assent or drowsiness.

'But we're quite content here,' she had said ingenuously as the two salesmen struggled to restrain their enthusiasm for the properties on offer. 'The owner has told us that we are welcome to live here.' The cheeks of the older of the two swelled as he forced a smile designed to enhance sincerity.

'I regret to tell you that plans have been put in hand to develop this site,' he said. 'We desperately wish to assist you in moving to acceptable and equally comfortable accommodation and can offer you generous financial assistance.' Mrs Ando looked towards her husband for support but, slumped against his back-support on the worn tatami mat, he had a bewildered expression and when he tried to speak a trail of saliva dribbled down his chin.

There was no sign of the white car when she reached her house. The door was ajar and she feared for her

41

husband. Dropping the shopping bag, she groped for the light switch as she slipped off her shoes and called out in the powerless, throaty voice of the aged. Her husband was lying on his futon, as usual, in the room cramped with newspapers, books and aids for invalids and dominated by the television and its stand. His head rolled on the hard, compact pillow and a shaky hand pointed to the package on the low table in front of him. The men in the foreign car had delivered a new set of brochures and an expensive box of seaweed-wrapped rice-crackers, a small gift, they had said, a gesture of goodwill.

3

A spurt of deep, purple liquid shot from the brain as the
nail transfixed the diamond-shaped head to the wooden
board. The wet, brown body wriggled in a desperate fight
for life, but a strong, practised hand held it straight
while another slipped a razor-sharp blade into the soft
flesh behind the head and opened the eel in one swift
movement, pairing it without splitting the body in two.
Separating the head and then cutting the carcass into
equal portions, he laid the strips of soft meat on a plate
next to a grill which lay across a bed of charcoal. The
patron's son, with his round face, puffed eyes narrow as
a pencil line, and a head of cropped, black, spiky hair,
was a younger image of his father. He had his back to
the counter, chopping spring onions and other vegetables
for the soup, and to the two customers who poured sake
for each other in the reckless Sunday lunchtime style of
men who lived alone. After an exchange of greetings the
patron retreated again to the kitchen and laid the strips
of eel, which he had joined into flat portions with splinters
of bamboo, on to the grill above the white-hot charcoal.
He brushed the meat with the sauce which dripped on to
the coals, firing clouds of pungent smoke that spiralled
upwards and out through a funnel into the alleyways.

'What makes a woman leave home, run away?' Araki
asked. 'Apart from another man.' The older of the two
drank down the thimble of hot rice wine and wiped
his mouth on his wrist before crooking his head, as
if to say that the answer required a dredge of the
decades of his accumulated knowledge and could not

be addressed in an instant. Yoshinori Kondo had been in journalism for forty years, the final fifteen on the *Tokyo Weekly* where he was in charge of research and records and acted as general adviser and consultant on legal matters, particularly the extent to which the laws of libel could be stretched. Here he had met Araki, and the recent arrival at the down-market end of journalism had befriended Kondo and exploited the vast file material and experience the old man had at his disposal. There was almost a kinship in their relationship, in spite of the quarter-century difference in their ages.

For Araki his departure resulted from an impetuous act of indiscipline, but, in the Japanese way, both Araki and the management agreed that his skills and desire for independence were better suited to the freelance world, an arrangement which sufficed to disguise the shared embarrassment and inevitability of the situation in the peculiarly Japanese way. Flush with a substantial severance payment, he had left the apartment in trendy Harajuku, and its bitter memories, and became the lodger at the home of the prosperous tradesman in Ikenoue, close to a Tokyo University Campus. Kondo was in his late sixties with grey, swept-back, thinning hair, and had a weary, wrinkled face which saw in Araki the son he never had. He admired the younger man's fiery independence, his refusal to accept blind conformity, even at the expense of job and marital security. And Araki for his part had stood beside his dignified, grieving senior when Kondo's wife's bones, crumbling and still warm, were trundled from the incinerator and placed on a long tray before the small gathering. After two days of wake at the family home, the closest relatives and, by special request of the grieving widower, Araki had gathered at the crematorium for the most intimate of Buddhist rituals, the most arduous of the funeral rites for Kondo's wife who had died on the first day of the New Year. Sifting through the powdery remains and the soft bones of the human form, his chopstick quivered in a nervous hand as he combined with a serenely composed Kondo to lift a symbolic, solid piece of bone and place it in an urn. It was from the throat, the Adam's apple, which was believed to take the form of a reclining Buddha. Kondo smiled at the fortuitous discovery and saw it as divine reinforcement of his feelings towards Araki. The former journalist was thirty-nine, and the skin of his round, plain face was a naturally pallid tone, and his lack of interest in a healthy diet in favour of a life-style of late nights, cigarettes and alcohol only served to convince those who knew him well that his interests were not wholly in his own preservation. With no formal employment, and the codes of dress and behaviour this would assume, Araki had let his thinning hair grow long and rarely found it necessary to wear a suit or tie. Kondo seemed to age as he spoke as if feeling the words he spoke. He turned the tiny carafe of warm sake in his fingers and lowered his head, perhaps remembering his wife.

Araki rephrased his question before Kondo could reply. 'If it's not a man, what drives a happy, busy fifty-eight-year-old to disappear of her own choice?'

'Sometimes they just get tired. They mostly wait until the last child gets married, by which time they're in their fifties, and having sacrificed their youth to their children and to a husband who was never home, or when he was he watched the television or slept, something snaps and they just want to be alone.'

Kondo let Araki refill the cup.

'The brittle thread that keeps them tied to reality and responsibility is strained when the man she has never known retires and there he is, still youngish but a stranger in the house she had thought her own domain. She sees him as unfriendly, and as useless as a broken washing machine, and just as expendable.' He paused to drain his sake. Then he said: 'There's a word for it.'

'Sodaigomi,' the two men said together, recalling the word used to describe the official classification of bulky refuse like old refrigerators or unwanted furniture which the local council would collect on request. They both knew it was also the word used to describe contemptuously the value of a retired white-collar salaryman.

'Where do they go,' Araki asked, 'when they finally decide to leave?'

'Most try to get as far away as possible, a thousand kilometres if necessary, to sever all neighbour and family connections. They might work in inns or cheap restaurants and live with their employers or other women in the same position.'

'What about suicide?'

Kondo shrugged.

'Possible, but unlikely. From what you say she, the Izumi woman, was comfortably off, in good health, and on the surface enjoying the care and pleasure of outside interests. Female suicide is usually a lot earlier, mostly by women in their late twenties with two taxing children and the normal inattentive husband and his demanding mother.'

They both drank, perhaps remembering the depressingly frequent articles they had written about young mothers pushing their children into the path of trains and then hurling themselves into oblivion seconds later.

'If they make it to sixty the worst is over,' Kondo was saying.

The waitress, another relative of the owner, laid in front of them with exaggerated enthusiasm the black and red lacquered bowls of steamy, sticky rice capped by strips of broiled eel, blackened by fire at the edges but now freed from their bamboo spits and basted in the sweet, thick sauce rich in soya. Araki sniffed appreciatively and stubbed out his cigarette. He and Kondo had patronized the small, family unagi shop in the old merchant quarter of Nihonbashi for many years, particularly on the hot and sultry nights in August when the smoke from the charcoal grill hung in the alley and tempted the throngs of shirt-sleeved pedestrians. Kondo sprinkled his eel with a layer of pepper while Araki refilled the sake cups and suggested a toast to the owner.

'And of course,' Kondo said, 'if it is suicide then there's likely to be a body, whatever the age of the person.'

'But if being older, and don't forget she wore a kimono regularly, she might have chosen a more traditional way of death.'

'There would still have to be a body,' Kondo said, 'even if she did seppuku.' He balanced a piece of eel on the end of his chopsticks and contemplated his own statement. 'Nobody guts themselves any more unless they're unbalanced and virtually a mental case like Mishima.'

'No, I don't mean seppuku,' Araki countered. 'What about the forest?'

'You mean the one near Mount Fuji. The one we wrote about.'

'Right. It would be the perfect place for someone with Mrs Izumi's personal profile to choose to die. Discreet and private, the place for an aesthetic kind of death.'

'A fanciful supposition,' Kondo said. 'I don't think the family are ready to hear that one yet.'

The article they had written for their employer, the *Tokyo Weekly*, was prompted by a police sweep of the edges of the huge, dense primeval forest known as Aokigahara, a hundred kilometres from Tokyo in the highlands between Mount Fuji and Lake Kawaguchi, which uncovered eight bodies in two days. This 'forest of no return' had become famous twenty years earlier in a novel which described it as the ideal place to commit suicide in secret. Since then fifty bodies a year have been found near the narrow pathways which cross the forest, leaving the curious to speculate on how many others have wandered deeper into the trees, where there are no landmarks to help the walker and where even a compass reading is distorted by magnetic lava in the region.

Kondo continued, 'What you're saying is that Mrs Izumi is one of our daily total of seventy suicides and one of those choosing to take the lonely, painful lingering death on a forest floor.'

Araki used his chopsticks to jab the air and emphasize his argument.

'If I recall, the reasons for suicide are illness, alcoholism, financial problems and mental breakdowns like depression. The missing woman suffered from none of these, as far as we know. What she may have suffered from was religious enthusiasm and the need for the supreme act of spiritual cleansing, something she could find in the forest at Aokigahara.'

The older man crooked his head in a gesture of disbelief.

'It's too convenient, and too much like a good story. Don't forget we're not journalists any more.'

'OK,' Araki conceded. 'Let's be clinical. Give me the probabilities for each of her possible fates.'

Kondo mashed the last chunk of grilled eel into the rice and shovelled the heap into his mouth, a hand cupped below to catch the loose bits dropping. Then he took a pen and jotted on to a paper napkin as he spoke.

'Seventy-five per cent,' he scribbled, 'she left home deliberately. Five per cent, she's had an accident and her body's not been found or perhaps not identified. I'll give you fifteen per cent for a suicide, but of the modern kind.'

'And the other five per cent?' Araki asked impatiently.

Kondo pondered, and put his pen down.

'She could have wandered off confused. And she might have been kidnapped.'

He raised an arm to halt his friend's obvious question.

'OK, but there's been no ransom demand.'

Elbow on the counter, Araki massaged his chin with a knuckle and said casually: 'And what about murder?'

Kondo drained the cup of sake and then scratched the top of his scalp, which shone with perspiration through the sparse grey hairs.

'Come up with a reasonable motive. This is Tokyo, not New York or London. Women are not killed in Tokyo for the contents of their purses.'

'Not even for five million yen?'

Kondo shrugged. 'Not even for that much,' he said confidently.

Araki beckoned for more sake and said: 'The police have no idea where she went after leaving the Tekkei Bank at around eleven-thirty on 28 February. They claim to have exhausted all channels of enquiry.'

'You sound like an official report,' Kondo said sceptically. 'But from experience, I think the police lose interest once they decide that foul play is not involved.'

'When will they close the file on Mrs Izumi?'

The old man sucked in air audibly.

'Well, she's been missing for just over a month. I'd say the active search will begin to wind down in another week or two, perhaps three since she's the wife of a leading businessman. Of course, the file will always stay open until she's declared legally dead.'

'When could that be?'

Kondo toyed with a slice of pickled carrot.

'Depends on the husband really. He might apply for a ruling after six months. Then again he might never give up hope of finding his wife.'

'Unless he wanted her dead.'

Kondo shrugged his shoulders.

'Would he give you two million yen if he wants you to find a corpse? The police can do that and it won't cost him anything.'

'He didn't give me it,' Araki said tersely. 'It was his daughter Mariko.'

'But her father agreed.'

'What could he say? "No, I don't want you to help find my wife." He had to agree with his daughter. The only problem was whether the money should come to me.'

Araki made a mental note to check if Izumi had insured his wife's life and then moved to another aspect of the case.

'I told you on the 'phone the wife was active on one of those new religions, the Honshinkyo. It seems she was on her way to their temple in Ueno, after a brief visit to her local bank, when she left home for the last time. Have you come across them?'

Araki knew he had, or had researched them, and he asked the question in the way he used to do when they worked together on the magazine. The old man seemed to be injected by a sudden burst of youthful enthusiasm and reached down from the stool for his shabby, black, two-handled briefcase. Then, on reflection, he left it alone and said, 'When people flooded to the cities they were immediately cut off from the close traditions of the village, especially the community spirit and the mutual support it gave everybody. Of course, the big companies act as their own "communities", their own life-belt, but the masses, the tradespeople and the millions of ordinary toilers have nothing to hang on to, no-one to approach for help. The wave of so-called new religions gave them this support. Honshinkyo's much like all the other post-war movements although it can be traced to a group of non-conformist Buddhists founded by a woman, a certain Etsuko Morozumi. It wasn't really a religion, more a movement, a large gathering of people who gave each other some kind of mutual support.'

'Some movement,' Araki opined. 'Mrs Izumi felt the need to see Go Morozumi four or five times a week.'

'That's Etsuko's younger brother. Honshinkyo started in 1951 or '52. It claims to offer Mrs Izumi and others like her a brighter present, let alone the exalted after-life of traditional Buddhism. In return for high personal commitment of mind, time and the purse, it promises its followers self-fulfilment, health, companionship and a feeling of purpose. It's more down to earth than other movements. Etsuko never saw herself as a living god possessed of a spirit, like some of the other leaders did.'

'What happened to her?' Araki asked.

'Nobody knows. The story was put out by the sect that she went off to India to live near her favourite guru.'

50

'Another missing woman,' Araki said with a chuckle, and then straight away regretted his words when he saw his companion lay his chopsticks across the half-finished dish of pickles and stare dolefully into his empty sake cup.

'Another round,' Araki ordered, beckoning at the young waitress with the empty beaker. Kondo was distracted, his thoughts on his own missing woman and the cold, childless house they had shared for thirty years until she had died painlessly alongside him on their futon.

Araki replenished the tiny, steaming bowl which the older man raised quickly to his lips.

'I think I'll wander over to the temple this afternoon,' Araki said. 'It can't do any harm.'

'I'll come with you,' Kondo said casually.

Araki waved a limp wrist through a hanging cloud of cigarette smoke.

'Not at all,' he said. 'I don't want to take you away from the magazine.'

The older man held his temple between the thumb and forefinger of one hand.

'It doesn't matter. They won't care.' His voice was flat and cold, but not bitter.

Araki rearranged the empty drink containers on the counter in front of him.

'I'm sorry,' he said. 'Was it because of what you did for me?'

'Goodness, no,' Kondo assured him, both knowing that the truth was somewhere in between. 'That was a long time ago.'

Araki noticed that Kondo's thin hair was ruffled and the crease in his trousers blunt. He sometimes went to the magazine's Shimbashi office on Sundays but to-day he hadn't. Kondo was saying: 'They brought in some young journalists and they seem to do their own research.' He searched for the words. 'They keep the information to themselves, on discs.' His voice rose as he sought to stress his incredulity at the development.

51

'They press a few keys and a year's research appears on the screen.'

'How long have you got?' Araki asked sympathetically.

'The Editor wants me to stay until the end of the year.'

'What will you do?'

The grey-haired, older man waited while the waitress filled them each a large mug of murky, green tea and then said:

'Take the money, move into a smaller flat. Yokohama maybe, like the one you and Yoko . . . '

Araki bit his lower lip, saddened at the memory and embarrassed for his friend at his unintended reminder of his neighbour and the place where she died so violently. He had never returned to the stereotype Japanese apartment, with its two low-ceilinged, cramped rooms and equally small kitchen and bathroom, except to gather his belongings and make a kind of peace with his neighbours. That was three years ago. He forced himself to sound cheerful: 'A two-room flat with kitchen and bathroom would suit you perfectly. The extra room will give you a place to keep your books and papers.'

Kondo nodded. Araki continued: 'If you can spare some time while you wind down why don't you help me with this Izumi case. Just till we solve it, or the police do, which is more likely.'

Araki thought his sad companion was going to cry when he said, 'I'll try and get away.'

'I'd enjoy your company.'

In the still air of the park, away from the main roads which surround this rare gap in the grey urbanscape of northern Tokyo, the perfume of fully opened cherry blossoms was quite intoxicating, even to the disinterested nose of Araki. The boughs of the cherry trees were cloaked by clusters of deep pinkish-white blossom whose weight dragged the branches down to a man's height from the ground. Even around the edges of the parkland there were few spaces not laid out with reed mats and picnic baskets for groups of cheery revellers. Some spots were being patrolled by advance guards who Kondo knew had been there since dawn, having been sent by their companies to secure a place to entertain important clients or their own chiefs, but most accommodated families lunching on onigiri rice balls and home-made sushi and copious rounds of sake and beer. They had taken their shoes off and squatted or sat around the food, their faces reddened by the drink and their inhibitions allowed to fall in public for a few hours. It was a perfect day for flower viewing. The sky was light blue with patches of harmless, listless, white clouds well separated and it was a warm, refreshing fifteen degrees centigrade with an imperceptible breeze. The rich, pink blooms were full and thick, obscuring their own leaves and blending into the blossoms of the next tree, their total fragrance forming a blanket in the still air.

The two men threaded their way between the happy groups, some of whom were becoming quite boisterous.

'Seven days,' Kondo said, as they passed the National Museum. 'From birth as a helpless wad of foliage waiting for its moment beneath the sun to a small pile of rotting petal on the ground. All in seven days. No wonder we Japanese see human life like the fleeting passing of the cherry blossom.'

'Don't tell that to Chris,' Araki said. 'When his Japanese friends go on about the superiority and sensitivity of our race he has to remind them that the wretched cherry blossom blooms again next year. He sees the cherry week as the only time the Japanese are allowed to get pissed in public and show any sign of human emotion. The rest of the year he sees us as playing out our pleasant, self-controlled roles as servants of the country whose destiny we have entrusted to those who have realized we cannot rule the world with guns but we damn well can with

53

semi-conductors, cars and a bottomless well of money.'

'What does he know?' Kondo said rhetorically. 'He's foreign.'

They exchanged a glance and then a smile. Kondo's was almost apologetic, but he found a reason to pursue a Japanese line of logic when a golden dome came into view beyond the park's outer fence and line of trees in the distance.

'We Japanese want fellowship, companionship, some way to believe in ourselves. The Shinto shrines and the Buddhist temples we have only offer the customs, the dressing-up bit, the ceremonies for birth, marriage and death. There's no belief in a single god, because that requires mental delusion, and so no divine ethical principles to guide our daily life, as there are in Christianity, even if the person doesn't practise any more. But in there,' Kondo said forcefully, pointing to the building settled on a slope and surrounded by a gravel forecourt, 'the people can talk freely and get some spiritual comfort from those in a similar position.'

The building was in three storeys, each with a balcony like a pagoda, and above the highest of these covered verandas ran a sloping roof covered with overlapping, silver-painted tiles which curled upwards at each rim. The incongruous edifice was made even more inappropriate to the nearby functional office buildings and shops by the gold-plated dome which rose above the flat roofs of the drab blocks behind it.

'There are other weird places like this,' Kondo remarked as they crossed the extravagant parking lot. 'Each sect tries to outdo the other in the degree of tasteless ostentation of its temples.' They followed signs which pointed 'observers' inside towards glass-fronted booths overlooking the sunken main floor of the building where groups of people squatted on mats laid out on what had the appearance of marble.

'One of them's the sponsor, the person who recruited the other or who's been assigned to be their teacher,' Kondo

54

said in a low voice, although the booths immediately adjacent were not occupied.

Araki peered out at the dozens of small gatherings, four or five people in each who listened intently to their teacher. Some of these leaders were waving a handbook while others were quoting from it. Most of the people, Araki observed, were in their forties or fifties and their clothes were uniformly sombre and basic.

'The key to the success of these movements,' Kondo said, 'is that they teach the newcomer to recruit others.' And then he added with cynicism, 'You can say that it is tantamount to ordering them to find followers or to collect contributions. Movements like this one have to keep growing or they die.'

Kondo tapped Araki lightly on the arm. 'That's Morozumi.'

The far side of the circular hall was cut away to make a stage which was backed with a gold tapestry inscribed with the huge characters for Japan and beside them the Chinese kanji characters for the Honshinkyo movement. Seated on a high-backed chair in the middle of the arcing stage, Morozumi looked short, perhaps average in height and appearance, not the sinister person Araki had expected. He had a flat, schoolboy face and a full head of carefully groomed hair which may or may not have been darkened. The throne was draped in a golden silk fabric and was reached from two sides by short curving steps from the body of the auditorium. With an arm hanging limply from the elaborately carved rest, Morozumi was receiving an orderly procession of believers who bowed deeply and spoke into their chests. A retainer with an ornate clipboard stood beside the leader and whispered something as each supplicant left and the next prepared his obsequious obeisances.

'It's almost imperial,' Araki said admiringly.

A trim young man in a business suit, with a prominent name tag on his lapel which made his subsequent introduction unnecessary, clasped his hands in front of his chest and bowed deeply. With a deft flick of his wrist he drew two name-cards from a pocket and proffered them in turn to Araki and Kondo. Neither felt obliged to accept or reciprocate with their own.

'May I ask who introduced you to our organization?' the man whose name was Ohta asked.

Araki said with uncharacteristic praise: 'Your spiritual activities are common knowledge.' The young temple front-man forced a grateful smile and sensed recruitment. He was quickly disillusioned when Araki's tone became serious and his language direct and uncompromising. 'But we are here to make some enquiries about one of your most active colleagues.' Ohta stiffened, almost crouching on the edge of the low chair, the two unwanted name-cards now damp at the edges as he held them nervously in the palm of a hand. He said: 'Who, may I ask?'

'We are trying to trace Mrs Masako Izumi,' he said, pausing to detect any change on Ohta's impassive features. There was nothing perceptible. 'She came here a lot and was due here around one o'clock on the day she disappeared.'

Ohta inclined his head and then looked through the glass partition at the crowded floor as if looking for help.

Araki persisted: 'She normally visited the temple every day. That would make her a very diligent believer if not a well-known member of your organization.'

'She was very important,' Ohta conceded. 'She was a sponsor and had the responsibility for introducing our ways to new believers and accompanying them on their home visits. She was a fine contributor.'

Araki knew that Kondo wanted to ask the same question. What was the temple doing to find Mrs Izumi? With their complex and tight network of believers, participants or simple contacts he had to assume that everyone had been ordered to be on the lookout. Was there no word of a sighting from the faithful around Japan? It occurred to Araki that, for whatever reason, the devout housewife might have found seclusion in the temple, hidden away

56

in some country retreat where she could find the peace of mind she sought. But surely that would be illegal, and Morozumi had already stated officially to the police that he was unaware of her whereabouts.

Putting the young man on the spot with deliberate callousness, Araki said: 'What do you think happened to her?'

Ohta rose from the seat and spoke in forced, nervous words.

'Thank you for calling. If you'll leave your card I'll see that your enquiries are passed on to my superiors. May I now show you out?'

Araki paused at the foot of the steps among the knots of people who were standing in the afternoon sunshine admiring the reflection on the golden dome before making their way inside.

'For caring people,' he said, 'they don't seem very concerned.'

Kondo shrugged and said: 'An old lady leaves the group, disillusioned, tired of fund-raising, knocking on doors, and all with little esteem or encouragement from her family. It can't be an unusual event in this kind of organization.'

'That doesn't sound right,' Araki said. 'She's been active in the temple for fifteen years. She must be one of the senior members.'

A flurry of activity distracted them. Looking towards the grand entrance at the head of the steps they saw Ohta pointing in their direction and the diminutive man who had looked so serene sitting on his golden throne now seemed clearly harassed as he tried to mix care with speed as he sidled down the steps ignoring the visitors who almost fell to the ground in obeisance when they recognized him. He began to speak even before reaching his goal and his voice was controlled and not a little menacing.

'You've been asking about one of my senior followers,' Morozumi said without self-introduction and with an abrupt pomposity to which Araki took an instant dislike.

57

'What is your interest in this matter?'

Araki put on his abused face, his eyes narrowing and his mouth rounding to force a tone of indignation which grew in his throat.

'I don't think I know you.'

Kondo found the scene a little ludicrous. The teacher, the leader of a quasi-religious movement which required him to be revered in royal tradition was caught out by someone for whom such contrived, abnormal behaviour was contemptuous, and when Araki failed to respond with the expected degree of deference or respect he was forced off-guard and looked angrily at the clutch of employees who had accompanied their leader in his abrupt departure from the temple.

He turned back to Araki and said: 'We should have been introduced. May I apologize and name myself as Morozumi.' He proffered a card and this time the amateur investigator reciprocated, although he exaggerated the moment by extracting his wallet and looking slowly through a wad of name-cards for one of his own. Kondo continued bemused at the scene and the way the believers on their way in recognized the beloved leader and slumped to their knees, their heads bowed, touching their pressed palms. The man himself ignored them. He looked much older in close-up. His face was gaunt and tense with wide-angled eyes over a high, thin nose. The hair was clearly dyed to a thick glossy darkness and was cut evenly around the narrow oval skull. He studied the rough-looking man in jeans and running shoes and then looked fleetingly at the name-card.

'Are you working for the police?' Morozumi asked, unable to elicit anything of importance from the card.

Araki was enjoying the superior role.

'Not at all. I'm employed by the Izumi family to add some more manpower to the search for the unfortunate Mrs Izumi. I can give some concentrated time to the case where the police can only look at the obvious, and the reason I'm in your temple today is that the missing lady was here often, was active in your recruitment drive and I have to believe that someone here must have known her well enough to understand her state of mind and her mental condition just before she disappeared. If people try to tell me that Mrs Izumi was merely a lonely old lady who looked to the temple as a lifeline and that she's history as far as the temple's concerned then I'm obliged to raise some questions about the moral obligations of those inside who proclaim and promise unachievable benefits in return for receiving their followers' personal wealth, if they happen to be rich, or recruiting and collecting money if they happen to be ordinary and poor.'

Kondo stepped back a metre, fully expecting the strong, young acolytes around Morozumi to be inflamed by his friend's inappropriate bluntness and manhandle him into apologizing. There was a movement, a reaction to the overt insult, but Morozumi anticipated trouble and raised a cautioning arm.

He said calmly: 'Her spiritual needs were taken care of here.' He pointed unconvincingly to the shining edifice. 'Who knows what tortures she suffered outside this sanctity.'

Araki forced a puzzled frown.

'Was she very devout? I mean, if she was troubled by something, family problems perhaps, wouldn't she have confided them to you?'

'Perhaps she wasn't given the chance to confide in us. But we've dedicated our mantras and prayers to her.' Morozumi broke away to touch the cheek of a middle-aged woman who was gripping the hem of his jacket.

'This is not the moment to discuss this sad event,' Morozumi said, his embarrassment enjoyed by Araki. 'If I think of something which may assist your investigation I'll call you.'

Kondo shielded his face as Araki tugged at the metal ring on the tin of beer and when the threat from the frothy spray had passed he said: 'Strange how Morozumi seemed so keen to find you and then said so little.'

Araki leaned back and drank, wiping an elusive dribble from his chin.

'He wanted to identify me,' he remarked casually, handing the foaming tin to his friend while reaching for another. 'Once his servant had told him I was asking about Mrs Izumi he had to know who I was. I wonder what incited him to rush out and offer help. Was it an overwhelming desire to find a lost parishioner?' He thought for a moment, a fist clutching the cold can to his chin. 'Or was it a need to find out how much I know?'

Kondo's belch interrupted a disdainful grin. 'We both know it was the latter,' he said. 'Only he doesn't know how little you know.' They laughed together and patted each other on the hips.

They had bought some tins of cold Kirin beer from a vending machine and found a patch of ground among groups of revellers who first looked at the intruders with red-eyed contempt. They mellowed when Araki toasted them in a country dialect he recognized and which gave him an affinity with the drunken cherry blossom viewers. When the breeze slackened, the rich perfume from the heavy, dark-pink clusters seemed to intoxicate the throngs who drank, sang and swayed beneath them. A man had vomited against a tree and the smell from his excesses overpowered the cherries' aroma when the breeze changed direction. The high, early afternoon sun played in the branches and warmed the passions of the people.

Kondo said, referring to Morozumi: 'He clearly sees himself as some sort of shaman, a real mystic. You saw the way he sat on his throne and the way his followers revered him.'

'I wonder what kind of hold he had on Mrs Izumi,' Araki said. 'Enough, perhaps, to force her to do something she couldn't complete successfully and make her run away.'

60

Kondo screwed an empty tin into the loose earth and made a gesture which said he had absolutely no idea.

Araki persisted in his search for a cause or direction for the Honshinkyo of Go Morozumi.

'Would you classify it with Tenrikyo and Rissho Koseikai and the other popular movements?'

Kondo shook his head.

'No. Morozumi's belongs to the neo-new, if that's possible. The older ones have become real popular movements, businesses almost, offering their followers a spirit of fellowship in return for support of the hotels, restaurants and resorts that the religious manage. The Honshinkyo is a lot more sinister and I believe that faith-healing is a strong factor in their attraction. Did you notice those groups of people lying down and someone kneeling beside them?'

Araki said he had seen the figures kneeling and kneading or stroking the backs of the men and women who lay before them.

Kondo continued: 'While prodding and poking, the enlightened servants of the master will be whispering their leader's promises of health and even a secure and happy after-life.'

Araki scoffed. 'In return for what?' He knew why but he let Kondo attempt to rationalize.

'If they don't have the income to make a regular contribution they are assigned to the fund-raising activities of the temple or the direct door-to-door soliciting for new recruits. Being both fervent and wealthy I would imagine the missing lady was an important contributor to Morozumi's finances.'

Araki opened two more tins and both men turned to watch as the first dispute of the afternoon was breaking out behind them. A man in a light raincoat was standing in the middle of some matting he had obviously laid out earlier that morning and was berating the swaying and lurching celebrators as they gradually encroached on his patch. He looked anxiously over heads in search of his

61

company seniors for whom he had been guarding a place for over five hours.

'They never stop, do they?' Araki said, nodding towards the harried salaryman.

He returned to the theme.

'How wealthy are the Izumis?'

'The company appears to be a success,' Kondo said, removing a folded piece of paper from his wallet and talking as he scanned his notes. 'I jotted down a few things from the handbook. The Izumi family own twenty per cent of the shares and they are currently worth about ten billion yen.'

'Who owns the rest?'

Kondo scanned his notes.

'Except for one City bank, the other major shareholders are trust and regional banks.'

'Could you do a proper scan on them? Check the financials, the main bank report, sales, profits.'

'Are you retaining me?' the older man asked, trying to contain his enthusiasm.

Araki patted the spot on his jacket where his wallet lay hidden.

'For a fee my friend, for a fee.'

4

In the rich light of a Tokyo April morning free of humidity and cleansed of air pollutants by a fresh, warm breeze, the house looked larger than it had on that night two days earlier when he had met the Izumi family at dinner. The cherries were in full bloom and would dominate the garden for another two or three days, but a few fragile outside petals had already broken free and speckled the grass.

The housekeeper was expecting him, though her cool, proper greeting was hardly the most appropriate for someone who was trying to help. She led him through the sitting room, past the dining room to the rear of the house and invited him to sit on the tatami in a large, twelve-mat room whose smell of freshly laid matting was not strong enough to mask traces of cigarette. Araki assumed it was also the master of the house's sleeping room, though he did not feel inclined to look into the cupboards for a folded futon.

'I hope I'm not intruding,' he said, watching as she knelt and served a cup of scalding, green tea. She apologized when he had to drop it sharply on to its lacquer saucer, making it rattle on the polished table. He was embarrassed by her exaggerated bowing, her assumption of guilt far beyond the severity of the misdemeanour. She was a pre-war relic in his eyes, a rare reminder of the demand for total servitude which dominated the relationships between the hierarchies and led to the blind submission of the wretched commoner and the soldier to those who demanded they give their lives for their country. He saw this again in the pliant behaviour of the legions of white-collar workers, the salarymen in their dark-blue and grey suits who, along with their dignity as individuals, gave their days and most nights and many weekends to the banks, trading companies and the securities houses and demanded nothing in return except to be kept in work from university to retirement.

Araki said calmly: 'Izumi-san invited me to look at some of the family papers.' The room, apart from the table and a landscape print and a calendar on separate walls, was bare and there were no documents awaiting inspection. The old woman did not respond to the prompt.

'There might be something in them to give me a clue to her whereabouts.' Still kneeling, she looked up and beckoned towards the paper-covered shoji doors which covered one end of the room.

'Please. When you've finished your tea, please help yourself.'

'You're very kind. But please rest for a moment.'

The housekeeper glanced nervously towards the door, a habit, Araki assumed, of the servant suddenly surprised by the guest who refused to ignore her presence. As she relaxed, her body sank into itself and she seemed to rest more comfortably on her frail limbs.

Araki leaned forward and said: 'Where do *you* think Mrs Izumi is? Is she with friends somewhere? In hiding?'

The old woman kneaded the knot of cloth she had made from the apron which covered her dark, shapeless work dress. Shaking her head, she raised her small, wrinkled face with its soya-bean-sized nose and actually looked into Araki's eyes.

'She's dead.'

Araki sipped the tea.

'The family don't believe so, or they wouldn't have asked me, employed me I should say, to find her.'

'They don't want to believe it,' she said with sudden openness. 'Perhaps they didn't know her.'

There was a sound in the house, a creak as someone stepped on a loose floorboard. The woman's eyes

64

darted sideways, full of tension, before softening as she measured the distance and concluded it was not close.

'That's Reiko,' she revealed. 'She's just woken up.'

Araki pushed his sleeve up. It was almost ten-thirty on his watch.

'When we were alone,' the elderly retainer said with intensity, 'Mrs Izumi and I were like sisters. She even called me Oneesan, older sister.'

'You've been with the Izumis a long time then?'

'Fifty-five years,' the woman Shimazaki replied, with a haste that suggested she was calculating her tenure in days, like a prisoner counting off the time until he is free. 'I was given to the Izumi family in the eighth year of Showa, eight years before the war began with America. The Izumis moved from Tokyo to Yamanashi and Mrs Izumi was born shortly after. The men in my family were in the army and had all gone to China.' She used the old word 'Shiina'. 'I was fifteen and a useless girl in a family of seven.'

Her voice betrayed little bitterness and her eyes, hollow and cloudy, stayed dry. 'I was given to the Izumis,' she repeated, 'to look after the baby.' She rocked slightly on her haunches. 'She was like my own. I fed and washed her and played with her for hours. We grew older, and the years changed our relationship. All the men were killed. There were bombs and fires and every few days another funeral. When she was eleven we climbed half way up Mount Fuji. She, little Masako, didn't understand that the orange glow in the distance was Tokyo on fire. She thought it was the sunset.' She smiled at the tragic memory. 'We came back to Tokyo after the war. The factory had gone, and the houses. Only the land remained. Her father, the last male in the family, built this house and started the business again. She was twenty-two when he died and he left her everything.'

Araki willed her to continue, to talk about the missing woman's husband Yasuo and how he had come to take his wife's surname, but again the sound of footsteps on

65

the old floorboards disturbed her concentration and this time they were closer.

'Obaachan!' Reiko's voice travelled easily through the frail partitions and called for grandmother, or little old lady in its familiar form.

Shimazaki rose awkwardly to her feet.

'Reiko wants something to eat.' Again there was no bitterness in her voice, only the sad resignation of those doomed to serve.

'Please take your time,' she said, motioning towards the shoji before shuffling away.

Araki drew the partitions aside to find a step leading to a carpeted strip of room which contained a desk and drawers and bookshelves reaching the ceiling. The layers of wall had been dutifully withdrawn and fitted into the sides of the building, leaving only the fine meshing between the house and the garden beyond. Araki was surprised that such a large, private property still existed in this part of Tokyo. Most owners had long ago succumbed to the tempting escalation of land prices in the metropolis and sold off their precious gardens to the developers. Many had let their old, wooden structures be torn down to be replaced by a smaller house in the shadow of a new mansion apartment block. Araki found the Izumi garden irresistible, seeing in it a lost generation. Below an overhang of willow he could see the still, dark water of a pond, its placid surface occasionally disturbed by the dorsal fins of the black and orange carp which broke through in the shade of the azaleas and then seemed to wallow and roll across to the sunshine and then rub their shiny scales on the moss which spilled down the banks and the granite stones that gave the illusion of a cliffside.

Araki sat at the desk and began to survey the pile of papers and photographs which had presumably been selected by Yasuo Izumi for his perusal. The drawers were all locked, which also suggested the stack of papers represented the limit of information available to him.

He held a recent, monochrome photograph the size of a postcard, away from the glare of a shaft of sunlight. Looking at the face of a solemn, round-faced woman in her fifties he searched in the eyes for the intensity of the religious fanatic, or in the mouth for the slightest of sneers, but saw only a gentle kind of strength. The strength, perhaps of a woman left with no male siblings and with the responsibility of inheriting a considerable fortune. What had the faithful housekeeper said about her mistress? When she was twenty-two she was left alone with everything.

He used the time it took to light a cigarette to search his memory for the words that had caused the strange daughter-in-law to receive the disapproving stare from her husband, or was it her father-in-law. Something about Masako, the missing woman, owning the property. He spread the documents impatiently, separating the photographs from the rest. Masako did not appear in any more flattering, posed pictures. Instead, she was lost among family members or friends where she was another unsmiling Japanese matron, mostly in a kimono. Were any of these people from the temple? He looked at the backs of the photographs but only the date and place had been left as a reminder, presumably, Araki thought, because none of the characters captured by the camera required identification. Araki recognized the family members he had dined with among the pictures of weddings and New Year visits to Meiji Shrine or the Asakusa Kannon temple. The documents Izumi had chosen to leave for his assistance seemed selected to help prove the theory of one of the grieving family that the matriach of the Izumis had sought solace in a hotel or lodging house near one of the properties the family owned or a resort they often visited. There were postcards from hotspring hotels, layouts of mansion blocks where Mariko and Shinobu had apartments financed by parental money and local government plans showing the dimensions of plots of land the Izumis owned. Araki scribbled some addresses into his notebook and stacked a batch of papers which he would take away for more detailed examination. He rattled the locked drawers and then looked angrily around the deceptively composed office and living quarters. The tokonoma alcove was bare and there was no tansu chest-of-drawers to hold the mistress's clothes. Araki strode to the cupboard and slashed the doors aside. A futon and its bedding in one and a row of suits, ties and shirts on hangers. The drawers below contained underwear, socks and handkerchiefs. They slept apart, Araki calculated with a nod of satisfaction, and this was the husband's room. Izumi had chosen a few pieces of information, scraps of family detail which would give the investigator a superficial understanding of the woman he had been paid to find and he had left them in his room, carefully locking away his own papers and the secrets of his own quarters.

He wondered where the missing wife slept: apart from the step down to the garden the only other exit was the door to the corridor. There was no door connecting directly to another room. He looked again in the cupboards, this time for a household safe or some other repository for the seals and deeds he knew could not be in the locked but easily penetrable drawers. A movement in the garden flashed across the light funnelled into the house, distracting Araki who had returned to the papers he had been given to help his search. He looked through the mesh and saw the back of a woman kneeling beside the pond, her head bent forward so as to be almost out of sight and from the heels that supported her buttocks he could see she was barefoot. Reiko stood up, threw a morsel of bread into the water and clapped lightly to shed the last crumbs.

She wore a white cotton, knee-length nightdress buttoned at the front and patterned in pink at the hem and around the edge of the long sleeves. She had not seen or heard him and stared ahead as if mesmerized by the reflections in the light of the rich cherry blossoms and the red of the azaleas around the pond. She barely reacted

68

when Araki stepped through the side of the house into a pair of wooden geta clogs which betrayed his presence as he walked awkwardly over the flat stone slabs which meandered through the carefully raked gravel towards her. There was no change of expression on the pale, thin face, no instinctive clutching of the nightdress at the throat, which might indicate a natural feeling of embarrassment or shame at being surprised by a relative stranger. It was her own garden, Araki supposed, and she had every right to walk in it in whatever state of dress she wanted. It was he who should feel some guilt for the deliberate intrusion but he had expected at least a startled cry. He wondered if she had had a calming glass of whisky with her breakfast, or perhaps a drink had been her only morning meal.

'I'm sorry to surprise you,' Araki said, pressing on with an explanation before she could run off. 'But your father-in-law invited me to look at some photographs and other papers which might help me find Mrs Izumi.' He waited for the response which never came and pressed on: 'I suppose I have to agree with the family opinion that she's temporarily confused and may have simply made her way to a familiar place or somewhere she likes and feels secure.'

Reiko looked once towards the house and said: 'Do you have a cigarette?'

'Of course.' He produced a packet and they lit up together. 'Should we go inside?' he said uncomfortably.

'It's warmer here,' she murmured, and although he had to concur that the old wooden house would retain the chill of the night hours after sunrise he could see by the way she hugged herself she still felt the cold in her flimsy nightwear.

'Where do you think I can look where the police haven't already been?' he asked.

The disturbed young woman turned and looked at Araki with what might have passed for the briefest gesture of contempt, as if to say that the answer was obvious, and then reached up to tap a ball of cherry

69

blossom hard enough to dislodge its outer ring of petals. They fell on to the water but the carp must have found them bitter as after one attempt to bite the soft flowers they rolled over and slapped the water in disgust.

Reiko smiled and shrugged her shoulders.

Araki said, searching for the words least likely to offend: 'If Mrs Izumi is still hopefully alive we think she's staying somewhere familiar, a hotel perhaps, near some family property. I see from the documents I've been given that there's family land in Kamakura and in Tokyo there's land in Nakameguro and apartments in Ogikubo and a house in Mitaka. I'll look at each of them.'

Reiko looked over his shoulder at the silent house. Araki turned and followed her gaze towards a silhouette in an upstairs window, a shadow which soon disappeared and could have been a play of light and then said: 'Where do *you* think she is?'

'She was only happy at the temple,' she replied, her voice expressing neither concern nor relief at the thought, and she turned and walked listlessly across the spiky, hardy grass towards the house. Araki followed obediently, wondering how to remind the young housewife, whose nerves were as tight as a drum, about her outburst before dinner two days earlier when she had corrected her father about the ownership of the family properties. Was it true that the land, buildings and billions of yens worth of shares in the family business were registered in the missing woman's name? He also wanted to ask what a young, married, childless woman was doing skulking about a garden in her nightwear, barely concealing her need for a strong drink. She had vices totally unexpected in the wife of a prominent businessman's son and none of the irritating, self-demeaning mannerisms or the elaborately affected speech of the humblest member of the household, the daughter-in-law. She plainly was not fulfilling the traditional role as caretaker of her husband's house and ageing parents, and if the latter had been one of her functions she had clearly failed. Araki chose his

70

words carefully, fascinated by the rich vein of mystery he managed to tap in his brief meetings with the family and concerned not to abuse the confidence he was trying to inspire. But he would have to wait. The housekeeper appeared at the opened wall and summoned Reiko to her late breakfast. Her parting words were almost childishly innocent, almost happy. Had she, Araki wondered, been able to impart some message, perhaps the one she had wanted to give last Saturday as she followed his departure with half a face from behind the sliding door.

The housekeeper had laid out more tea in the reception room in anticipation of his prompt departure, but Araki paused in the office-cum-sleeping room to peruse the photographs again, his attention on one which showed a group of women, including Mrs Izumi, around the un-smiling figure of Go Morozumi in front of his ostentatious temple. When he joined the old woman he made it clear he intended to return the small bundle of pictures and documents he had stashed into a folder. He was pleased she did not retire automatically but sat uncomfortably at his invitation on one of the armchairs by the table.

After an exchange of pleasantries, Araki's face tight-ened and he said: 'Did Mrs Izumi always wear a kimono when she went to the temple?'

The woman's head lowered and twisted to one side.

'Mostly,' she said firmly.

'The same one.'

'She has twenty. Perhaps twenty-five. But she had two or three she wore regularly.'

'Which one was she wearing when she left home for the last time?'

The old spinster appreciated the finality of his words, even though he had chosen them by accident.

'The dark brown one.'

Araki scratched the loose hair on his scalp.

'What puzzles me,' he said, 'was why nobody remembers seeing a middle-aged woman anywhere after she left that bank around eleven-thirty.'

71

'The police haven't found anyone yet,' she said in explanation. 'After all, kimonos are not all that rare, confined though they are to elderly women by day and the bar hostesses at night.'

'Do you know what she planned to do with the five million yen she withdrew from the bank?'

Araki detected a tone of disapproval in an otherwise dispassionate voice when she muttered about obligations to the temple, the results of fund-raising, personal contributions, gifts and seasonal payments.

'It was not a large amount for this family,' she concluded.

'But a year's salary for the average Japanese,' he added.

They turned and twisted through the lanes, between the high, protective walls of the prosperous houses of south Tokyo, Chris complaining that a policeman had asked him to show his alien's identity card as he was perceived to be loitering.

'It seems a bit obvious,' Araki said, 'but since everyone assumes Mrs Izumi is living happily in some familiar hotel or family-property we have to check them first.'

'Won't the police have done that already?'

'A month ago, certainly, but they're waiting for her to reappear with a story about amnesia. Or for somebody to find a body.'

Chris asked: 'Where should I go?'

'Take yourself to Nakameguro, to a plot of land between Komazawa-dori and the station. Here, I've marked it.' He passed a creased map to Chris as they queued for their tickets. 'See if it's a house or a block of flats and check the tenants' names. Write a few down and we'll check them with names in the family records. Talk to a neighbour or two and the shopkeepers. Look for a hotel in the vicinity where an old woman with fading faculties can sit and watch the family possessions in private. Play the gaijin looking for a Japanese friend. Don't speak too fluently.

We meet tomorrow night at the Roman. I'm going to visit the bank and then look at the flat in Ogikubo where the married daughter lives and before I see you and Kondo in the bar I'm going to see a bank manager and a policeman.'

Araki had wanted a quiet evening, a couple of hours of thought, a study of the locations of the Izumi property and the planning of a trip to each of them. Some, like the land in Kamakura and the villa in Kawaguchi would have to be the object of a special trip, but he planned to see all of the bits of real estate to eliminate the theory that the confused owner of all of them was in hiding near one favourite investment. The Tanaka daughter watched disapprovingly as her father's tenant hauled a mixed case of beer and whisky up the outside steps to his apartment. She had liked the invitations to his late-night drinking sessions but had despaired at not being the object of his affections, feeling like a decoration and later like a servant when she found herself pouring drinks and calling for the take-out food on which Araki and his friends seemed to survive. And she did not like his friends, most of whom were like Araki, early middle-aged, heavy smokers and drinkers and lacking in family responsibilities. The foreigners were slightly better, but when they drank they wanted to play sex games instead of falling asleep like Araki's Japanese colleagues. And there was the excitement of deceiving her parents and the boy across the street in the general goods store, the one who had been chosen to be her husband next year.

Araki called his former wife, always hoping his son would answer but expecting and usually receiving the curt tones of the woman he had met in university and married for love. Yes, Mitsuo could play in the baseball game in the sand-lot Araki had arranged for the coming Saturday but he would have to leave by five, and a car would pick him up, as he had to attend evening school at seven. Mitsuo was eleven. Araki was nearly forty and

73

the sallow skin he pinched close to the mirror was slow to flatten. The ring of fat bulged under his shirt like a sumo wrestler's mawashi belt.

The summons was thinly disguised as an invitation and the voice barely hid the irritation, presumably at having to speak into Araki's answerphone. The recording device was a luxury he retained, although its usage had peaked years earlier when he left the magazine and enjoyed a brief period of notoriety. He felt obliged to request Araki's presence in view of the fact that the former reporter had been retained at some cost by one of the family and should be at the disposal of any of them if a meeting could assist in finding his mother. It sounded very formal.

Araki was uncomfortable in a suit and the one he wore was an unconventional, dark-green colour and he had owned it for ten years. He guessed correctly that it would be appropriate to wear at the venue chosen by his host. Ken Izumi was late and Araki waited not unhappily at a reserved table in a private booth of a members' club for middle-level managers called The Piper below a twenty-storey office complex in Hibiya, opposite one of the entrances to the old park and within sight, at least from the eighth floor and above, of the Imperial Palace. Young women in short tartan skirts and frilly blouses served drinks and a variety of cold snacks, and one of them anticipated the tardy host's predilection by setting the table with a bottle of Johnny Walker Black Label and the accompanying ice bucket and bottles of soda water. Araki asked for Kirin beer. The glass was refilled for him twice before the figure of Ken Izumi approached, an apologetic smile on his face and obviously enjoying the greetings of recognition from the staff. He held a hand across his double-breasted, grey business suit in a slightly imperious gesture and met Araki with a truncated bow which petered out as he slumped into the soft, low cushions.

'Difficult times,' he said by way of apology. 'The yen had just hit a hundred and twenty-three in Europe when I left

74

the office. Up from twenty-four fifty here this morning.'
Araki was not an avid reader of economic news but the
rising yen was a national issue, and he could not avoid
the trade debate raging between Japan and her main
trading partners. By forcing the dollar down, the logic
went, the cost of America's imports would rise and, little
by little, fall in volume. It seemed to ignore the fact that
most of Japan's imports were raw materials and since
they would become cheaper they would help keep the
cost of processed exports down as a result. The younger
Izumi leaned comfortably in the chair, waving a cigarette
dismissively as he spoke.

'A half yen rise in the Japanese currency will eventually cut our overseas sales income by half a million
dollars.'

Araki nodded sympathetically and agreed with his
host's suggestion to abandon beer for the Johnny Walker.
The antipathy he felt towards this confident, aggressive
man, perhaps due to his failure to mention immediately
the matter of his mother's disappearance, was starting to
rise to the surface. Was it nervousness, embarrassment or
deliberate callousness that caused Ken Izumi to put the
country's trade balance before the fate of his mother, the
reason for this hastily called meeting? The whisky was
beginning to taste thin so he topped it up without the
aid of the waitress. Araki watched the son pat his short,
permed hair and look around and wait for someone to
scurry over and light the new cigarette gripped between
those thin, weak lips. He decided to let him talk, even
prompting him to do so, waiting until he mentioned his
mother and wanting to catch some flaw in the detail,
some hint that someone was lying, and to compare his
statement with the succinct and disturbing note Kondo
had left in his apartment during the day.

Izumi Electric, Kondo had written, joining up the first
two ideographs to make 'Izumiden' in his peculiar short-
hand which assumed the reader was familiar with the
abbreviated form, was a large company but not known

to the ordinary Japanese because it made bulbs, lamps and light fittings virtually unnoticed by the public as they are brand-named products in the cars and lorries that host them. Look closely at one out of four cars on the roads in Japan, Kondo had written, and you'll find the kanji for Izumi moulded into the perspex light coverings and the rims of the bulbs and fittings used in the motor industry. Figures just released for Izumi Electric showed sales for the year ending in March were fifteen per cent down and analysts forecast a further twenty-five per cent fall in the current year. Izumi had stayed onshore when competitors had set up cheap manufacturing plants abroad, and was falling behind. Kondo's note turned even more precise and disturbing in its implication. Izumi has issued capital of five billion yen, of which sixty per cent was traded on the first section of the Tokyo Stock Exchange among the giants of the Japanese industrial scene, and another twenty per cent was held by three of the thirteen City banks and five less grand, but nevertheless significant, major regional banks. And then Araki reached the point of what he thought was becoming an unnecessarily verbose narrative. His host was talking about profit margins and the importance of maintaining a market share in a world where Koreans and Taiwanese entrepreneurs were chipping away at Japan's competitive edge. But Araki was thinking about the last line of the note from his friend Kondo. The remaining twenty per cent of the Izumi shares, worth a nominal billion yen, was held by the family, but in the Tokyo stock market they were worth ten times their face value and in the books of the legal authorities they were registered in the name of Mrs Masako Izumi.

'Was your mother involved in the day-to-day business?' Araki asked, trying to link the information about the missing woman's immense shareholding with her son's monologue.

Ken Izumi's mouth contracted into a disdainful scowl. He said: 'We respect the role of women in our society and

76

that's to run the household and support those who fill the rice bowls. None of the women in our family take part in the management of Izumi Electric.' His voice was emphatic and slightly menacing, as if he resented the question and found it offensive.

Araki recalled the contrasting women he had met two days earlier in the Izumi household. Only the younger daughter, Shinobu, fulfilled the stereotype her brother had specified, with her look of pained acceptance as the wife of a bureaucrat husband she never saw and the standard brace of children enjoying that brief spell of freedom before demands of the education system overwhelmed their childhood and condemned them to a teenage world of cramming schools and midnight studies. And her sister Mariko, unusually forward for an unmarried Japanese. A woman with a career in fashion and at twenty-nine almost past the conventional marriageable age. It did not seem to bother her; she was single-minded and determined, the proof being her tenacity in pressuring her father to pay Araki to find her mother. And then there was Reiko, hardly the obedient spouse of a successful businessman, more the desperate runaway, living on cigarettes and booze and the occasional scrap of sympathy. And what role did the ageing housekeeper play in this complicated family? She was the least significant, yet she knew the most.

Izumi was saying: 'My father's the president and senior managing director. I'm on the board and I have responsibility for our exports.' He did not have to add that barring some boardroom revolt he would be the next president when his father decided to retire or take the honorary chairman's position.

'Of course, mother was interested in our business, because it was the family business, but she was gracious enough not to interfere.' With still no clear expression of sympathy that might cause him to stop and reflect on the horrible possibility that his mother might be dead, Izumi continued. 'Mother has led an independent sort of

77

life since we grew up, not that she did very much.' He exchanged a brief look with the waitress who knelt to refill the glasses. Her eyes were highlighted in black and darted expertly from the drink to the attentions of her chief guest.

'She messed about with one of those trendy religions. Gave them money, promised them land. Throwing our money into the river would be more worthwhile.'

Araki felt no compulsion to play the passive guest.

'Your mother's named as the main, private shareholder in Izumi Electric. Surely she had to have some influence, however small, on how the business was directed. A passing comment over breakfast, a note or two on the monthly trading figures. And I have to assume that she was free to spend the rewards of her position on anything she fancied, even these trendy religions.'

Izumi scoffed contemptuously.

'We never ate breakfast together,' he said. When Araki was not amused he continued, spreading his hands across the table to emphasize his point.

'Mother's name on the shares is an expedient. For tax purposes. It is not unusual in wealthy families.'

'And the property,' Araki said. 'Is that also in your mother's name?'

The businessman had paused to snack on jelly-fish and chopped, roasted pieces of chicken and cold salmon steak and drank deeply between each mouthful.

Araki looked for a reaction in the other man but unlike the western face, where the slightest change of mood caused an eye to widen or a cheek muscle to crease, the oriental was a mask of taut, wrinkle-free skin and eyes that said nothing. The younger Izumi, it seemed to Araki, had made a decision at that instant but it was not betrayed by his expression. He wiped some grease from the corner of his mouth and laid his chopsticks across the plate.

He said: 'I asked you to spend an evening with me so that we could get to know each other, and to explain to you what the family thinks. I have not succeeded in putting over this message and if you're not busy I'd like to go somewhere quieter.' He looked at his watch without reading it and smiled as Araki shook his head nonplussed. The place was full and the smoke and bits of conversation from the tables around them, separated only by a low divide which hid all but the bobbing black heads of the customers, drifted over. Izumi signed the bill on the way out.

'We can walk,' he said, joining Araki after passing some instruction to a driver in a black Nissan President. 'It's at the Hibiya end of the Ginza.'

It was the kind of night-spot Araki had been to rarely during his journalist career, and always at times when he had written something complimentary about a politician or a company president and at their expense. The guests at the Kana, on the second floor of a building he did not recognize behind the Hankyu Department store, were of that category. Most were in their sixties, born before the Great Kano earthquake of 1923, but there were others, like Izumi, the sons of the powerful and wealthy, who were allowed to display the rewards usually only enjoyed by those at the head of the escalator. The hostesses who served drinks and sat with their guests were clad in evening gowns of subdued colours and had been carefully selected for their attractiveness and maturity. There was no giggling, or touching of clients' knees or the exchange of ribald puns and jokes that typify entertainment in most of the thousands of bars in the floating world on a normal Tokyo evening. Araki knew that the women were former actresses and singers whose media usefulness had ended in their late teens. Their hair was carefully groomed and shoulder length. The dyed hair and miniskirts and the flitting between tables of drunken salarymen were missing. The Kana catered to the senior élite, who paid for the company of women but on their terms and in their time.

79

With the help of a stern man with eyes almost closed and wearing a dinner jacket, they were shown to a circular booth which almost enclosed the seats which were covered in mauve mock velvet and surrounded a low, glass-topped table. His host, Ken Izumi, and the head waiter were talking, their heads close. Araki looked for the source of the quiet orchestral music but he supposed the speakers were disguised in the sound-proofing which gave the walls a padded look. There was a small raised floor which Araki knew was not reserved for karaoke bawlings of the customers of less exclusive venues.

'There's a vice-minister in the next booth,' Izumi said, as if to impress upon his guest the exclusivity of the surroundings. 'But this is mostly a businessman's refuge.'

There was no subservient kneeling by the tall, well-proportioned woman in a short, electric-blue satin evening dress with thin shoulder straps, who appeared with a tray of drinks and deposited it on the table. She sat with Izumi and they shook hands limply.

'This is Araki-san,' Izumi said, motioning towards his guest.

'Mayumi Maeda,' she said, her eyes closing as she inclined her head.

Araki reciprocated.

'Is your father well?' she said, returning to Izumi and leaning forward to begin her serving duties.

Izumi chuckled.

'As well as ever.' And then remembered the gravity of the moment, adding quickly 'in the circumstances'. Mayumi's face turned mournful and her voice betrayed what to Araki was exaggerated sincerity.

'And your mother. Is there any news?'

'Regrettably no. That's why Mr Araki is here. My sister thinks he can assist the police in finding her.'

There was something unpleasant in his tone and it was quickly becoming clear to Araki that the son of the family did not support his sister's initiative, but he had no idea why he should take time out to entertain the investigator in what was becoming a lavish manner. The woman had high cheekbones which seemed to shine beneath the carefully made-up face. Her mouth was wide and the lips lightly coloured in coral red. She was clearly a confidant of the Izumi family, at least the menfolk.

'It's a tragedy,' she said, addressing Araki but speaking to her patron. 'But when they find her the family can take care of her properly. It's all she deserves.'

She poured the drinks, including a weak whisky-water for herself and sipped it once during the conversation about the qualities of the missing lady and the efforts that everyone will make once she is found.

Dulled by the liquor, it took time before Araki realized Mayumi was talking like a member of the family but when he did he said: 'Everyone thinks Mrs Izumi was carried away with her fascination for the Honshinkyo and is now alone in some familiar surroundings contemplating her reality and may return shortly to resume her peaceful life at home.'

'Then I'm sure she's in good care and waiting for the most propitious moment to reappear,' the hostess said.

Two similarly mature, attractive women moved silently around the room and smiled diffidently when they recognized Izumi. One of them considered stopping to talk but only until she saw Araki's doleful, cynical expression and the frozen smile on their senior colleague Mayumi's face. She apologized and saw her escape in an elderly, frail businessman who was being escorted to his favourite seat and would appreciate another fussing beauty.

The charade was over, Araki thought, rubbing a tired, watery eye. The son had tried to buy his trust and would no doubt shortly suggest the course Araki ought to pursue. It came much sooner than the former journalist could have predicted. By their smiling asides to the staff, the two men who approached were obviously known at the Kana and they paused only to seek directions to the booth where their friend Ken Izumi was entertaining Araki and enjoying the company of the most attractive

81

of the hostesses, Mayumi Maeda. Araki felt very tired, as much from the whisky which always seemed to stay at the brim of his glass as at the impossibility of the task he had assumed. He hoped his state of mind had not betrayed itself to Izumi: it was after all only his second full day in the family's employment.

Araki thought it was a coincidental encounter, not unusual in an exclusive private members' club, but there was something about the speed at which they finished the preliminary exchange of greetings and sat comfortably in the armchairs and the way that Mayumi, as if by pre-agreed script, excused herself.

The two men were in their thirties and both had carefully cut short hair and dark, well-tailored suits. One was introduced as Sugita or Sugishita, larger than the other, whose name Araki heard clearly as Yano, his face rounder and his fingers short and stubby, like his frame. Araki knew exactly what they were. Where Izumi exuded the toughness of a businessman and a sharp intuitive mind to go with it his visitors displayed only a meanness in their humourless smiles and unintelligent faces. And they were too sardonic and casual to be the kind of playboy sons of the rich who might normally carry wads of banknotes on nightly circuits round the bars and clubs. When Mayumi had departed they placed their outstretched hands on the table as if to reinforce the sincerity of their bows and performed an unnecessarily prolonged foreplay, offering their words of deepest regret at the continuing unfortunate situation and proffering a sincere belief that Mrs Izumi, their friend's mother, would be reunited with her caring family. Araki's eyes ran across the rows of fingers but none of them were mutilated at the tips. They were polished front-men and not the tattooed street troopers. When the respectful exchanges had ended Izumi allowed another hostess to pour whisky for his guests before dismissing her with a sharp smile.

Araki was slurring slightly when he asked pre-emptively: 'What business are you in?'

He addressed Yano who, through his sharper reactions, seemed the senior but faltered at the question and looked fleetingly at Izumi for a lead.

Araki smiled to himself, trying thereby to quell a mild sensation of fear in his stomach, and drew a mental picture of the exit while trying to remember where exactly the Kana Club was.

Flustered, Yano said: 'Property investment advice. And sometimes we finance our own developments.' There was a sarcastic undertone in Araki's overly polite, almost feminine use of the language, missed by all except Izumi, when he said: 'Do the Izumis happen to be your clients? You act perhaps on their behalf?'

Izumi, the son, raised a hand.

'He is aware,' he said, addressing the two men Araki believed to be yakuza, 'of our property interests.' And after taking time to light another cigarette he added: 'And my mother's special interests.'

Araki savoured the implications of his knowledge and the fact that his host felt obliged to disclose it to the visitors. He looked at his watch.

'Don't let me stop you,' he said, 'but it's time I went home.'

Izumi protested mildly but saw Araki off without rising, merely a wave with one hand while the other gripped the back rim of the sofa.

Araki passed the discreet room where the bills were carefully prepared and found a short stairway leading to the toilet. His swollen bladder ached. He had drunk a lot and he breathed heavily as his head lowered and nodded involuntarily, a bent forearm supporting his body against the patterned tiles of the back wall. The first splash of urine and the noise from the automatic jet of cleansing water masked the opening of the door.

The two men swiftly checked the pair of cubicles and then took up positions on either side of Araki at the unpartitioned urinal. Araki acknowledged the first as if it were a chance meeting with someone he had already half-forgotten and then blinked when he saw the other man, the broader of the two, at his side and smiling as he thrust a hand ostentatiously through his open flies.

Sugishita produced a muted greeting but said nothing when the first spurt of pale liquid struck the edge of the step and splashed across Araki's shoes. On Araki's left Yano grunted, looked up in relief and playfully flicking his penis lost interest in the arc of urine as it hit the back of the urinal and rebounded in spots on to Araki's trousers and shoes. Araki tried to stem his own emission but kept having to release and watch in disgust as the two men he had shared drinks with minutes earlier seemed unaware of the mess they were causing at his feet. Araki finally broke away and made for the washbasin opposite where he was soon joined by Yano who made an ostentatious display in front of the mirror, unbuckling his belt and flattening his shirt inside his trousers. Uneasily, Araki splashed water on his face and saw through the mirror the grinning face of Sugishita, his arms folded across his chest.

'Many thanks for your help with the Izumi family problems,' Yano said, his face contorted as he took an exaggerated interest in an imagined blemish.

Araki mumbled something modest in reply.

'But it seems to me,' Yano continued as Araki braced himself for some words which might explain the hard men's crude behaviour, 'that the police are doing everything in their power to find Mrs Izumi.' He yanked the zip of his pants, and then said:

'As friends of the family we are very concerned about the emotional stress they are under and want to help them come through this trial. As our clients and friends we owe it to them.'

'As real friends of the family,' the sharper of the two was saying, 'we do not think there's any need for you to open the wounds again. The police are doing all they can and we suggest they be allowed to continue their efforts to find her without further embarrassment from others.'

*   *   *

The open-backed delivery truck had been stolen in
Yokohama, its licence plate switched for a Shinagawa
number, and left in a multi-storey car park near the west
exit of Shinjuku Station. Walking up the rear stairway
to the fourth level, the shorter of the two men removed
two pairs of transparent surgical gloves from the pocket
of his zip-up jacket and handed one to his stockier, taller
companion who cursed impatiently as the sticky material
snagged his fingernails. There was only a scattering of
vehicles in the bays but his head moved round slowly and
rhythmically across the dimly lit, open concrete cavity.
The other man knelt by the truck and twisted the rim
of the inside headlight until it gave sharply in his grip
and came away in rapid twisting movements. Senses
alert, he felt around the inside of the bowl until his
fingers struck the obstacle he expected. It was awkward
through the gloves, but his nails finally held beneath the
wrapping tape and he prised the tiny package away from
its hiding place.

'Hurry,' the other man said, quietly but urgently, hearing on a level below the dull drone of another vehicle.

'Let's go,' the shorter man said, separating the two keys
he had found in the lamp and opening the truck door with
one of them.

Both men stared ahead as they moved in the midnight
traffic along Yamate-dori. It was busy, the bars and restaurants had emptied and the taxis and hire cars were
taking Japan's drunken businessmen on the painful last
lap of their evening out with clients. They drove carefully
as there were few commercial vehicles of their size on
the road and to be stopped would have needed a difficult
and desperate attempt at escape. Passing Nakameguro
Station, its platform lights ablaze still, they turned right
into Komazawa-dori and pulled into a narrow lane where
the main road curved on a winding hill. The maroon
Toyota Corona was parked in a recess in front of the
crossed pillars of a Shinto shrine. They drove slowly past

the car, the man in the passenger seat fingering the key in his pocket for reassurance. 'Left here,' he said, after they had crossed a drainage canal and entered a local shopping precinct.

'Remember it now?' he said to the driver, laughing.

The driver grinned.

'I almost knocked the old woman over about here,' he said.

The other tensed.

'Careful,' he urged, seeing two men emerge ahead of them from a cellar bar and lurch aimlessly into the road. One of the drunks acknowledged his precarious meanderings with an apologetic wave towards the headlights that threatened the two of them.

'They won't remember us,' the driver said confidently. 'They can hardly stand up.' He turned the lights off as he turned into the lane without pavements and slid the gear into neutral and let the truck roll forward of its own momentum. A lamp in the porch cast a funnel of light into the street but the house stood alone on the edge of the plot of land that had been surrounded by a fence of hollow block concrete.

'Ready?' the driver asked.

'Yea,' the other man said, sliding out of the cab and tapping the door as he closed it as silently as he could.

The driver checked the mirror and ran his vision along the houses set back in a neat row to his right. He then drew the seat belt across his chest and locked it into position and opened the door until it hung loosely on the catch. Ramming the gear stick into first he pressed the accelerator and braced himself as the truck screamed towards its target. 'Yoshi!' he roared, as the tyres bit the tarmac. Approaching the porch of the house, his arms stiffened and his body tensed as he swung the wheel sharply to his left. The truck hit the fragile gateposts and bounced up the short flight of steps and crashed into the wooden stays of the porch, the bumpers reaching the front door, pressing it inwards with enough force to snap

86

the hinges. His sensations were dulled from the blow to his head as it struck the windscreen on first impact and he could smell dust and feel the drip of liquid, obviously his own blood, when unseen arms eased him out of the truck on to the rubble of the house's entrance. The big man half-carried the other and they were within metres of the Toyota before lights popped and the first suspicious neighbours made tentative moves to discover the origins of the sudden explosion of noise outside their windows. Inside the wooden dwelling, an old man felt a sharp sting in his chest and surge of pain from the left shoulder down to the wrist. His wife rushed to the futon and clasped the tired, sallow face of her husband to her lap. 'It's all right,' she murmured over and over, tears cascading down her cheeks.

5

He had to invoke the name of his retainers before the manager of the Tekkei Bank, a small, local savings institution in a busy shopping street, agreed to an appointment. Araki had wondered why a family of the Izumi wealth should use a bank of such little stature. The father, Yasuo, had replied that it was used exclusively by his wife, saying that she preferred to keep her everyday affairs away from the big City and trust banks that financed the business and were intimately aware of enough family details already. Put on hold, and listening to an innocuous jingle, he had been kept waiting long enough for the secretary to find a spare spot in the diary of a busy banker to meet someone who offered no potential as a customer. Or enough time to check his bona fides with the Izumi family.

The branch manager's name was Nakata and he had a flat, broad, square face and a small, almost bridgeless nose on which his glasses rode uncomfortably and required frequent, unconscious adjustment. His smile was obsequious, a result no doubt of constant use, but it faded quickly when the conversation turned to the customer. Mrs Izumi, he said, had withdrawn five million yen at around noon on 28 February. The account, as the police were perfectly aware, was in her sole name and used for small personal accruals and disbursements.

'But on the twenty-eighth you met Mrs Izumi personally,' Araki said. 'Did you meet all your customers when they made withdrawals of that size?'

Nakata looked despairingly over Araki's shoulder and through the window into the banking hall where a handful of customers waited for their number to be called to the counter. 'The Izumis have been valued clients of this institution for almost two decades,' he said with conviction. 'When any of them appear at our bank they are invited to take tea with me.' Sitting before the manager, Araki realized he had not been asked to sit at the table and there was a diminishing likelihood that the clerk in the lime-coloured outfit would appear with a cup of green tea, a small but normally obligatory gesture of welcome. Araki recalled that even when he interviewed the most intractable targets of his investigations, and they knew his intentions, the offer of refreshment transcended personal feelings.

Araki said: 'Did she say what she intended to do with the money?'

'Of course not,' the manager said, barely concealing his disdain. 'The movement of a client's cash is of no interest to me, particularly of someone like Mrs Izumi.'

'How often did she come to the bank?'

Nakata shrugged. 'The police know all this.'

'I'm sorry,' Araki said, shifting the chair. 'I haven't had the opportunity to interview the officer in charge of the case yet.' And for effect he added: 'Mr Izumi is arranging it, I believe.'

Araki was gratified that the bank manager understood the implication of his unexpected visitor's reasoning and replied accordingly.

'I apologize,' he said, 'but the matter has caused me great personal sadness and as the last person to have seen the missing lady I feel somehow personally responsible for not having recognized some sign.' He sought for words. 'Some sign of instability in her behaviour or something to indicate that she was going away. A suitcase perhaps.' Araki watched as minute bubbles of sweat traced the other man's hairline across his scalp.

89

'I don't understand,' he said, his voice deepening. 'How could you have been the last person to see Mrs Izumi unless she walked out of your branch and was knocked over by a bus?'

'Excuse me?'

The thin damp trail soaked Nakata's greying sideburn and trickled towards his jaw.

Araki held the unimaginative banker on the hook a little longer.

'If you were the last one to see her it implies you know for certain she disappeared after seeing you and she's talked to no-one since she withdrew five million and walked out of your bank. It is curious no-one reported seeing a late middle-aged woman in an outmoded kimono in a restaurant or the underground. Even a taxi-driver. Her photograph was in all the newspapers and weekly magazines, not to mention on television.'

'I'm sorry,' Nakata said, in a tone of conciliation which amused Araki by its exaggerated efforts to win him over. 'I was probably being a little dramatic. Everyone interviewed me, the police and some reporters, as if I was the last person to see Mrs Izumi. In the absence of anyone else admitting having met her or talked to her after leaving my bank I suppose I was.'

'I understand,' Araki said softly, his hands on his thighs as he rose to his feet.

'You've been most helpful. Thank you for your time.'

A young female clerk saw the brief courtesies of departure from her desk in the general office and leapt to open the manager's door, closing it again after aiming an instinctive bow towards her chief. Alone again, the bank manager lifted the telephone off its tray. Araki had almost reached the waist-high security gate when he stopped, his conscientious shepherdess almost stumbling into him.

'Excuse me,' he said, brushing past her and another visitor already being ushered towards the manager's office. He opened the door without the politeness of

90

a knock. The bank manager was leaning back in his comfortable, springy chair, his attention not on the door and the intruder's return. The telephone was cradled on his shoulder while his hands moved through a thin, black file of papers. In his surprise, he juggled the instrument, staring blankly at Araki before muttering something into it and returning it deliberately and self-consciously to its rest.

'You must excuse me,' Araki begged. His voice drifted as he tried to picture the person on the other end of Nakata's call. Why should he hang up abruptly when a hand over the receiver and a request, polite or otherwise, for Araki to wait outside for a minute would have constituted a normal response in the circumstances? Nakata could only produce a feeble 'yes'.

'It slipped my mind completely to ask what seal Mrs Izumi used for the five million yen withdrawal. Was it her registered seal?'

'No it wasn't,' the manager said, his reply sharp and definite, more a denial than contradiction, which Araki found unusual. 'She used an everyday seal for the normal banking business. Like you or I would use.'

'Did you notice if she had the registered family seal with her?'

Nakata shook his head and his first words were stammered as he pursed his lips and stumbled for a conclusive reply.

'I'm sure she hadn't. It would have been foolish of her to risk the family seal if she didn't need to for some important transaction.' It was suddenly important for Araki to know where the seal was and whether the missing woman had it with her on her last day in public. As the nominal owner of most of the Izumi wealth he had uncovered so far, the registered seal was the official symbol of that ownership and the only instrument which would recognize legally the transfer or sale of the individual assets registered in her name. It would be specially carved and larger than the pencil

91

thin chops bought off the shelf and used to sign receipts or confirm a dozen daily transactions. The registered seal would also be kept in a safe or secret place. Its possession conferred to the holder all the wealth it had the power to authorize.

'Well, if you're sure she didn't have it,' Araki said. 'Anyway, you would have told the police if she had brought it with her,' he continued, and apologized again for the intrusion.

Araki was bothered by the fact that this small, local money shop was the missing woman's last known stop. The entrance was a single, automatic door conspicuously painted with the bank's name and logo, and he was bowed out by a middle-aged uniformed man whose role doubled as a token security guard and the person who assisted customers in finding the appropriate counter for the service they required. He had a practised, ready smile which probably hid a genuine capacity to help; and he would have been about the same age as Mrs Izumi. Although in the street and with the door stuck open in its rut by the pressure of his feet, Araki turned and invited the doorman to join him.

'It's regrettable,' he said, as if he were talking to an old friend. 'We still haven't been able to find the lady who disappeared a month ago, one of your customers.' He looked over the man's shoulder to see if his conversation with another member of the staff had drawn the manager from his office. Behind the rows of desks and the heads of the clerks as they leaned forward, deep in concentration, he could just see the corner of Nakata's office and make out the shoulders of one of the people who had followed him for the next meeting.

'You mean Mrs Izumi?' The doorman's chin dropped to his chest as he muttered a selection of regrets.

'I wonder where she went from here,' Araki said hopefully. The man was too simple to be suspicious of the stranger's intentions. Araki continued: '. . . The station's too far for a woman of her age to walk comfortably so I would assume she caught a taxi or bus.'

The older man stepped aside and greeted a customer by name, for which Araki was thankful, as the helpful guard did not see the need to follow her into the banking hall.

'I was saying that Mrs Izumi probably took some form of transport from the bank.'

'I really don't know,' the old man hissed.

'Did you see her leave the bank?' Araki asked expectantly.

The man was beginning to have doubts about the status of the slightly scruffy person he had not taken seriously as a customer anyway.

'Are you with the police?' he asked suspiciously.

'No, I'm with the family.' Araki found a name-card and gave it to the reluctant doorman. 'It's important I know what she did the moment she stepped out of your bank. Please tell me what you told the police.' Araki's voice was deliberately edged with a remote touch of intimidation, enough he hoped to impress the doorman to speak openly but without arousing the verbal techniques of defence he might expect of a more intelligent person.

'I told them honestly that I didn't see anything odd. I knew the poor woman, have done for fifteen years. If it was raining, and even if it wasn't, I used to find her a taxi, and she always had a gift for me in July and December.'

Araki raised an arm, halting the tributes to Mrs Izumi from the grateful functionary.

'Did you find her a taxi on the day she disappeared?'

The older man shook his head.

'We were too busy that day,' he said, his brow creased and his voice betraying a suggestion that he thought Araki might be hinting at a lapse in his responsibilities. 'She bowed towards me but I couldn't help her because I was helping a customer.'

Araki asked: 'So that was the last time you saw her?'

'Yes it was.'

'You didn't see which way she turned when she left the bank?'

The uniformed man scratched his scalp through the thick, well-groomed, greying hair. Something had tripped his memory.

'Well,' he said, his hands on his hips as if angry with himself. 'The door of the bank opened and she stood on the edge of the pavement. I tried to hurry the customer I was talking to but he kept asking me more questions. I looked through the door a couple of times and she was still there and I still thought I had the time to find her a taxi.'

'And did you?' Araki asked, his excitement growing.

'I walked the customer over to the current account desk and when I went back to the door Mrs Izumi had gone.'

It was useless to ask how or where and Araki simply asked: 'Did you tell this to the police?'

'Excuse me?'

'Did you tell the police that Mrs Izumi probably caught a taxi or was picked up in a car?'

The doorman looked bewildered.

'They didn't go that far with their questions. I just told them I saw her leave the bank.'

There was nothing to show that the plot of land, a quarter the size of a football pitch and worth several billion yen in this central Tokyo site, belonged to Mrs Masako Izumi. There was a small sign attached to one of the pillars on the fragile perimeter fence, explaining details of plans to develop the plot as a mansion block with each floor reducing in size as it rose to eight storeys, but the Chinese character for 'Izumi' was not present. Chris had relied on the accuracy of the map Araki had given him as his enquiries at Nakameguro Station and even the police box on the corner of Komazawa Road failed to locate a property nearby registered in the name of the missing woman. Not unusual, Chris could imagine Araki saying. It was not likely a landowner would advertise his or her title to a vacant lot but would wait until it was developed and the owner's name could be attached to it in perpetuity. The empty site, overgrown with ugly weeds sprouting amongst a scattering of rubble and pieces of rotting timber was a few minutes' walk north of the station in a triangle between the main arteries of Yamate and Komazawa roads. On two sides its walls were less than a metre from grey, weathered six-storey housing blocks with futons airing over the balcony rails and pot plants adding a welcome touch of colour to an otherwise drab and typical urbanscape. From the top floors of both buildings thin signs had been draped, proclaiming in huge, fierce red characters the residents' right to sunlight and their opposition to the proposed mansion. Their protest would be futile: under existing legislation no exception could be made which would give these citizens any rights not accessible to the other millions of Tokyoites who lived in clean but cramped and airless flats and houses throughout the metropolis. Narrow lanes separated the plot from the tiny front gardens of private, barely detached dwellings and it was not until Chris rounded the corner that he saw the house. Its wood was dark brown and the rippling tiles on the roof made of authentic ceramic. It was obvious that the houses on the same site, which seemed to be the property of Masako Izumi, had been torn down and only this weathered relic defied the developer and stood incongruously on a patch of derelict, débris-strewn land.

Tokyo is not a city where people gather in the street to chat. They work, shop or stay indoors. Chris had long since recognized a street group as a sign of trouble and he hesitated when he saw the loose assembly of people, mostly women, their arms folded, their faces drawn in patient, morbid expectation. Approaching the scene, and attracting the first suspicious glances he had warned Araki a gaijin could expect, Chris saw what was drawing the crowd. A small truck was embedded in the façade of the building, its rear wheels raised off the ground as the impact had driven it deep into the porch. A dozen policemen bustled around, some discouraging the inquisitive, others completing measurements and writing the results on clipboards while a towtruck waited nearby, conspicuously blocking the narrow road. Chris knelt down, rubbed dust off a dented mailbox and scribbled the name of the householder into his notebook. Ando, he wrote.

Araki's mind was alert, although he craved a cigarette and planned a beer and a bowl of savoury noodles before he met the missing woman's younger, married daughter at the apartment the mother owned in Ogikubo, thirty minutes away from the central district of metropolitan Tokyo and almost an hour by public transport between the Izumi home and this four-storey block built for dentists, doctors, the best bar hostesses and the children of the wealthy. There were few people on the orange westbound commuter train as it lurched gently a few minutes ahead of the next, a yellow ten-car train which stopped more frequently along the Chuo-line that bisected the capital. He thought of the trousers that he had stripped off and thrown in anger on to his terrace when he reached his flat, and the two friends of the Izumi son who had looked blankly at the wall as they urinated on his clothing. Did Ken Izumi put them up to it, he wondered, as the shadow of yakuza crossed his mind for the first time in what he had assumed was a simple example of a disappearing middle-aged female.

The apartment house was set back from the main road and its intrusive noise, and protected from the view of a private hospital and a tall, functionally grey block of flats by a narrow lane and a border of tall, full ginkgo trees, whose leaves were nevertheless mottled and withered by air pollutants. It had orange-coloured, square-tiled walling which also covered the verandas on each floor and the building was raised on concrete stilts to allow some parking space for the residents at ground level. Shinobu Ohashi was expecting him but even so the thin lips were pulled into a frozen, embarrassed smile which told Araki that she feared the gossipy tongues of her housebound, female neighbours. The two children were

96

at their different schools but signs of their occupancy were pleasantly in evidence in the shape of discarded pieces of Lego blocks and the residue of sticky tape on the panelled doors where drawings had been temporarily hung in full childish pride. Otherwise, the clinical cleanliness of the room, with its carpets, western dimensions and carefully placed chairs and magazine furniture, and the absence of a television set, suggested that the family relaxed elsewhere, probably in a tatami room with a low table under which their knees could rest when the family had an occasional meal together. Araki asked about her children and boasted about his own son, who was about the same age as their daughter, while Shinobu served western tea in the style of the tea-room, the bag still in the cup. A piece of lemon in the saucer removed from him the choice of having his drink with milk or without. He lit a cigarette and hoped his hostess would notice there was no ashtray on the rosewood coffee table. But Shinobu was distracted and wanted to talk. She walked to the window clasping her hands and looked out at the empty side-street. She told him in a quiet, controlled voice that the children were too young to appreciate the extended absence of their grandmother and how they expected her to return from holiday with some toys or traditional country gifts for them.

'Your husband must also find it very disconcerting,' Araki said, tapping a growth of ash into his free palm and rubbing it into his trousers. He was trying to un- cover another scrap of detail which might connect with something else in his growing stock of facts, but some- how it was not always the verbal disclosures of his subjects that revealed a useful or even vital chip of information. In Shinobu Ohashi's plain, colourless face, with its slight, twisted smile of grim resignation, he saw the shallowness of her husband's concern and the sparse degree of co-operation and support she could expect from him. Ohashi would be on the verge of a promotion to one of the prestigious bureaux in the

97

Ministry of Finance, an apt appointment but merely the next natural stage along the career path which had begun at the right kindergarten and progressed through those junior and senior schools which tuned their curriculum to the numbingly competitive entrance requirements for Tokyo University, from where he graduated and sat and passed the demanding public servants' examination. By now he was qualified to join the élite, beginning with a first appointment at the National Tax Agency and later the Ministry of Finance. The ultimate consummation. The last thing Ohashi wanted was a mother-in-law with a wandering mind and suicidal tendencies and her family and relations analysed in the media. His arranged marriage to Shinobu Izumi joined a political family, his father being a prominent Lower House member of the Diet, with that of a senior business leader and major contributor to the ruling Liberal Democratic Party funds. It was a classical, perfect union.

'He's desperately sad about the events,' Shinobu said, almost apologetically, joining him at the table but still oblivious to his need for an ashtray.

'I don't want to intrude into family matters when I'm not sure my questions are relevant,' Araki said uncomfortably, when the required pleasantries were finished. The ash on his cigarette bent and fell on to his trousers. He rubbed it into the fabric, but Shinobu Ohashi was staring dolefully at the sweet, green rice cakes she had placed by his tea.

'I don't think there's anything new I can tell you,' she intoned. 'There was a lot of publicity when my mother was declared missing. The newspapers were very helpful, of course, but those dreadful magazines.'

Araki thought of Chris and hoped he would have a sheaf of newspapers and magazine cuttings when they met that evening.

Shinobu's Japanese was polite in the extreme, controlled and laced with honorifics that softened the harsh

98

reality of the event and effectively obliterated any hope of a significant disclosure. She talked again of her assumption that her mother was alive and suffering from a temporary mental affliction, but she was hardly convincing. There was a strained tone of doubt even in a voice which had repeated a story so often that the speaker really did believe it to be true. It was when she talked of her mother's presence at the family discussions on the future of some property or other the family owned and the way she would ceremoniously withdraw the vital registered seal from the safe and personally stamp the orange chop on to the document of disposal or acquisition that Araki knew he was not looking for a confused, menopausal woman with fading mental faculties and a driven desire to find oblivion or a kind of inner peace sitting at a lonely window somewhere in Tokyo's urban wilderness.

He asked: 'But did she ever say to you or your family that the property – the land and the apartments you own, and which are registered in her name – was getting to be too much for her to cope with?'

Shinobu's face was furrowed with pain, as if every suggestion that her mother was anything other than a completely rational human chipped away at her own credibility, even her loyalty as a daughter, and it threatened her own mental stability. She shook her head and found brief respite and comfort in the tea. Araki leaned forward. He had to know about the seal.

'Is the hanko missing too?' he asked, a shade harshly, and perhaps prematurely but he was tiring of the grey mists, the obfuscation and the fact that no-one, apart from Mariko Izumi herself, had come forward to volunteer information. The others seemed embarrassed, even hostile to his role, and after the previous evening's events in the toilet of the Kana Club he had to believe that the whereabouts of Mrs Masako Izumi was the subject of conversation outside the woman's family. 'I mean the registered seal, the important one.'

99

Shinobu looked over her cup, as if the location of the registered seal, the key to billions of yens' worth of assets, had not occurred to her yet. Perhaps it hadn't, Araki surmised. Perhaps her grief was such that the base thought of so much money had not interrupted her solace. Araki tried to help. 'In your mother's absence, who would take care of the important matters, important enough, say, to need the principal seal?'

Shinobu caressed the near empty cup before speaking.

'My father I suppose.' After a second or two of thought she said, this time with more conviction, 'Or my elder sister Mariko.'

Araki perceived the change and spoke in a controlled, polite voice.

'Why would it be Mariko-san and not your father, or your brother for that matter? Why should a daughter, a woman of the family, decide business issues? Issues I mean that related to the family holdings as opposed to your father's electronics company.'

Shinobu fussed with the cake dish, while Araki walked across the room and found an ashtray on the Swedish-style bookshelf. She apologized for her lack of attention: Araki waved it away.

'You're obviously not familiar with our family circumstances, Mr Araki.'

'Then I think you'd better tell me.'

The officer in charge of the Izumi case had the luxury of a corner room with two solid walls, on one of which he had hung a map of metropolitan Tokyo showing the boundaries of each police division's responsibility. On the other he had fixed a calendar and a small indulgence in the form of a photograph he had taken himself of the Grand Torii gate at the Ise shrine one warm summer evening at sunset when the air over the sea was unseasonably free of mist. Beyond the line of private cubicles and meeting rooms was the open-plan work space. The fourth-floor window which ran the length

of the new police headquarters was double-glazed against
the noise of traffic which crawled in distant silence like
mechanical toys along the outer moat of the Imperial
Palace. The policeman introduced himself as Sasaki, and
the given name as written on the identity tag pinned
to his shirt pocket could have been read three or four
ways, but Araki thought it was Terao. He was a short
muscular man with dark, penetrating eyes in a flat face
tanned a deep olive. His grey-peppered hair, cropped to a
neat, uniform length, added to the tough image belied by
his stature.

The detective was naturally circumspect at having to
account to a stranger for the fact that after a month the
police had nothing to show for their efforts. He could
have felt insulted, belittled by the man he knew to
be a failed journalist, but who was confident enough
to believe he could succeed where the police had so far
failed. A stack of files lay in front of the policeman and
served, Araki guessed, to show him how much work had
in fact been done. They were simple folders that would
fit into racks of hanging holders in the steel security
cabinets which split the huge expanse of open office
where uniformed and civilian staff worked at rows of
joined-up desks. Like the appointment with the missing
woman's bank manager, the interview with chief detective Sasaki had required the personal intervention of
Mariko Izumi. He was polite without being enthusiastic
and the abbreviated bow of greeting told Araki that
he would receive every courtesy, but no more. Araki
was sensitive to the other's loss of face and offered
to share anything he might discover but which had
so far eluded the official investigators. In this way he
hoped to draw from Sasaki a summary of the search
so far. He described his visit to Nakata, the manager
of the bank, and told him about his conversation with
the security guard and the strong possibility that Mrs
Izumi had been picked up outside the bank. Sasaki was
not impressed.

101

'We have considered that,' he said looking at his watch. 'Though we can't determine that the bank was the last place she visited. Elderly women are like the rest of us. They don't stand out.'

'But she was wearing a kimono.'

Sasaki raked his sharp bristles on his head. Araki persisted: 'This is 1988. Hardly anyone wears a kimono outside the inns and clubs.'

'Let me tell you something,' Sasaki said, leaning forward. 'A few weeks ago I was on a bus going through Ueno when I saw an old woman on a bike totter out of a side road and collide with a van. I'm sure you know how we Japanese reacted.' He waited for Araki to think and then continued: 'She wasn't badly hurt, just bruised from the fall and a bit shocked, and, by the time I got the bus to stop and crossed the road, she was already sitting up and looking bewildered. But do you know that nobody went to help her. They either watched like morons from a safe distance or hurried by in embarrassment. If our countrymen won't help a woman in pain, what chance is there of asking them to remember seeing an anonymous old bird in a kimono?'

Araki knew the policeman was right. As a nation we confine our relationships to the groups which nurtured us: our family, schools, company and perhaps a residents' association. Outside of these, nothing matters, or even exists.

Araki asked: 'From your experience do you think you, or we, can find her?'

Sasaki stood up and walked to the map. Stooping slightly he examined the red-tipped pins stuck in various locations. He turned to Araki.

'We find eighty per cent of the people reported missing by their relatives. Ninety-five per cent of those we find are still alive.'

'And the others?'

'Suicide mostly, and of course accident victims.'

'And murder?'

102

Araki knew that the experienced policeman had considered the possibility that Mrs Izumi had been killed by other causes than accident or suicide. Sasaki returned to his desk and slipped a beige file, a thin folder compared with the others, from the pile.

'When all normal routes lead nowhere, you have to consider the abnormal,' he said predictably, opening the file with a flourish and flicking through the loose, flimsy sheets. He paraphrased the texts.

'My officers made a rigorous inspection of the potentially hazardous parts of the house and the vicinity but found no trace of human remains.'

'Isn't there a well behind the house?' Araki asked, remembering a sign on the outside wall of a shed which cautioned the visitor about an electric pump inside.

Sasaki removed a pair of wire-rimmed glasses from his drawer and fitted them carefully just above the bulb of his nose. He peered at the documents and flipped them like a cashier counting money until he found a hand-written note and pushed it towards Araki. He said: 'We obviously looked at the well, and all other places a person might fall accidentally, or otherwise, and not be found.'

Araki quickly scanned the writing, and officer's report of the search. 'Under the veranda?'

The policeman nodded and smiled instinctively.

Sasaki was not an impulsive investigator, surging like some of his less experienced colleagues at the first signs of circumstantial guilt, and any emotion he felt remained behind an impassive, almost disdainful expression which he could hold in the most trying circumstances. He was known to share his compassion between the victim and the villain, but only when the former was an innocent, uninvolved citizen and not a loan shark or landlord whose greed had pushed someone to the edge. If the guilty showed real remorse, he would side with him in court. When a confession was drawn by persuasion Sasaki would plead before the bench of judges

103

for a sentence which would offer the best chance of rehabilitation, and such was his reputation that a fair hearing in the jury-free courts was ensured. With the obviously guilty, unrepentant criminal he was harsh, his interrogations vibrant with menacing brutality and the requests to the prosecutors for sentences severe in the extreme. His fiercest campaigns were against the organized gangsters, the yakuza and the youths who took their inspiration from the massive organized crime syndicates whose activities ranged from drug-peddling, prostitution, loan-sharking and protection rackets to the murky world of semi-legitimate political fund-raising and corporate blackmail.

In his pensive moments, alone with a bottle of home-town Fukuoka sake, Sasaki imagined his apparent demotion to the investigation of less violent crimes was the result of pressure from sources he could not identify but knew existed. The calls this time had started within hours of confirmation that the Izumi woman had failed to return home or stay at any of the places that might be expected to offer her lodging. First his superintendent had called to order him to find her and followed his call with a written instruction. A politician from the Liberal Democratic Party faction of Shinobu Ohashi's father-in-law had telephoned his support through an aide, suitably diluting, Sasaki thought cynically, the sincerity of the sentiment. A few days ago a business colleague of the missing woman's husband called to exhort the policeman to greater efforts in the search. Sasaki found himself apologizing and would later regret it as the warming sake released his emotions. He cursed the implicit threats that hung thinly disguised behind the politeness and platitudes. He knew he would find the Izumi woman, though he could not begin, even after a month of intense search, to say by when. And now the appearance of this roughly dressed man with a mandate from the family and an arrogant attitude to the requirements of protocol and position would seem to be another message that his efforts were being questioned. He regarded Araki with controlled resentment and his lack of professional qualifications a personal insult. He found his questions belittling, as if he had not considered the obvious possibilities and solutions that Araki was raising. But he had to appear interested, concerned and above all co-operative. He had agreed to see Araki the day following the call from Mariko Izumi, giving him little time to evaluate this new personality. He had worked late the previous evening, consulting the data bases on three police computers and telephoning the divisional record centre in six locations in Tokyo. When Araki's name began to appear on his screen and the microfilm transcripts telefaxed to his office at midnight his own memory was stirred and the events of summer 1982 assembled themselves like a mosaic. Araki was a friend of policemen, but he had betrayed their trust when he pursued a murderer from the Yanagida yakuza syndicate and brought embarrassment to the force. But he had to admire the man's tenacity and ultimately his expressions of humility and responsibility for the death of an innocent citizen he had dragged into the affair.

'Are they paying you?' Sasaki asked bluntly.

Surprised, Araki just grunted and motioned with a hand.

'I don't mean to be rude,' the policeman said, shutting the file forcefully, 'but sometimes people are driven by a sense of mission, rather than, say, base economic reasons. It sometimes leads them to injudicious decisions and un-helpful intrusions.'

Araki looked into the sharp, intelligent eyes across the table, knowing that the harassed police officer had been busy in the last twenty-four hours, though not on the Izumi case.

The detective continued: 'Are you working alone?'

'I have a couple of friends helping me.'

Sasaki gestured towards the general office and the rows of clerks with telephones at their ears or files under their

105

arms, hoping Araki would understand his use of the headquarter's personnel to make his point.

'Every police station and corner box in the country has been looking for Mrs Izumi. It's a tragic situation and she is still a priority case. She has to be found.'

Araki was surprised by his forcefulness. Was he being pressured from above? Araki believed he was. Wives of top businessmen do not disappear while leading lives of comfort and security. They die, divorce, go mad or are kidnapped, but they don't disappear in a society where family matters, changes of residence and status are recorded at official levels in local government registers, at tax offices and at the local police boxes attached to most of Tokyo's urban railway stations and intersections.

'I agree,' Araki said condescendingly, 'and if I can help I will.'

He made to leave, having fulfilled the need to introduce himself and make known to the detective the sponsors of his mission as the grieving family of Mrs Izumi. Sasaki walked with his visitor to the lift.

He said: 'I trust you will take me into your confidence if you discover anything useful to my investigation.'

'Of course,' Araki said. He then turned, as if sensing a new dominance. 'Have you seen the registered family seal?'

The policeman stopped. 'I don't understand,' he said, his reaction somewhere between confusion and suspicion.

Six people in the lift waited patiently as Araki held the touch-sensitive doors.

'The private family assets,' Araki said with deliberate, precise words. 'The family's wealth is under the control of the missing woman and her power is in the formal registered seal, carved in the name of Masako Izumi.'

Someone in the lift coughed, just loud enough for Araki to relax his hold.

'What relevance does the seal have?' Sasaki asked, although he was aware of the conspiracy theory the other man was suggesting.

'If it's murder,' Araki said, stepping into an empty lift, 'it's absolutely relevant.'

'He pissed on my foot,' Araki growled, his face flushed with anger. 'The fucking yakuza pissed all over me.'

'They don't have to be gangsters,' Kondo said, allowing himself a rare smile at Araki's expense. 'They sound to me like the usual ill-mannered sons of private company presidents. Like Ken Izumi himself. They're out most nights spending money which would otherwise go to taxes.'

'But they warned me,' Araki snapped.

Chris waved away the assumption with a broad sweep of his hand.

'You were as drunk as they were,' he told the audience, touching off another bout of laughter in the cellar bar Araki had made his own for over a decade. A clutch of stools with sensible back supports around the counter, half a dozen tables in a line and the same number of wall booths gave little intimacy to the customers, but it was not the kind of bar that needed it. Mama Yoshida's claim to have been a Kyoto geisha, and as a result had taken as her patron a cabinet minister, was not disputed in public, but her regulars knew she had simply sung and danced in the hot-spring and hotels in Yamanashi Prefecture where her guests were drunken salarymen on weekend trips or local councillors on junkets. Mama-san had a large, round face with a permanent smile and was not too fat to circulate frequently and tease the men. More often though she sat, like today, on the end bar stool, revolving in half turns in a dress which was too tight and short for such a large, mature woman. She squealed with delight at Araki's discomfort. The only customers who were not regulars sat red-faced in a booth, enjoying spasms of their own ribald, eye-shutting

107

laughter separated by moments of intense conversation when their heads almost touched.

They snacked on warm, sweet potatoes coated with soya-bean paste, and picked on chewy strands of dried squid. Araki waved a chopstick, a gesture Kondo and Chris took as a sign to clear a space in front of them and place some reference papers ready for the discussion to come. Their usual sessions in the Roman were releases, comprising hours of self-effacement as each bravely absorbed the friendly mockery the stories of their embarrassing incidents produced. The Japanese do not laugh at the misfortunes or mistakes of others without implying the deepest of insults and it was refreshing for Kondo to learn from Chris and Araki, who had absorbed the habit of the West during his year abroad. But Araki saw no humour in the events he had just unfolded. The incident in the toilet of the Kana Club was interpreted by Araki as a deliberate threat and now, in the relative privacy of the booth, the other two respected the former journalist's intuition and shared his disquiet. Araki let one of Mama Yoshida's two girls fill their glasses with whisky and water and waited for her to leave. He then stunned them with his deduction.

'One or more of the people we've met know where Mrs Izumi is.'

His friends knew better than to mock or dispute him until the essentials of his argument had been bared. He lit a cigarette and used the time to search for an opening remark.

'I don't know what happened to her,' he said defensively. 'But we're talking land. We're dealing with billions of yens' worth of property, buildings and of course cash and shares. I don't know what the English language press are saying,' Araki said to Chris, 'but you can't open a Japanese newspaper without seeing the latest statistics of the rises in land prices and stories about the plight of the ordinary citizen who can never now hope to possess enough land to build a house or earn enough money to buy an apartment.' Chris nodded his understanding. Until a year or two earlier the ambition of the working man was to retire with a lump sum payment and buy a house in the suburbs or his home town. Or he could borrow at low interest after a few years at work and pay off the loan over his lifetime and leave the mortgage obligation to his children if it was necessary. But in the last two years massive speculation and entry into the property and construction markets of organized crime syndicates and dubious realtors had pushed the price of the initial investment far beyond the ordinary Japanese. The latest estimate, Chris recalled, said that a Tokyo resident must pay about fourteen times his annual income to get on to the property escalator. He thought that three or four times was the normal gearing in London. Araki was picking out quotations from newspaper clippings Kondo had researched for him. '"A small three-room flat in a working-class condominium in the suburbs of Tokyo costs fifty million yen."' It was an easy mental calculation for Chris to translate it to two hundred and twenty thousand pounds. '"Condominiums offered for sale in Tokyo's twenty-three boroughs have an average price of seventy million yen, fifty-eight per cent higher than a year ago."'

He laid the paper down and added: 'The two daughters, Shinobu and Reiko, live in apartments at the luxury end of the scale and they're worth about a hundred million yen each. What's that in pounds, Chris? Half a million?'

The Englishman nodded.

'The land and buildings in the main family house are worth at least ten times that,' Araki continued, and returned to the news cuttings.

'"Housing land prices in 1987 were an average of seventy per cent higher than a year earlier. This trend has continued into 1988."' Clutching his drink, he saw he had the rapt attention of his colleagues.

'Imagine please the value of the Izumi land in Nakame-guro, in Kamakura, the office and factory sites, and half

109

a dozen other places in and around Tokyo.' Kondo had raised a hand limply off the table but Araki begged to continue.

'The single, sole owner of all this wealth, and I haven't even mentioned the cash or the shareholding in the company, is the missing woman, Masako Izumi.' And for even greater effect he added: 'She is one of the wealthiest private property owners in Tokyo.'

The three of them reacted when the door of the bar was opened carelessly, rebounding off the wall, by a pair of well-dressed visitors, but relaxed when Mama Yoshida greeted them by name.

Araki leaned forward, drawing his friends into a huddle.

'She is also heavily insured, around five hundred million yen, but a few million pounds is neither here nor there.' He said the last part of his sentence in English for Chris's sake.

Kondo had caught the train of thought much earlier, but he let Araki proceed, again for Chris's benefit.

'Apart from the eldest daughter Mariko, who employed me in the first place, the rest of the family describe the missing lady as unstable, menopausal and other not very complimentary words. I myself feel we are looking for someone who is mentally very sound, personally very happy and financially very astute.'

Chris asked: 'Why do you think someone we've met knows her whereabouts?'

Araki drained his glass and refilled it himself.

'She disappeared just over a month ago and during that time you have to believe that some major transaction, some item of business, has arisen which would have needed her seal, her authority. As far as I know, no such deal has been identified to me, but then if someone else has the registered seal we would never know what's been done in her name. The possessor of the seal owns the goods.'

'Where is the seal now?' Chris enquired.

110

'Logically the husband should have it, unless she kept it locked away or had it with her when she disappeared. I told the police about it today and they are going to look for it.'

'Surely,' Chris said, 'the husband is wealthy in his own right. He wouldn't have to kill his wife for her money.'

Araki smiled at his friend's ingenuousness.

'There are not many murders in Japan,' he said. 'But a surprising number involve the killing of a spouse for the insurance taken out on his or her life, or simply for the wealth owned by the other partner. Kondo-san. Tell Chris what you know about Yasuo Izumi.'

'Very little,' the old sleuth said, meaning he had learned a lot but it was not enough to satisfy him. He fidgeted with a sheaf of papers before speaking. 'He's sixty-one, married Masako in 1952 and took over the company five years later when he was thirty. It couldn't happen nowadays. We're coming back to the bureaucrat businessman not the entrepreneur.' He felt better after this quip on the current level of economic vigour. 'The prosperity of Izumi Electric was guaranteed first by US military procurements for the Korean War and then the vast insatiable demands of the motor-car industry. But the equity and the collateral for the bank loans came from his wife, whose family name he took on marriage.'

Chris interrupted, fascinated yet confused by the man with no name.

'Where did he come from, this brilliant entrepreneur? Who was he? What was his name before he married Masako Izumi?'

Kondo shifted in his seat.

'I haven't been able to gain access to the Izumi family records,' he confessed, a mild chuckle hinting at the illegality of such a move. 'But I'm looking into it. Just remember,' he said, mostly for Chris's benefit. 'It's not unusual for a man to adopt his wife's family name on marriage if her status and business interests merit the action. It normally wouldn't generate a mention in the

111

press. The Thirties and Forties in Japan were periods of extreme social turmoil and confusion. I suspect that Yasuo was a talented orphan found by acquaintances of the Izumis and married to their daughter on the condition that he change his name in order to preserve the prestige and reputation of the family.' Kondo paused to sip his drink and shuffle his notes until the paper he needed came to the top of the heap.

'Izumi, or whatever his name was then, would have been eighteen when the war ended and was probably under arms and ready to go overseas and fight for the Emperor. Someone called Masao Yamada appears on the payroll of Izumi Electric in 1950 and I believe he was the man who went on to marry the president's daughter.'

Araki leaned back, stroking his chin as he weighed the implications of Kondo's unfolding family story. He knew better than to question the accuracy of the information or how it had been obtained. Araki knew that during thirty-five years in journalism Kondo had given hundreds of favours to colleagues, politicians, bureaucrats and people of the street for which he had yet to receive the reciprocity such favours implicitly entailed. In the last two days Kondo had cancelled out a couple of these unwritten, timeless obligations of giri and it was unprofessional and un-Japanese to pursue their origin. Twice a year, in July and December, all adult Japanese bestowed on those of superior rank a gift which would express their appreciation for favours done and yet to be done. A person of humble means might have a few packets of gift-wrapped sugar or fruit juice from a local grateful tradesman while the general manager of a giant trading company like Mitsubishi could have a spare room crammed with vintage wines, whisky and smoked salmon. Kondo had requested an early, intangible present. He was talking: 'As you both know well, there were fierce labour disputes in the early years after the war.'

'From what I've read,' Chris said, 'it was more like a communist uprising.'

Kondo complimented Chris without condescension on his knowledge of modern social history but said he felt 'uprising' was a touch exaggerated.

'The communists and militant workers were stunned to be released from prison by the conquerors of Japan and even more surprised at being allowed to gather in groups of more than seven and organize themselves. They took full advantage of the political and social freedom bestowed on a populace who had been told to expect violent retribution from the victors. Food riots in the immediate post-war period, and I remember them clearly, arose from genuine shortages that had people in Tokyo breeding rats for food. But the leftists joined the demonstrations and later organized them, the needs of the people not being amongst their real objectives. Every company at that time, and however much it was struggling to survive, was gripped by labour unrest which led to strikes and violent confrontations with management and the police and military forces who tried to maintain order. Some time in 1950 a man called Masao Yamada came to work for Izumi Electric. I don't know how this came about but what is certain is that he joined the managerial level almost straight away and I hear from a source that he led the company's efforts to suppress the workers' revolt.'

Araki was beginning to guess what Kondo was leading to, but it was Chris who unwittingly raised a few issues when he said: 'But he couldn't have done it alone.'

Kondo looked around, instinctively and suspiciously. He leaned forward and spoke: 'When the labour disputes and strikes turned violent the Americans had no idea how to equate their espousal of the democratic principle of freedom for Japan with their desire to suppress what they had come to believe was a communist insurgency. What they did was to look to the militant wing of the new conservative government for help. Unfortunately, the leaders of these right-wing groups were in prison for their wartime excesses but many were released from long sentences on condition that they organize their gangs and

113

lead them against the workers, a task they relished and accomplished by intimidation and outright force. The rightists were naturally rewarded for their work.'

Araki knew the elements of the story and was distracted by the arrival of two strangers who paused unusually long to survey the bar before letting one of the girls lead them to the corner booth. The mellow enka folk music and the highback seating, Araki noted happily, would stifle the already muted voices from their own booth. Chris remained fascinated by Kondo's revelations and asked how the gangs were paid off by the Americans.

The scholarly Japanese sucked in air noisily.

'They accepted money and the authority which allowed them to operate in clearly defined areas. You know very well,' he said, his comments aimed at Chris, 'that Japan has been carved up amongst six major syndicates and their affiliates and fellow travellers. The boundaries we still see today were drawn at the time by the godfathers of the Yamaguchi, the Sumiyoshi, the Umeda and the rest were called upon to help the government. A few of the old ones are alive today; their legacy of political influence-peddling and power-broking certainly is. What we are seeing now though,' the old researcher said, warming to the topic even while Araki's concern about the new customers in the end booth grew, 'is that the boundaries are breaking down as the gangs seek new opportunities which are national rather than parochial. Drugs, prostitution, gun-running, legitimate business manipulation. These are lines which do not respect frontiers.'

Chris spoke slowly as he struggled to get the word order, the opposite way round to English, correct.

'Are you saying, Yasuo Izumi was Masao Yamada, the guy who put down the labour revolt at Izumi Electric and went on to marry the boss's daughter and become president?'

Kondo sipped lazily on his near-empty tumbler. His head was nodding gently when he replied.

'Yes.'

114

'And those two clowns who pissed on Araki could be the heirs to syndicate connections of Ken Izumi's father?' Chris's grammar faltered and his sentence was awkward, but the question was precise and frightening in its implication.

Kondo spread his hands in reply and said:

'It would not be surprising.'

'It's called "jiage",' Araki said, and left Kondo to explain the Japanese version of forced eviction, which used a range of tactics from firm persuasion to outright violence, while he pondered the possibility of a connection with his mission. It seemed unlikely. When Chris had described the lone, old house, on an otherwise neglected plot of land, with a truck embedded in the porch, he reached the obvious conclusion. Jiage.

'When house prices exploded during last year,' Kondo was saying solemnly, 'it was only a matter of time before the yakuza and their quasi-gangster camp-followers joined up with the willing real estate agents at the lower end of the integrity scale.' Chris was impressed by his older friend's passion and conviction. He had of course read about 'jiage' in the English language press but he let Kondo continue with his colourful account.

'Persuasion, suggestion and downright threat are in the armoury. The yakuza see it as an opportunity, another business line.'

The Englishman raised a hand, the one without the flute of beer.

'But surely they're not interested in property development, and all that it entails.'

'Precisely,' Kondo said. 'Their only interest is in money and that comes from turnover. They buy a plot of land . . .' and before Chris could ask the obvious he qualified his statement ' . . . with ready finance from insignificant but cash-rich savings banks, like Tekkei, who are keen to find lending opportunities. Sometimes the land is re-sold before the documentation for the first deal is completed.

115

When the package includes new construction on occupied property, enter the yakuza and tactics which they are more familiar with.'

'Aren't there laws against this rather obvious form of rip-off?' Chris asked with frustration. The relationship between the underworld and the state never ceased to fascinate him. And anger him. The police knew who ran the three thousand gangs and had the names on file of eighty-five thousand men who claimed affiliation to them. It irked him to read of highly visible public gatherings of mobsters at welcoming parties for colleagues on their release from prison or at the funeral of an aged patriach. The official tolerance of blatant organized crime confused and irritated him, but in the absence of muggings, rape and other disorganized street crime perhaps the situation was an acceptable compromise.

'There will be new measures in this case,' Kondo said in response, and reading the Englishman's mind perfectly. 'The authorities are concerned because the yakuza are moving into an area which brings them into conflict directly with the public. That demands some action.' He shuffled his papers again and produced a long, twisted cutting.

'From November,' he intoned, his face contorted as his weak eyes peered over his glasses to scan the tightly stacked vertical characters, 'the Real Estate Business Law comes into effect. And as of now the forty-seven prefectural governments will refuse to grant real estate licences to underworld organizations and their members.'

'I suppose they write "gangster" under profession when they apply,' Chris said with sarcasm.

'Of course not,' he replied testily. 'All applications are referred to the police who vet the names.'

Araki snapped his note-pad shut, a gesture which told the others he considered the conversation had drifted away from the problem of Mrs Izumi's disappearance. A very confused, red-faced salaryman was being escorted to the door by his two marginally less drunk colleagues. Mama Yoshida fussed attentively, her bulky frame hardly making the progress of the swaying trio any easier.

Araki lit a cigarette, the burning match dwelling in his hand as he spoke. 'I'd love to know who that bank manager was telephoning when I interrupted him,' he said. He paused to drain his glass. 'I'm going home. You two can stay if you want.' But neither did, and listened while Araki explained his plans for Wednesday and issued instructions to his foreign assistant and tasks for his more sedentary researcher. 'Let's earn that money.' He arranged a tidy pile of notes and coins on the table. 'Heavy rain's forecast tomorrow. It should finish off the cherry blossom for another year.'

6

The room smelled antiseptically clean, with a faint, mellow odour, like that of a freshly washed and powdered baby, around the occupied bed. In the space between the bed and the wall, a stack of medical equipment, centred on a cardiac monitor, warned of the grave condition of the patients interned beside it. In one small darkened window a line of green electronic dots ran across the screen, its tiny, intermittent hops giving visitors their only real sign of optimism. The old man lay asleep, perfectly still except for the quiet motion of his heaving chest. A tube trailed from a nostril and his mouth was open grotesquely wide, as if desperately seeking air. The starched bedsheet was drawn down and bunched at his waist and his green clinical wrap lay loosely open, exposing a child-like tortured chest. From behind the bed a metal shaft protruded from a machine and from its end a thread of spiralled wire led to an electrode which lay embedded below the wrinkled skin near his fragile heart. A glucose drip fed nourishment through a tube into Mr Ando's flaccid arm.

Mariko had responded without hesitation to Araki's request and had gasped into the telephone when he told her about the day before the incident at the home of one of her mother's tenants. She confessed she had not seen the article on an inside page of the morning press and said that in all honesty she would not have recognized it immediately as her mother's property. Mariko's own involvement was barely more than a provider of advice on where to buy furniture and household equipment for the places her mother owned and managed. Now, as she drew a chair alongside the bed and took the old lady's hands in hers Araki saw the compassion he had sensed was real. She had drawn her long, straight hair loosely at the back and held it with a modest rubber band. Her plain grey skirt and matching long-sleeved jacket complemented the sombre mood of the occasion but her presence seemed to brighten the atmosphere. The elderly housewife clutched the warm, living fingers of the visitor in her own fragile grasp and without looking up placed the clenched bunch in her lap. Releasing one of her hands, but still holding Mariko's with the other, she leaned over with a tissue and wiped away a dribble of saliva from the corner of her husband's gaping mouth.

Araki stood, head bowed, by the door and after an exchange of greetings and words on the condition of the patient moved with Mariko and Mrs Ando to a visitors' rest area at the end of the corridor. He eased the pain of his questions and sought the frail woman's trust by addressing her through Mariko.

'I hear Mrs Ando has been harassed at home several times recently.'

The old woman nodded, but her mind was elsewhere. Mariko said quietly, 'They had three or four visits from a realtor and a string of telephone calls in between.' She had clearly been given a lucid history.

'The suggestion was that they, the Andos, would be more comfortable in a small apartment, one catering to the needs of the elderly and the disabled. They came up with the offers of finance, removal expenses and even a hot-spring holiday when the contract was signed.'

'Sorry,' Araki interrupted. 'When did all this start?'

'She's not ready to make a formal statement to the police yet,' Mariko said protectively. 'I'll try to help her.' Turning to Mrs Ando she murmured, 'I think you said about five weeks ago?'

The old woman nodded, uttering a polite affirmative.

'About the time your mother disappeared,' Araki said to Mariko.

'Yes,' Mariko replied gloomily, wishing her helper could choose a word other than 'disappear'. 'But there haven't been any visits for ten days. It's just that the calls have increased. Worst of all, they've started calling during the night.'

The older woman stirred, her face rising defiantly even as she kneaded and massaged her bony hands together, and she begged to speak.

'They asked about my husband's health,' she croaked. 'They said he was bound to improve if he moved to the highlands where the air was cleaner and the water purer.' Although her skin was blotched and creased with age, her eyes were clear and her gaze flitted between Mariko and Araki, of whom she was still suspicious. But the burden of her husband's care, and now this frightening intrusion, showed when the pale light washed through the mesh curtains and brushed her face. Her head rose slowly and apprehensively as a nurse backed quietly out of her husband's room and it slumped when she went the other way.

Araki leaned forward, searching for the words which would not alarm her further.

'Did the men who visited you ever suggest that something unfortunate might occur if you and your husband didn't move?'

Mrs Ando twisted her head and sucked in air softly.

'What about the telephone caller?'

Again, her face contorted with doubt, but after a moment she remembered something. Another intake of air, this time noisier and sharper and followed by an uncharacteristically angry tone to her normal self-effacing voice.

'What were his words?' she said to herself, straining to remember. ' "To your advantage", or was it "in your personal interest"? Yes, something like that. "To your advantage and in your personal interest".' Content that at her age she had been able to make a contribution, especially the product of what she feared was a fading memory, she smiled obligingly.

Araki asked, 'Was it always the same man? The visitor.'

'Men actually. Two of them.'

'Did they leave their name-cards? I think the police would like to talk to them.'

'Why should they?' she asked, suddenly suspicious and defensive. 'They were very polite. They always brought me a present.'

Araki exchanged a glance with Mariko and at once regretted his bluntness. Mariko reached out and took the frightened woman's hands, finding in her grasp the cold fingers of a woman who feared authority, who remembered the visits to her school and the awesome demands for loyalty, obedience and sacrifice in the name of the Emperor by the men in uniform. Now she was unable to see through the ready smiles, the perfunctory gifts and the transparent concern and find a link between the kindly men in suits and the ruthless attack on their house which had almost killed her husband.

'I think my mother would like to know who's been talking to you about her house,' Mariko said gently. 'Your house. You know my mother would not want you and your husband to leave. She had no plans to develop the land while her tenants . . . while her friends still lived there.'

Mention of Mrs Izumi, her landlady, caused the old woman's features to tighten.

'It's so sad,' she snuffled, opening a laboured monologue of polite regret on the fate of her compassionate benefactor. 'She came to see me every month without fail.' Araki moved to speak but the old woman was talking as if in a trance, her eyes fixed on the ashtray by Araki's hand, and answered the question he was preparing to ask.

'She came to the house two days before I read about her in the newspapers. I gave her the rent as usual. She thought it a bother for me to have to send it through the post. She is right, of course. My knees can be very painful. It's all I can do to help my husband.'

121

For a while, her pity was transferred to the woman who owned the house she lived in and who visited as a friend rather than as a landlady. Mariko spared her more questions. She said to Araki, 'I collected the rent myself last month and of course we discussed my mother. They were quite close. Mrs Ando says that Mother was completely normal two days before she left.'

Araki raised a palm to each of the women.

'Don't be offended by my question,' he said, 'but is Mrs Ando also a member of the Honshinkyo sect?'

'You mean,' Mariko said with an edge of testiness. 'Did my mother try to recruit Mrs Ando into the religion?'

'Not exactly,' Araki said with momentary embarrassment. 'But it would be useful to establish your mother's religious conviction.'

Mrs Ando almost enjoyed the exchange and seemed pleased to intercede.

'I'm a life-long member of Tenrikyo, which is much older than Izumi-san's temple, and we spent many hours discussing our beliefs. We respected each other's.'

A doctor approached and spoke quietly to Mrs Ando. She rose to leave amid a profusion of apologies for the bother and nuisance she had believed herself to have caused.

'I'm sorry, Mrs Ando,' Araki said, emerging from a short bow. 'I'm not sure you told us whether the real estate agents left a number for you to contact them.' She could have hurried away to her husband's side, clearly in receipt of some new information on his condition. Instead, she looked at Mariko, who smiled instinctively, and picked through her deep handbag, producing a purse from which she extracted a card.

'Do you think I should tell the police?'

'I think it would help,' Araki said, scribbling on to his notepad, 'but you should also alert the property agent of the situation and suggest you discuss the matter further.' Mariko shot a puzzled and worried look at Araki. The confusions of age, concern for her husband and an innocent

122

ingenuousness still prevented the elderly woman from associating the solicitous representations of the rogue realtors and the venomous attack on her house. 'But you needn't trouble yourself. Izumi-san here will represent you. I'm sure her mother would prefer it that way.'

Mariko hesitated only momentarily, picking up Araki's plot and reassuring the grieving woman who could not divert her concentration from the door along the corridor. Hospital regulations required her to sleep near her husband and on discharge, whenever that was, she agreed to accept Mariko's offer of temporary accommodation at a nursing home her new landlady would find. Before reuniting with her husband, Mrs Ando rehearsed and practised a conversation she was about to hold.

Sharing an umbrella, Mariko clutched Araki's arm as they skipped around the puddles on the short hike to Meguro Station. They stopped under the awning of a tobacconist while Araki stooped to tie a loose shoe-lace. An unbroken trail of rain dripped on to her partner's thinning scalp and down his neck but failed to interrupt his task. She smiled at him, tucking herself into a dark-blue, belted raincoat with a high collar restraining her hair. As they left the hospital, Araki admitted that he had no clues as to her mother's whereabouts but the more he learned of the family's circumstances and the dominant financial role of Mrs Izumi, the more he was convinced she was not the victim of a mental disorder. Mariko, at first, was shocked, but her reaction was quickly replaced by mild relief. Apart from a lifelong inability to cope with telephone numbers and memorize addresses she considered her mother to be in complete control of her faculties. She was persuaded by Araki that the move to possess the Nakameguro plot may not be coincidental and if it was it should be eliminated from the case.

The old Mrs Ando had played her part immaculately. It was hardly a surprise for Araki to find that the name-card gave no address. It identified the bearer as Terashima, Property Consultant, and the telephone number engaged an answering machine, no doubt difficult to trace. Mrs Ando spoke clearly but self-consciously, almost relishing the intrigue. She told the recorder that she would like to discuss the proposals Mr Terashima kindly made but because of her husband's ill health she would like to meet him elsewhere. If convenient to him she had some business in Ginza the following day and perhaps they could meet at eleven in the lobby of the Imperial Hotel. She was particularly interested, she added teasingly, in the retirement homes in Chofu. 'Isn't it dangerous?' Mariko had asked while they rehearsed. Araki begged her co-operation, explaining that there would be no meeting. Mrs Ando was needed only to identify Terashima. Mariko should also attend, along with Chris Bingham.

As the shortage of space commands, shopping centres are built around and above major railway stations and at Meguro a moderately tall store of modest pretensions also housed a clutch of economy restaurants. The couple beat the midday rush by a few minutes and ordered noodles in a cramped eatery with few tables. Mariko teased a wayward strand of hair and stirred the steamy, spicy broth when it arrived in three minutes.

'Do you really think my mother's disappearance is connected to the land she owns?' Mariko asked with some trepidation.

Araki sought for words which would not alarm her but he had already hinted at the connection. 'Someone is trying to obtain possession of your mother's land.' Mariko's mouth was close to the bowl but as if paralysed she froze, letting the twirls of dripping noodles slide from her chopsticks into the broth.

'Why?' she asked uncompromisingly.

'As you know the jiage tactics are usually initiated by the landowner who wants to exploit the land's real value. I have absolutely no doubt your mother is not that kind of person.'

124

Mariko's head slumped. She declined his offer of beer, preferring the soothing warmth of the deep mug of green tea. She looked up.

'Why can't you be at the hotel tomorrow?' Mariko said with evident disappointment.

'I'll bring Chris but I have to see Morozumi at the Honshinkyo temple. Chris will look after you, and Kondo, an old friend of mine, will be close.' He felt a sudden twinge of envy for his English friend, who found Japanese women so appealing. 'But I'll call you later. Tell you what I've found, if anything.' She thought for a moment, looking at him with clear, tear-drop eyes.

'Please.'

Yoshio Suwano looked through the reversed characters of his own name on the window which was marbled by streaks of rain. Below him, a swarm of umbrellas massed at the crossing, their occupants hidden but for a trace of coat and the shoes of the front rank. When the light changed the troop moved in orderly march from the Kasumigaseki side towards the office buildings in Toranomon. One black umbrella broke away from the column and hurried sideways before stepping over the low crash barrier.

'I think he's here,' Suwano said to the other two.

'About time,' the shorter man barked, flicking a sleeve to reveal his watch. His name was Yuji Inaba and he was the founder and president of Inaba Kensetsu, a construction company whose fame in the sector came from the building of luxury apartments on narrow and improbable parcels of land in urban Tokyo and surrounding conurbations. As an impoverished youth in his native Saitama Prefecture, bordering metropolitan Tokyo, Inaba had run errands for a local crime syndicate whose principal source of income in the 1950s was the supply of day labourers to the explosive demand of the post-war construction industry. He was not a career yakuza and on an earn-and-return understanding borrowed money

125

from his patrons to finance his own tentative property purchases which led from simple real estate business to construction and land development. He had long ago repaid his financial debt, but moral obligation would never end. A short, broad-framed man, Inaba's face was flat and round with lined, purple lips and pitted, weathered cheeks. His small hands were hard, rough and scarred, like those of the workers he joined on site when he felt an urgent need to wield a pick or shovel cement. He hitched his trousers and joined Suwano at the window.

The third man was much younger, barely thirty, and possessed the cool, assured confidence of a man with authority. His dark, tailored three-piece suit covered a trim, muscular body and his thin boyish face and bright, nervously intelligent eyes gave a deceptive impression of the character beneath. Shigeo Goto held a filter cigarette ostentatiously between thumb and forefinger and allowed his lips to fold in a mildly contemptuous manner.

'He's taking unnecessary risks,' he said, addressing his words to the opposite wall.

Suwano and Inaba joined him around the table, where the green tea had become tepid.

'He said he had to talk to us together,' Suwano responded, his voice low and controlled, suggesting he was tired of explaining the reason why the meeting had been called.

'It's still risky,' Goto said, almost amused by the implication. 'A banker, a realtor, our friend the carpenter and, well, me.'

Inaba guffawed. He enjoyed the way the young mobster described him as a 'carpenter', harkening back to the time when all structures were made of wood and the term accurately described a builder. Goto's oyabun boss, Shimpei Endo, had approved his loose relationship with the syndicate which took Endo's name about the time Inaba incorporated his first construction company. When Endo was serving a ten-year jail sentence for conspiracy to murder and related crimes in the late 1960s it was

126

the young, wealthy entrepreneur Inaba who saw that decades of accumulated obligations and debts in favour of the gang leader were acknowledged and called upon to ensure that Endo lived well in prison and that no-one took advantage of his temporary absence to poach on his territory. The political debts were the easiest to collect and at the lavish party in a leading Tokyo hotel to celebrate Endo's release from prison, at least three cabinet ministers were represented by aides and four members of parliament actually appeared themselves.

The banker still held a dripping umbrella when he entered the room and seemed reluctant to release it to the woman receptionist who had led him to the meeting.

'Dreadful weather,' he said, addressing the room at large. 'It's ruined the cherry blossoms.' He slapped his clothes with the outside of his hands. His face was damp from rain and sweat and he squinted to adjust the thin-rimmed spectacles which slipped along his greasy nose. He bowed curtly to Goto and the realtor Suwano, who barely hid his impatience while motioning the visitor to a vacant chair. When he recognized the elderly figure in the poorly fitting suit as the founder and president of Inaba Construction, Nakata lowered his torso from the hips, his head stabbing towards the floor while his chin brushed his chest and the palms of his hands rested on his knees. He returned to an upright stance only after a series of bows of decreasing depth, reciprocated by brief nods from the man of higher rank and superior age. The wealthy builder respected the bank manager, grateful for the loans the small savings bank had quietly extended for the construction of a string of mansion blocks on the river side of Setagaya Ward. As a man, Inaba loathed the banker for his wretched subservience.

A clerk brought a fresh cup of green tea and placed it before Nakata. Her bow was instinctive, her eyes diverted and distant, and she retreated backwards with a stooping motion. The tea was steaming hot and a pale green

127

in colour, as if the boiling water had barely disturbed the thorny shreds of leaf.

'I hope the situation has changed since you spoke to Suwano-san yesterday.'

It was the syndicate's representative Goto, his eyes on the banker, his words icy as he interrupted a further exchange of pleasantries. He leaned back in his chair, a thumb lodged in the pocket of his waistcoat while with the other he spun a ballpen expertly over the knuckles of his spiny, long fingers. The bank official was clearly distressed, even intimidated, by possession of illicit knowledge on the arrogant man's identity and already a collar of sweat had formed across the crown of his broad forehead. His voice was wary as he responded in carefully structured language.

'I regret the situation is as I told our colleague,' he said cautiously, indicating the realtor Suwano. 'We, the Todoroki branch of the Tekkei Sogo Bank will be audited by the Ministry of Finance within two weeks.' His voice ebbed. 'It could be next week. Even tomorrow.'

Suwano motioned with a cigarette. He said, 'Kindly explain the problem for Inaba-san's benefit. I only gave him an outline.' Nakata looked at the imposing face of the construction company president but averted his eyes when he spoke.

'My institution, the Tekkei Mutual Savings Bank, has lent eleven billion yen to Suwano Land. Suwano-san lodged his promissory notes with us last week and the money had been drawn down to his instructions.'

'That's more than double the value of the Nakameguro plot,' Inaba said casually. Suwano gestured nervously towards the neatly dressed Goto.

'There are some other deals,' he said.

Inaba nodded knowingly. 'Of course,' he agreed. 'And the problem.' Nakata's nerves began to show. He placed on the table the bowl of tea he had raised almost to his mouth.

'Because of good experiences in the past, and my abso-lute confidence in Mr Suwano's reputation,' he intoned,

'I overruled normal procedures and authorized with my personal seal a loan for which the documentation was incomplete.'

'Incomplete?' Inaba growled. 'How do you mean, incomplete?'

Nakata sought for words but Goto rose from his chair and walked to the head of the table and pre-empted the banker.

'What he means,' the arrogant young mobster said expansively, 'is that the security for the loan, in the form of the deeds to the Nakameguro property and another plot the Izumis are selling, are not yet available to his bank.'

'Why not?' Inaba asked bluntly.

To Inaba's distaste, the disrespectful Goto leaned over his shoulder, his breath sharp with tobacco.

'Because', the younger man said, 'the registered seal is missing.'

The banker eased into the conversation. More politely, he explained.

'Mrs Izumi is the sole title owner of the land and her regrettable disappearance makes completion of the formalities impossible because the registered seal seems to have vanished with her.'

'Or she hid it somewhere,' Goto suggested malevolently.

Nakata tapped his brow with the back of a hand.

'I had hoped,' he said in faltering words, 'that the issue would have been resolved by now. I said at the outset, late in January I believe it was, that we had to have this deal agreed and documented by the end of April.' He looked at the tiny frame of his watch. 'Just two weeks from now. The official audit I anticipated in January is scheduled for an unspecified date in the very near future. The loan transaction we have concluded with Suwano Land must be properly secured and documented before the Ministry of Finance officials descend on us in force.'

The real estate dealer's eyes passed around the table.

129

'So you can see that Nakata-san has a few days before the authorities discover an improperly authorized and unsecured loan.'

Inaba said hopefully: 'They might miss it. Surely they can't look at all the outstanding lending deals your bank has put on the books.'

'They'll find it,' Nakata said gravely. 'That's the type of deal they'll look for first.' He reminded the others that the largest savings and loan bank in Tekkei's peer group had been liquidated and its president and chairman jailed for just such transactions and another case was at this moment before the prosecutors.

Inaba tried to be helpful. Turning to Suwano he asked ingenuously, 'Can't you return the money until the inspection's complete?'

Nakata's face, lined with tension, cracked into a smile of hopelessness. 'The deal's on the books. It's recorded in a dozen places. The loans department, credit, disbursements, customer relations, the funding section. And of course Head Office. Everywhere it shows the documentation to be in order for internal purposes, but when the ministry inspectors check through the files all they'll find are three promissory notes signed by the president of Suwano Land. They won't find the property deeds. And with respect,' he said, bowing tentatively from the shoulders towards Suwano, 'the notes are obviously not prime names so I can't even re-discount them in the Tokyo money market.' The harassed bank manager slapped the table in frustration. 'After what happened with the Heiwa Sogo and the others I should have expected the audit. I must have those deeds,' he pleaded. 'Within seven days.'

Suwano sympathized with the banker's predicament and ushered him to the door with some final words of comfort. 'We hope to have better news for you shortly. It would be very embarrassing', he added earnestly, but with a threatening overtone which was not missed on the banker, 'if my company were seen in a perjorative light by the authorities.'

Extracting his umbrella from the stand, Nakata halted, as if pondering the other man's statement, but something had jogged his memory.

'Someone came to the bank yesterday,' he said, his head inclined loosely as he struggled to compose his thoughts. 'He said he represented the Izumi family and asked specifically about the family seal.'

The pen Goto had been toying with fell on to the table. He stood up abruptly, the chair scraping the floor loudly. 'I know about the man,' he said dismissively. 'Some former journalist hired by one of the daughters.' He strode across to Nakata, his eyes narrowed, dark and cold, and his lips curling downwards at the corners.

'What did he want to know about the seal?'

It was a demand rather than a request, and the damp bristly hairs on the banker's neck went cold.

Nakata shivered again, recalling the shock when Araki returned to his office unannounced and interrupted him as he tried to speak to his contact. Fortunately, he had been left on hold and believed he had not been overheard saying anything he might regret. He looked at the man he found distasteful and chose his words carefully.

'He asked me what kind of seal Mrs Izumi used for her regular transactions with my bank.' Nakata shrugged, fingering the release button on the umbrella handle. 'The usual simple stamp for day-to-day business I told him, and then he wanted to know if she had the registered seal with her.'

Goto took a step nearer the banker.

'And did she?' he asked harshly.

'I didn't see it. She used her everyday seal to take out five million yen.'

And as an afterthought he said: 'Of course, the registered seal could have been in her handbag.'

'Baka!' the syndicate man said after the office door closed on the bank manager.

'What a fool!'

131

'He could be dangerous,' Suwano said cagily. Goto scoffed. 'He knew nothing more than he said today.'

Inaba chuckled without humour.

'Everybody's looking for the seal.'

Goto moved to the window. He thought he could identify the figure of the Tekkei Bank manager scurrying across the intersection as the rain intensified and the sky darkened to obliterate anything beyond the Toranomon crossing. He spoke quietly, his eyes stopping on each of the conspirators. 'We've bribed the local government officials with women and presents and scared an old couple almost to death. We're not just talking about Nakameguro. We need that seal for the other five deals as well.' He held his chin.

'One of them's got it,' he murmured. 'And Araki might lead us to it.' He looked towards the sinister heavens and said softly, 'If it's raining like this here, what's it like in the mountains.'

The wheels of the worn Toyota crunched the coarse gravel and rolled wearily towards the parking bay in the empty forecourt which stretched from the temple to the main Ueno station road. There were stretched, human-form shadows in the brightly lit arched entrance but no believers climbing the imposing bank of steps, slippery with rain and glistening in a funnel of light. There were other cars, Araki noticed when his eyes had focused to the artificial glare of the arc lights around the perimeter, but very few. He stared through the mist at the heart-shaped grill of a dull-coloured BMW and two black Cadillacs a few bays away. Araki was early, fifteen minutes before the time the voice on his answerphone had requested. It gave him time to appraise the day and draw energy from a cigarette and the explosive information Chris had passed to him.

Chris was always conscious of his foreignness, and when Araki asked him to spend the day watching the comings and goings at an insignificant bank in a district

132

where the only white foreigners were on advertisements he had protested. 'I stand out like a sumo wrestler in a ballet school,' he had said, and Araki had to sympathize. A foreigner parading with no apparent motive in front of a bank would attract the police within two hours. 'Once you've identified the chief manager,' Araki said, 'ease off and find somewhere to observe the door. I don't particularly want you to follow him, just watch his behaviour, notice who he's with, does he lunch with a junior, a woman, alone or with a customer.'

'Do you think he knows something?'

Araki's hands opened in a gesture of hopelessness, but hardly had he started when he slammed a fist into the other palm.

'He must know something. He was her local banker for years and he was the last person to see her in circulation. His behaviour with me was weird and he was nervous. Bank managers usually aren't.'

Nakata arrived at eight-thirty and Chris almost bumped into him as he walked in front of the bank in a kind of reconnaissance. The doorman bowed deeply to the man with the broad, square face and flat, bridgeless nose and imposing briefcase. Araki's description had been accurate and the more reverent gestures of recognition by the staff confirmed the identification. A coffee shop opposite the bank gave him the narrowest view of the Tekkei's entrance and Chris had two sessions there interrupted by a stroll on either pavement. Boredom was taking its toll and he had tried flirting with the waitress. He almost missed the departure of the manager Nakata and would have lost him completely if a taxi had been immediately available. Instead, tucked under his umbrella, Nakata hurried to Todoroki Station, giving Chris enough time to catch him and lounge casually near him through a short journey before a change to the underground and a thirty-minute ride to his final destination at Toranomon.

'Did you see which office he went to?' Araki asked anxiously.

Chris shook his blond head inadequately. 'I couldn't dive into the lift with him. He would have remembered a gaijin during the journey. But he was nervous. He kept dabbing his brow and I don't think it was to mop up the rain.'

Araki tugged the collar of his windbreaker against the wispy traces of rain and took the steps in pairs. His heart beat faster from the unaccustomed stress on an overweight and abused body and at the thrill of the day's findings. Chris had caught him on the telephone in the half hour he spent in his apartment between the hospital meeting with Mrs Ando and a car trip to Kamakura, the other side of Yokohama. He had lain on a cushion, stretched on the tatami, playing back the answerphone tape and sipping a plastic tumbler of Nikka whisky. There was only one call, and it asked him to appear at the Honshinkyo temple at nine that night and apologized for the abruptness of the invitation and the lateness of the assignation. It was then that Chris called with his report. He had not really wanted to make the Kamakura trip himself but Chris had no car of his own, and drove Araki's only reluctantly, and the site owned by Mrs Izumi was eight kilometres from the nearest station. He would not ask Kondo to spend three or four hours struggling on public transport, however efficient and frequent the service.

The old Corona lurched, its engine racing enigmatically before coughing alarmingly when the traffic slowed abruptly on the underpass leading to the Yokohama by-pass. In the next hour he stopped twice to peruse the chart he had found at the Izumi house and had enquired on three occasions before finding the slip road and a track leading to the fenced-off site. There was no gate and he was forced to tread the soft ground until he found where the mesh fence, a token indicator of private property beyond, met a bank of birch and cedars with thick overhanging foliage which blocked out the light. He eased himself through the gap and trod around the

134

trees until he came to a dirt track which ran between them. From the crown of the rise Araki had a magnificent view of the town below him and beyond the beach in the distance the Enoshima island causeway. He wondered where the boundary of Mrs Izumi's land was and why he should feel bothered in this unusually spacious tract of woodland. And then he saw the cause of his unease. He sunk to one knee and traced with his fingers the cross pattern of a heavy vehicle's tyre engraved in the soft earth of the track. He mused too long and the two shadows approached silently and engulfed him.

When he reached the broad entrance, overhung with an ornate carved balustrade, like a gigantic lip, the figures he thought he had seen from the car park had gone. The summons to the temple had puzzled him until he recalled during the slow crawl back to Tokyo from Kamakura the parting words of Morozumi three days earlier, a few metres from where he now stood. 'If I think of something which may assist your investigation I'll call you.' And so here he was. Where was Morozumi? The thick door gave after a firm push and Araki followed the lights of the curving corridor around the central deserted arena to a reception area with a pair of lifts. Still no Morozumi or his people, though he was convinced his presence in the elaborate building was known to the occupants even though he saw no cameras. A blue light above one of the lifts erupted, grasping Araki's attention, which was acute and edgy. He stood back as the lights hopped down the scale and mentally tracked his retreat through the eerily empty recesses of the golden temple. It was Ohta, the young well-dressed man who had greeted them on that original visit and now invited Araki into the lift.

The lift opened directly into a penthouse with floor-to-ceiling windows on three sides giving a sweeping view of metropolitan Tokyo, the skyscrapers of Shinjuku, with their patchwork of lights, rising like prongs from the otherwise bland urbanscape. Morozumi was wearing a light mauve yukata as a dressing gown with a broad sash

135

around his hips and tied in a traditional draped knot at the back. The gaunt, tense face Araki remembered from their first encounter was notably more relaxed and he saw why. One corner of the room was host to a circular glass bar with a quartet of stools made from bamboo. Araki noted the traces of water in circular patterns on the sheer surface of the bar and knew he was in a very private place.

When Ohta had withdrawn to an adjoining room, Morozumi slid behind the bar and brought up from a hidden shelf a bottle of malt whisky and an ice bucket, pouring generously from the first and offering Araki the option on the latter. Araki felt vulnerable, and uncomfortable still in the shoes which he had not been invited to leave by the lift. He wondered who, apart from Ohta, occupied the rooms beyond the doors at the side of the bar. Was it the two well-built characters who escorted him from the Izumi property in Kamakura that afternoon?

Morozumi seemed to read his thoughts. He said, 'I hope my assistants didn't frighten you this afternoon. They had instructions to be most courteous to you.'

Araki accepted the glass.

'They were expecting me?'

'Sooner or later,' the head of the sect said smugly. 'I anticipated your tactics. When they called and told me you had arrived I felt I owed you an explanation.'

'You certainly do. To me and to the police.'

Morozumi's face tensed.

'The police have no interest in my affairs,' he said with gritted teeth.

'They might like to know,' Araki said defiantly, his confidence growing as he drained the whisky, 'what your people were doing on private property. Land in fact which belongs to one of your believers.'

Morozumi accepted the remark, and its accusatory inference, with a nod and a pause to straighten the fold of his kimono. He took Araki's empty glass and left it with his own on the bar.

136

'You'd better look at this,' he said, leading his guest through the doors beside him into a room with a similar expanse of glass, this one overlooking Ueno Park on one side and an imposing segment of golden dome of the main chamber. Ohta was reading a magazine with the help of a single standard lamp but leapt up when his master approached. He moved smartly to the darkened central part of the sparsely furnished room dominated by the outline of a massive chest or table with its collapsible sides folded down. As the other two men watched – Araki with trepidation – Ohta uncovered a concealed box of switches and knobs and began to turn and press in sequence. Spotlights in the ceiling illuminated the structure which, when its top had slid apart and fallen effortlessly against the sides, was revealed to be a large hollow rosewood display cabinet. Ohta pressed again, and with a barely perceptible purr the contents of the case rose slowly from the inside. Araki watched Morozumi, who seemed lost in himself, watching the melodramatic little spectacle no doubt for the hundredth time in a trance-like state. A square model building appeared, intricately carved in what looked like jade. The entire outer edge was a rim of three- or four-storey apartments with tiny balconies and the interior was dominated by a rotunda surrounded by a border of tiny glass-like trees. Even on this minute scale the resplendent bowl rose above the buildings like an enormous rising sun. On one side the row of flats was broken by a high slender arch beneath which rested a statue, on a scale twice life-size. Araki did not have to lean far to realize the statue represented Morozumi, his arms outstretched, reaching to the sky. Hillsides of tiny glass trees fell away from the multi-coloured mosaic garden and the play of light on an opaque pale-blue, glassy material Araki could not identify, simulated the ocean beyond.

'That's your plan for the Izumi land in Kamakura,' Araki said.

'That's my dream,' Morozumi retorted, still seemingly in a daze.

137

'Has work started?' Araki asked, craving a cigarette and looking around hopelessly for an inviting ashtray.

Morozumi returned to his normal state and shuffled to the window, staring pensively towards the silent snaking trains tracing trails of light in constant motion in and out of Ueno Station.

'There are a number of formalities to complete,' he said carefully, 'and they require the presence, or the legal authority, of Mrs Izumi who has agreed generously to lease the land to my movement for a token consideration. Until then work cannot proceed.'

Araki raised a hand, and was about to describe the clear evidence of the recent movement of heavy-duty construction vehicles on the site. As the two Morozumi aides marched him firmly back to the perimeter gate Araki had, thanks to the muddy conditions, seen the deep ruts all along the access road and guessed that the tyre tracks belonged to more than one vehicle. He remained silent.

Morozumi was rocking on his feet. Staring at the lights outside, he said, 'If you locate our believer, for whom we are offering our prayers unselfishly, you should deliver her to those who can most offer her the comfort she will need.'

'To you?' Araki asked with an irony not missed on the other.

Ohta shifted uncomfortably next to the model.

'Please remember clearly what you have seen and heard,' the leader of the faith said, retreating briskly through a rear door.

Shaking with an inner torment at the blatant exploitation he saw in the actions of the Honshinkyo head, Araki fumbled for a cigarette and wished the match he held unsteadily could fire the hideous edifice that stood with its crown of gold bathed in a halo of artificial light. He would not remember until, when a final cigarette burnt a groove in the tatami by his head as he drifted into sleep, that he had promised to call Mariko Izumi.

138

7

An hour before the appointment with the realtor Terashima, Araki drove Chris to the Imperial Hotel, leaving his car in the covered semi-circular forecourt. With a curt wave he acknowledged Kondo who sat in his Toyota on the exit ramp of the underground garage. Mariko was bringing Mrs Ando.

'And that must be her,' Chris said, pointing beyond a huge flower centrepiece to a woman standing alone beneath a row of clocks on the farthest wall of the expansive lobby. Chris's eyes had been drawn to the lone figure with the anxious, urgent expression. Her clothes were casual and loose in case, Araki suggested, they had to move out quickly, and her bag hung from long straps across her. Chris saw that Araki's description of her elegance and charm was not exaggerated.

'This is Chris Bingham,' Araki said. 'He's a trusted friend and he'll stay with you. You'll be safe.'

Chris introduced himself in Japanese and to his surprise, and even more to Araki's, she replied in confident English, with a faint American drawl.

Mariko smiled at their embarrassment and said, 'I went to school in the States. The University of Hawaii, if you call Hawaii the States, Mr Bingham.'

'We've no choice, though I believe there are more Japanese on the islands than native Americans. By the way, I'm from London.'

'I can tell,' she said. 'You have an English accent when you speak Japanese.' He could have taken it as an insult, but her tone was genuine and her comment on the Englishman's deficiency in her language judged his accent not his ability.

Araki watched her in fascination. Speaking English her voice changed to a deeper, less deferential pitch, freed of the need for feminine platitudes of respect.

'Where's Mrs Ando?' he asked, suddenly remembering.

'Toilet,' Mariko replied, checking the time.

Araki wished them luck and moments after his departure the elderly woman emerged from between the banks of lifts. She was quite chirpy, the condition of her husband had improved overnight, and to Chris's consternation she had left the hospital early, returned home and dressed in an immaculate, maroon kimono.

'We're supposed to be inconspicuous, on surveillance,' he said despairingly to an amused Mariko, who led them up a central stairway to another smaller waiting area, from the balcony of which they had a clear view of most of the lobby. They would be undetectable as long as the real estate broker called Terashima, if he appeared as Mrs Ando had requested on the answerphone, patrolled the area looking for a woman he expected to find downstairs. In any case, Mariko pointed out, a kimono was not out of place in the Imperial, which played host daily to parties, weddings, receptions, fashion shows and self-conscious couples in their finest clothes, aside a marriage go-between who brought them together for the first time in the lounge of one of Tokyo's most luxurious hotels.

'That's him,' Mrs Ando said with conspiratorial relish, pointing to a thin individual with a light beige raincoat over his arm in the centre of the main lobby.

'Are you certain?' Chris murmured, drawing the old lady away from the balcony.

'Of course,' she said confidently. 'I met him several times.'

Chris rested a Nikon F-9 on the balcony rail, its zoom fully extended, the flash unit in place. Terashima smoked and paced over short distances, and when he stopped to check his watch Chris pressed the shutter button. The

140

stab of light went unnoticed in a place where souvenir photo-taking was commonplace and Chris followed up with two more when Terashima moved towards them, his mounting irritation distracting him from looking upwards to the source of the flashes.

Turning to Mariko Chris said, 'Take Mrs Ando out through the coffee shop at the back and accompany her to her home, or to the hospital, wherever she wants to go.'

'When I finish what I have to do I'm going to Araki's,' Chris said, his eyes on the figure below who had checked his watch several times and was now at the reception desk, presumably asking if there were any messages for him from a woman who was thirty minutes overdue. 'He should be back by two.'

Wondering if Araki was working on her mother's disappearance she asked, 'Where is he?'

'He called me last night to say he was going to Kamakura again.'

'Kamakura? Again?'

Chris quickly confirmed their quarry was still in the lobby and spoke quickly to the beautiful, confused woman.

'He went to look at the land your mother owns in the hills outside Kamakura. He said he had to go back again today urgently.'

Mariko made to leave, taking her frail charge by the arm.

'Is Araki . . . reliable?'

'Reliable?'

'I am not being rude,' she said, struggling for words. 'Is he looking for my mother in . . . a correct way?'

There was no time to reply. The man in the lobby was stalking towards the main entrance, tripping past the stacked luggage of a tour group assembling to depart.

'Wait for ten minutes,' Chris said urgently, 'in case he has a car and a driver outside.'

Kondo sat in the battered Toyota, ignoring the pleas of the uniformed bell-boys to give way to the airport bus and the stretched limousines that had precedence in the front drive. Terashima could choose to walk towards the Hibiya underground station or take a taxi, in which case Kondo would pursue him in Araki's car and Chris would follow in a back-up taxi. If he chose the train Chris would be with him. The Englishman came out, a few metres behind the thin man who was slipping into a raincoat and waiting in the short line for a taxi. Throwing a glance over to Kondo, Chris anticipated his turn in the queue and motioned to the driver of a yellow and green fleet taxi to open the automatic door. The driver, a stocky unshaven man, looked round disapprovingly at the gaijin who asked him in fluent Japanese to follow the white private cab pulling out from the kerb. 'I'll give you an extra thousand yen,' Chris said, leaning over the back rest, relaxing when the driver grunted his agreement.

Kondo, unused to driving, was labouring with the unpredictable Toyota and the complexity of the lanes along Hibiya-dori, and he let the white taxi gain a dozen car lengths on him. Poorly positioned, he watched Terashima's car melt into the off-side lane with a view to a right turn at Uchisaiwaisho and was relieved to see Chris in his mirror two cars behind in the same line. He held his breath as the light changed from green as the quarry's vehicle entered the intersection, but relaxed when Chris's driver, evidently warming to the task, swerved in close pursuit. Kondo almost caught up with them at the next crossing but the three lines of vehicles became embroiled in a routine game of evasion and lane-swapping when a large delivery truck pulled up sharply in front of the Japan Press Centre. The white private taxi braked but escaped the mêlée, leaving Chris stranded and frustrated as his driver hung through the window, begging for a slot in the solid traffic and seeing his thousand yen bonus evaporate. Kondo found himself in the outside mainstream and almost collided with the white cab as he swept by. A right turn brought them alongside the shell of the burnt-out New Japan Hotel and when they passed the complex of hotels and restaurants around the Akasakamitsuke intersection Kondo had his first inkling that his pursuit might not be secret. The other car hesitated on the approach to the three lanes and at the last moment chose to swerve left, bumping over lane dividers and heading deliberately at speed up the incline towards Aoyama. Kondo swerved, forcing a van to brake dangerously and attracting the attention of a policeman standing passively below the underpass. He decided to pull over to the side of the road, his ability to control Araki's car and follow another totally shattered. He saw what he thought was Chris's taxi flash past but by then he was considering his excuse.

8

'Will you have to give the money back?' Chris asked, his voice thick from last night's drink and lack of sleep.

'No.'

Chris mistook Araki's uncompromising and uncharacteristically inadequate response as a reflection of his own fatigue: they had been together talking and drinking above the Korean barbecue where Chris lived until four that morning. The Japanese had vented his anger and frustration at the failure of his paid colleagues to follow the dubious land agent to his lair but as the evening progressed the recriminations evaporated into significance. The telephone call he had received from Mariko at the peak of his verbal tirade suddenly rendered knowledge of the man's whereabouts of immaterial value. There was an important new development Mariko Izumi had said.

The Japanese was struggling to hold his ten-year-old green Toyota Corona on the slippery surface of the two-lane metropolitan expressway at the point where it joined the Chuo highway ten minutes west of Shinjuku in the heart of Tokyo and where the noise-absorbent barriers stood alarmingly close of the roadway. At the legal speed limit of seventy kilometres an hour, the old car's engine coughed intermittently and at ninety its control grew loose and unresponsive, even without the threat from the treacherous tarmac. At least the traffic was in his favour. Across the barrier two lanes of vehicles limped towards Tokyo in another endless Friday morning rush-hour.

It had rained for two days with the intensity of a September typhoon but without the squalls and violent winds. Flights had been cancelled and fatal landslides reported within thirty kilometres of Tokyo. The playing fields below them as they crossed the Tama River at Hachioji were flooded to the point of being unusable. In the baseball field nearest the bridge only the pitcher's mound stood out in what was now a lake. The river tore past in surging, brown torrents reaching up to the very lips of the ruptured banks. Araki had welcomed the break from talking to apologetic and depressed relatives and their ambiguous and confusing emotions. As the rain washed his terrace and formed a pond in the lot behind the building he had time to contemplate the Izumis and search for an excuse for the behaviour of the son's so-called friends in the toilet of a very expensive Ginza bar. He was sure they were the new generation yakuza, distinguishable from the ranks of salarymen by the cut of their suits and the trim of their neat, permed hair, not by the tattoos and mutilated fingers of their seniors. And did the nervous bank manager Nakata have a legitimate business reason to visit a small real estate broker called Suwano? In land deals it was usually the middle-man who went to the banker to petition for finance. In letting out his feelings, Araki had grilled his two mercenaries with a violent need to know where the man called Terashima, another real estate agent, was going when he caused his taxi to veer away and leave Chris and Kondo stuck at a red light in separate vehicles. Was there a chance it could have been Toranomon, the location of Suwano's office? 'No,' said Chris. 'The taxi didn't seem spooked and was driving towards Shibuya at normal speed.'

'Yes,' said Kondo, with confidence. 'He thought Terashima in the target cab knew he was being followed and was taking a roundabout route to Toranomon.'

Kondo seemed to be rejuvenated by the tasks Araki set him, displaying the same diligence he had showed as a researcher on the magazine where they had both worked. Now, in retirement, he had the relaxed enthusiasm of those who have a choice. It took only time, and Kondo

145

had it in reserve, to piece together a crude background for the man who had married the missing woman and taken her name. A family with wealth but no male heirs searched for a solution. The war was over and a street smartness superseded education. The Izumis had assets in the form of land which they could mortgage for cash and they had the shell of the electric goods company and its impoverished employees desperate for work. When the company was on the move, there was a workers' revolt, inspired by outside agitators. It was put down by a man known as Yamada. Kondo could still find no lead on Yamada's birth or early youth but he remained convinced that on marriage he took his wealthy partner's name. Izumi was a gifted entrepreneur and in the 1960s, when Japanese names began to be recognized in New York and London, he was talked about in Japan in the same circles as Honda, Morita of Sony and Matsushita and others who revelled in the freedom of the moment and enjoyed, if that was how the post-war period of poverty and devastation could be described, a release of expression. Apart from Tsutsumi of the Seibu Group, there were no individuals nowadays, Araki mused ruefully, only the faceless, humourless bureaucrats who plotted Japan's strategy for world economic domination and the uncomplaining salarymen, the slaves and who formed the backbone of the banks, trading companies and producers which constituted Japan Incorporated. If the name of Izumi was not familiar to the consumer it was because he produced the lights and electrical fittings that lay moulded anonymously in the cars and trucks that began to flood the roads as the nation marched to prosperity. The equity for the enterprise had come from the president's wife's family and the security for the first vital loans from the land that had been later freed of its liens as the company prospered and was back in the name of a woman who might now be dead. A purveyor of religious comfort, family members of dubious loyalty and a shady property group all saw themselves as heirs to the legacy.

146

Sleek, turbo-charged saloons glided past in the fast lane, tails of spray falling on the Toyota as it lumbered up the long incline which began outside Hachioji and would take them a thousand metres up to the highlands surrounding Mount Fuji. Each crest revealed the distant mountain ranges, each distinguished, according to distance, by varying grey and mauve layers of misty coloration. But the great mountain itself was saving its majestic form for later.

No. He wouldn't return the money, he thought. In fact he had mentally spent it, the million two hundred thousand he would have left after giving Kondo and Chris four hundred each would give him at least two months' breathing space. A trip, perhaps to California and London, to the campuses he had roamed for a year and had opened up a life of freedom and expression which unconsciously destroyed his Japaneseness, and the irrational sense of uniqueness he had been taught to believe in since childhood. The telephone call at eight that morning was almost a relief. He would need time to find the unfortunate lady but most likely the authorities would do so first or she would appear by herself. When Mariko Izumi called to say they had found something in Lake Kawaguchi, not her mother the police had stressed, he felt as though he had contributed something to the search that now seemed over. He may have prompted the police to step up their search and as a result the case may be close to solution.

Mariko said the police wanted the family to identify an article of clothing and she had asked Araki to make his way to the lake. He had protested mildly as he felt awful, wondering why he had slept in his clothes, but when she paused and said haltingly that it would help her personally he relented and apologized for his lack of consideration.

'Do you know the area well?' Chris asked, when they passed Lake Sagami far below them, a snaking reservoir from whose steep sides rich, green cedars, pines and maples rose in dark packed banks.

147

'I climbed Fuji when I was in high school and I've driven round the lakes a few times. Never really stayed though.'

'Interesting coincidence about the house.'

Araki twisted his head towards Chris.

'What house?' he uttered.

'You said the Izumis had a country villa near Lake Kawaguchi. If she is in the lake it sort of confirms that theory everyone seems to have that she chose somewhere familiar to go and die.'

Araki thumped the steering wheel with the heel of his hand. 'I thought the house was in Kawagami,' he said with unusual self-criticism.

At Otsuki he swerved off the highway into a service area. While Chris went to buy drinks Araki rummaged through the papers lying across the rear seat. When was the villa mentioned, where was it and why hadn't he been to see it?

'Have you found it?' Chris asked cheerfully, returning with tins of soft drink and some rice balls wrapped in sea-weed and dripping with soya sauce.

'Yes,' Araki said quietly. 'You were right. It is Kawaguchi.' He showed Chris a map and some hastily scribbled notes – illegible to the Englishman – that he had written after the dinner with the Izumis the previous Sunday.

'The father, or somebody, talked about a villa near the lake. It was when they thought Mrs Izumi had gone off in some deluded state to a familiar place.'

'They might be right,' Chris said, as Araki pulled on to the road where it forked left in the direction of Fuji and its highlands.

'But probably not,' Araki retorted. 'Izumi said the villa was for his own private use. He entertained business clients after a round of golf or went there for quiet strategy meetings with his senior managers. It was out of bounds for anyone else, including the women of the family.'

148

The resort town of Kawaguchi, on the south side of the lake, was still an hour's drive from the mountain but the vast bulk of the volcano, with its perfect cone and upper slopes still covered with snow, imposed itself like a powerful sentinel. They skirted the town and crossed a toll-road bridge which split the lake before turning on to the road which wrapped itself around the expanse of water. The mountain was there again, a misty, haunting apparition. They passed through hamlets with tidy vegetable plots carved from the slopes and stepped in neat rows as far as the tree lines above the houses. Below the road, concrete sluices had been built to direct mountain streams into the lake, where they emerged delta-like on to dark, pebbly beaches just wide enough to hold the skips and rowing boats for visiting fishermen. After the incessant rains, the streams were more like rolling runways which plunged down the artificial channels, dragging roots and assorted débris with them. The car rounded a sharp bend and on one of the lake beaches they found their goal.

A motor-cycle policeman stood by the roadside directing traffic past a row of police cars, their warning lights flashing to discourage the casual observer away from the activity on the lakeside beach behind some wild ferns and thick shrubs. There were also private cars pulled on to the verge and Araki parked at the end, next to a clean, black Mercedes. Before they could leave the car, an ambulance drew in front of them, a reminder of the ominous nature of their journey. There were at least thirty people, mostly men, in contemplative knots around a small plot fenced off on three sides with a hastily built head-high construction made from tarpaulin. The policemen who noticed their arrival looked suspiciously at Chris. Approaching the groups, Araki gestured with his head towards people he recognized. 'He's a superintendent in the Lakes Police,' he said, motioning towards a clutch of uniformed police, one of whom was clearly the leader. 'That's the family over there.' The daughter Shinobu was wearing a dark, sombre suit as if she had expected the body of her

149

mother to be dredged from the lake and had dressed appropriately. Yasuo stood slightly apart with his son, his neck bobbing and hand gesturing at his side as he emphasized a point. Reiko was with them but her mind seemed elsewhere. An elbow rested in the hand of her other arm which she clutched across her chest as if she was cold. A cigarette burned harmlessly in her fingers, drawn by the twists of breeze drifting off the lake.

Chris said: 'There's Mariko. She's looking great.'

'For Christ's sake,' Araki hissed. 'Her mother might be lying on the bottom of the fucking lake over there.' He had never come to like the way his foreign friends based their conversation opening on a subjective comment as to whether the object of their talk was ugly or attractive, applying the criteria to either sex. But he knew Chris was right, and seeing Mariko for the first time in a static pose among people and nature made him forget for the moment the purpose of the trip. Someone moved as Chris spoke, leaving Mariko alone and fragile by the lakeside, her hands sunk deep into the pockets of an open light-weight coat. Wisps of hair, shining auburn in the light, blew across her finely shaped, thin face as she looked anxiously towards the makeshift police compound. The heels of her shoes had sunk into the ground but she was still a head taller than her sister and Reiko, who stood near her, still smoking and kicking pebbles into the lake. When Mariko saw Araki, her mouth opened into a near-smile and she walked over and bowed lightly in recognition.

'You're very kind,' she said.

'Not at all. I wish I could help,' Araki replied.

As she turned towards the makeshift police enclosure, Araki saw how the breeze ruffled her dark straight hair and the sun's rays lightened it into auburn.

As they moved towards the family group and the policemen Araki asked: 'What have they found in the lake?'

'I believe it's a kimono slipper.' Mariko's voice hesitated, and she looked towards the pebbles at her feet. 'They wanted to do some tests, take some pictures and

150

whatever else the police have to do before they let us see it.'

Araki and Chris stayed with Mariko but the uniformed police drew a cordon around the family group and kept the civilian onlookers away. Some were obviously journalists and Araki recognized Takemura from one of the more lurid weekly magazines.

'Oi, Oi,' Takemura shouted, his head bobbing up and down and face spread in surprise as he tried to attract the attention of his old colleague and competitor.

'What have they found? A body? Is it hers?'

Araki stepped protectively between Mariko and the crude gesturing of the journalist. The scene in the tiny compound was almost comically anti-climatic. The family had joined a quartet of policemen, one of whom was Sasaki, the cold, solid detective in charge of the Izumi case, and they were gathered around a cross-legged table. Araki stood on tiptoe, peering between the shoulders of Yasuo Izumi and his son. On the table, and the object of everyone's intense concentration, was a split-toed kimono shoe, a grey-brown colour, with one of its two thongs torn from the base. A uniformed police detective, intent on enforcing his jurisdiction as representative of the Lakes Police, invited the family members to scrutinize, cogitate and decide whether the flimsy item of clothing had belonged to their mother. One by one the family of the missing woman moved to the table and leaned over to inspect the shoe.

'Please look carefully,' Araki heard a policeman saying. 'If it has been in the water for some weeks it may have lost most of its original colour.'

'It might have been brown, or even orange,' another voice said. 'Does anyone remember, or might guess, what colour zori Mrs Izumi was wearing when she left home?' There was a conversation among the family members and some noisy drawing of breath from the men. The two sisters, who did not live in the family home, were not expected to know the colour of their mother's footwear on

151

a particular day but could only offer their thoughts on her dress sense and favourite combinations. Araki wondered where the housekeeper was. She of all of them would be the most likely to know how her mistress dressed and even what she was wearing on her last day with them.

The first to offer an opinion was Yasuo Izumi. Araki could see his head moving slowly from side to side as he said: 'It's not hers. I'm sure of that.'

His son looked at his wife who said she could not say one way or another, adding by way of excuse that she was not usually awake when her mother-in-law left home every day. Her husband said he had to agree with his father, mainly because he could not imagine any reason why his mother should be in the Kawaguchi area under any circumstances. Araki could think of one but he stayed silent. It was Shinobu, the nervous married daughter, who surprised Araki by saying that her mother may have possessed a pair of the brownish kimono slippers similar to the exhibit before them. Under pressure from her father and desperately hoping for an optimistic outcome she conceded that the possibility of it being her mother's was negligible. Inspector Sasaki moved around the table, partly to impose his authority and to thank the Izumi family for coming such a long way at such short notice. He said his men would search the lake area a little longer but the family's evidence would ensure their efforts would not be prolonged unnecessarily. Araki waited with Chris for an opportunity to inspect the slipper while the family filed past to where more policemen waited and journalists jockeyed for a better view. Concluding that the shoe was not their mother's, the family were able to reassure each other and relight the fading candle of hope that she was safe. Each greeted Araki except, he noted wrily, Ken Izumi, his pleasant host of only four days earlier and who now passed him with a stare through narrowed eyes and a knowing nod, certainly not a pleasant greeting.

152

Inspector Sasaki greeted Araki formally but with a warmth that was missing at their first meeting. Even the appearance of the foreigner caused no more than a mild lift of the eyebrows. It was manifest that the policeman was more comfortable in the field than in the sterile confines of his office. His voice was commanding and resolute as he set about ordering the packing of the slipper and the care which must go into its transportation to the laboratory in Tokyo. He seemed to read Araki's mind.

'Well it was worth a try, I've got so little to go on.'

'May I ask who found it?'

They had left the compound and were walking towards the water's edge.

'A very sharp-eyed young man,' the policeman said with admiration. 'He was loading his rowing boat at dawn for some fishing when he found the shoe on the water-line. He thought it odd to see it among the usual plastic bottles, beer cans and cigarette ends. It was very commendable of him to call the police. My colleagues in the Five Lakes Police were perceptive enough to relate the find to the Izumi case.'

The air was cooler and their side of the lake was in partial shadow from a slick of oily black cloud moving listlessly towards Mount Fuji, whose crown was already swathed in its own wrapping of dense cloud. Further along the shore, on a smaller patch of beach, four men in scuba diving suits were heaving full tanks of air, lamps and flippers on to a broad, powerful rubber boat.

'How deep is it here?' Chris asked in confident Japanese.

The detective drew breath noisily.

'Thirty metres, they say.'

Again he anticipated the next question.

'We would be negligent if we didn't make a thorough search, including the bed of the lake.' He gestured towards the other policemen. 'It's a big lake and they tell me there is some underwater activity which causes

153

currents.' And in desperation he added: 'We can't drain the damned place.'

He heard his name called.

'You have to excuse me,' he said.

Araki followed the detective on a winding course around the swampy patches and through the knee-high weeds to the bank at the edge of the road where the cars and police vehicles were parked in a line. Some had already started their engines. The journalists looked disappointed and their photographers snapped shots at random but with no great purpose. Araki was in the family group whose visibly relieved members were waiting in turn to address Inspector Sasaki. Yasuo, the patriarch, spoke for the others: 'We are all grateful for the help you and your policemen are giving at this sad time for us.' He was bowing deeply and his traditional and inflexible words of contrition faded to a dull mumble as his jaw lodged itself against his chest.

The rituals finished, Sasaki went off to talk to the press while Ken Izumi sped away with his wife and married sister in the black Mercedes. His father, Yasuo, left with Shinobu in a chauffeured Nissan executive saloon. Mariko was standing by Araki's old Toyota when he and Chris reached it. She looked relieved to see them but as they neared her they could see the tension and anxiety of still not knowing were carved on her face; her body was tense and she held her handbag in front of her, the knuckles on her hands white as she alternately gripped and released the fabric.

'I'm sorry I brought you here,' she said, her voice firm and sincere, contrasting sharply with her father's perfunctory remarks to the policeman.

Araki flapped a wrist. 'There's nothing to apologize for. I'm working for you and your family and I had to be here.'

Mariko returned her hands to the pockets of her long coat and opened and closed the flaps in a futile gesture. She looked towards the lake where the insulated

154

heads of the divers bobbed like seals alongside the floats of their boat.

'I'm sure she's not in there,' she said hopefully, more for her own consolation than the two men.

Beneath the coat she was wearing a dress of beige and black diagonal stripes, loose but not enough to hide the contours of her model's body. Long, straight legs, narrow waist and the slightest of swellings in the dress where the tips of the broad collars met over her breasts. Yes, he could see what excited Chris and caused him personal anger because he could not rid himself of his own Japanese innate suppression of emotion. Affection, sensuality and the expression of human feelings escaped him even after years absorbed in western culture. He did not want to tell her about the lake and its depth and the depressions and enclaves which could trap her mother and hold her for ever. Better to let her and her family go on believing sincerely that their beloved matriarch had not thrown herself into the comforting eternity of the black waters.

'Will you be all right driving home?' Chris said kindly. 'Perhaps you ought to rest for a while.' He touched her lightly on the sleeve. Araki wished he could transmit his compassion so easily and fluently.

'No, I'll be fine,' Mariko replied, recovering her composure and fishing in her handbag for her car keys. 'I have to get back to the office for a presentation this afternoon. Are you coming?'

Chris was about to say that he would ride back with her and Araki would follow them but Araki's reply was quick and unequivocal.

'No. We'll wait around the lake for a while and talk to a few people. Probably have some lunch in town.'

Mariko seemed disappointed: so did Chris. She made to leave and Araki stopped her. 'One small thing,' he said, a cigarette unlit in his fingers. Mariko turned.

'Yes?'

155

'Why didn't the housekeeper come along with you? I would have thought she was the most likely one to know what your mother's dressing habits were.'

Mariko looked puzzled for a moment and then said, as if recalling someone else's excuse.

'Father does not like the house left alone. He's almost paranoid about it. If there was any doubt about the shoe he planned to have her see it in Tokyo or wherever they are going to take it. I suppose that won't be necessary now.'

The piece of paper he sought was in the folder on the back seat of his car among the others he had taken from the drawers in Masako Izumi's desk. It was lodged in a sheaf of surveyors' reports and land developers' plans which had been miniaturized and photocopied. Taking the papers would help him to identify the property which the family, or Mrs Izumi as it was turning out, owned and where, the popular theory went, he might find a tired and dispirited old woman seeking some last desperate attachment to a recognizable sanctuary. Studying the documents in his apartment, he had been more interested in the land and buildings she owned in the Tokyo area, the Nakameguro tract with its sinister overtones and the mansion flats of her two daughters, and had ignored the plot outlined in red and lodged high on a mountainside above Lake Kawaguchi, probably less than five kilometres from the spot by the water where the family had gathered to reject the possibility that the trivial piece of footwear floating among the garbage belonged to the missing woman. He looked at the place on the plan and then surveyed the view outside in search of bearings. From the position of the bridge which crossed the lake he concluded they were not far from the turn-off leading to the villa.

'You navigate,' Araki ordered, tossing the diagram to his companion as he pulled away from the verge. Chris sniffed.

156

'I thought the chalet was out of bounds to anyone except Yasuo and his son. We ought to be back in Tokyo trying to find who bought that land in Nakameguro from Mrs Izumi.'

'We'll do that next,' Araki said tersely. 'While we're here let's eliminate one more refuge the old lady might have resorted to.'

They drove in silence for a while, Chris's gaze darting between the chart and the road landmarks.

'Slow down a bit,' he growled in street Japanese. 'I'm looking for a school on the right.'

Araki moved down a gear and said: 'Did you notice a white BMW among the cars at the lake?'

'No. Why?'

'There's one about three hundred metres behind us. Two vehicles away.'

Chris turned, watching the sleek, broad saloon with smoky black, opaque windows close in as the traffic slowed for a light.

'Probably just a rich kid's toy,' Chris said.

'I know. But it picked us up just after we pulled off the verge at the lake. It made the same five turns as we did.'

The road had strayed from the lake – though they could still see it through the houses and across the fields on their left – and narrowed where it passed by a cluster of buildings, before curving sharply and passing between compact and carefully tended vegetable fields, all green with young plants but saturated by the rains of the last two days.

'Pull into that restaurant,' Chris said, indicating an old, weathered house ahead advertising noodles on an incongruously large, and as yet unlit, neon sign clamped to the corner of the building.

It was a tight fit. The restaurant boasted another sign which said 'drive-in' in phoneticized English but it was close to the road and, although the bays were empty, Araki had to slow almost to a stop before he could ease the

157

Corona into a space. The two men waited motionless until they saw the BMW pass and then twisted their heads to watch it round the next bend and disappear.

'I find something very odd,' Araki said as they sat at a plastic-topped table in the roadside café, a simple plate of curry and rice and a beer in front of each of them. Chris stirred the mild, spicy mixture with his spoon.

'What's that?' he said, topping up his colleague's glass.

'When we were standing around that table staring at the slipper as if it were alive, only one of the five family members gave a definite yes or no as to whether it belonged to the Izumi woman. Do you remember who it was?'

Chris spooned a mouthful of curry and fukujinzuke pickles.

'Easy. It was her husband, Yasuo. So what?'

Araki played with the frothy bubbles of condensation on his beer glass.

'I was married for eight years,' he said. 'Obviously nothing compared to Izumi and his wife, but if you had asked me at any moment during those eight years what colour shoes my wife owned, or specifically what colours she didn't own, I would not have had the slightest idea. The same with her clothes. I could never have said that she didn't have a white sweater or a pair of Dutch clogs. It goes without saying that I couldn't possibly tell you what she was wearing yesterday.'

Chris pondered the statement and then said: 'Perhaps Izumi was a more considerate husband than you.'

Araki smiled at the quip, knowing that considerate was not an adjective applied to Japanese husbands under any circumstances. Ironically he could in fact remember what his former wife had worn on their first formal date as third year students at university. It was spring and she was wearing a long-sleeved purple sweater with a V-neck and grey jeans with the pockets and creases outlined in black. With the fluency he had acquired from a year in California and London, he had led the English language

158

debating society and edited its magazine. Kaoru had helped him organize the schedules and plan the topics and arguments and she seemed to respond to his individuality and casual non-conformity. When their relationship was accepted reluctantly by Kaoru's banker father, it was to everyone's relief that Araki accepted a place on the career escalator at one of Japan's major daily newspapers. But even Kaoru knew that he would never be moulded and subdued to produce the unprovocative and reassuring form of journalism that Japanese society had evolved for itself. When he provoked a scandal by corrupting a government official in the search for information on an issue of defence he broke the unwritten code which dictated that the press was there to assist with the creation of a consensus of opinion by propagating the official line given to them at collective press conferences. His dismissal put pressure on his marriage and it ended quietly with a properly negotiated divorce.

'Let's go,' Chris said, pushing the bill to Araki.

They paused where the gravel drive met the road and they both looked without talking for the white BMW among the passing traffic. They drove back to the village and turned left at the school. Stray, torn cherry blossom petals wafted across the windscreen and some of them stuck for an instant before the slipstream tore them away.

'Don't talk to me about the brevity of human life, just like the poor old cherry blossoms,' Chris said.

Araki looked over once and smiled.

The narrow road rose steeply, with patches of cultivated land on each side. The Corona shuddered as Araki eased the gear stick into second and then into first when the road forked upwards, leaving the clutter of farms and holiday villas on the left as it snaked up along an even steeper climb beyond the tree-line of packed pines, spruces and white larches. They stopped on the crest of a curve against the strip of metal which offered token protection against the ravine below. A mountain stream murmured unseen, and a solitary mail box reminded them of human habitation nearby. Behind them the great mountain dominated the scene, its body invisible in the play of light which fused it with the reflection from the lake but left the snow-capped cone stranded in space like a cloud. Chris estimated that the dotted line on the map was a track or access road not much further past the point where this road bent left a kilometre or so further on. They drove on and the road turned inland and narrowed, so that in places the branches of the densely packed trees touched. They had met no other traffic since they began to climb fifteen minutes earlier but they felt a disorientation of time and space in the psychodelic atmosphere of flashing lights and shade where the sun broke through the leafy roof and danced on the road in tune to the speed of the car. Araki braked hard when Chris bellowed and the car skidded past a narrow turn-off. The Englishman had seen a board nailed to a tree and he had seen the ideograph for Izumi next to one he could not recognize.

'You read it "so",' Araki said, reversing the Toyota alongside the sign. 'It means chalet or villa.'

'Not very wide is it?' his friend commented.

Araki turned the car into the access road.

'It's for people who know their way there,' he said cynically. 'Or have a map – not for strangers.'

Almost immediately Araki pulled into an arc of space bordering a coppice of beeches.

'What's the matter?' Chris asked.

The Japanese turned the engine off and walked to the back of the car.

'Let's wait two minutes,' he said as Chris joined him.

In the placid air, even the sudden dash of birds rustled the branches and caused the two men to look towards the disturbance.

Chris paced the road: Araki propped himself against the boot, his ears alert.

Chris turned and said: 'He was probably looking for the nearest love-hotel. The lakeside route was his best choice.'

'It's too early,' Araki said, staring ahead, and then adding. 'Even for a Japanese.'

'But surely you don't follow somebody in a white BMW when . . . '

But Araki leaped away from the Toyota and ordered Chris to silence.

'Shizuka!' he said. 'Silence.'

They stood immobile, as if stricken by a paralysing ray and when the sound of their own body movements and voices had subsided they concentrated their hearing. Somewhere there was a drone, a barely perceptible low hum. Chris looked ahead but decided the sound was not coming from the direction of the chalet. It was on the main road, from below them on the road down to the lake.

Another command from the Japanese.

'Get in the car.'

The rear tyres spun on the soft dirt of the verge and then threw up a spurt of mud as they gripped on firmer ground. Araki drove back to the main road and pointed the car down towards the village. The other vehicle passed them at the place they had stopped on the bend. It was a post-office light truck and its engine strained at a high pitch on the incline.

'That's why we could hear it from where we did,' Araki said, relieved.

'What did you do that for?' Chris asked.

'What?'

'Race off down the hill towards the noise of the van. It could have been the BMW.'

Araki slowed the car and turned it deftly in three movements. He smirked at Chris.

'If it had been the BMW I didn't want to be caught going in the same direction on a private road to no-where.'

161

They chortled together, as if they had cheated the executioner, and drove back to the tract which would lead to the Izumi lodge.

Once upon a time, a patch of forest had been cleared and levelled, and a Swiss-style wooden chalet with a broad sloping roof had been built on solid, concrete stilts. The view from the veranda, which ran the length of the lodge, was magnificent. An unimpeded view of the sacred mountain and the placid lake, like a silver carpet, at its base. The paved road continued into the trees and Araki wondered aloud whether there were other villas whose owners had managed to find in Japan an exclusive kind of privacy.

'There was only one sign,' Chris noted, causing Araki to compliment him on his perceptiveness.

The place was obviously unoccupied. The storm windows around the house were all drawn and the veranda chairs folded and stacked against the wall. Araki rapped ostentatiously on the door under the porchway at the side of the building while Chris surveyed the exterior and the sheds which housed a generator and probably some tools and leisure furniture. Had there been anyone in the chalet the pair might have found an excuse for their presence hard to find. Chris came across the Japanese on one knee, an eye against the keyhole which he was probing with some instrument or another.

The Englishman looked over his shoulder, at the road which led away from the isolated, lonely villa, and said, in a distressed voice, 'What are you doing?'

'It doesn't look very complicated.' His wrist turned. 'I wish I had that implement,' he said, the words stretched each time he strained to find the catches inside the lock. 'A locksmith gave it to me years ago.'

'We came to look the place over,' Chris pleaded. 'Not break into it.'

'You're right,' Araki conceded. 'I couldn't get in anyway.' He stood and looked around. 'Let's check the terrace.'

162

The front of the house was in shadow as the sun fell away behind the mountain to the rear but the lake and volcano stayed radiant in the late afternoon sunshine.

Chris started to protest but Araki was already hauling himself on to the crossed supports of the veranda. Overweight and badly built for climbing, Araki had reached the rail but had to rest his body over it while he found breath to make the final effort to pull himself across and fall on to the terrace. Chris found it easier. He was slim and twelve years younger and managed to land on his feet after the last hurdle. Araki prowled the terrace, probing the firmness of the amado rain windows and looking for signs of weakness. There were none. He stood facing the view, his arms resting on the rails of the veranda.

'I don't know where she is,' he confessed, shaking his head in desperation. 'But this place stinks.' He spoke in English but he used the Japanese word 'kusai', at the end, emphasizing the odorous implication of the word with a disdainful contortion of the face.

They climbed down and walked towards the car.

'What's on the other side?' Araki asked, remembering he had focused his efforts on the front porch.

'A couple of sheds,' Chris answered casually. 'And there's another door.'

Araki was leaning over to open the car. He looked up.

'But it's tight shut,' Chris added, when he sensed his colleague's heightened interest.

'I'll have a brief look,' the Japanese said. 'Wait here if you want.'

Araki rattled the locks on the two lean-to buildings and probed the lock on the rear service door and again gave up in frustration. His attention fell on the blue, solid tub which would hold the sacks of rubbish for what Araki assumed were infrequent collections. Chris joined him as he circled the container as if it were alive and posed a threat.

'Nothing here, is there?' the Englishman suggested.

163

Araki lifted the lid. They recoiled at the same instant, their faces contorted in disgust at the vile odour of putrid flesh.

'Jesus!' Chris exclaimed, reading the other's mind. 'Surely not here!'

Araki held one hand against his face and approached the bin with trepidation. He peered in and then heaved it on to its side. It rolled on the spot until the weight inside stabilized it, and through the untied mouth of a grey plastic rubbish sack pieces of moulding food and odd bits of paper spilled on to the path. Araki dragged the bag clear of the bin. It had been punctured in places, accounting for the smell which had now dissipated in the open air.

'How long has it been left?' Chris wondered.

Araki smirked. 'I've been working in garbage for the last ten years but I'm not sure I can age the stuff.'

Chris joined him in the joke.

'Two weeks or so.'

'At least,' the Japanese said, carefully lifting the bag upright and drawing two ends together to make a knot.

'What are you doing?' Chris asked bemused.

'We're taking this with us. Grab one end. I don't want to tear the bottom of the sack on the gravel.'

Chris reluctantly hoisted the side of the bag off the ground and as they moved towards the car he was still protesting.

'What do you want this crap for? You can have mine if you like. At least a bag a week.'

Araki ignored the offer and spread several layers of newspaper in the boot.

'If the stuff's been there long enough there might be a trace of Mrs Izumi or her belongings.'

'Like a leg,' Chris said in jest.

'Might be,' the Japanese said. 'Or her head.'

Chris's exasperation was clear in his voice.

'Why don't you just tip it all over the ground. We don't have to cart it back to Tokyo. If she's in the bag, let's know about it now.'

Araki closed the lid on his malodorous cargo. He said: 'I don't plan to leave any sign of our visit and if we spread a carpet of garbage in front of Izumi's house, I for one am not going to pick it up again.'

'Where are you taking it then?' Chris asked.

'Your flat.'

At the first pharmacy they passed after leaving the expressway in Tokyo's Shinjuku district Araki stopped to buy a pair of rubber kitchen gloves which he tossed into Chris's lap. Before his passenger could demur, Araki enquired: 'Do you have some disposable chopsticks?'

'Yes, but . . . '

'A spare rubbish bag.'

'I think so, but this is disgusting. Where can we empty the stuff? I don't have a terrace.'

'Use the bathtub.'

Chris chuckled ironically. 'Of course, the bathtub.'

'And when you've had a good look, re-bag it and send it out with your own rubbish.'

Chris saw another catch. He said: 'Aren't you going to help?'

Araki checked the mirror with a prolonged gaze and became serious.

'After I drop you I'm going straight to the Izumi place to try and get to the housekeeper.'

'The slipper bothers you, doesn't it?'

'More and more,' the Japanese murmured.

He felt familiar enough with the surroundings and sufficiently confident of his relationship to let himself through the roofed gateway without announcement. The air was still and in the shade of the plum and cherry trees it was lightly chilled. The cracked stones were slippery with fallen cherry blossoms and a carpet of shrivelled petals covered the garden giving it an aspect of unusual neglect. It was almost half past five when Araki rang the bell in the porchway of the Izumi house. He thought he could detect a musty odour of rotting garbage on his

165

clothing, but perhaps it was just unwashed. The bell sounded in several places inside and made a shrill echo as if it were ringing in an empty house. But Araki knew she was there; and he asked himself why she never seemed to go shopping or be out visiting friends. Why hadn't she stopped off somewhere on the return trip from the lake to celebrate the happy fact that the slipper in the water did not belong to her mother-in-law? When she finally opened the door it was obvious to Araki that she had seen him arrive and had hurried to brush out her hair and wrap herself in a yukata, which hugged her slender frame. It had not been around her long enough for the last fold to start to loosen itself below the sash. He also thought he saw traces of make-up below her eyes where there had been none at the lake or when they met over dinner or the day following when he had studied the missing woman's papers.

'There's nobody in,' Reiko said strangely, as if she herself did not exist.

'I know I'm troubling you,' Araki said with sham embarrassment. 'But I'd like to speak to you or your housekeeper.'

She still looked puzzled, as if trying to recognize the visitor.

'May I come in Izumi-san?' Araki pleaded formally.

She stood above him as he stood in the sunken entrance hall and watched as he removed his shoes without a real invitation. He waited in hope for the usual civilities but in the end opted to reach over himself to a low stand with a dozen pairs of guests' slippers tucked into holes cut into its side. Next to the slipper stall, Araki noted, was a tall umbrella stand which, apart from these articles, held some golf-clubs the men of the family used for putting practice on the garden lawn. Next to that was a cabinet with sliding doors for the family shoes.

Reiko led him to the lounge with its western furniture where they had all met the previous Saturday, six days earlier. The atmosphere in the room was heavy with

166

smoke, although the walls of the house had been drawn aside, leaving only the insect mesh to filter the grey trails of floating ash into the cool spring late afternoon air. A half-crushed cigarette smouldered in an ashtray beside half a dozen predecessors. Araki felt at one with the smells and thought he could detect the familiar odour of whisky although there was no glass left for him to find. She could be attractive, Araki considered, watching how she held a sleeve while she cleared sheets of newspaper before sitting across the rosewood coffee table, her legs crossed beneath the loose folds of the kimono. But the neglect was in the sallow, undernourished skin webbed in grey creases at the corners of her mouth, and the dark eyes which, in spite of the mysterious thin trace of blue liner, looked weary and abused.

'The housekeeper is out shopping,' she said vacantly.

'You must be relieved about the shoe,' Araki said.

Reiko shrugged, pondering a response.

'It might have been better to have resolved the situation,' she said finally.

'Your husband believes the police will,' Araki said. 'That's the message I got from him the other night.'

Reiko looked surprised.

'Monday night,' Araki added. 'We went out to a few bars. He had two of his friends with him.' He lingered on the word 'friends' and looked to see if she was curious. 'He's certainly got stamina,' Araki said with exaggerated envy. 'I couldn't have got up early after a night like that.'

'I wouldn't know,' Reiko said disinterestedly.

'Did you know he was with me?'

Reiko smiled vacantly at the futility of such a question.

'I saw him today at the lake for the first time in three days,' she said, and before Araki could pry she added: 'Business. Friends. The usual things.'

Araki nodded knowingly, his own long absences from home as a restless, combative journalist having contributed to the breakdown of his marriage to an intelligent

167

woman who refused to accept the traditional role of a subservient, forgiving wife.

'I'll get you a drink,' she said, adjusting the folds of her yukata and not waiting for his reply.

He had plugged the widest tear with a ball of newspaper but a fluid, a yellow bile, oozed from the hole and the putrid stench of decomposition hung around him. Chris manoeuvred the rubbish at arm's length up the outside steps of his modest apartment block which was squeezed between a complex of bars and restaurants across from the Yamanote railway line running from Shin Okubo to Shinjuku. He had taken the three-room flat on the introduction of a drinking friend of Araki's who had waived the right to key money in return for a tenant who would not object to the nocturnal movements in the adjoining flats. Chris had no complaints, and in the eighteen months of his stay he had befriended the girls, their benign yakuza minders and the frumpy, retired hostesses who ran the bars, restaurants and love-hotels in this popular bright, bawdy entertainment district. The day after a long evening of drinking, Chris would often find Araki splayed on an old futon in his cramped living room, snoring loudly in the clothes he had arrived in. The three apartments rested on a Korean barbecue restaurant, whose pungent fumes wafted nightly through the rooms, and a late-night snack bar with singing equipment in its basement.

Chris heaved his smelly burden into the squat bathtub and ripped the bag down one side, exposing the heap of rubbish. He needed a break and backed into the kitchen, carefully sliding the door shut against the stench and poured himself a glass of neat Suntory whisky, a drink he kept normally for Araki's exclusive use. He drew on the rubber gloves his friend had considerately bought for the task ahead and found an unused garbage bag, which he shook open, and a pair of wooden disposable chopsticks. The thought of sorting through the mess, even with covered hands, nauseated him. Piece by piece, and as carefully as if he were lifting explosives, Chris picked out scraps of paper, mostly tissues and food wrappers, and after a tight-lipped, quick inspection he dropped the stained tatters into the new bag. Lifting a congealed mess of rank, mouldy noodles and what looked like chicken bones with remnants of stringy, half-chewed flesh, Chris could only wonder at the motivation of his Japanese collaborator. Was it tenacity and an almost fanatical attention to detail which had identified him as the complete journalist with a national newspaper and later as a ruthless and unsentimental investigative reporter for the popular magazine? Or perhaps a revival of his uncompromising refusal to be intimidated by what he saw as attempts to deter and frighten him. Qualities, Chris reckoned, dropping a filthy beer bottle into his bag, which are unappreciated in the passive, manipulated world of Japanese journalism, and had led directly to his dismissal from a newspaper and a popular magazine. Or was it sheer desperation at the lack of progress in his search for the missing woman? Whatever the reason, Chris found this task sickening and pointless and retired to the kitchen for another deep draught of whisky, delighting in the way the rich aroma of the alcohol overwhelmed the foul stench of the garbage.

Reiko returned with a single glass and a dish of slim, savoury rice crackers.

'I think I'm keeping you away from your business,' Araki said out of courtesy. Reiko's head was bowed and she seemed to be searching for the courage to speak, and when the words came they were deliberate and carefully weighted.

'I do have an appointment,' she said. 'But you're welcome to wait for my father-in-law. He has to return early to change for a dinner.'

Araki calculated the time he would have to himself in the house. Yasuo had left the lakeside at twelve-thirty and would have dropped his daughter Shinobu in Tokyo around two before going to the factory in Shinagawa. It was now almost five-thirty. Araki wondered what 'early' meant to a man like Yasuo Izumi. He wanted ten minutes alone in the house.

'If you'll excuse me,' she said. 'I have to prepare myself and change.'

'Of course,' Araki said, and then decided to gamble on her nervousness and he hoped that in her haste she would not try to look too far into his motives.

'I would like to see your mother-in-law's room,' he said, and before she could object or ask why he added: 'I examined her papers in your father-in-law's room but I did say I would like to see where she lived and try to get a feel for her habits, dress sense, that sort of thing.' He tossed the words across to her in a matter-of-fact way, aimed at pressuring her to agree. It worked. After a flash of hesitation, she checked her watch instinctively and led him down the familiar creaky corridor, past the room and office-cum-den overlooking the classical laid-out Japanese garden, to a tatami room next to a bathroom. Araki thanked Reiko and urged her to complete her preparations to leave.

The atmosphere was stale in the low-ceilinged room and Araki guessed the rain doors had been left unopened for days, perhaps weeks, since the occupant disappeared. He found the light switch. It was a friendly, cramped room hung with prints of European impressionist paintings and colourful drapes drawn aside at the outside wall. A dressing table with a hinged mirror and small drawers had been cleared and stood next to a door which Araki assumed connected it with the bathroom. He made a mental note of the layout and then moved swiftly to the object of his visit. Then he thought he heard a shuffle of feet in the corridor and waited, his hand in the groove which would open the sliding door of the cupboards. He breathed deeply and eased the door aside along its smooth ruts. It was the mirror image of the tidy racks and packed drawers he had found in her husband's room a few days

170

earlier, only here the hangers held dresses, skirts, jackets and blouses, unsurprisingly in browns, navy blues and dark, check patterns. Lower shelves kept a small collection of shoes, the toes pointing outwards, others still kept in their original boxes. Araki grunted his disappointment and moved to his side, rearranging the doors until he exposed a concealed heavy tansu chest which he knew would contain the Japanese wardrobe the missing woman preferred. Grasping the two black iron rings, he drew the deep top drawer open. Inside, there were at least ten immaculately folded kimonos, including two formal black examples with the family crests sewn near the collar in a tiny white circle. Unable to be washed or ironed without damage, the pure silk garments were separated by sheets of soft white paper. The kimono shoes, more like padded slippers with simple thongs which split the feet between the big toe and its neighbour, were in their original flimsy boxes, fifteen in all, and marked meticulously as to colour, some with handwritten Chinese ideographs, others with the maker's coloured disc. More in hope than expectation, Araki lifted the lids from the three boxes marked by hand or colour for brown and purple and when he found they were all occupied he flipped open the rest with mounting frustration. They were all filled with the appropriate shoes. He knelt down and rummaged on the floor at the foot of the cupboard and in the crevices between the shelves but there were no empty boxes. He stood up and drew the doors together with a sharp crack. There should be an empty box. A woman of precise habits like Mrs Izumi did not leave kimono slippers, so easily soiled, lying around when not in use.

Reiko was already dressed and waiting for him in the lounge. He was astonished at the difference. Her natural dark auburn hair had been brushed and smoothed until it shimmered like pure silk; she had pampered her face with a touch of colour and glossed her thin lips a strong coral orange. Her eyebrows were extended and her narrow, dark eyes highlighted with thin, sharp lines.

171

She wore a long-sleeved, lime-green beltless dress which was moulded to her slender frame and ended above her knees. Flesh-coloured tights concealed and shaped the pale legs Araki had noticed at that first meeting with the family and fingernails painted a salmon red completed the transformation. She looked relaxed, her head moving sensibly with the conversation, her hands controlled, and Araki used the closeness of an offered cigarette to sniff for alcohol. She looked so passive, so languidly apathetic. Araki had one card to play and if somehow Reiko had something to hide he knew he would expose it now. He led her to the door, mumbling apologies while his eyes searched the hallway, and lowered himself into his shoes. Bending down, he contorted his face into a false grimace.

'Is there a shoe horn?'

Without waiting for a reply or positive assistance, Araki hobbled across the sunken tiled hallway towards the shoe cupboard: 'Please don't bother coming down,' he said pre-emptively, before dropping to one knee. 'I'll find one in here.'

Behind the sliding doors was the carefully segregated footwear of the men and women of the two families who shared the house. The men's selection of formal and casual shoes, mostly in black leather or dark browns, was neatly presented, the toes pointing outward, and all polished or dusted, a daily task no doubt performed by the aged housekeeper at the same time every day. The women kept less footwear in this cabinet, presumably, Araki thought, because it was easier to match shoes with clothes at their leisure as they dressed and then carry the footwear to the door. But there were some shoes amongst the plastic garden slippers and the pair of wooden geta clogs. His eyes scanned the dark corners and recesses.

'I think it's on the left,' Reiko said helpfully. She craned her head forward but fortunately made no move to step down to help him. Amongst the shoes and cleaning equipment in the last section were two shoe boxes.

172

Through his side vision he saw the flickering image of Reiko, her suspicions growing as she moved along the step for a better view. Drawing the flatter of the boxes off the shelf, Araki stood up and held it towards Reiko. He did not miss the way she gripped the edge of the door and looked around helplessly for support. The box was clearly old and used obviously to protect regularly worn shoes which were easily soiled. It was plain white, except on one end where details of the maker and origin were printed above a patch of colour, and was flatter than usual because it was made to hold kimono slippers. The sphere was deep brown, copper in colour. The box Araki held out towards the bewildered woman was also empty, a point he emphasized by tilting it towards her and separating the layers of tissue-like paper inside. He dropped the box at her feet and reached again into the cabinet before she could offer some form of protest. He pushed each shoe or obstacle aside, knocking a pair of brushes and wiping cloths on to the floor in a single-minded search for the contents of the box. He knew he would not find them.

Reiko had lost her nervousness and watched, almost bemused, as her visitor tidied up below her. When he had replaced the cleaning materials, he stood up again, the empty box again in his hand. His voice was harsh and a little menacing.

'Would your mother-in-law have worn these when she went out that last time?' He tapped the empty container. 'I mean the ones that belong in this box.'

Reiko shrugged.

'I have no idea. Nobody controlled her wardrobe.' The silence told her Araki was not satisfied and expected a more considered response.

'Yes, I suppose she would.' Reiko confessed, smoothing her fingernails.

'You saw the slipper they found in the lake?'

'Yes.'

'Is it your mother-in-law's?'

173

Reiko shifted uneasily from one foot to the other, searching for a refuge.

'By the time I saw it,' she said evasively, 'everyone had decided it wasn't hers. Who am I to disagree?'

Ignoring the rhetorical question he sought her eyes and held them when he raised the box and asked: 'And what do you think now?'

'I think nothing,' she replied, by way of dismissal.

There was not much left, a few scraps of papers stuck amongst the mess that had sunk over the weeks to the bottom of the bag and which oozed from tiny holes into his bathtub. Chris tugged a paper with his chopsticks and gagged. The bottom of the black bag was a living mass of maggots rising and dipping in the decomposed meat or, from what was barely discernible amongst the stench, possibly fish. The smell drowned his senses, and he gagged again. He dropped the chopsticks and the pieces of paper, and with breath held deeply in his chest he lifted the last bits of the mess from the bath and eased it into the new bag. Possessed of an uncompromising desire to rid his flat of the smell, the presence of decay, he secured the flaps of the bag in a stack of knots and carried it down to the back of the building where he left it amongst a heap of similar discards from the restaurant and the bars. The first table barbecues of the evening had been lit and the welcome aroma of burning meat was already on the staircase as he returned to his flat. He opened the rear window wide and breathed the fresh, mildly heavy spring air, and then the front door which gave on to the narrow communal veranda overlooking the street. There was a slat behind a grill in the bathroom and he could not remember whether he had opened it or not. He had, but there were still stains and unidentifiable wastes on the floor of the bathtub, including the chopsticks where he had dropped them. He used the hand shower to flush the mess down the drain and then picked up the soiled chopsticks disdainfully and dropped them into another rubbish bag. He stooped down, then knelt on the cold tiles, his face close to the stem of the toilet where it was rooted to the floor. He only heard the telephone after it had rung for a minute.

Araki hurried along the quiet side roads which ended abruptly where the suburban railway divided the tiled homes from the flats and clusters of shops and restaurants around the station concourse. His body shook with impatience and excitement when pedestrians and vehicles were halted by the monotonous plinking of the crossing warning bell and another loaded commuter train curved between the tidy tenements and modest wooden houses alongside its tracks. Salarymen in dark suits, many with open beige raincoats, and a swarm of office girls poured through the turnstiles and joined the orderly queues for the local buses. An early evening scene at three hundred metropolitan stations. Araki was desperate to share his discovery and debated within as to whom he should call first. He chose the central police station but Inspector Sasaki was not there.

'I can have him located if your request is urgent,' a distant female voice proclaimed, but Araki had already begun to have his first doubts. They grew as he returned the telephone to its rest after thanking the formal voice and leaving his number. One empty container hardly constituted conclusive evidence that the slipper in the lake originated in the Izumi house. Could he please match one rotting piece of footwear with its point-of-sale box? He smiled to himself at the thought. Two hundred and thirty million feet in the country and that meant a lot of shoes and their boxes. He chortled again, and then a calming seriousness overcame him. But only a fraction of women wear kimonos regularly . . . Someone coughed behind him, an elderly man with a thin moustache and sparse beard dotting his chin who had chosen Araki's position in the line of fifteen red boxes as being the most likely to be vacated first. He was right and wrong. Araki

175

raised a hand, chopping the air apologetically, and turned his back on him.

'Come on Chris,' he growled. 'I know you're there.' He turned again to reassure the man whose immobility of age prevented him from moving spritely along the line as telephones became available but his eyes passed over his shoulder to the figure approaching him across the street against the general flow of people. She walked quickly, her bright lime dress covered to her hips with a loose long-sleeved jacket with a broad collar. He heard Chris's voice in the ear-piece, but he was riveted on the figure of Reiko Izumi as it changed direction towards the bank of ticket dispensers.

'Chris,' Araki said urgently. 'I'll call you back. I'm going after Reiko.'

'Hang on please,' Chris's voice was pleading. 'I found something in the rubbish, a . . . ' But his words were redundant as Araki deposited the telephone in the hands of the old man and dashed for the ticket machine, rummaging for a coin as he ran and watching the back of Reiko as she passed through the barrier. In the background, unseen behind the station façade, he heard the dull rumbling of an approaching train.

She sat on an end-of-row seat, staring without seeing through the window across from her. The urban line train slithered between the houses, the carriages lurching around tight bends, picking up commuters on its way. Araki leaned on a rail near the door, ready to exit should his quarry leave suddenly, engulfed in a mass exodus. Two changes and forty minutes later she chose the northern track of the Yamanote Loop and alighted among the crowds at Shinjuku. He was confident she had not recognized him at that stage. With his blue baseball warm-up jacket, faded slacks and sneakers he was not to be mistaken for a salaryman, with uniform short clipped hair, dark suit and two-handled briefcase. He was of average height, with the prevalent pale olive skin and the larger squarer continental shape of head

176

and he faded easily into the broad cross-section of Tokyo society which passed through Shinjuku on ten different lines or stopped there to work, play or shop. But he came close to losing her in the orderly chaos in the crowded subterranean concourse where Reiko disappeared among the bobbing black heads. She clearly knew the route and had no need to check her progress to find the right exit among a dozen choices. Araki was stranded in the cross-march of people, jostled in that curious Japanese impolite and unapologetic way, and then his luck returned. The back of a woman's head rose above a group of junior high-school students, the girls in sailor suits, the few boys in black, high-collared uniforms with silver buttons. It was Reiko.

Above ground, in a cool, still, April evening, Reiko fell in with the knots of revellers, mostly in Araki's late thirty-forties age group, wandering leisurely in search of pleasures in the earthy, hectic entertainment district known as Kabuki-cho. Araki found it a simple task to follow Ken Izumi's wayward wife as she walked without demurring and without being distracted by the touts and the temptations of a thousand cabarets, strip clubs and a range of encounter parlours. Matching her stride a few metres behind, Araki felt the first touch of doubt. Was this the same woman he had met barely a week earlier, unkempt, lethargic but liable to sudden fits of emotion and anger, or had he been deceived by appearances and had somehow found himself following an innocent bar hostess on her way to work? Araki had to scurry to beat a pedestrian light. It had to be Reiko, he reasoned. Both women wore the lime-green he had seen on Reiko at the Izumi house earlier, when the touch of make-up around her tired eyes told him he had interrupted her preparations for departure. Taxis dropped groups of giggly salarymen next to flashing, portable neon stands or narrow cellar entrances advertising their presence with huge, blown-up photographs of college-age girls with grinning, alluring faces and suitably short skirts.

177

Reiko moved deeper into Kabuki-cho, her safety never in doubt in the streets whose integrity was maintained by the same yakuza syndicates that managed the pleasure houses on every side. She paused to talk to a miniskirted beauty with trailing, wet-look hair, bright rouged lips and high, dominant cheekbones. There were fewer revellers in this area, where the bars offered a less garish, more discreet and discerning invitation, and had Araki not recognized them from earlier days he might have assumed Reiko's contact was another woman. He knew the painted creature was a man even before his head rocked back, unleashing a deep unfeminine cackle and exposing his uneven teeth, discoloured with badly applied lipstick, and a grape-sized lump flashed above the high collar of a crimson and white striped blouse, the final betrayal of the wearer's sex.

Araki pretended to study a menu and then edged closer, finding a doorway almost opposite the bar where Reiko and her transvestite friend had finished with their greetings and had become serious. If her face mirrored her gay companion's, Reiko's expression would also suggest a weighty topic, perhaps even dangerous. Then her head turned instinctively, causing Araki to retreat into the shadow of the doorway, but the woman's action was more a prelude to a surreptitious act than a gesture of alarm. Araki moved closer to the dubious security of a high-sided automatic drinks dispenser and longed to hear the pleasant thump as a can of beer responded to his selection. He ran his tongue over dry lips and through the flickering images of the passers-by he saw the Izumi daughter-in-law extract a small package from her shoulder-bag and pass it in one movement to the man in the leather miniskirt who, with equal dexterity, slid it into his own bag which hung from the crook of his arm. If there were parting words or gestures between the two they were lost to Araki who noted the name of the gay bar and moved off in pursuit of Reiko, now heading towards the more conventional entertainment

178

sections. The transvestite smiled to himself as he entered the cramped noisy bar of stools and half a dozen tables. He lit a cigarette and when he opened the padded door and leaned out to throw the dead match into the road he saw, in the temporarily deserted street, two figures walking away from him. One was Reiko: the other could have been the man loitering across the road from the bar while he was talking to her.

Araki assumed Reiko's mission was completed with the exchange of a small package with the transvestite and was preparing mentally for another trip to the lake where the kimono slipper was found. They were progressing in the general direction of Shinjuku Station and when he was tempted to finish the evening at the Roman, a mere ten minutes' stroll away, he saw the slim figure of Reiko drift sideways and disappear into one of the narrow passageways which housed friendly snack bars and late-night jazz coffee shops with regular clientèles. The usual stacked neons illuminated the entrance to the alley but inside the only light came from the handful of cafés and stand-bars themselves. There was nowhere in the musty corridor for Araki to watch unobserved the evening meal of the woman he had believed was a frustrated, housebound recluse with uneven domestic habits. He was hungry himself, having taken nothing since the hurried plate of curry with Chris seven hours earlier at the lake. The choice on the main drag was limitless but Araki picked a smoky yakitori bar whose corner stool gave him an angled view of the mouth of the alley through a window with the bill of fare stencilled in neat, broad columns on it. Perched comfortably on the high chair, the tips of his shoes touching the floor and his senses mellowed from a deep drag from the glass of warm sake, Araki realized how tired he was. The short, shallow night's sleep in drunken disarray on Chris's spare futon showed in the dark borders around his eyes. He had also shared in the Izumi family's tension at the lake and generated personal anxiety at the father's hideaway villa in the hillside woods above it when the temptation to break in was overwhelming. The dash to Tokyo, driven by sudden suspicion, and the confrontation with Reiko about an empty shoe-box had heightened his feeling of stress and sense of foreboding and misgiving. And now there was an irresistible drive within him, one which smothered his body's need for rest. It had nothing to do with the disappearance of Mrs Izumi but he had to know why the sallow, hard-drinking daughter-in-law had transformed herself into a well-dressed, desirable woman and where she was going unaccompanied in a district of night pleasures. He sucked on the Hi-lite and blew a funnel towards the charcoal grill where it mixed with the pungent soya fumes from the skewers of chicken pieces. He watched the passageway through the letters on the window and toyed disinterestedly with his food.

Reiko, the wife of the heir to the Izumi Electrical conglomerate, was greeted as a regular customer and offered a choice of seats at the counter or one of the three tables. There was only one other customer, a bar girl in a bright, cheap kimono whom Reiko knew because their timetables seemed to coincide at this cheap snack bar. She greeted the familiar face with a nod, a silent expression of camaraderie before both embarked on some inevitable episode in the floating world that evening, and sucked noisily from the contents of a bowl of buckwheat noodles. Reiko raised the cup of hot, green tea to her lips, more in gesture than in need, and waited until a bowl of clear soup and the shallow dish of soya sauce had been placed in front of her before she made her move. A perfunctory excuse to the patron and she was in the lavatory with its western style bowl and tiny washing sink which expelled a sharp jet of water when the toilet was flushed. Closing the lid of the toilet bowl, Reiko sat down, her body heaving, and fumbling in her handbag, her mind racing ahead of her actions. Opening the hard cover of a plastic container the size of a pencil she extracted and then assembled a syringe. She breathed deeply to

180

steady a trembling hand and unwrapped a tiny package containing a pair of ampoules of clear liquid. She pierced the tip of one of them with the syringe and brushed the spike, with its cargo of ecstasy, along her left forearm, towards her elbow, in search of the vein. She tensed her bent arm until the already scarred tissue beckoned the needle. There was a knock on the cubicle door.

'I'm sorry,' a woman's voice said sincerely.

'A few minutes,' Reiko said tensely.

Reiko flinched, she always did, when the needle pierced her skin, but the warm feeling was almost immediate. When the phial was drained, leaving a tiny bubble of blood, she dismantled her lethal equipment tidily and then finished her task by smoothing a patch of skin-coloured elastic plaster over the self-inflicted wound. Her breathing slowed and with eyes shut she leaned back against the water tank and for a few seconds thought of freedom.

Perhaps she would not appear, Araki reflected. Perhaps she had reached the place where she was to spend the evening, either working or in someone's company. He paid a modest bill and paused to light another cigarette. Had he foregone this action he would certainly have collided with Reiko Izumi. As it was, he parted the noren curtain over the doorway and watched her appear from the darkness and turn back into the road, her jacket open and her green dress almost luminous under the dazzling night lights. There was, he noticed, a purpose in her stride and her head was higher, not buried in her coat. She had rounded another corner and when he hurried to fall in step she had gone. He chased the forms of unaccompanied women and ran his eyes into coffee shops and restaurants and in passing the gap between two buildings saw what he thought was Reiko's figure at the top of an iron fire-escape. Before he could focus his attention she had disappeared behind a door. He threw the cigarette angrily into the gutter. A tout in a faded tuxedo approached Araki, as he would any single man or group.

181

'Live sex,' he insinuated, contradicting the neon outside the SM Club which advertised only an enticing strip show, including foreign women.

'Only four thousand yen.'

Araki walked in front of the panelled door and then a neighbouring sex shop. He looked up at the windows above the adult venues. Art photography and fashion art consultants and other nebulous descriptions were stencilled on to the crystal. He found a side entrance which would give access to the upper storeys but as far as he could tell the stairway in the alley belonged to the strip club. Having lost his quarry and feeling exhausted, physically as well as mentally depleted of ideas, he reached for his wallet. Izumi money he mused, handing four sharp notes through a low, arch-shaped hole in the wall to a fist. Only the jaw and mouth of the face beyond were visible.

'In the basement,' it ordered.

The stage was semi-circular and broken by a catwalk which thrust into the audience who sat in rows six deep around the small stage and its phallic protrusion. All the seats were taken and so Araki joined the knots of men standing on the stepped floor at the back of the room. Above them through the window of the control room, an unseen figure manipulated the strobe lights and toned the music to the particular performance of the stripper. A strapping man with a cynical scowl was a redundant bouncer. The audience, all Japanese men apart from a pair of white foreigners, and a woman there for the thrill with some male colleagues, were obedient to the signs which urged them not to talk during performances. The air was thick with smoke. An act was ending. An overweight dancer with imperceptible eyes and flabby, unappealing breasts was posing for the customers who in turn borrowed her Polaroid camera for a price and took their personal picture from whatever angle they desired. One young salaryman leaped on to the stage and embraced the naked stripper. Embarrassed, a broad grin on his flushed, animated face, he stood barefoot while a colleague steadied the camera and recorded the moment. Time dragged and the men standing were becoming impatient. Araki bought a beer from an over made-up waitress in a black uniform with miniskirt and moved along the wall towards the main stage. Finally the photographic model left the stage amid timid applause.

The lights began to flash and music flowed from hidden speakers. The next performer sashayed on to the stage to the rhythmic, ethereal sounds of a group Araki recognized but could not name. The voices spoke of deep love but in a ghostly echoing stereo sound. The woman wore a sheer, long-sleeved blouse pinched at the waist with a sequined belt attached to a strap which split her harem pants at the crotch. Araki struggled to identify the trance-like music to which the woman's body seemed to attach and move obliviously. A pink veil masked much of her face leaving only a pencil line outline to the eyes which were all but shut to the spectators. Beneath the blouse, her breasts were small but firm and pointed. The men in the front rows leaned forward as she reached behind her to separate the blouse and let it fall from her body. The lights flashed, illuminating parts of her body in turn but not giving the viewers time to enjoy a particular bit. She danced to the music, the minutes passing, and then suddenly spun twice and gracefully slid to her knees in front of a chosen voyeur, inviting him with a hand motion to tug the strap which would dislodge her belt and the thong between her thighs. The others envied the chosen one and admired the serious way he approached the task, like an actor in a modern Kabuki yarn. Unsmiling, and with a practised hand, he slipped the hook, and with that his fantasy faded, the sparkling support still in his hands as the woman spun away and stepped with a ballet dancer's poise and control from the loose transparent trousers. She was on Araki's side of the stage, a few metres away, hovering over the unmoving heads, rolling her body from the waist and caressing herself with swift, flowing movements.

She wore a wig, Araki realized, shaped like Cleopatra's hair with a low front fringe which, with the veil, obscured all but the eyes of her real face. But what could she see through those narrow slivers? She seemed to be moving by instinct, oblivious to the eyes that ravished her. The women Araki had known in the clubs often said they came to ignore the clients and dance for themselves. Across the room, by the door on the wall was a list of the performers, ten, maybe twelve names, Araki thought. She would not be using her real name but he would check her professional title on his way out. The stripper held the spot near him and had a hand in the thin band of white, satin briefs. It was a comfortable body, slim and long-legged, where the norm was squat and boyish, and her breasts small and prominent. Again, a balletic stance, first one leg and then the other as she slipped off the panties, her left arm outstretched for balance. Araki leaned forward, mesmerized. The song finally came to him. It was the Bee Gees, singing 'How Deep is My Love' in multi-phonic sound. He drained a beer and yawned. He would see one more act and go home, a return trip to Lake Kawaguchi now seeming even more urgent, more important. The dancer was interpreting the hyperbole of the song's claims of love with alternate waves of her hands across her body in Arabian fashion. She swept the audience with eyes that stayed shut, almost grazed by the veil which ran from one ear to the other and down to below her chin and which was now her only item of clothing. The music slowed, and the dancer's girations responded to the changing rhythm. When it stopped, she thrust her pelvis towards the audience and reached upwards to grasp the air in a triumphant climax. The applause was universal but was brief as participation was promised in the second part of her act and the menfolk were impatient.

Araki heard nothing, the music fading from his consciousness as he stared transfixed at the performer and the left arm which rose in supplication as the music faded. He cursed the flashing lights which broke his

184

concentration and continuity of vision and then, like the music, they stopped, leaving the woman under a funnel of spot-lighting on an otherwise dark stage. Araki barely noticed the tepid applause. His eyes were on the arm, precisely the discolouring or blemish near the elbow. He searched the recesses of his recent memory while the stripper stooped to recover her silky trousers, pausing to let a guest press her breast and teasing him with mocking groans of ecstasy. The satin panties lay at the edge of the stage where the nearest handful of men waited eagerly for the call to help. Impulsively, Araki moved from his cover and sidled between the low chairs and mildly protesting gogglers. The bouncer unfolded his arms at the back of the room. The woman still seemed to be performing with minimal emotional involvement and showed only passing interest in the usual dark figure from the audience who, with passions inflamed, leapt at the chance to earn a brief grope, enough perhaps to entice him back and to enhance her personal reputation as well. Araki retrieved the scanty garment and held it aloft. It was little more than a satin crotch on a colourful elastic thread. He placed it into an open left hand and waited while the stripper completed her short triumphal circuit of the stage before stopping in front of him. He could almost touch the tiny piece of material which did not quite match in colour the skin it was attached to. The woman mouthed something but was otherwise silent. At the Izumi house a few hours earlier he had noticed a break, a minute lump, in the skin of Reiko's arm beneath the sheer sleeve of her blouse.

'Dō itashimashite,' he said clearly, assuming she had thanked him for his help.

'It was no trouble at all.'

A jolt seemed to rack her body. The eyes that had stayed closed during the trance-like dance opened above the veil and pierced the retreating figure of Araki. Without looking back again, he knew they belonged to Reiko Izumi.

9

The road peaked and curved and began a downward
loop towards Kawaguchi town and the lake. Crossing
the bridge which spanned the hour-glass-shaped water
at its neck, Araki could see in his rear-view mirror
the volcano's snow covered cone and high slopes with
their sharp ridges of bare rock. Chris had called Araki's
rooms until at last, around midnight, he was there
to answer and they could exchange details of the rewards from a busy day. The Englishman's find was in
a wrinkled plastic bag on the back seat of the Toyota.
His face had creased in disgust as he recounted finding
the soaked strip of paper which was heading for the
new disposal bag when he was drawn to the Chinese
ideographs on the torn scrap. They were almost illegible, the green print washed away or diluted into
the white of the paper. There had been four multi-
stroked letters and the last two clearly read 'ginkō',
the Japanese for bank. The first of the other two was
impossible to read as the paper was partly torn away
at the edge. The second fascinated him and he carried
it carefully to his table and examined it under the
light and the magnifying glass he had used, since he
had been a student in kanji writing, to unscramble
particularly complex characters which might differ from
another by only one or two minute strokes of the pen.
When he finally made contact with Araki he was able
to tell him that the second of the characters could
be read 'kei' depending on the pronunciation of the
first, which eluded him. If the first was 'tetsu' then

the four characters could be read 'Tekkei Bank'. He had waited for the other's praise, but heard only the mounting excitement in his voice.

'An envelope from the missing woman's bank,' Araki said. Unnecessarily he added: 'They always give you an envelope when you draw money from a Japanese bank.'

'Or a box of tissues,' the Englishman said chuckling.

'Only when you put money in,' the other said, and they laughed and enjoyed the euphoria of what was a strange and interesting find. Araki's smile evaporated.

'That muck this was in,' he said, weighing the precious find in his palm when they met that morning.

'It could have been a month old. That tells me that Mrs Izumi was in the chalet with five million yen in a Tekkei bank envelope.'

On his knees in the moist soil at the edge of the lake Araki looked up towards the densely packed trees that hid the Izumi villa the missing woman's husband used. A retreat which the family had said was forbidden to its female members. On his feet he joined Chris in scavenging among the plastic bottles and misshaped débris and armed with a long-handled trowel swiped at the clumps of broad-leaf weeds that grew in thick patches between the rivulets of water. The scuffled sand and patchwork footprints, reminders of the previous day's gathering of family, police and pressmen, gave him point to begin his own search. His mind told him it was a futile quest but he was desperate for answers in a case which had thrown out only questions. Chris moved roughly in parallel, prodding the earth with a stick and occasionally bending to examine a dirty piece of detritus. Araki arched his back which was beginning to stiffen.

'I've missed something,' he remarked in Chris's direction.

The Englishman heaved the stick like a javelin along the deserted shore, a gesture he hoped would express his boredom and lack of conviction at the course Araki was taking. He favoured giving the scrap of envelope to the police and leading them on a search of the chalet, but

Araki overruled this option saying that Inspector Sasaki had already looked at the mountain house as a possible refuge and had found no evidence of occupation by the missing woman. The policeman had obviously seen no reason to look in the garbage bin.

Araki was continuing: 'When we drove up the mountain yesterday to the villa, what did we do? We stopped didn't we?'

'Come to think of it, we did,' Chris said, following with his eyes the road which tapered into a slim, white gash as it disappeared into the trees above the village.

'Do you remember why?'

They were walking with the lake on their left, prodding the soft earth, a few metres apart.

Chris stood erect and remembered: 'You wanted to wait in case that white BMW we saw when we ate came up after us.'

'That's right,' Araki said fervidly. 'But there was something else but I can't recall what it was.'

They reached an area of patchy, coarse grass which ran down a mild slope to a stream. The waterway was too broad to cross in a single leap and here, at its death in the lake, it was swollen from the rains that had lashed the region earlier that week. Bits of wood, forlorn, solitary cherry petals and other natural débris raced by as if propelled by some underwater motor whose conveyor belt stopped abruptly when it reached the lake, leaving its disorderly load to bob helplessly in the still water. Araki's mind raced as he watched a torn branch shoot into the lake on the current and then drift sideways, pushed by the breeze, until it floated lazily on to the shore. He looked upstream where the nearest crossing point was a rough path over a double-barrelled concrete culvert which guided the flow between a clutch of flooded paddy fields and the tennis courts adjoining a pair of dilapidated apartment blocks. Chris was already scrambling up the slippery bank to the bridge when he heard Araki call his name. The Japanese was on his

188

knees, a half metre from the water-line, stirring the earth carefully with his spade.

'Look at this,' he said, a keen triumphant edge to his voice as he brushed aside dirt from a flat object which looked like a piece of old wood. Chris watched it emerge from its sheath of grime.

'Is it the other shoe?'

'No it's not,' Araki said without disappointment, handling the object like a fragile piece of pottery. He looked up at Chris. 'It might be more than that,' he said, laying it across his palm, where its slender bulk reached as far as his wrist. 'It's a wallet.'

Chris lifted the discoloured, soft case from his friend.

'It could be a purse or a small handbag.'

'No it's not,' Araki said firmly. 'The owner might carry a bag as well, but this one could hold some emergency money or valuable document and you could keep it in a coat pocket, like a wallet.'

Chris knew what the Japanese was thinking. He said, 'Or in the obi of a kimono.'

'Precisely,' Araki said, gently opening the flap on the wallet and feeling through the damp fabric with his fingers. He tossed it to the ground in disgust. It was empty.

'Women often tucked a small purse in the belt of their kimono,' he said by way of explanation. 'They could feel it under the tightness and I suppose it gave them a sense of security.'

'Could it be hers?' Chris said hopefully.

Araki breathed noisily, stood up and lit a cigarette. The smoke hung languidly in the still morning air.

'Let's walk upstream a bit,' he said, snapping open a plastic shopping bag and laying the treasure he had retrieved carefully inside.

The stream cascaded down a weir, creating churning frothy white-capped whirlpools, and then disappeared below the bridge which spanned the main lakeside road. Scrambling on to the bridge Araki greeted a farmer

189

who had stopped his Komatsu mini-tractor to watch suspiciously the foreigner and his Japanese companion poking around among the pebbles and weeds. When Chris asked whether the stream was running at normal levels or not the weathered face showed him a mouth of gold teeth. The fruit grower smiled again, the crow's feet in the corners of his mouth deepening. He was in the rare position of possessing knowledge others needed. 'Three times normal,' he growled proudly, warming to his first foreigner.

Where the violent stream passed between the houses and cultivated enclosures concrete walls had been constructed to control the flow and maximize the land available for crops and housing. They assumed that anything caught in the current at this point, floatable items such as slippers and purses, could be carried unimpeded through the culverts to the lake. There was enough of a path for them to walk in single file until the houses and compact fields above the rim of the gorge were replaced by foliage and the shadows of tall trees. The final evidence of civilization was a hamlet which took them by surprise when they thought the stream had finally become its own master of the mountain. They had come suddenly into another artificial gully and a curtain of water confronted them, tumbling down a straight concrete wall. Chris marvelled at the ingenuity of the locals; their determination to tame even the most insignificant course of nature. They climbed the steep border of the man-made waterfall and from the clearing at the top could see through the trees the thatched roof of a farmhouse, and in the distance a more modern two-tiered structure with bright orange tiles on both levels. There was also a fierce smell of animals and a small détour disclosed a shed and corral where a dozen domesticated wild-boar piglets romped in their own filth under the lazy eyes of a bloated sow.

They returned to the stream which curved away from the hamlet and disappeared among the packed slopes.

190

The two men were exhausted by the climb but the excitement of the find drove them on, their exhilaration only tempered by trepidation at the possibility of converting Araki's suspicions into reality. High above the lake, now visible only intermittently, the stream came down the mountain with menacing ferocity, dropping in noisy torrents over the lips of craggy waterfalls before gliding deceptively to the next. In places the edge of the waterway was impassable, where roots hung from eroded banks in tangled meshes in the water. The two men scrambled up through twisting undergrowth before descending again over loose, slippery soil to the river's edge. Chris rested, breathing in the crisp, fresh mountain air, and watching how the funnels of sunlight seemed to bring the stream to life as they bounced on the ripples. But Araki was already out of his view, beyond the next bend, his hands on the solid lips of an old, weathered long-abandoned culvert pipe half-buried in the stream which ran through and around it. The trees on either side leaned like drunken sentinels, their branches almost touching. Araki wasn't moving. His legs were apart, making an inadequate bridge between the thin strip of water between the old culvert and the bank. His feet had sunk into the mud but he seemed oblivious to the discomfort. He was staring at something Chris could not see and when he heard him approach he raised a cautionary hand. The narrow channel was in darkness from the shadow of the culvert and the tangle of roots and the leaves and other débris trapped in the passage. Chris clutched a branch and hung close to Araki's shoulder, his eyes following his colleague's free arm. It looked like a bundle of old cloth, the same dark colour as the earth and roots into which it blended. Chris hauled himself along the branches and gnarled hanging vines until he was above the blockage. He found his chest heaving, not from the physical effort or the pain in his hands from the thorns, but from what he knew he would find.

191

'Is it her?' Araki called, his voice competing with the echo from the water gushing through the tunnel.

'I think so.'

'What?'

'Yes,' Chris shouted.

Araki pulled himself alongside Chris and then lower, where he gripped a root for support. The 'bundle' was the back of a head and an upper, clothed torso. The rest of the body was underwater, the arms buried in the mud or trapped in the roots, and the legs pinned by the force of current beneath the culvert. A gust of wind stirred the water, releasing a stench which engulfed them, forcing them in disgust from the edge of the stream, their faces buried in the sleeves of their jackets.

Clusters of wild mountain cherry-blossom petals, some fresh, others faded, had accumulated in the sheltered parts of the corpse. A few fresh pink petals were trapped in the stiff, lifeless fingers of a hand which rose pleadingly from the water.

For a while the only sounds were the murmur of the stream and staccato chirping of the forest birds. The two men exchanged knowing looks, their flesh cold, their senses dulled.

The forest was very still, even the birds seeming to maintain a respectful silence, but in the cold, unbelieving numbness of the shock the low rumble high above the two men almost passed unnoticed. Araki was first to hear the sound, looking up and down the stream before he realized the muffled sound came from a vehicle on the mountain road they had taken to the villa the day before and which was now directly above them, a few hundred yards away. It was an uphill scramble rather than a smooth climb, their exhaustion hampering the pace as they picked and tore their way in silence through the lush undergrowth in the dark world under the canopy of trees. A cleanly snapped branch or a depression in the

192

knee-high entanglements drew an exchange of glances between the two men and initiated a brief, optimistic search for pieces of torn clothing. It had been over a month and traces of a body being dragged to a secluded watery tomb or a woman stumbling to a lonely suicide would have been obliterated by the forces of nature. The final obstacle, after what seemed like more than the actual thirty minutes, was to crawl up a steep bank of grass and ferns, dotted with patches of yellow and purple wild flowers, before they rolled over the two-tiered split crash barrier on to the road that began at the lakeside and snaked up the mountain and on past the villa.

Chris sat on the verge, his head in his hands, in a state of physical and mental exhaustion. The body, the colour of the roots it lay entangled amongst, was the first corpse he had seen, and his mind raged as it sought an explanation for the image of sudden transition from a living, thinking, eating human being to a lifeless piece of earth. His head lifted slowly, his nostrils filling with sharp, cool mountain air, and took little interest in Araki, who was pacing the road, his head tossing one way then the other. The Japanese returned to stand by the low fence, his senses now sharp, his ears alert. When the light wind eased, stopping the leaves ruffling, and he himself was motionless, he heard the faint murmur of the unseen rapids deep in the valley. Chris called to him.

'Come on. We need a telephone.' And he started down-hill on tired legs.

'Eh!' Araki barked. 'We're going this way.' And with a wide sweep of his arms he indicated the opposite direction. Chris knew where he meant.

'There's got to be somewhere nearer than the Izumi's place,' he said despairingly.

'The villa is closest,' Araki said and set off. 'There must be a 'phone.' On his heels Chris said, 'How do we get to it? We break in I suppose.'

'Right. We have the best excuse.' When angered, Araki reverted to Japanese, and he turned on Chris with uncharacteristic venom.

'There's a body down there in the stream,' he said, pointing across the valley. 'It's been there a month or more. I'm shocked, frightened and angry and when I come across a house I bang on the door and plead to use the 'phone. When I find the place is empty I make an executive decision and break the door down. We're wasting time. Let's move.'

Chris said nothing, just shrugged his shoulders in surrender.

A hundred metres before the turn-off to the hillside retreat, where the road narrowed so much that the branches of the cedars and pines on either side crossed and twisted, Chris signalled a halt.

'Down at the lakeside you asked me what we saw on the way to the villa yesterday. If we saw anything special or unusual.'

'Yes,' Araki said. 'I think I meant the sound of running water when we stopped to check the map.'

'Do you remember that?'

Araki followed Chris's outstretched arm towards the red box on its perch by the roadside.

'That's right,' he murmured. 'We heard an engine, and a post-office van stopped to make a collection. At first, I thought it was that bloody white BMW we saw near the restaurant.' They laughed together, but Araki became serious, circling the post-box as if he were stalking a dangerous animal.

'I wonder,' he said in soft undertones to himself. 'She was in the villa. An envelope from the bank she'd been to was left in the garbage.' He rubbed his temples and sucked in breath. Turning to Chris, he said, 'How many envelopes did she have from the Tekkei bank?'

'That's true,' the Englishman said slowly. 'She had two. One was in the rubbish. What happened to the other?'

'Come on. Let's get to that house.'

194

After a burst of sharp raps on the door of the deserted house Araki leaned against the lock, testing the tension and pondering the possibility of an alarm.

'You said it didn't matter,' Chris said provocatively. 'Let's just get on with it.' Araki looked around once, clenched his teeth and hit the door with his shoulder. It rattled and shook but did not give way.

'Together,' Araki growled. The two men drew breath, stepped back and threw themselves forward. They hit the door with joint force of a hundred and forty kilos. It gave quite easily, a sharp crack, a half-second of resistance and the door rebounded against the hard rubber stop.

Chris turned the light on.

'The 'phone's over there,' he said, motioning towards a table beneath the stairs at the centre of the chalet's open main lounge. If the rain doors had been opened the whole of the front of the chalet would face the lake with the view the two men had seen the previous day when Araki had strolled the broad veranda. At one end of the room was a table with chairs for eight and a door leading to a small kitchen. The rest was furnished simply with comfortable leather chairs around a low table, a drinks cabinet and a television on a stand which had shelves for golfing trophies. The darkened oak-panelled walls were decorated with photographs of Mount Fuji in different seasons and a wood-block Hokusai print with the same theme.

Ignoring him, Araki lifted the pictures before moving to a methodical search with his hand between the cushions of the chairs.

'That's enough,' Chris urged, with a vehemence which surprised Araki.

'The woman you were employed to find is dead. Our role has finished. Do you hear me? Finished.' He strode to the stand beneath the stairs. 'Do it now or I do it,' he growled.

Araki dragged his fingers across a moist, thinning scalp. He nodded ruefully before patting a cushion back into shape and walking across the room, his lips puckered

195

petulantly. Lifting the receiver, he said, 'What's the code for Tokyo?'

A minute later, Araki replaced the instrument on its bar and turned to Chris.

'We've got about fifteen minutes before the Lakes Police can respond to Inspector Sasaki's call from Tokyo and reach us up here. Let's use it well.'

Chris raised his hands in surrender.

'OK. We've done our duty. What do you want me to do while we wait?'

'Take the bedrooms. Look for any sign that Mrs Izumi was here.'

'But it would have been a month ago,' Chris protested.

Araki was already on his knees, pressing the floor-boards. He looked up.

'When news of the body being found so close gets out this place will be the focus of the investigation. It'll be stripped.'

'Then why are we doing it?' he said to Araki's back. 'Let's leave it to the police.'

Araki led the way to the kitchen where they set about the cupboards, jars, packets and their contents.

'Not only the police,' Araki said cryptically. 'Whoever was with her before she went, or was taken off, to die, will want to sanitize the place in case the poor woman left something damning.'

'She already did,' Chris said.

'What?'

'The piece of envelope in the garbage.'

They went to the second floor where there were three tatami rooms and a separate bathroom with a toilet. Apart from futons, blankets and wraparound yukatas for the male guests, two of the rooms were empty, the air musty and warm. The two men moved quickly to the other. It was stocked for occupation by the host with spare clothes and the cabinet above the washbasin of the private shower room held a supply of bottles, lotions and tubes. Araki was looking through the drawers of a

196

walnut tansu chest, rummaging among the sports shirts and underwear.

Chris called from the walk-in shower closet.

'Hey! Look at this!'

Araki joined him, pressing against the wall of the tiny cubicle. Chris held up a jar of white cream.

'I thought this was a bolt-hole for the Izumi men,' he said.

'What is it?' Araki asked.

'This is skin moisturizer. And that's nail-varnish remover.'

Araki grinned. 'Perhaps they lived out their fantasies here. In which case they'd need these.' He drew his hand from behind his back and with a mischievous flourish waved a crumpled piece of sheer grey fabric.

Chris whistled.

'They weren't Mrs Izumi's,' he said irreverently, as Araki stretched the panties between his fingers.

For Chris's benefit Araki flipped through the drawer of clothing.

'All women's,' he guessed. 'And young.' He closed the drawer carefully and turned to Chris.

'Where did you hide your dirty magazines when you were a teenager?'

The Englishman shrugged. 'Can't say it was ever a problem,' he said lamely.

'Come on,' Araki said impatiently. 'We all had something to conceal from our parents.'

'I can't remember particularly. The bottom of a pile of books and toys. Inside a mattress.'

'Precisely,' Araki said firmly, pacing the room and looking for a hideaway. 'In the west you've got a house full of cupboards in three times as many rooms as we have, and then there's the attic and the garden shed. Here,' he said, straining to reach the corners of the bedding cupboard, 'we're more limited with space. Check in there,' he ordered, indicating the head of the L-shaped room furnished with two low bamboo chairs with foot-rests

197

and which would function as a private veranda when the rain doors were drawn, while he himself disappeared down the stairs.

Chris checked the walls for concealed cavities and squeezed the cushions on the chairs in desperation. Araki returned with a heavy-duty screwdriver he had found in the kitchen and forced it between two of the tatami mats in the main bedroom.

Chris looked aghast.

'We came here to make a 'phone call,' he remonstrated. 'Not to tear the place apart.'

'If there's anything hidden, it's under here,' Araki insisted, lifting the first light, rectangular slab of tightly packed reed matting from its shallow sunken bed. Then another, and another. The bare spaces gave up years of dust and shreds of paper but nothing obviously concealed deliberately beneath the soft matting.

'Are you going to rip up the other rooms?' Chris asked, glancing at his watch. 'They're all tatami on this floor.'

Another slab, the size of a small table, gave under the lever.

'No need,' Araki said. 'The other rooms are for guests. They'd never risk leaving valuables in them.'

It was a large room for a recreational villa, containing twelve uniform mats which served as the standard measure.

'They don't fit back flush with the ground,' Chris said as he struggled to reassemble the pattern of the mats Araki was discarding. 'They'll be able to tell that . . .'

Araki raised a stilling hand. Chris fell to his knees beside him. Araki slid a dusty grey envelope from beneath the last mat but one. Then it was Chris's turn to silence his partner.

'They're here,' he uttered.

They both heard the urgent screech as tyres bit into loose gravel and scrambled to assemble the remaining mats and press them flat to the floor. Chris bolted through the door while Araki skipped barefoot around the room,

198

tidying and closing the cupboards and drawers. He heard feet on the stairs and moved to meet them, a freshly lit cigarette in his hand.

Chris's face was paler than usual.

'Is Sasaki with them?' Araki whispered.

The Englishman beckoned downstairs.

'It's not the police.'

Araki bounced a glance off the other, tucked the envelope into an inside jacket pocket and strode towards the stairs followed by Chris, who was trying to say something.

Deprived of fresh air by the solid belt of storm doors around the villa, the atmosphere in the broad lounge was stale and still, but there was a disturbance, a faint odour of flowers. Araki recognized it and sought the source in disbelief.

The figure stood near the far wall of the room, straightening a photograph.

'What are you doing here?' Araki demanded thoughtlessly.

Hands in pockets, Chris joined his colleague. The Japanese face, he had read, was a mask, a camouflage which hid the true and the real feelings of the bearer, and as he looked into the features of the newcomer he seemed to be staring into a mirror. He saw no look of surprise, desperation, sadness or relief, no movement of the eyebrows or tightening of the muscles around the lips which might suggest fear. The expression confronting him questioned his own eligibility for being there.

'It did belong to my mother,' Mariko said, 'even though she wasn't allowed to use it. I suppose I have a duty to ensure that the family interests are maintained. By the way, what are you doing here?'

'I have some news for you,' Araki said drily, his mind racing as he fought for the appropriate words. They stuck in his throat and Chris's presence embarrassed him. A sound disturbed the silence. A low, purr which grew

199

to a fierce howl as it approached the house. Then the siren was still.

His disclosure seemed unnecessary. His face told her what he had to say. She sat on the edge of the sofa, clutching her knees. Without looking up, she said, 'You've found her.'

10

Araki stood on the narrow terrace watching a trio of boys in the lot below, slapping the palm of their outsize baseball mitts as they crouched in the dust, refusing to surrender to the dying light. As coloured lights appeared in the area of the railway station and beams from car headlights swept the ground, they finally succumbed to the inevitable and ambled off with their gloves and metal bats. The worn envelope lay alongside a lacquered bowl of sushi, half of it abandoned and drying to the point of being unpalatable.

In the four days since he and Chris had found the body of the woman the police had sought for four weeks, Araki had seen members of the Izumi family only in passing. The police interrogation was straightforward and favourable to the pair who assisted them in their investigation and had not embarrassed the authorities by denouncing to the press what might have been interpreted as their incompetence. Many of his former colleagues in the popular weeklies were given one of the most lurid stories for months. They repeated the headlines of a month earlier, comparing the speculative conclusions they made at that time, that Masako Izumi had been kidnapped and killed, with the official verdict that she had died for reason or cause yet to be determined. The immediate motive was seen as robbery. The woman had five million yen in her purse when she left the Tekkei Bank and for some reason, as yet unknown, visited a chalet near Lake Kawaguchi which she owned but left to the exclusive use of her husband and son. A solitary elderly woman waiting at a lonely, mountain bus-stop became a rare statistic in Japan – a murder victim. A local vagrant, the magazines speculated, perhaps the one known to live rough in the area and who stole eggs and occasionally exposed himself to the farmers' wives. The police were leaning towards suicide, citing the frequency with which older women chose to end their lives by losing themselves in the tomb-like security of a densely packed forest. But they were at a loss to explain why the handbag was found a kilometre away, on the fringes of the bamboo copse and not on the direct route she might have taken if suicide was on her mind as she dragged herself from the road down to the valley bed. The police were grateful for the help of a civilian employed on a temporary basis by the Izumi family to make private enquiries on their behalf. He was able to supply information which suggested the dead woman had been in the villa retreat before, or on, the day of her death.

The autopsy was a sad, perfunctory detail in the tragic story. The body was obviously the missing wife of the president of Izumi Electric but the conclusive identification came from dental records as the state of the corpse, beneath the remaining scraps of kimono, bore witness to a month immersed in mud and water and ravaged by the creatures of the forest and river bank. Whether she had stumbled down the mountainside in a mindless, deliberate search for oblivion or had become a victim of a callous pursuit and vicious attack the police would not speculate. The body was far too decomposed. Internal organs were still being examined but the authorities saw no reason not to release the mortal remains for proper disposal.

Araki tipped the envelope and let the contents slip on to the tatami. Would they be thankful, he asked himself with a rueful scowl, if they knew he'd taken, stolen to be exact, some documents from the villa which could be conceived as evidence if there was a murder investigation. He slumped heavily on the mat, his hands aloft holding an empty tumbler and a bottle of Nikka whisky like the branches of a cactus. He shuffled the four photographs into a square and poured a glass full of Nikka.

The couple in the adjoining apartment were arguing, the man trying to impose his domination by using guttural demeaning Japanese, his wife refusing to succumb to his rough bullying. From the street came the sounds of Tanaka and his daughter clearing the boxes of vegetables. Araki drank deeply and lifted the nearest photograph. It must have been taken at least seven, possibly ten, years earlier. The hair was longer and straighter and the skin unnaturally green as the picture's colours faded and fused over time. But it was definitely Mariko. She was wearing a loose, flower-patterned short smock, and stood on a beach with a clump of palm-trees in the background. Araki assumed it had been taken in Hawaii when she was a college student there. Her right hand was raised in a wave to the photographer but only the upper part of her left arm appeared. The rest went off the picture. From the way it extended away from her shoulder he could only speculate that she was holding the hand of another person, something he could never prove. The photograph had been cut cleanly in two and the other half was not one of the remaining three from the envelope he had found hidden in the chalet bedroom.

He only recognized the woman in another of the photographs because he had seen an enlarged copy in an Izumi apartment a week earlier. It showed the family gathering at the wedding of the younger daughter Shinobu to her high-flying bureaucrat husband. Had the picture not been in the Ohashi flat when he visited he would not have known the woman in the Shinto bridal gown with her broad, flattened turban and face painted so thickly in white like the traditional geisha so that the features were obliterated. The third picture showed Reiko, the stripper with syringe marks on her arm and wife of the future president of Izumi Electric, stretched on a collapsible garden chair. There was surprise on her face, as if the photographer had crept close and taken the picture

203

without her consent. The last photograph was different from the others, in texture and composition. The rim had a faint blur and the colour lacked the sharpness and finesse which would come from proper processing. It was a Polaroid instant picture and it portrayed a woman and a man in a moment of pleasure, she on his lap, him with his head thrown back, his face contorted as he enjoyed the situation. Araki smiled, lit a cigarette, and congratulated himself on his memory, particularly when he recalled that on the night he met the woman he was half-way drunk. The man was Yasuo, patriarch of the Izumi clan, if not possessor of the instrument that determined its family wealth. The woman was Mayumi Maeda, the senior hostess and confidante of the Izumi menfolk at the Kana Club. She had an erotic attraction, Araki remembered, with firm, high cheekbones and lips which formed a heart with a slight pout. In the photograph she was completely naked on the president's lap, her right hand between his legs, no doubt the cause of the expression captured by the camera. She was looking towards the photographer with a kind of 'Is this the pose you wanted?' expression. There was a rap on the apartment door. He knew who it was.

A day earlier he had attended the final rite at the Izumi home when family and relatives gathered to offer a Buddhist farewell to their departed matriarch. Beneath the black and white bunting which bordered the porch of the Izumi house, company employees manned a table, accepting slender envelopes containing condolence money and recording the names of the mourners. Araki joined the slow-moving lines shuffling up the steps to the house. The rich, woody odour of smouldering incense drifted across the lawn and, as he neared the door, the low, monotone drone of the death sutra held the mourners in respectful reverence. When Araki's turn came he knelt before the coffin, which was closed and covered with the appropriate white flowers of death, and dropped the pinches of incense into the burning tray as custom required. Among the squatting rows of relatives and friends, he saw all those who had dined with him two weeks earlier. When he rose to leave, his eyes caught those of a sharp-featured man with his hands in his pockets standing away from the mourners. It was Yano, one of two men, the smarter, thinking one, who had splashed him with urine in the toilet of the Kana Club. The man Araki believed to be a yakuza slid behind an opaque sliding screen.

Mariko stood in the doorway now, almost apologetically. As Araki had left the family wake, shortly before the coffin and its contents departed for the crematorium, the elder, unmarried daughter had taken his arm, requesting a few moments of his time to make a formal expression of gratitude for his invaluable assistance. He had said he would be at home the following day. Vestiges of respect remained reflected in her sombre black jacket over an equally austere but tight skirt which was moulded to her model's figure. When she looked over her shoulder, down where the Tanaka's daughter watched suspiciously and jealously, her clothes stained with fruit-skin rubbings, her hair matted with perspiration from a long day's work, Mariko's unbuttoned jacket fell open to reveal a flame red shirt with a broad-winged collar. Mariko demurred when Araki stepped back to invite her in.

'If I might make a suggestion,' she said coyly. 'I would like to invite you and Mr Bingham to a farewell dinner.' A red border under her eyes told of tears, and dark shadows below them testified to brief, restless dream-filled sleep.

'That's not necessary,' Araki heard himself saying. 'I did what you employed me to do. I'm just sorry the conclusion was so undesirable.'

Mariko's chin dropped to the rim of the fiery blouse, then rose proudly. She said, 'You succeeded where the police didn't. At least my mother can now rest peacefully. And I think she would like me to show some appreciation. Is Mr Bingham here?'

Araki forced a grin.

'He doesn't live here, you know,' pondering a response. 'He's doing a bit more research for me.' Mariko bowed apologetically. Araki did not want to tell her that his English assistant was on his way to a gay bar in Shinjuku armed with a description of the transvestite her sister-in-law was friendly with.

'I have a taxi waiting,' Mariko said. 'If you're not busy, perhaps you would join me.'

Araki hesitated. Two days' growth of beard, little more than a wispy scattering of stubble, decorated his pale, worn face.

'Give me a minute,' he begged, 'and I'll change.'

His natural shyness had evaporated and as he entered the bar in Shinjuku two-chome for the third time in four nights he received the enthusiastic welcome Araki had told him to encourage. It was in sharp contrast to that first, tentative visit to the thriving homosexual world Japanese society pretended did not exist. While his Japanese friend had attended the funeral rites for the woman they had found together, Chris had followed a hand-written map to a bar in a neon-lit block across from Isetan department store. Had he not been briefed, the transvestites lounging in front of their bars and clubs were provocatively dressed, attractive young women. A thin, trim man in a black leather mini-skirt and matching jacket and short, natural hair shaped into a curl around both high cheekbones blocked the narrow entrance. Chris assured him that the bar was recommended in a gay's international guidebook. A short, stick-thin man in a knee-length pink cocktail dress listened to Chris's plea and was so impressed he drew a clutch of colleagues and introduced the hairy foreigner in a deep drawl as a friend. Chris breathed deeply. He crossed the door step, amazed at the confusion of beauty and gender. In the smoky, dimly lit room he could easily have been deceived. The man in the fancy wig Araki had watched exchange

206

packets with Reiko Izumi was sitting on a stool on the bend of a curving counter bar in the windowless salon. Shelves behind the bar were lined with bottles, bearing tags with the names of their owners who would drink from them over time. Otherwise the bar room of red and black synthetic leather panelling was unadorned except for a lifeless air-conditioning unit above the door which was opened into the street. A short line of plastic-topped tables hugged the walls. Chris sidled between them to a stool. His target was wearing a red latex leather skirt and a tight, padded white blouse whose stiff collar covered his Adam's apple and held his firm, feminine jaw imperiously erect. The night's wig was shaped into what was popularly known as a 'wolf' cut, long at the back and shaped at the sides to cover the cheeks, the tips almost touching at a point just below his nose. Between snatches of chit-chat with a man in casual slacks and a light sweater hanging lazily over his shoulders and short pulls on a long filtered cigarette the transvestite mimed to the shrill entreaties of a Michael Jackson record, playing through hidden speakers at a volume not powerful enough to need a raised voice. The Japanese had observed Chris's arrival, approved of his admittance and opened the conversation with a plea for the tall, bony foreigner with the curly blond hair and pale, smooth skin to relax and enjoy Japan's hospitality. A fragile barman with a twitchy smile poured drinks and listened to the trite overtures of his resident host.

'Your Japanese is excellent. Have you been in Japan long?'

Chris started to tell of his temporary research project with the Tokyo magazine and his subsequent decision to return but the Japanese, who introduced himself as Hayato, was keen to discuss the physical differences between western and eastern men. Chris had hung his jacket on the back of the bar stool and Hayato soon embellished his thesis by running his fingertips across the folds of soft golden hairs which coated Chris's forearms.

'Do you get many foreigners here?' Chris asked perfunctorily, gripping a coin in a white-knuckled fist as Hayato leaned over so close he felt his warm, sour breath.

'We don't really let them in, unless they speak Japanese. Even then they don't know how to behave, what to do here.' The Japanese put a hand on Chris's thigh, just above the knee, and left it there. 'There have been a few,' he continued, 'but they were like you.' Chris almost heaved, disgusted by the man's physical deviation and at the pleasurable sensation his hand caused.

The bar filled after ten, the air-conditioning was activated and the smoke extractors hummed monotonously. The gay drinkers were in good spirits and they welcomed their straight male clients and real women customers with exaggerated exuberance. Chris saw there was a stairway leading to a basement and which he had not noticed earlier. As midnight approached, the flow of guests to the stairway grew. Most were men in street clothes but there were also some real women who Chris guessed from their kimonos and showy cocktail dresses were cabaret girls looking for a non-threatening environment for a last drink and endearing company on their way home. Chris resisted Hayato's mild passes and made no reference to the area below, which was apparently the preserve of the regular clients. He had to wait until his third visit before he was invited downstairs. Hayato did not pressure his untried friend, and was content to flatter and attend him, introducing him to the other resident hosts, including the one whose voice was naturally high and whose neck was smooth and unbroken by a male's prominent voice-box. Chris struggled to control the flow of whisky, to stay sober enough to take in the characters, watch Hayato's sudden disappearances, fend off unwanted advances without offending anyone, and look out for another swift, passing visit from Reiko Izumi. On his third visit, around ten-thirty, Hayato invited him to the cellar, the place which had attracted his curiosity almost to breaking point. Men in men's clothing came in from the street

208

and disappeared down the sharp, unlit stairway. None left by the same route while Chris was there.

'It's only for our special guests,' Hayato said with a mischievous smile, his voice ludicrously deep as if thrown from elsewhere into these attractive female features by a hidden ventriloquist. 'We like to be sure first,' he added, leading Chris demurely by the hand. At the foot of the stairs, separated by a drawn curtain was a cooled room with a low ceiling, throbbing with slow, soul music and dark except for a play of white beams in which cigarette smoke swirled like trapped spirals of mist. Chris coughed, and when his eyes adjusted he saw couples dancing, or rather shuffling, in tight formations. The strobe lights gave a mechanical, clockwork motion to the movements and Chris had to strain to see what to the unknowing were heterosexual couples in the early stages of intimate foreplay. His host led him to a bar and gave him a whisky. From there the Englishman could see another entrance, or exit, and through the gloom a row of small rooms, no more than cubicles, partitioned from the corridor by hanging curtains. The flimsy barriers were drawn across a couple of them.

'Rest places,' Hayato said helpfully, noticing Chris's curiosity but misinterpreting his motives. A good euphemism, Chris thought. He wanted to sound out the transvestite about the swift visits of the heterosexual female called Reiko Izumi but watched in horrified fascination at a couple, one half a colourful, grotesque simulacrum of his assumed sex, the other a properly turned out middle-aged salaryman. There was no camp badinage, or ribald sexual exchanges, only the straight-faced understanding between a supplier and his customer. As Chris watched transfixed, the lights dazzling patterns on the dancers and the hands that roamed over bodies, couples drifted past him with hardly a glance at the tall, white stranger and went into the cubicles. He felt a hand passing between his legs, searching for his fly. Again, a sickening feeling of revulsion overcame him as he absorbed Hayato's bitter breath and unequivocal offer with its underlying basic, cheap plea.

'Do you want to dance?' the Japanese said, and then he inclined his head towards the corridor. 'Or do you want to be alone with me?'

Chris brushed the hand away, cursing Araki silently and swearing to himself that even the extra money would not buy him again for this kind of service.

'I don't make the scene,' he replied uncomfortably. 'I like a more relaxed party. You know, sharing a shot or two in private with a friend.' He looked across Hayato's shoulder. Some of the men were lounging against the wall with their partners or friends. Chris could not tell whether they were high on stimulants or a less common drug. Hayato took Chris's reticence as bashfulness and not rejection. He had met many such men before. As the senior host he was the leader and example for the others and rarely took customers to the cubicles any more, leaving that duty to the team he had trained. Besides, he was looked after by a pair of senior bankers from two top City banks and a junior government minister and his side-job selling amphetamines to clients gave him a comfortable income which he was saving to buy a plot of land and a chalet. Meanwhile, he lived in a cheap, discreet apartment where he rarely took his clients or lovers. But this was a rare opportunity.

'I understand,' he said, a hand again straying to Chris's knee, shooing away with the other a colleague in a blonde wig and a bare midriff between a halter top and his tight yellow hot-pants.

'I think I can leave early tonight,' he said hopefully, raising his wrist close to his eyes and reading ten-thirty on his watch. 'In about half an hour. My apartment's tiny but much more convenient than a hotel. And it's not very far.' Hayato brushed an imaginary irritation. 'And it will be fun,' he insisted. 'I've got all kinds of things.'

* * *

The taxi drove north-east, against the rush-hour traffic fanning out to the suburbs, and after twenty minutes stopped outside a low, wooden building separated from a brightly lit shopping street in Mejiro by a path of raised stones bordered by a strip of finely raked gravel with a double-tiered grey lantern acting as a gate.

'I haven't eaten well for four days,' Mariko confessed, paying the driver against Araki's weak protestations. 'I hope sushi's acceptable.'

It was warm in the restaurant and Mariko was slipping the jacket from her shoulders before the manager had finished a spasm of obsequious greetings.

'I thought we could take the counter,' she said, easing herself around a diner on to one of the last two stools around the L-shaped serving ledge. 'We can choose what we want instead of the set courses they serve at the tables.' Mariko was greeted by name by the chief itamae-san, who bowed across the counter, displaying a bald scalp bound by his knotted headband. There was an atmosphere of exclusivity in the restaurant. The straw-coloured tables, separated by screens, gave token privacy to the customers. Lanterns made of opaque rice-paper stretched between slender wooden frames hung from the low, latticed ceiling. Bordering the counter, was a perspex shield under which the day's selection of fresh uncooked fish and shellfish was exposed on a carpet of dark green and purple seaweed covering a bed of ice. The rear of the shield, away from the customers, was open. On the back wall, the name of each type of fish and sea creature on offer was written in ornate, complex Chinese characters with the price of a single two-piece helping beneath it.

'Beer?'

Araki grunted, commenting on his thirst. He would have preferred whisky.

A medium bottle of Sapporo Dry appeared within seconds, delivered by a pleasant girl with prominent canine teeth stretching her thin-lipped face. The stocky itamae assigned to the half-dozen customers at the end of the

211

counter had a broad smile and the narrowest of puffy eyes. He squeezed a ball of soft, wispy seaweed and placed the fresh wad of the dark-green sea vegetable in front of his new guests, alongside a small dish of soya sauce and a mound of green horse-radish.

'A little sashimi to start with?' he asked suggestively. 'Some slices of fish?'

Mariko drew her hands in front of her. A pleasurable gesture.

'And some shellfish,' she said enthusiastically.

Araki felt deeply for the woman and her behaviour. Her forced conviviality so soon after the funeral of her mother, as she showed her gratitude for the person who had ended the first stage of her suffering, overwhelmed him with sympathy. They were half-turned towards each other, their knees touching lightly as they leaned to pick up their glasses. Each small movement from Mariko released a soft, flowery hint of perfume and freed her breasts, which rose and moved beneath the blood-red silk blouse, creasing the delicate fabric with shadowy ripples.

The chef was busy. As they spoke about the funeral, a few slices of hard raw abalone with its rich, pure taste of the ocean, a pile of chopped orange-pink ark shell, still wriggling with freshness and a block of soft, sliced white scallop, were placed on the bed of edible seaweed on the counter in front of them.

Mariko snapped her chopsticks apart with almost childish glee and picked a glob of grated horse-radish which she dropped helpfully into Araki's soya sauce. She then stirred a similar amount into her own dish. He wanted to help her overcome the pain and sought for a topic which had nothing to do with land, religions or missing seals. But when he spoke his hand strayed to his jacket, past the lapel and inside to the thin envelope holding the four odd photographs he had found in the Izumi villa.

'What took you to Hawaii?' he asked casually, dousing a piece of abalone on both sides in the soya horse-radish mix and scooping it to his mouth.

212

If there was suspicion in her expression or voice Araki missed it.

'It wasn't so unusual. I went to a private school in Tokyo for the daughters of the wealthy. It was Catholic in fact, though not many of us were Christians, either before or after. We had money, we travelled in the holidays and learned to drive as soon as we could. Some of my friends, me included, wanted to study abroad.'

'How did your parents feel about that?' Araki asked. 'Once you leave the shores of Japan you're lost to the system for ever.'

Mariko smiled.

'Shinobu was turning out to be the traditional daughter. You remember Shinobu.'

'Your younger sister. Yes, of course.'

'My parents gave up on me early on. They married Shinobu to a bureaucrat with a bright future and she dutifully gave them grandchildren. A boy and a girl, naturally.'

They chuckled, poured each other beer as custom required and together attacked the mound of chopped shellfish.

Araki asked, 'Why did you come back from Hawaii? Wouldn't you find more opportunities there among the expatriate Japanese?'

If there was a moment in their two-week-old relationship when Araki thought he saw in her face the briefest of expressions which said she regretted his presence it was now. He had a picture in his pocket of this woman in a country he was certain was Hawaii and his question was asked in all innocence. He did not expect her to give him a clue as to why the picture had been mutilated to extirpate the identity of her companion. He tried to back away. He continued,

'It's not easy for a woman to come back from the States or Europe and re-adjust to life here.' He knew that the pressure on the Japanese woman from her family and

213

employers to marry at twenty-five is intense and irresistible; and while polite conversation at this difficult time was his aim he would like to know how she had avoided the marriage-children stage and was close to that age which would make her socially unsuitable as a bride. She seemed to accept his questions as innocuous.

'You're right,' she said, stirring the soya-radish mix with a chopstick. 'They treat you differently abroad, especially if you're a woman. Not differently really,' she said correcting herself. 'They treat you with what by their standards is normal. When I got back from Hawaii I wanted to help change the role of Japanese women here, change the perception from being not just decorative tea-makers whose only hope for personal fulfilment outside of marriage to a salaryman is to become a bar girl in the water trade. To do otherwise is to abandon any chance of marriage and you're left to pursue a lonely career.'

'I'm glad you chose a proper job,' Araki said playfully. 'I can't picture you at a night club.' She threw him a glance which told him she knew he was lying. With her long, straight legs, her above average height and naturally round, bright eyes in an angular face, alive with intelligence and vitality, she was almost a race apart from the masses of short, round-faced women with featureless faces on which they insisted on applying unnecessarily large quantities of make-up, almost always too white for their pale skins.

From the viciously sharp edge of his slender knife, the smiling itamae slid four slices of pink, marbled tuna fish, pieces cut from the fatty area around the fish's gills, on to the counter. He followed the tuna with a fan of tiny, raw, sweet prawns, stripped of their shells except for the tails.

'So you went into the fashion business,' Araki said, recalling their first conversation. 'As a model?'

'Design. I studied it in the States and joined the Shoda Group. Through a connection of my father. But I think I would have made it without his influence.' She used

214

the corrupted English word for connection, now invariably shortened and pronounced in Japanese as 'con-eh', unashamedly, and she was proud to have become a senior partner on merit.

They ate the oily, rich tuna, chewy and tender, almost like the best Kobe beef, and the prawn mouthfuls. Mariko was relaxed, the trials of the recent days obliterated for the time being. She asked him if he wanted to change to sake and ordered a large pot before he could reply. 'It goes better with the sushi,' she said by way of excuse.

The toothy waitress hurried away and to the chef across from her, who was already kneading a ball of vinegared rice in the palms of his hand in anticipation, Mariko commanded.

'Nigitte kudasai. Please make some sushi.' And to Araki, 'What would you like to start with?'

'Sea urchin.'

'And I'll have the horse mackerel.'

'Uni to aji,' their chef confirmed.

At eight o'clock the sushi shop was full and from then on gaps at the counter would appear and tables become vacant. But now it was animated with parties receiving fifteen varieties of raw fish and shellfish in sliced sashimi style without rice on a serving tray in the shape of a fishing vessel, covering half the table. There followed a selection of sushi, the mouthfuls of soft rice with multi-coloured slivers of fish as a cap and served on individual flat wooden boards with a square leg at each corner.

'What now?'

Araki wondered whether she meant the next selection of raw fish or the next stage in the case, which, if the term of reference of his employment were strictly followed, had ended for him. He opted for the latter, picking his way around her sensibilities.

'I had hoped you would allow me to assist you further.'

Mariko looked puzzled. The plum-purple piece of mackerel lay on its wad of rice wedged between her

215

chopsticks close to her lips. She returned the food to the soya sauce dish.

'Perhaps it's appropriate that you offer the police your full co-operation. I understand there will be a full investigation.'

She straightened her back and breathed deeply, as if strengthening herself for the next effort.

'Here. Drink this,' Araki said, with unusual tenderness, pouring from the sake flask into the thimble-sized cup he held aloft for her. Her sad brown eyes engaged his own as she sipped the warm rice wine.

'Thank you,' she said. 'And now you.' She reciprocated the gesture.

They went back to their food and finished it greedily.

'Should we have the salmon roe?' Mariko said, pointing to the carton of bright orange eggs through the perspex shield which protected the refrigerated display of un-cooked sea-food.

Araki nodded, smiling.

Mariko beckoned the chef.

'Ikura, please.'

Araki said, 'I will disclose to the police everything I know. How Chris and I came to the conclusion that the slipper in the lake belonged to your mother.'

'But how did you know it was hers?' Mariko asked eagerly.

Araki sought for time by lifting the rice ball, heaped with salmon eggs and wrapped in a band of emerald green crispy seaweed. Dipping it in the soya sauce he chewed it whole, while searching for an explanation.

Finally, he confessed, 'You gave me free access to your parents' house and so I went over there last week and found an empty shoe box with a colour strip which matched the description of the kimono slippers your mother was wearing when she left home.' He neglected to tell her that her own father had alerted him by vehe-mently denying that the slipper in the lake was his wife's. No husband could ever be so sure that a piece of clothing

216

belonged or not to his spouse. Nor did he mention the presence of Reiko, who watched him make the discovery, making her own hurried departure for the pleasure dives of Shinjuku, a plaster over a vein marking the motive for the journey to the floating world.

Araki continued, gently, cautiously, aware that an injudicious comment could break the woman's brave façade of deep composure. 'I think I know what your mother did on the last day she was seen alive.'

The couple next to Mariko made a move to leave. A call for the bill, an exchange of pleasantries with the serving staff and embarrassed apologies as the man accidentally nudged Mariko's chair. The minor commotion ended and Mariko's attention returned to Araki. The slight over-bite over the thin lips of her downward curving mouth gave her face a natural sadness which her companion found mesmerizing. He lit a cigarette, waiting for her reaction. His mouth was dry and he craved another beer.

'Please tell me,' Mariko said softly.

'If I tell you, I have to tell the police.'

'Why can't you?'

Araki toyed with his chopsticks.

'Because it's pure conjecture,' he said.

'But you were right about the slipper,' Mariko reasoned. 'You might be right about her movements that day.'

Araki looked at his employer with compassion.

'You're right,' he said purposefully. 'Perhaps I owe it to you to tell the police what I think.'

'Can't you tell me?' Mariko asked, with a strange urgency.

Araki's mind was slightly confused by drink and by the disarming woman whose long fingernails, painted in delicate pink, grazed his wrist even as he fought to disclose nothing.

Mariko reached for her handbag on the ledge below the counter and extracted a special gift envelope.

217

'It's very little,' she said, extending the bulky packet towards him on the fingertips of both hands. 'A million yen,' she continued, relieving him of his curiosity. 'I hope it covers the expenses you have incurred in the past two weeks.'

It would, Araki calculated, leaving the first two million she had given him free to distribute among the three of them. The extra million was needed, as he called to mind the one hundred and fifty thousand yen he had handed the man from the planning and development section of the Kanagawa prefectural bureau with responsibility for land around the proposed site of the Honshinkyo temple. It had not taken him long on that second unplanned dash to the coastal region south of Tokyo to identify the senior individual in the teeming local government office. A few concerned enquiries, assurances that his interest was not hostile, and Araki had the functionary amenable to a request for some details of the proposed developments on the hills overlooking the Kamakura beach and the bay beyond. It was not really an illegal enquiry, merely that of a concerned citizen anxious to know the limits of the proposed development. It had been almost a week since this second visit to the coast and still there had been nothing from the inoffensive civil servant who had received about a month's salary from the gullible sleuth from Tokyo.

Araki bowed self-consciously.

'More sake?' she asked, pouring in the manner of the water-trade, supporting the base of the slender pot, the fingertips of the other hand directing the lip to Araki's cup.

'Is this farewell?' Araki wanted to know, tipping the envelope towards her before sliding it into the inside pocket of his jacket. He used the formal word for 'gift of separation', a telling gesture in a country of gestures and which suggested the parties might not meet again.

'Let's eat a little more, if you're still hungry.'

218

He was. The portions, arriving in pairs, were pleasantly short on rice and covered with thick slices of fish or wrapped in bands of seaweed and topped with a deep layer of fish eggs and spongy sea urchin. Mariko ordered conger eel which was grilled lightly and brushed with a sweet soya-based sauce. Araki asked for langoustine prawns and the itamae took the creatures still wriggling from a box of sawdust, stripped them deftly of their heads, shell and pincers and placed the two transparent bodies on to rice and placed them before his customer. Mariko giggled uncontrollably, clutching Araki's arm to stop herself from falling off the stool, when one of the morsels suffered a posthumous nervous spasm and appeared to jump off the rice as Araki lifted it towards his mouth. The pat of rice between his chopsticks disintegrated, some falling on his lap, other grains falling back into the dish of soya sauce and again drawing guffaws from his beautiful companion and an understanding smile from their chef. Mariko raised a portion of her eel, a hand spread protectively beneath it, and fed Araki.

The restaurant was emptying, the families and the businessmen departed, leaving a handful of couples absorbed in each other or drifting between light and serious conversation. The staff had begun to pack the unsold fish in muslin and scrub the cutting surfaces: and the waitresses were topping up the pots of green tea, hoping it would be the last time. Mariko was confused by drink and pleasantly distracted, Araki hoped, from the awfulness of the last few days.

'A night-cap?' she offered.

'I wouldn't mind a beer,' her companion said, 'but I think they want to close. Let's go somewhere else.'

Mariko called for the bill. The itamae-san filled in the last items on his pad and presented it to Araki with a respectful bow. Araki made for it but Mariko took it gently and paid it at the door.

Araki stretched and yawned noisily as he waited for his patron. The evening was cool and clear, a three-quarter moon dominating a cloudless sky. He nodded his thanks when she joined him and they helped each other over the irregularly shaped stones and laughed when they reached the deserted streets.

'Where should we go?' Araki said, hopefully scanning the street for a welcoming neon sign or red lantern which might suggest an intimate piano bar or snack.

'My place,' Mariko said, clipping her bag shut. 'I live near here. That's why they know me in the sushi restaurant.'

The blue address plates over the doors of the larger buildings told him they were near the upper loop of the Yamanote train line, a symbolic feature which divided inner and outer metropolitan Tokyo, and when they passed in front of the Chinese restaurant, with its imposing façade of tiered balconies, he knew Mejiro Station was near. Mariko led him to a three-storey mansion block in a quiet street lined with young gingko trees. It stood on solid concrete stilts to give off-street parking space for the residents' cars as the law required. Araki saw the outline of Mariko's fiery red Celica, subdued under the pale reflection of a night security light. There was only one apartment on each floor, testifying to the wealth of the tenants. The owner, probably an actor or a doctor, lived on the lowest level, with a foreigner on the second, his company paying a million yen or more a month for the privilege. Mariko had the third, another asset in the name of her dead mother.

Mariko was relaxed on the short rise in the lift, laughing with authentic zeal as Araki compared without malice or envy this sound, architecturally designed building with his own modest rooms whose walls seemed to amplify even the most intimate sounds from the adjoining dwelling.

'That must make entertaining quite interesting,' she said mischievously, her delicate floral perfume almost drowning the whiff of sake which neither noticed.

'You don't have such problems,' he reposted, tapping

220

the panelled walls of the dimly lit hall as the lift doors folded shut behind them. She fumbled in her handbag while Araki admired the thick, richly varnished door.

'Do you always leave the lights on?' he asked casually, indicating a sliver of light along the floor.

Mariko's face was contorted with fear: she shook her head. 'Never,' she whispered with rising trepidation. Araki tried not to betray the thumping in his own chest as he took the key from her trembling fingers.

'You might have left it on by accident,' he said without conviction. The drink may have emboldened him as he did not consider retreating. He slid the key into the groove, deliberately prolonging the action, making a noise with the door handle, hoping to offer an intruder, if he was in the apartment, the chance to assess the danger and avoid a violent, unpredictable confrontation.

'Is there another way out?' he whispered.

'The fire-escape. Through the kitchen.' She was more composed, but held Araki's arm tightly. He pushed the door with his fingertips, watching intently as the triangle of light filled the hall. Mariko stared in disbelief at her companion when he leaned against the wall and made the first instinctive stoop to remove his shoes. She tugged his sleeve and he desisted. Facing them was a cabinet, and to its right the main lounge they could not see. Mariko jerked the handle and the cupboard door gave with an echoing click. She reached inside and extracted a slim, folded umbrella which she gave to Araki, whose uncomprehending look told her that he found the flower-patterned weapon less than menacing while seeing the logic of holding something, even a token deterrent.

'Where's the light?' he whispered, entering a lounge where the shapes of chairs and other pieces of furniture took on threatening silhouettes in the darkness. He ran a clammy hand up the wall, his heart threatening to break out of his chest, and Mariko's sweet breath telling him she was near. The muted, metallic sound of a door closing in a nearby room jolted them upright.

'The kitchen,' Mariko hissed, almost with relief. 'The back door.'

Araki leapt forward, gripping his weapon in the middle of the shaft. Blindly he barged through the first open door, halting just as abruptly to let his eyes adjust to the pale light of what was Mariko's bedroom. Below the closed curtains of a solitary window a table lamp cast a pool of light over the contents of her bedside drawers which were scattered in careless heaps on the floor. He felt a tugging on his jacket sleeve and heard an excited voice urging towards another room. The kitchen door smashed on its hinges as Araki crossed the room and tore at the more solid, metal-framed door opposite and stepped on to the ledge of an iron, rust-coloured fire-escape. There were rasping sounds on the steps below. The man was near the bottom of the escape, which zigzagged between the floors. The top of his head bobbed between the steps. He was a heavy man, otherwise he could have taken the steps two at a time. Safe from the possibility of reprisal, Araki took careful aim and hurled the umbrella downwards, accompanied with a cry of 'thief' and a useless demand for him to stop. The missile was thrown more in frustration than real intent to harm but it hit the flat crown of the low concrete wall that projected the compound and which the fugitive had somehow mounted and was now straddling as if it were a horse. A spark from the impact pricked his wrist, startling him, and as he slid over the wall he looked upwards. It was a stupid, careless reaction. Both faces were illuminated; Araki's in the ghostly glow of a single, high density security light on the landing and the other by the beam of a pair of headlights which scanned the neighbouring buildings as they turned into the back street and rested on the intruder. The two men stared at each other motionless, like rabbits caught in a piercing light, their faces frozen in an expression of mutual recognition: Sugishita, the heavier of the two men

222

who had urinated on his shoes in the Kana night-club. In a theatrical moment, the headlights were extinguished and the body disappeared over the wall, followed by the slamming of a car door, muted urgent voices in the evening quiet, and the screech of tyres biting on tarmac. Araki was surprised at his own agility as he too skipped the steps and scaled the wall before sliding into the street. Figures had appeared on the balconies of nearby apartments but quickly withdrew. Araki looked for traces of the man but in the hopeless darkness found nothing except the blunted umbrella. He looked up, ready to reassure Mariko with a wave but she was gone.

He walked round to the front of the block and buzzed on the interphone. Mariko's voice crackled through the speaker. Araki moved to the plate glass doors but the opening mechanism was not activated.

'I'm sorry to have troubled you,' the voice said, it was barely audible.

'Are you hurt?' he thought she said.

Apart from a bruised knee, Araki was almost exhilarated by the experience.

'Fine, thanks,' he intoned. 'Just need a wash before the police arrive.'

The woman's voice took on an unexpected, formal tone.

'Could I ask your forgiveness this time, Araki-san, but I would prefer to be alone to meet them.'

Araki was stunned. The woman he had laughed and joked with, and comforted to the point where she had invited him to her apartment, was now a stranger, dismissing him with the same polite aloofness she might apply to a noodle delivery boy.

His mouth closed on the tiny, grey box.

'They'll need a statement. I can give them a good description of the man . . . '

Mariko's voice was distant, almost pleading.

'Please understand. It's very important I face the authorities alone.'

Araki nodded to himself and blew out air.

'Fine. I'll call you.' He made a helpless gesture with his arm.

'Araki-san?'

'Yes,' Araki responded lamely.

'Thank you for being with me this evening.' Before he could respond, reciprocate her compliment, there was a click and the buzz died.

There was a crowd of salarymen in front of Mejiro Station, touching, bowing, giggling. There had been a party and some of them were vomiting silently alongside sheltered walls while others pondered the journey home. Araki eased his way through them and called Chris, only then remembering the mission he had set for the English-man and, smiling, replaced the telephone. Mistakenly, he pressed a button and received a ticket marked 'child' and tore it in two. His mind was on Mariko, on her fear, her vulnerability and her sudden rejection of his support. Where earlier she had craved his help, and generously paid for it, she had in the end spurned it. Why? The tone of her voice had risen in politeness to an aloof, impersonal level, the way the young graduate recruits announced the destinations of lifts in department stores. He had expected a drink and a long talk, during which their relationship would be strengthened and secured as they exchanged private intimacies. Her grief would lower her defences, heightening a desire to share it and be comforted. Araki had relished the trust she had placed in him and had worked to fulfil the task she had paid for generously. He patted the bulging envelope in his jacket pocket. And suddenly she was somebody else. He turned towards the emptying station forecourt and then it hit him. He had the answer. He turned round, brushed aside a compliant drunk, and slipping the ten-yen coin intended for Chris into the slot he dialled her number. Seven, eight, nine bursts of distant unanswered droning electronic sound. He slammed the handset onto its rest. Pushing the same, confused salaryman aside he dashed

224

across the road against the pedestrian crossing light. A policeman stepped out of his box to make an example of this socially unacceptable person, but Araki was already out of his sight, running down the dark lanes to the squat block of luxury flats he had so recently abandoned. 'She wasn't alone,' he told himself. 'She isn't alone,' he corrected. There was another intruder in the apartment. God, he'd been stupid. He should have known from her voice. Whoever it was had been surprised by their arrival and forced to hide as Araki rushed in pursuit of an accomplice who escaped through the kitchen. It was in her voice. It was new to him, too polite, each word clipping the end of the next, edging it with an unnatural staccato. Was she being held captive, forced to send him away, a knife at her throat? He skipped up the steps and lunged at the interphone button. Again, the humiliating betrayal of silence between each electronic plea. Abandoning the bell, he pressed the glass door with two hands and then despairingly fell back. He retraced his steps, looking in vain for a light in the front windows and then to the rear where his expectations were similarly dashed. He was contemplating a flurry of options, favouring police action rather than a destructive forced entry using bricks and perhaps a scavenged length of pipe, when a woman emerged from one of the houses opposite and approached him, nervously bowing on the move, and a wary expression on her beakish face. Excusing herself she said, 'Are you looking for the young woman who lives on the third? I saw you return together earlier,' she said sheepishly.

I bet you know everything, he thought, but was thankful for her help.

'That's right, I have to talk to her urgently.'

With a hiss of breath and a twist of the neck she showed the degree of her concern and the hopelessness of the situation and said, 'I'm afraid she left the building a few minutes ago.' And to justify the timeliness of her observations she added, 'I was putting out the garbage.'

'Was she alone?' Araki asked calmly, but with urgency.

'Yes, quite alone.'

Goto's fist hit the dashboard. His normally clear, intelligent eyes had a feral ferocity which he directed to Yano behind the wheel and Sugishita in the back of the black saloon, nursing grazed thighs through torn trousers with a damp handkerchief.

'How the fuck did you let them catch you inside,' he stormed.

'A policeman on his rounds,' the sour-mannered driver insisted. 'He was checking all parked cars, taking down their numbers. I had to move on. The Izumi woman and her friend happened to arrive while I was circling the block. I just didn't see them.'

Goto, who had joined them in front of an office block near Sagamo Station, weighed the consequences. He turned again to Sugishita.

'How far had you searched?' he demanded to know.

The paunchy yakuza shrugged his shoulders.

'I was just finishing in the bedroom. I didn't have time to put her things back.'

'You had to search her underwear thoroughly,' Yano said without humour.

Sugishita smirked.

'Fools!' Goto shrieked, freezing the faces of the bungling burglars.

'We're two or three days away from exposure,' he hissed, reminding the others of the Tekkei Bank's manager's appointment with the Ministry of Finance inspectors. 'Once those auditors work their way into the records and find the unauthorized loan they'll burrow away like demented moles until they find enough evidence to prosecute the bank.'

'Nakata should be able to stall them,' Yano offered.

'No way,' Goto scoffed. 'He's scared out of his mind.' And then ominously added, 'We may have to remind him of his responsibilities.'

'What about the scruffy guy?' Yano asked, rubbing the

tip of a cigarette with the car's lighter.

'You two were persuasive,' Goto said sarcastically. 'It seems he was inspired to greater efforts and went off and found the old woman's body.'

Yano drew on his cigarette and blew a funnel of smoke at the windscreen. He accepted Goto as his leader but their ages were the same and he could not respect him as his oya, his senior and object of his loyalty. He had made an error when, as a junior enforcer only two years since being recruited from a motor-cycle gang which tracked the Yokohama waterfront, he drew a knife on a civilian customer of an Endo-gumi managed bar. At his trial before the elders of the gang he had offered the index finger of his right hand, falling to his knees as he begged permission to mutilate himself. They had all laughed at him. The syndicate chief, Shimpei Endo, reminded him of their new image: the business suit, longer hair, less swagger and less conspicuous tattooing, and warning him that violence was ordered by his superiors when appropriate and otherwise was only used when provoked by street fighters from other gangs where territorial superiority was the cause. He was ashamed of the punishment: extra bodyguard and chauffeuring duties. When he stood up and took his place among the semi-circle of retainers he found himself next to Goto who was grinning in his own smug and condescending way, waving a hand and wiggling his fingers at the humiliated acolyte. He knew that were it not for that single incident, a rash move arising from inexperience and poor leadership, he would have been equal to Goto in status, if not higher. He adjusted the mirror, fixing the station forecourt in the image, knowing that there was the customary police-box on the other side of the magazine stand, and turned towards Goto.

'We only pissed on him,' he said. 'If you'd let us use some proper powers of persuasion I guarantee you the money he got from Mariko would be back in her account within half a day.'

Sugishita nodded in agreement.

227

'As it is,' Yano continued, sensing an advantage, 'this guy Araki's still sniffing around. He was at the funeral: he's dating the bereaved daughter.'

'He might have found the seal himself,' Goto interrupted quietly. 'He might see more in it for himself than the couple of months' salary she gave him.'

'Give me ten minutes with him and I'll find out.'

'You may have to,' Goto said, looking at his watch which told him it was close to midnight. 'Take me home. Meanwhile, we have to eliminate Reiko Izumi from suspicion.'

Yano pulled out into the deserted road, a swell of anger and resentment barely concealed. Another order from the upstart. He suppressed his overpowering hatred by breathing deeply and focusing his attention on the infra-red glow of a train of tall lights heading, like themselves, towards the west.

From the back seat, Sugishita was saying, 'She's just a harmless junkie. She doesn't have the fire-power up here,' he said, tapping his squarish skull and laughing. 'She wouldn't know what to do with a family seal.'

'Maybe,' Goto grunted. He knew why his patron had married the pliant child-woman, the 'gift' from the father's relatives about which nothing was ever said. She was accepted without outspoken objection, though he knew about her free-time excursions to the darker side of Tokyo, her addiction to amphetamine stimulant drugs and her predilection for exhibitionism in seedy strip clubs.

'What bothers me,' he said as the neon lights gave way to the fluorescent tube lighting along the Koshu Kaido, 'is her relationship with that transvestite mob.'

'They're her suppliers, aren't they?' Sugishita offered.

'Probably,' Goto said. 'I wonder if it's any more than that?'

Sugishita stretched his arms across the rear seat.

'Lots of women go to those places,' he said knowingly. 'They feel safe.'

'It might be worth checking a bit deeper,' Goto said in parting.

After the door had slammed and the car, with Sugishita now alongside his colleague, was travelling back to central Tokyo, Yano assumed the dominant role.

'If we find the seal we're made,' he said, more to himself than to Sugishita whose senses were drifting towards sleep. The overweight minor hoodlum rolled his head from side to side, trying to fight the drowsiness that was causing pleasant hallucinations. He struggled to stay alert, to maintain respect before the man he had been assigned to follow, obey and protect for the past two years. Sugishita was the nephew of the leader of a minor gang in Omiya and had been given to the senior branch in Tokyo in return for a sister who married the Omiya boss's son. A high-school dropout of limited intelligence and even less potential, little was expected of him beyond total loyalty. His first assignments were in Ikebukuro clip clubs, persuading reluctant salarymen to pay ridiculous prices for a dish of rice crackers and a tepid beer. Twice he faced charges of undue use of force and was once indicted for attempted murder, a charge not proven by the police but which marked him as a member of the violent wing of the yakuza syndicates. He resented the humiliation of his senior and told himself he would strive to protect Yano, whatever the cost. He was desperately tired, drained emotionally and physically by the discovery and flight from the apartment belonging to the Izumi younger daughter, but his senior was burning with purposefulness.

'Where are we going?' the drowsy yakuza said.

'Shinjuku two-chome,' the stone-faced Yano answered. 'Let's see what those queers know.'

It was a warm, clear night and the Tokyo University students had begun to occupy their lodgings around the Komaba campus a few days ahead of the start of the first semester. The cheap eating-houses, with their huge red, ribbed lanterns indicating their modest cost of fare, lined the narrow streets and the tireless teenagers replaced the hordes of frustrated salarymen who responded to an unwritten curfew and caught the last suburban trains any time after eleven o'clock. Araki sat at the counter of a smoky red-lantern café crowded with Tokyo university students, Japan's future élite. Their confidence was infectious. They knew that the examination hell was over, the year-long cramming, the hours of study beginning from the time the student could walk and form a meagre sentence. The safe had been opened and after four years the ministries and the top banks and trading companies would compete for their minds. Araki sipped his sake, swivelling his body on the loose stool and envying the optimism of the separated groups of boys and girls. His own university was one level down from Tokyo, but at least Keio was first tier below it and all its graduates found employment. It was also the place where he met his former wife, whose father, a prominent banker, reluctantly agreed to marriage entered into from a 'love' match, a concept he found unnatural and degrading. He would only add his consent after she agreed to undergo two token 'omiae' where she met young men chosen by a 'go-between' as most suitable for her marriage partner. By coincidence, both men worked for her father's bank.

In the narrow, tidy lanes the delicate scent of azaleas, freshly released by a short, gentle drizzle, flowed between the front gardens, little more really than crammed, lushly planted strips between the low walls and the wooden or concrete houses. Passing into the deserted shopping precinct, his legs were heavy by the time he reached the forecourt which during the day displayed the boxes of fresh fruit and vegetables of his landlords. He slowed his already labouring pace as he approached the building. A snatch of light drew a broad triangle on the ground and as Araki made his way to the access staircase on the outside of the house it contracted to the briefest sliver and there was a sharp click before it disappeared. He

230

stopped briefly, pondering whether to surprise the figure no doubt fixed to the other side of the door. He was too tired and tossed a cigarette butt into the gutter.

He normally forgot to close the windows when he left his room and whether he did or not the tatami matting, fusuma room dividers and walls always exuded the stale reminder of tobacco and in places the greasy odour of burnt cooking oil. Araki had already slipped his shoes and lit the gas ring in his kitchen before he sensed the difference, a subtle change in the atmosphere. It was less acerbic, more agreeable. But it was different. He reached into the drawer beside the sink and grasped the handle of a broad chopping knife, his neck suddenly cold, his chest heaving. With almost everything at right angles, it is hard for an intruder to hide in a Japanese house. There are no doors to hide behind and in Araki's modest flat all the partitions were sliding fusumas or thinly framed shoji covered with opaque white rice paper through which the outline of a body would appear. He edged towards the darkened room he used as a living room, with the television, bookshelf and low sofa and matching chairs. His senses were heightened, his fear rampant. He gripped the knife but knew he could never use it. The room was still and unoccupied. Beyond it was the only other living quarter: the six-mat room he used for sleeping and lounging around. The night was clear and the full moon was bright enough to penetrate the curtains and illuminate the bedroom in a ghostly grey pallor. The shoji was open a third of the way along its rut and as his eyes adjusted he saw the oneness of the light was broken by the outline of a body, its two legs lying with toes bending inwards towards the floor. He retreated to the kitchen entrance, his mind racing, and he argued with himself on a rapid escape or a hushed telephone call. Reassured by the stillness he saw the danger recede. He approached his bedroom again, easing the shoji further along its rut with the knife. There were dark shadows on the floor, ebony pools around the body. He stepped back

231

two paces, his eyes fixed on the shape in the other room, and tugged twice on the cord hanging from the ceiling. In two flashes the room was filled with light which cascaded into the next room.

The figure on the floor stirred, rising from a flat position on to its side. To his relief the pools of 'blood' around the body were small pieces of clothing: a scarf, part of a blouse, the rest trapped beneath the inert figure. The thin quilt was tucked under her armpits and her long hair, naturally curled at the tips, rolled over her bare shoulders. Araki smiled and retreated to the kitchen. Teri Tanaka had fallen asleep waiting for him, he assumed, stripping off the sticky shirt and his trousers which were smeared with dirt and scuffed where he had slid over the wall. So that was the light he had seen, he thought. It was Teri who had slipped out of the shadows as she used to, using the master key her father kept on a hook near the door, to let herself into his apartment. It was like an escape for her, promised as she was to the shopkeeper's son opposite. She would clean up the mess after one of Araki's small talk and drink parties, see the guests off and massage him as drunken, noisy sleep overcame him in the early hours. At some hour, he never really knew what time, she would return to her father's house below. She had already taken two approved trips with her fiancé and her parents believed, with the wedding only months away, that the young lovers were sharing romantic moments when really she was mothering their tenant. But she hadn't fallen asleep before, Araki realized, a frown creasing his dripping brow as he sat, knees beneath his chin, in his plastic bathtub, a shower head in one hand, under a cascade of water. She must have been pretending he concluded, his powers of deduction clouded by tiredness and the depressant effects of the alcohol. The door of the Tanakas had closed only moments before he had let himself in. He was standing dried and naked in front of the sink and the small mirror on the cabinet above it, contemplating a shave, when the door behind him slid open. Whether his surprise came from embarrassment at his vulnerable, flabby nudity or the impassiveness of the visitor, who failed to smile or retreat at the sight before her, he had no time to contemplate. She stood there holding with the tips of her fingers the empty shoulders of a cheap yukata gown bearing the name of the long-forgotten inn it was stolen from. She was wearing a crumpled copy. Her hair had lost its sheen, strands were matted in places, and her face was drawn and streaked from dried tears.

'I couldn't return to my apartment,' Mariko said, oblivious to her host's nakedness.

'How did you get in?' Araki asked, turning to let her hang the kimono over him and wriggle his arms into the sleeves.

'The Tanaka-san's daughter remembered me.' He drew the folds around himself. 'I could only find this one,' she said apologetically offering him a thin, black cord. She held her own gown together loosely with her free hand. 'She was kind enough to let me in. I must give her some cakes.'

So Teri wasn't coming out, Araki thought. She was just waiting until I came back and had been surprised by a new visitor. Just checking. He followed Mariko back to the sleeping room where she squatted dejectedly on the futon, feebly gathering pieces of clothing and shovelling them behind her in an unconscious gesture of modesty. Araki sat and propped himself against the wall.

Her chin was slumped forward.

'Would you like a drink?' Araki offered helplessly.

She looked up.

'Some tea please.'

'Green or brown?'

'Green please.' Which was just as well, because he remembered too late he had no western-style tea in the flat. When he returned with the two steaming cups and an ashtray, Mariko had found a comb and with tilted head was straightening her hair.

233

'Where did you go when you left your apartment?' Araki asked.

'I went out to walk and think. I couldn't stand being in the place, in my bedroom. It was defiled.'

'A neighbour I spoke to said you were alone.'

'You came back?' She looked up, startled.

'Your voice was very odd when I called from the station. As if you were being told what to say. I thought there was another one in there threatening you.'

'There was no-one else.'

Araki lit a cigarette and coughed as the bitter smoke rasped his dry throat.

'You knew him as well, didn't you? The man who ran down the staircase.'

Mariko nodded, knowing it was futile to pretend any longer.

Araki said, 'His name is Sugishita.'

'Is it? I've seen him a few times. Never really spoken.'

'With your brother?'

Again she nodded.

'Did you know he's in a yakuza group?' Araki could not yet prove it, but he was certain.

Mariko sipped greedily at the tea.

'His behaviour was different,' she admitted.

To Araki, that meant 'yes'.

'When you get to my brother's level of business,' she continued 'you are the company president's son, the future president in fact, and you mix with a very high political, business and pressure level of people. The boundaries are very blurred, as you know.' Mariko yawned.

'Would you like to sleep?' Araki asked.

Mariko leaned backwards, resting on her hands. Her untied kimono drifted apart, revealing the swell of her breast. She did not seem to notice.

'I'd like to talk,' she said, 'but perhaps it's a little late for you . . .'

It was almost two in the morning, an hour now

234

meaningless given the arousal of his senses and, increasingly and unintentionally, his body. He waved away her concerns. 'Please. Just speak freely.'

'When I asked you to look for my mother it was, somehow, a last resort. The police followed their normal procedures, my family thought this was enough, and meanwhile there were people, the Honshinkyo temple for example, who looked to me, as the eldest daughter and perhaps heiress to some of her beliefs, responsibilities.'

'Land, money, shares?' Araki offered.

Mariko gave a sardonic scoff. 'So you know,' she said.

Araki nodded. 'I could only guess. The men have complete control over the family electronics business, and the women, that is your mother, Mrs Izumi, managed the inherited real estate assets. If she . . . ' and the word came reluctantly from him. 'If she passed away, then the responsibility, the use of the family seal, would fall according to your family tradition to you, the older daughter.'

'You're not going to stop, are you?' she asked by way of convenient interruption.

Araki was suddenly distracted by a baby's cry in the adjoining apartment. Its low whine soon became an agonized screech and he hoped his conversation in the still, early morning had not awoken her.

'Sorry?' he said.

Sensing his concern, Mariko lowered her voice.

'You're going to press on with some kind of investigation into my mother's death.' When he did not respond immediately, she continued, 'Surely the police . . . '

Araki raised a hand.

'I have a theory,' he said, 'which I might be on the point of proving.' He tried to restrain his enthusiasm, his trust in the woman who had employed him having slipped in the last few hours to the point of being negligible. 'Chris. You remember Chris? The Englishman with me at Lake Kawaguchi. He's out at this very moment, looking into one particular point which I find odd.'

235

Mariko looked unconvinced. She tugged the edges of her gown together and lowered her eyes.

'I owe it to your family to tell the police what I know and believe,' Araki persisted.

'Can't you tell me first?'

'It might be painful.'

Her sad, tired, slender eyes seemed to penetrate his defiant intensity.

'I'd like to know. I think I have a right to.'

After a pause, he nodded in agreement. 'As you wish, but I have to show you something.'

He watched as she heaved her tired body on to her knees and rested before rising. She tried to restrain the unbelted gown but had to support her body with one hand, and as she rose after a few seconds' rest on one knee it fell apart, revealing a long and straight leg from the ankle to the dark triangle between her thighs. Araki led her to the sofa in his living room and beckoned her to sit. He fetched a handful of papers from his desk and the envelope from his jacket and laid them on the glass top.

'We are not a very complicated family,' Mariko was saying. 'I don't want anyone to be hurt.'

Araki stifled a sardonic scowl and excused himself.

'Would you like a stronger drink?' he called from the kitchen, above the baby's muffled crying.

'Please,' she answered, simply and surprisingly.

Araki tugged at the ice-cube tray embedded in its own thin layer of solid leaked water. He glanced through the half-opened door at the strong, confident woman temporarily cowered and looking as fragile as a child's origami paper crane. He had never met an uncomplicated family, one without tensions or sibling competition and strains which occasionally rise to the surface and manifest themselves in public. And he had never met an uncomplicated individual, the kind Japan's consensus society wishes to create and mould. A cabinet minister is seen by the public as a faceless politician, just as a line-up of impassive and unsmiling males, in the company photograph, are

236

indistinguishable by appearance. The janitor, journey-man clerk and the chairman are physically interchange-able. But when the politician is indicted for bribe-taking or giving, the veneer is stripped and his vulnerability and individuality exposed. Behind their wall and the soothing cherry trees, beneath the appearance of well-earned re-spectability, the Izumi household was a dormant volcano which had begun to rumble and smoke as the magma swelled and boiled on its way to the surface.

Mariko wanted to know what he thought of her family. He would tell her. He joined her again with two full glasses of Nikka and ice.

'Let me tell you what I believe happened. If it hurts you I'm sorry in advance. If you feel you want to stop me to criticize or ask questions may I respectfully ask you to wait until I've finished.'

Mariko leaned forward in a kind of apologetic bow and then curled her legs beneath her on the sofa, the glass of whisky nestled against her chest.

Araki's body had craved sleep when he left the students in the late-night café but in front of this beautiful, vulnerable woman it cried to stay awake.

'On Tuesday, 28 February at eleven-thirty in the morning, your mother left the Tekkei Bank, taking with her five million yen in cash in two envelopes.' From one of the buff folders on the table he removed a soft transparent plastic packet containing pieces of the Tekkei Bank money envelope Chris had found in the rubbish bag at the Izumi villa. 'She almost certainly had the family's registered seal and was due to be at the Honshinkyo temple in Ueno where she was scheduled to stamp the seal on a document which would lease her land in Kamakura to the temple. For a token one thousand yen and indefinitely. But someone she knew met her outside the bank and they drove to Lake Kawaguchi and your father's villa in the mountains there.' Another movement revealed the top corner of a dirty piece of newspaper, the date clearly visible. 'February 27,' Araki read. 'This was also among the garbage. It tells me somebody was in the chalet around the time of your mother's disappearance.'

Araki paused to drink.

'At some stage she left the chalet on foot, probably refusing a lift because she was angry and intending to walk to the road and seek help in getting down to the village which had a bus service into Kawaguchi Town.'

Mariko was listening to the last moments of her mother's life and as Araki talked in a dispassionate, journalistic drone she forced herself to listen, while her thoughts flew between the impact of the words and the image of her mother's face when she last saw her and the memory of the agitated voice on the telephone just before she left home for the Tekkei Bank.

'She had almost reached the end of the chalet's access track, she may even have turned into the road, when she realized she was being followed.' He broke off his narrative to swallow the last of the whisky and pour another over the remnants of the ice.

'She hurried down the hill and suddenly remembered the registered seal. Don't forget that this small piece of carved ivory is the key to the Izumi fortune. Whoever holds it possesses billions of yen, whether or not he or she is its legal owner. She sensed the pursuers somewhere behind her and thought quickly. She wasn't the semi-senile, religious freak some of your family wanted me to believe. But she was absent-minded. You said so yourself. When I came to dinner you said your mother could barely remember her own telephone number. But on that mountain, faced with the greatest threat to two centuries of family prosperity, she had to remember something. Turning right from the villa road, and a few hundred metres down the mountain road, there's a layby with a mail-box which must serve the scattered houses for a long distance around it. I saw it the first time I went to the chalet with Chris after the search for your mother in the lake and then I saw it again last Saturday after we found her in the ravine. At that moment I began to understand. I realized the same possibilities your mother saw in February when she must have been struggling through the slush and the snow. She must have taken the seal in her hand and considered throwing it into the frozen undergrowth but then, when she came upon that same red post-box, she was reminded of an envelope in her handbag. Although it was a cold February day your poor mother was hot in her kimono and her heart must have been beating to the point of bursting. The only address that came readily to mind was her own and she scribbled it on the other Tekkei Bank envelope in her handbag.' Araki stopped in the middle of his speech. Mariko looked concerned. Araki suddenly asked himself why Mrs Izumi had left one envelope in the chalet and according to his theory kept the other in her bag. He continued. 'She deposited the packet in the post-box and moved as fast as she could in her kimono down the road. At some point her aggressors caught up with her.' He spared his visitor his theory on the details of her mother's assault and death in the icy mountain stream. Instead, he followed the trail of the letter.

'The envelope should have arrived in your parents' house on 2 or 3 March. I doubt it would have arrived the next day. Somebody in the Todoroki house paid the stamp charge, recognized the handwriting and considered the position. Don't forget your mother's disappearance had by this time been recognized and reported.'

'Well, I wasn't at my parents' in the mornings. I did go later every day to comfort my father,' Mariko said defensively.

Araki leaned forward, like a cobra ready to pounce.

'There's the second delivery,' he said accusingly. 'You could have recognized your mother's scrawly handwriting on the envelope and taken a suspicious interest in its bulky contents.'

Mariko's eyes opened defiantly.

'Why should I have come to you if I already had my mother's family seal?'

Araki fired back. 'Your mother had to be found without the seal in her possession. If you already had it, you could argue that she gave it to you for safe-keeping and by definition you, as holder of the registered seal, became her legal successor.' Mariko cupped her face but there were no tears left, only a silent motion of her head. Finally, she looked at her tormentor and said, 'Do you really believe I have the seal?'

Araki shook his head in reply.

'Then why is it so important?' she insisted.

The apartment was strangely quiet. The baby had gone to sleep again and the drone of cars and the thumping of taxi doors had ended as the night entered that graveyard-still period a few hours before the dawn.

'It's important,' Araki said, 'because your mother died for that seal. I have absolutely no interest in the damn thing but I am determined to find out who killed her. It certainly isn't the person who has it now.'

'Who's that?'

'Your sister-in-law.'

'Reiko? Impossible.'

'Is it?' Araki asked, pouring another measure of his cheap whisky.

'When the men have left for the office she's the only family member left.'

'What about our housekeeper? Mrs Shimazaki,' Mariko said triumphantly.

Araki shrugged off the challenge.

'She's too loyal and too old for intrigue. It has to be someone who knows how to use the seal and needs the money it could be worth.'

'But Reiko doesn't need the money,' Mariko said scornfully. 'She only had to ask and Ken would give her pocket money. Not that she spent much. You saw how she dressed when you came to dinner.'

Araki wondered whether she was genuinely innocent of knowledge about her sister-in-law's nocturnal habits or whether she was being protective of an unseemly aspect

240

of her behaviour which they all tolerated. Either way he had to disclose what he knew.

'Reiko is a user of stimulant drugs, amphetamines, she may even be an addict. I've seen the way she tries to hide the bruises on the veins. She picks up the capsules from a gay bar in Shinjuku, shoots up somewhere and then drops into a cheap strip joint where she hides behind a veil while she performs. Surely the family knows what she gets up to.'

Mariko gave another despairing sigh which said that yet another family secret was lost.

'Yes,' she said forlornly. 'We knew that Reiko liked to let off steam. Women have to do something.' She glanced at Araki's sceptical expression. 'Some drink and I know a lot of married women who go to "host" clubs. They pay for the conversation they never get at home.'

Araki nodded understandingly. 'But stripping!' he said.

Mariko sank into the cushions.

'Your sister-in-law has put your family seal into the hands of some Shinjuku low-life homosexual junkies who'll put it out to the highest bidder.'

'Why hasn't it surfaced yet?' Mariko asked dispassionately. 'It's been more than a month.'

'I don't know when she handed it over,' Araki confessed, his confidence ebbing as his own doubts rose on the realization that his theory on the fate of the religious housewife and her invaluable seal was founded entirely on supposition. But he was convinced in his stubborn, life-long way and, when Mariko persisted with her scepticism, his mental concentration, worn by physical fatigue and dashed by Mariko's logic, was about to crack. Mariko was saying,

'But what business could my mother have had in that chalet?' she asked scornfully. 'Unless she was kidnapped. She was on her way to the Honshinkyo temple the day she disappeared. I told you before. We are not a complicated family.'

Araki's face flushed as he strove to control his anger.

241

The nerves in his face twitched and the words flowed through gritted teeth.

'Don't tell me a family worth forty or fifty thousand million yen is not complicated!' he growled, as the baby next door began its senseless wailing again. 'Perhaps your mother was being blackmailed.'

'Fool!' Mariko screamed, suddenly alert and defensive. 'My mother is blameless. We all are.'

Araki leaned forward, his thin, straggly hair falling over his veined forehead, anger and frustration etched on his pale, olive face. He emptied the contents of the other brown envelope on to the glass table-top. The photograph which showed the high-class hostess from the Kana Club sitting naked to the waist on her father's lap fell face up towards Mariko. Before words replaced the look of horror on her face, Araki had turned over the sharply cut photograph of the beautiful woman herself, divided enigmatically to suggest she was not alone on that Hawaiian beach. And finally, together, the picture of the unsmiling family at the wedding of Shinobu and her bureaucrat and the solitary Reiko, surprised as she sat at rest in the garden chair. Mariko ran her fingers across the glossy images, as if the hidden reason for their existence would transmit itself through her touch.

'Who gave you these?' she demanded to know in slow, deliberate words.

Araki had nothing to hide, only to discover. He said, 'Nobody. I found them at your father's villa. Just before you arrived.'

He stood and stretched his elbows backwards. He rolled his head, yawned, and still standing he stabbed at each of the photographs in turn.

'Whoever has kept these,' he said, 'and your father and brother are the only candidates, must have some hold over one or more of the subjects. Please tell me what your secret is.'

His voice hid no malice, perhaps only a trace of betrayal, but Mariko responded violently, her cheeks flaring, her words distorted by uncontrollable passion. Strands of damp hair stuck limply to her face.

'I asked you to find my mother, nothing more. You found her and I'm grateful. Please now forget us. Leave the Izumis alone.'

A brief silence was followed by a dull tapping from the neighbouring apartment. They both looked instinctively towards the back wall.

'I'm sorry,' Mariko said in a kind of half sob.

Araki moved across to the sofa and sat on its edge. Legs curled beneath her, Mariko seemed to retreat into the soft fabric.

'Is it a gaijin boyfriend?' he said gently, 'a white lover unacceptable to your family? Come on,' he urged. 'You have to tell me. There's not much time.' Mariko's narrow, angled eyes snapped open.

'For what?' she said with sudden clarity.

Araki toyed with an empty cigarette packet and said, 'Your family seal is sooner rather than later going to appear on documents which sell or transfer land, houses, apartments and goods which are currently in your mother's name. If someone in your family possesses the seal then there won't be any suspicion. He or she will simply be carrying on the family interests. That person has ensured the compliance of his immediate family by possessing some very embarrassing information on each of them. In short, blackmail. You're not an uncomplicated family, Mariko-san, you're a devious, complex group of people and one of you is an accomplice to the murder of your mother.'

Mariko's knees were pressed into Araki's thigh and felt cold under the thin cotton yukata. She stirred, ignoring his accusation and sat rigidly facing the table, adjusting her robe as she spread the photographs like a hand of cards.

Without looking at him she spoke.

'He's the father of my child and yes, he's a gaijin.'

There was no theatrical change in the air, no expression

243

of apology or surprise from Araki, only a slight shift in his
position. Mariko was sadly amused at his discomfort and
chose to follow through with her explanation.

'It was an affair in my last semester at the University
of Hawaii. I had tried to restrain myself with men until
I returned to Japan to work but there was something
irresistible in the moment, knowing I had only a few
months of freedom left. Only a Japanese woman can
understand this, Araki-san.' Araki nodded understandingly. 'I might have been looking subconsciously for a
reason to stay away from Japan, to remain in a society
where I was an individual. For a while I couldn't bear
the thought of returning to my family and the pressures
from my parents and relatives to marry after a couple
of years' work at some menial job. Getting pregnant by
a white foreigner whom I loved was a relief once the
shock had worn off.'

She had already answered the question as to why she
had not yet married.

'Where is the baby now?' he asked.

'Baby? He's almost six.' Behind the words, and the
misty, dark eyes was the image of a lost child.

'He's still in Hawaii. The father left the islands after
graduation, when I was three months pregnant. Can
you believe it? I came so close to suicide that autumn.
My family has relatives in Hawaii, they're now second
generation, nisei Americans. They live on Oahu and are
bringing up Steve as their son. Perhaps one day . . .'

Mariko sank back again, this time her legs straightened and her arms went limp. Araki brushed the other
photographs into the envelope and returned to the room
where he slept and smoothed the futon Mariko had been
lying on when he arrived.

'Please,' he said, through the shoji screen. Mariko
stirred and looked towards him as if wakening from a
dream. He offered a hand and helped her walk unsteadily
to the mattress. His own tired body stirred from the
warmth and faint flowery smell of the body which clung

244

to him for help. As he lowered her on to the futon he drew the loose folds of her creased gown together, his knuckles brushing the ripples of skin. From the in-built cupboard he dragged the other futon and wrestled with it between the two rooms. To make enough space in his tiny, cramped lounge he would have to push the table against the sofa and jam a chair beneath the desk. The mattress engulfed him and slipped from his grasp. The noise roused Mariko, who rolled towards him and spoke.

'It's more comfortable here,' she managed to say, gesturing at the tatami mat next to her futon. A moment of consideration, enough time for Mariko's eyes to close once more, and he shuffled the mattress alongside its twin. He slipped off his trousers and sank down beside her, leaning over to pull the quilt up to her shoulders before drifting easily into sleep.

11

Chris unfolded the scrap of paper and studied it under the lights of the station's low roof. He looked around the open plaza, with its central roundabout of bushes, and matched the carefully written symbols with the grey, modern office block to his left and the fried chicken franchise at the entrance to the covered web of streets on the other side. A few scattered neons still blinked defiantly but it was gone twelve-forty-five when the last train west had dropped him at Nakano and the general bars and restaurants were shut. A line of weary men and overdressed bar girls waited patiently for a taxi. As instructed, he followed an alley of clubs and cafés, and when it widened into a street of weathered, packed wooden dwellings he looked for the corner and the road which would take him back towards the railway tracks. He startled an old man bringing down the shutters of a noodle shop when he sought confirmation of his whereabouts. The building he wanted stood alongside land ripe for development and the two nearest blocks were recent constructions: a kimono school for marriageable women and an academic crammer. In front, across the narrow road, was a shabby squat building bordering the Chuo-line tracks. It belonged to the national railway administration and like the schools was in complete darkness. Hayato's building, on three floors with a broad fire-escape zigzagging at its side, stood curiously alone and quiet in an otherwise typical, cramped urbanscape. Two tubular telegraph poles, as tall as the building itself, rose erect, drenched in cables which criss-crossed the street. A drinks machine stood incongruously between them, its base well rusted. While by day the street would bustle with students and railway employees, at night there was a silence which Chris knew was suited to Hayato's lifestyle. Even the solid, rain-stained block was largely unoccupied, if the blank post-boxes were to be believed, further evidence Chris thought that the building had little more life before demolition. He walked up gingerly to the second level, the stairway giving on to a communal veranda at the rear of the building, desperately trying to create the possible scenarios he might face.

Knock gently, the transvestite had said, and don't worry about the noise. None of the apartments on his floor were occupied, the owners elsewhere while the terms of sale were agreed. The other flats housed students whose habits were as irregular as Hayato's and noise was never a neighbourly issue. A car pulled up near the building and Chris leaned over the rim of the parapet. Across the open patch of rubble, in a tight corner view, two men made a quiet exit from their vehicle. Chris watched, looking for purpose in their movements, some deliberate action which would tell him whether or not they were strangers to the area. He pulled back when one of them looked up, but relaxed when the other opened the boot and tugged on a bag of golf clubs. The Englishman approached apartment 224 and knocked softly. He reassured himself that the walkway was deserted by retreating to a central pillar from where the chilly, empty veranda and a side view of the block appeared in its stark reality, illuminated only by the pale light of a half moon in a cloudless spring sky. He returned to the unopened door and knocked again, this time letting his hand twist the knob and quietly ease it open. A breeze brushed his hair and he saw the billow of the curtain from the open window and the terrace on the street side of the block. The dark shape of a bearded man sat upright, its silhouette sharp in a room illuminated only by traces of pale moonlight. Chris called Hayato's name and searched for a lightswitch. The air held traces

247

of cigarette smoke and an odour he could not identify. He shouldn't be there, he told himself, almost hearing his heart thumping. But the invitation was irresistible and if Araki's theory was correct the Izumi seal had been exchanged for stimulant drugs and was in the transvestite's apartment waiting for its moment to reach the market. Draw him out, Araki had ordered, earn his confidence while trying to persuade him to give up the seal in his own interests, otherwise the police would be told. The light he needed hung above the silent figure, a trail of cord swaying beneath it. 'Who are you?' Chris wanted to scream, but the words were merely breath as he approached the face of a man whom he saw in the half-light was kneeling on the tatami matting, away from Chris on the far side of a low table. It was Hayato and his mouth seemed to be leering at him in anticipation.

Chris inched near and with arm extended pulled the cord. The light directly above Hayato's head flooded the room, casting grotesque shadows on the hidden parts of his face. The beard Chris thought he had seen was Hayato's auburn wig which had been stuffed at its crown into his mouth, forcing the fixed leer the Englishman thought was for him. Chris circled the pathetic body, horrified. It was squatting naked on its haunches, hands tied together behind it with a strip of te-nugui hand-towel. Hayato's hairless torso was painted with rivulets of shiny, fresh blood. Chris moved as if controlled, his body and mind in slow motion until gradually the danger of the moment heightened in his perceptions. How fresh was the blood, he speculated. Hayato had no more than an hour and a half alone after they had separated at the gay bar. Chris's bowels loosened and his body chilled. Have I interrupted the killers, his other self screamed? He threw a glance at the terrace and the gap in the sliding window door, the width of a human frame. His next reaction was not altogether instinctive, rather a considered defensive move. He lunged forward, dragged the door together and threw the latch. Behind him there was a muted thud and he spun round in terror. Hayato had moved and was lying on his side, his lifeless eyes fixed on the short table leg. The door's vibration had disturbed the corpse's delicate balance and sent it toppling sideways, blocking Chris's exit. The Englishman looked down in distaste as he leapt over the body and made for the door.

A rasping metallic clatter shook Mariko from a short, light sleep which needed little to disturb it. Araki was already awake, shaved and dressed and was watching Mariko with a mixture of lascivious pleasure and growing concern. When she woke at the noise, he leaned across, a calming hand on her shoulder.

'It's only an earthquake,' he said casually, and they both listened and watched apprehensively as the lantern lampshade swayed and the weak joints on the wooden door jambs creaked. The rolling tremor rose in intensity and within ten seconds abated. 'Not strong enough to stop the trains,' Araki remarked. 'But it's the second this week.' Then he remembered the solid ferro-concrete mansion block he visited fleetingly the previous evening. 'But you'd have hardly felt them if you were at home.'

Bright sunshine and the sounds of crates slamming against concrete told Araki it was still only early morning, and Tanaka his landlord was back from the fresh vegetable market at Tsukiji. Mariko showered and pulled on the black and red combination she had left where they had dropped, grimacing at the creases and the clinging smell of smoke. Someone pushed the morning mail through Araki's letter-box. It was probably Teri, aiming for another look at the person she assumed was sharing Araki's futon. Araki weighed a beige, swollen envelope on his palm.

'Is this all there is?' Mariko called from the kitchen.

'Sorry?' Araki said, happy to hear that the unrestrained confidence had returned to his companion.

'The contents of your refrigerator are as follows: half

249

a green pepper, a broken egg with shell in a saucer, an opened pot-noodle, six cans of beer and some stale milk.'

'Is that all?' he said, distracted by the light mauve surveyor's documents which spilled from the envelope.

'No,' the voice came again. 'There's a slipper.'

Mariko appeared in the room, her hair brushed straight to a bright sheen, her face forming a puzzled look. When she saw he was squatting by the futons, engrossed in some documents, she left the apartment, returning in minutes with a bag.

'I've a meeting with your father at noon,' he told her. 'I'll take you home first.'

'That's not necessary,' Mariko replied. 'I've caused enough embarrassment to you and your neighbours.'

Araki waved an arm dismissively. 'The neighbours are used to it,' he said. 'And it's not a bother. I can have you home from here in twenty minutes.'

Mariko made a simple breakfast of omelette, coffee and fruit juice and left the 'fridge with a small supply of eggs, milk, bread and butter.

'There's a new leader in the race for your mother's seal,' Araki said, as they crawled between traffic-lights along Meiji-dori.

'Who?' Mariko said, concerned at the suggestion and at the sliver of daylight along the bottom rim of her door.

'As you well know your mother had title to the upper slopes and peak of a mountain in West Kamakura, overlooking Sagami Bay. She promised the land to the Honshinkyo for their country temple headquarters. You know, Go Morozumi?'

Mariko nodded, emitting a soft sigh of resignation, and said she had met him on several ceremonial occasions with her mother but it was only a casual relationship.

'Morozumi needs your family's registered seal on the agreement which would lease him the land for a token sum. He's already tried to explain to me how committed your mother was to the project and how important it is for it to go ahead.'

250

Mariko said, 'When the seal turns up, I'm sure we'll go along with my mother's wish. It would be a kind of memorial.'

'I've no doubt it will turn up,' Araki said confidently, braking hard and sending a wave of vibrations along the Toyota's ageing frame. 'The question is when and in whose hands.' He turned off the main road, the engine racing unhappily as the gears lowered. 'If your sister-in-law, Reiko, has sold it in return for drugs then you'll be getting a call soon. It might not be too much. Twenty, thirty million yen. Or someone else in your family might have it already and is holding it until the moment's right to find it and then he or she will bargain its possession with the rest of you.'

Mariko indicated a side road.

'The Kamakura plan is not what it seems,' Araki was saying solemnly, easing his reluctant vehicle around the tight corner. 'I went down to the site last week after I'd seen the model Morozumi has built in his Ueno temple.'

Mariko's head turned.

'I found fresh tyre tracks from a heavy vehicle and signs that the timber was being cleared.'

'Isn't that normal?' Mariko suggested.

'Firstly, there shouldn't be any activity,' Araki insisted. 'The deal's not been signed off legally by your family. Secondly, the police might be interested to know that the work is in the wrong part of the mountain. The temple, and Morozumi's statue to himself, were supposed to be near the peak.' He stopped the car across from the garage entrance of Mariko's apartment block and looked at her for a reaction to his outburst.

'There's more,' he said, indicating the envelope on the back seat. 'They are the plans for the site. The temple has a prominent place but there's also permission to build sixty-two villas and two low-rise hotels. Some monument!'

'How did you get them?' Mariko asked, unfolding the sharp-cornered plans.

251

'A hundred and fifty thousand yen,' Araki said almost proudly. 'About a month's salary for the functionary in the Kanagawa land registration bureau.'

He expected a show of admiration, if not gratitude.

'Did I pay the bribe?' Mariko asked incredulously. 'Have I helped you break the law?'

'You gave me the money originally,' he answered blandly. 'Unconditionally as I recall, and you have no more financial obligation to me. In fact, you've been more than generous. But there's been a murder and if I can help to solve it I will.'

Mariko tossed her head back and opened the reluctant door. Her feet were touching the ground when she turned round towards Araki.

'I'm sorry,' she said. 'I'm tired and anxious and would like to ask you a final favour.'

Undisguised by make-up, Mariko's skin had a soft, porcelain smoothness and her dark brown eyes lay in a bed of unblemished pearl whiteness.

'Of course,' Araki said, looking at his watch. 'But your father . . . '

'It will only take a minute or two. Would you please wait while I check my apartment. I'm sure it's all right, but I would feel better if . . . '

'Please,' he said, and when she had gone he shook a Hi-lite from a crumpled packet and lowered the back of the driver's seat. When Mariko had gone to the local shops to buy breakfast he had called Chris but there was no reply. He had more success with Kondo whom he had not seen or talked to for three days. His old mentor hoped to have some inspired news and demanded to meet Araki later that day. Araki knew he should drop out now, leave the case completely to the police who may or may not put the puzzle together and track down the killer of Masako Izumi. What the police had disclosed, and it was not much, was disturbing. The newspapers said the police were looking for a well-known local vagrant who may have murdered the victim as she walked along the lonely,

252

freezing, mountain road with five million yen in her purse. They also speculated on the possibility of Masako Izumi's suicide, citing the loneliness of the Japanese housewife, whatever the economic circumstances, and her strong connections with a mystical and predatory pseudo-religious order. None wished to speculate that the dead woman had entered the family villa with the money but left it with only an empty envelope and the family seal.

Araki was planning in his mind the conversation he was to have with the widower when Mariko Izumi emerged from the garage entrance, her hair trailing behind her in the fresh, late April breeze. Her face was alive with tension. She beckoned Araki with urgent, agitated waving. He squeezed himself from the seat and dashed with her into the garage where Mariko's crimson Toyota Celica was the only occupant of the half-dozen bays.

'They've been back,' she gasped. 'Look at the tyres.'

Araki was about to say that a flat tyre was not uncommon but he saw that both the tyres on the driver's side were flat and when he peered into the gap between the car and the wall he found that the offside front wheel was not only flat but had been punctured and slashed.

'Why me?' Mariko pleaded. 'I don't have the wretched seal.'

Mariko's Celica was a compact, powerful two-litre, twin-cam model, as the stencilled writing below the spoiler proclaimed, but now it was as helpless as a beached whale.

Hands on hips, Mariko looked desolate.

'I'm not staying here,' she said. 'I'll go to Shinobu's.' Her sister's name triggered an after-thought. 'No. I'll find a hotel.'

'Wherever you go let me take you,' Araki said. 'But I have to meet your father first. It sounds impolite, but if you wouldn't mind waiting in my car.'

253

Mariko smiled gratefully and watched him stoop his stocky, out-of-shape frame to examine the wheel cavities of her car. She wondered at the source of his enthusiasm and was beginning to feel the first stirrings of suspicion. He wasn't a policeman, yet he had risked his body in her defence, and what he was doing now was entirely at his own expense. She felt warmth towards this unkempt and impetuous man whose ambitions seemed to stretch no further than the next cigarette. Or perhaps they did. Perhaps the lure of the seal was irresistible, even for one of society's dropouts like Araki and his two friends, the pensioner and the foreigner. In a moment of extreme vulnerability he had drawn from her the secret of her child. But he had shown no signs that he wanted to abuse the knowledge or her body.

Araki waited in the hall while Mariko packed a travel case and changed into jeans and a loose pink shirt half-way buttoned over a plain white vest.

'Someone wants you immobile, at least enough to make you easy to follow,' he concluded, as they drove south through the congested heart of metropolitan Tokyo to the low-lying sprawl of warehouses, factories and garbage incinerators around Tokyo Bay.

'Do you visit your father's factory in Shinagawa often?' Araki asked, pulling up sharply at a crossing over the Keihin Kyuko railway.

'Twice in the last twenty years I think. The last time was the fiftieth anniversary of the founding of Izumi Electric. It's more than a factory,' she corrected. 'It's our Head Office. There's an assembly plant with it but the main production is done in Fujisawa and Ofuna.'

'Not far away,' Araki noted.

Mariko stayed in the car, a discreet distance from the drab, squat, concrete factory and office complex which backed on to the quay of a deep-water canal. A clerk led Araki to the executive floor whose corridors were decorated with copies of Impressionist paintings. In the ante-room was an original Utrillo, a gilded, finely carved

254

frame and deliberately elaborate name-plate attesting to its authenticity in case the viewer was in doubt.

Izumi senior did not pause to bow, simply inclining his head as he directed Araki to a soft, leather couch which sank under his weight. Izumi placed himself in the dominant position in a matching armchair across a glass-topped table. Green tea was served during the exchange of pleasantries. Izumi thanked Araki for the invaluable assistance he had given to the police.

'You were very clever, Araki-san,' Izumi said, easing an ashtray towards his visitor. 'May I ask how you were so sure my poor wife was in Kawaguchi?'

'You confirmed it,' Araki said blandly.

Izumi's boyish, unlined face looked weary, the silvery lines in his thick hair broader, more pronounced. 'Me,' he said, only mildly disturbed. Araki continued.

'You tried to convince us that the slipper they found in the lake was not your wife's. You tried too hard. Your wife's disappearance seemed to embarrass you. That sent me back to your house to look at the shoe cabinet. There was an empty box for kimono slippers in your wife's colours.'

'Who let you look around?'

'Your daughter-in-law. Reiko.'

Izumi stood up languidly. He looked out of the window, between matching warehouses where containers were being loaded on to barges for the short trip to a freighter in Tokyo Bay. The room was panelled in dark rosewood with a window running the length of one side. A silk scroll trumpeted the company's battle slogan in broad strokes of the calligraphy brush and a notice embedded in thick glass commemorated a recent dollar Eurobond fund-raising issue.

'The police have theorized that my wife was killed by a tramp for the five million yen she had in her handbag. It seems a reasonable explanation to me but no doubt it doesn't satisfy you.' He slumped in the chair. Izumi's voice betrayed him. It showed him less

255

than convinced and he imitated Araki's silent, insolent sideways head movement in grudging anticipation of his reply.

The former journalist turned investigator glowered.

'There's a cold, vicious conspiracy to remove your family's personal wealth from under your eyes.'

The older man wriggled uncomfortably and forced a patronizing smile.

'I understand,' he said, 'that we are looking at plain, simple murder.'

'Try adding blackmail, fraud and intimidation with violence,' Araki reposted, 'and you're getting closer to the reality.'

Izumi scoffed. 'You're a journalist, or you were, you're always looking for a scandal in any potentially newsworthy story.'

Araki's hand moved to the inside pocket of his zip-up jacket.

'The wretched weeklies,' Izumi was saying, 'won't leave us alone. I'll have to tell the police.'

Araki wondered which of his former colleagues from the sensation pedlars had sensed that there was more to be uncovered behind a murder and robbery of a wealthy Tokyo woman.

Araki said: 'In this case the scandal has oozed to the surface in spite of your family's best efforts to keep it down.' He withdrew the envelope and laid it on the table, waiting for Izumi to see it and resume his seat.

'I know about your daughter-in-law's addiction to amphetamines and your daughter's love-child in Hawaii.'

Izumi's eyes filled with contempt. Araki continued.

'Your younger daughter's stability with her élite bureaucrat is also her Achilles' heel. They want nothing to happen, not even a family bereavement, which will harm your son-in-law's career path through the ministries. Someone knows the Achilles' heel of each of your children. He possesses enough facts to hold his victims in perpetual, pathetic submission.'

'And you think that I'm that person? I'm the black-mailer?' Izumi said incredulously.

'Until I saw this photograph, yes,' Araki said, indicating the slim envelope. Izumi was anything but stupid and uncovering only the tip of the colour frame was enough to tell him what it portrayed. He leaned back into the soft fabric and toyed with a cigarette, ignoring the persistent feeble purr of the table telephone.

Finally, Araki said coldly, 'Answer it.'

'Moshi, moshi.' There was a pause. 'Thank you. We're just finishing.'

Araki retrieved the picture and stood up.

'When were you last in the Kawaguchi chalet?' he asked pleasantly.

'Chalet? What do you mean?' He thought for a moment. 'I really can't remember.'

Araki sensed the still air and did not hear the muffled sounds of engines from the yard. Something was wrong. Izumi's response was odd, curiously sincere. The evasive-ness he had expected was missing. He frowned towards the company president.

'The villa. The place you and your son used exclus-ively. Could I ask you to try and recall when you last used it?'

Izumi ran his fingertips along his sharp hair parting.

'About seven years ago at a guess,' he said. 'It could be earlier.'

'Seven years?'

'It's my son's,' the Izumi patriarch said. 'He needed his own place and that was his. He had exclusive use of it. Of course, it was in my wife's name.'

Nakata looked up when a flicker of movement in the banking hall distracted him for a moment from the letter he had nearly finished. A secretary offered to take it to be typed but he said it was personal. When he was satisfied, he sealed it in an envelope and put it into his briefcase and left the office to the puzzlement

257

of the same secretary who failed to find an appropriate entry for the time of day in the manager's diary. Two more days, the line of informants had told him, before the Finance Ministry inspectors were going to arrive unannounced at his branch. Nothing unusual in that. He remembered an audit five years earlier when he was deputy manager in a southern Tokyo branch. After three days, the ministry inspectors had found a handful of minor flaws in the documentation and procedures and had enjoyed a handsome party at the Tekkei Bank's expense. The team that would henceforth ask for the books and loan accounts of his bank would be different. The savings and loan banks, small fish in a financial group which held eight of the world's biggest ten banks, were in disrepute. Their loans were under review and the largest of their peer group, the Heiwa Sogo Bank, had been dissolved following illegal real estate deals authorized by the senior officials of the institution. The Tekkei would be the next, Nakata assumed, his mind rambling as he changed trains indecisively until he found himself on the quiet platform of Ebisu Station. Yamanote-line trains, ten yellow, square-fronted carriages long, rushed into the station in methodical, precisely timed, eight-minute intervals and came to a stop alongside the allotted boarding grids painted on the platform. Nakata checked the letter in his briefcase and moved to the head of the platform. Another train passed him and stopped; near him, a railway guard with a lamp perhaps wondered why this salaryman had let yet another train go by. Nakata breathed deeply and placed his case on the ground. He moved to the edge of the platform and thought about his superiors and the condemnation they would heap upon him. He was comforted by the thought that everyone would then praise him for taking responsibility for the shame. He crossed the yellow safety line, his mind relentlessly raging from images of his sons to the trial of shame he would otherwise face. The flat face of the next train

258

bore down on the station, the driver's hand gripping the decelerator, ready to apply the brakes. The recorded voice above the platforms repeated its message with dispassionate monotony, advising the direction of the train and asking passengers to wait behind the yellow line. A woman stepped forward to warn the nervous, distracted salaryman. Perhaps it was the restraining gesture which gave him the nudge he needed. Nakata breathed deeply, finding a momentary hallucinatory release and hurled himself into the void. His body did not reach the rails. It was hit in mid-air by the train, the head crashing through the windscreen to the horror of the driver, the torso destroyed and carried by momentum down the track until, broken, it slid inevitably between the rails.

Shimpei Endo chewed an imaginary irritation on his fingertips and extended the bent knuckles in front of him as he examined his work. He had an owlish, almost comical face, exaggerated by the pair of outsize rimless glasses he wore in his classically built home in the Tama suburbs. His fragile, wiry frame was clad in a sober, dark grey kimono, the form of dress he preferred except when attending political and business parties. He had always been an urban yakuza, his three-hundred-strong syndicate controlling bars, clubs, massage parlours and love-hotels in the entertainment areas of Tokyo, supplying stimulant and amphetamines to their customers and providing sensible protection services where required. The Endo-gumi was pledged in allegiance to Japan's largest crime syndicate which supplied the Thai and Korean bar girls, the drugs and the fire-arms that were occasionally needed to maintain territorial rights, across two-thirds of Japan's prefectural districts. Endo considered himself a patriot and a contributor to Japan's prosperity. He financed construction firms, supplied them with labour and found them investment opportunities. He supported government politicians and Sumo wrestlers and appeared at

259

appropriately private fund-raising and other parties with them.

In the garden, through the opened side of the old, sturdy, wooden house, a gardener trimmed the domed layers of the cedars and larches which bordered a rising, manicured lawn. On the crown of the lawn stood a man in a grey cotton suit, arms folded, watching the street which ran past the house beyond the high concrete well. At the rear of the house was a wall which separated it from a children's playground and dense copse. An Endo guard sat on a bench near the sand-pit in the playground studying a racing paper.

Shigeo Goto arrived late, bowed in apology and joined the twelve men squatting around the dark teak table headed by his oya Shimpei Endo. His own follower, Yano, was explaining the circumstances which led to the killing of the homosexual. Sugishita, staring at a spot on the table, sat next to his accomplice, pleased with the reaction so far. Endo was seventy-two and his voice cracked as he sought to articulate his judgement.

'The death doesn't worry me,' he said dismissively. 'What worries me is that you failed to find the seal and still don't know where it is.'

Yano's eyes met Goto's, which were expressionless. The other men smoked and sipped green tea served by a middle-aged woman in a kimono who glided around the room, ignored like the black-clad scenery-movers in a Kabuki play. 'I'm sure the Izumi woman's the key,' Yano began, only to be interrupted. 'That's Ken Izumi's wife?' one of the gathering, a round-faced, pale man with loose strands of long hair like a stereotyped professor, said quizzically.

Goto saw the puzzlement on most of the faces around the table.

'The Izumis are our friends and colleagues,' he said, a thin, unamused smile cracking his lips. 'These two,' he continued, waving a hand towards Yano and the hard Sugishita. 'These two believe that Reiko Izumi found the seal and was using it to finance the drug addiction which we all know about.'

Endo's cheek twitched.

'Well, did she or not?' he said. 'You killed a guy to find out. What did he tell you?'

Yano lowered his head and recounted in deliberate, polite Japanese the events of the previous night.

'We knew where Hayato lived. We supply stimulants to almost all the gay clubs in Shinjuku two-chome. It wasn't hard to find out where the most senior transvestite of his bar lived. We'd been in his flat for half an hour, almost finished a search and found nothing when the man himself turned up, earlier than usual, if our information on his movements was correct. He obviously had a date.'

Sugishita scowled with pleasure, remembered the look of surprise on Hayato's painted face when he found a knife playing at the rim of his wig.

'He was shit-scared,' Yano said humorlessly. 'We cut him a little and asked for his co-operation. We told him we knew he was supplying Reiko Izumi with amphets and supposed she had given him the family seal to sell back to the family as if it had been lost when her mother-in-law disappeared. It was incredible. The wretch claimed he had no idea where the seal was. He wasn't very coherent.'

Goto butted in. 'Because you two fools had almost stabbed him to death.'

Yano cast a thumb towards his harder companion.

'The cuts weren't deep. They just scared him.'

'So why did you kill him? If he didn't know anything,' someone asked.

Yano said: 'His mind was going. We were struggling to keep him quiet. He kept asking for his gaijin.'

Ten pairs of eyes reacted.

'Asking for a foreigner?'

Yano addressed the gathering.

'He was out of control by then, we had to shut him up with his wig.'

261

'That's when I strangled him,' Sugishita said with mistimed and inappropriate enthusiasm.

'It must have been his date,' Yano said. 'He died before he could tell us.'

Endo wafted the air with a paper hand fan in the shape of a shell. He said: 'Did you wait and find out?'

'It was too dangerous. It's a quiet place but not permanently. We couldn't risk another interrogation.' There was silence for Yano's explanation. 'He almost found us there. We watched him arrive from the doorway in the building opposite.'

Endo tossed the fan on to the table and rose to his feet as if on a spring. He shuffled out of the room, returning minutes later with a newspaper. He handed it to Yano and resumed his place at the head of the table.

'Is that him?' the oyabun asked.

Yano looked closely at the photograph of Chris Bingham with Araki at his side, captured as they left a police station after questioning about their discovery of Masako Izumi's body. Yano sucked in air and crooked his head, handing the newspaper to Sugishita.

'I'm eighty per cent sure it's him but these foreigners all look the same. What do you think?'

His hard-faced, tough companion frowned, his dark, oily skin glistening.

'It's him. That's the gaijin we saw.'

'You're positive?' a senior syndicate member asked.

'Yes,' Sugishita said, with exaggerated nodding. 'That wavy gold hair's the thing.'

At one they looked towards the oyabun.

The old man twisted his head at the table.

'We have caused two deaths,' he intoned cautiously. 'Masako Izumi's was regrettable. We misunderstood her strength of purpose and her will. If she had co-operated with her family she would be alive. The other is insignificant. And we still don't have the seal.' As he rested in thought, the door at the end of the tatami

262

room slid open and a young well-dressed foot-soldier bowed himself in. His voice was urgent with tension.

'Oyabun,' he said, falling to his knees and bowing again.

'Excuse me. There's been a suicide at Ebisu. The police believe it's Nakata, the bank manager.'

A simple flower arrangement of white irises and bamboo leaves in the tokonoma alcove accentuated the stillness and the unreal calm that followed the simple statement.

Shimpei Endo tucked his hands inside the kimono sleeves.

'Have the ministry inspectors arrived at the bank?'

'They haven't,' the messenger confirmed.

'Then we still have a few days. Do we still have a tail on Araki?'

Goto said they did.

'Where is Araki now?'

The new arrival spoke.

'He's in Shinagawa at the office of Izumi Electric. The eldest daughter is with him.'

Endo nodded knowingly.

'And the gaijin? Is he with them?'

'He isn't.'

'Do you know where he lives?'

The messenger looked towards Goto and his team.

Goto said: 'No, but we can find out.'

'I believe,' Endo said with penetrating authority, 'that those three, the two Japanese and the gaijin, know what is happening, though not necessarily who is doing it. They probably have the seal or are close to finding it. Let's talk to them. Somewhere quiet. Perhaps the valley chalet in Hakone.'

'But Mariko-san?' Goto queried.

Endo removed his glasses.

'We have the authority,' he said casually, thereby condemning another member of the Izumi family to the attentions of his corporals.

263

Mariko was pacing the pavement impatiently and when
Araki came running from her father's offices, she seized
his collar.

'Have you got a diary? A calendar? There's something
I have to check. It might be important.'

Araki urged her into the car.

'There's something I want to check too. This is it.'

He did not see Mariko's face contort as he swung
recklessly into the traffic. She looked disbelievingly at
the picture of her grinning father and the naked woman
draped across him.

'I've been incredibly stupid,' Araki said, castigating
himself aloud. 'I was convinced your father was behind
the plot to remove your mother from control of the family
money. He ran the business but it wasn't enough. I was
sure he also wanted the status that came from land
ownership and real-estate dealing.'

Mariko was still holding the Polaroid picture as if it
were a disgusting piece of garbage.

'Who is this woman?' she hissed.

'She's the mama-san in a Ginza bar. Your brother's
a member.'

The beautiful woman was oblivious to the rattling of
her door and the erratic, violent manner Araki was
steering his wreck through the disciplined traffic. He
crashed a gear in anger.

'Your father is innocent. I should have realized all the
main characters in those photos were being controlled,
blackmailed. Whoever's doing it arranged the murder of
your mother.'

The cold, brutal words went unheard. Dark stains
spread on to the collar of her pink shirt and her head
rocked gently. She was alone with her thoughts for
ten minutes when she gripped Araki's arm with sudden desperation, burying her face in the soft fabric
of his jacket.

'We'll find him,' was all he could manage.

264

They drove in silence along the main arteries of the capital. Araki hoped that Chris was in possession of the seal or had convinced the transvestite that it was in his interests to find it. He turned on the radio, which emitted a feeble, distant crackle. He had forgotten about the recent loss of the aerial.

The traffic was a fuming line of vans, cars and awkward buses, and the pairs of policemen watched stoically on the approach to the Ikenoue Station. Araki rolled up the window and eased his car into the alleys he knew would take him to the waste ground behind the Tanaka food store and their apartment.

Mariko tensed.

'Is something wrong?'

'The traffic's too heavy. Too many police.'

Araki drove on to the rough ground and parked where the children would heap their jackets on Saturdays to make home-base in their ball-games. They approached the street from an alley and watched unobserved from behind a stack of fruit and vegetable trays. Uniformed police with clipboards were interviewing passers-by and in the centre was the solid form of Inspector Sasaki, his hands folded across his chest, his eyes roving the shop and home and the apartments above. They were about to disperse and when the policemen reported their findings to Sasaki they drifted away after a crisp salute. Mariko's body stiffened as she prepared to move out, but Araki restrained her.

'If they just wanted to talk to me they could have 'phoned instead of sending half the Tokyo police force. I'd like to know what they want me for before I hand myself over.'

A solitary policeman remained, a hand resting comfortably on his pistol holster as he positioned himself on a corner of the forecourt where it met the street. He was almost hidden by Tanaka's light truck. Shoppers were moving again and all three Tanakas were inside the shop serving.

'Choose your moment and walk casually in front of the shop and up the staircase.' Araki pressed a key into her hand. 'I'll need a jacket and tie for the Kana Club tonight.'

Mariko looked at him astonished. Araki continued, 'There's a brown envelope on my desk, please bring it. And if you're not disturbed, play back my answerphone.'

'Is that all?' Mariko said with inoffensive sarcasm which Araki missed.

'If you can do it, ask someone what the police were doing here.'

'What? No, fine, I understand,' she said. 'Where will you be?' 'Near the car. Ready to leave when you get back.' Mariko drew herself up and stepped among the stacked display of fruits and vegetables. Teri, the only person who would recognize her was deep in the shop and so she casually prodded a basket of plums and then skipped unnoticed up the side stairway.

Yano used a red telephone outside a coffee shop nearer Komaba than Ikenoue.

'Are you still with him?' the deep, uncompromising voice at the other end said.

'No, we're not,' he replied, glancing at the grey Mercedes, its engine purring blandly across from him. 'The police are everywhere. Morikawa went in on foot and he's called in to say that they're looking for Araki to ask him about the foreigner.'

'Keep him in view. We pick him up tonight.'

'He's still not alone,' Yano said.

'Mariko?'

'Yes.'

There was a momentary pause before the voice spoke conclusively. 'We'll take her too.'

Araki left the cover of the fencing when he saw Mariko ambling towards his car, a bulky but light department store bag under her arm.

'Get in,' he said urgently, tossing the bag into the back seat and slamming her door. 'Someone's been watching the car.'

'The police?' Mariko said, giving the door a reassuring tug.

Araki shook his head and teased the Toyota into life.

'No. A fellow in motor-bike gear, pretending to look for an address. I noticed him near your father's office. Don't look round,' Araki warned as they cruised Yamate-dori towards Shibuya. 'He's behind us.'

Mariko looked at the mirror on her side of the car and when they crossed the lanes the leather clad figure with a blue helmet veered with them, as if attached by an invisible cord. Araki turned towards the Dogenzaka hill but at the last moment swerved in front of a bus on to the expressway ramp. The bus driver trumpeted a protest.

'Where are we going?' Mariko asked, her body easing back into the seat.

Araki paid the toll and said, 'There's somewhere I want you to see.'

The traffic was heavy as usual, moving slowly but relentlessly along the elevated road which snakes around metropolitan Tokyo, almost but not quite stopping as feeder roads joined it and the exit ramps jammed.

'Have you been here before?' Araki asked, as a smiling, uniformed attendant let them into the temple's broad expanse of gravelled parking ground surrounded by a fence of bamboo sticks. There were few free bays and only a scattering of people. Mariko looked up in awe at the columns, the tiered balconies topped by the gold-plated dome. She stood for a moment, chewing the inside of her lower lip.

'Once, years ago,' she said. 'We were on the way to somewhere so I didn't really take it all in. It looks different now.'

They walked to the foot of the steps where Araki had had his first confrontation with Go Morozumi, the high priest of the Honshinkyo.

Mariko seemed mesmerized.

267

'Is this where the money went?' she said rhetorically. 'All those millions.' They mounted the elaborate, spreading stairway.

'Your mother wanted to give him more,' Araki said, slapping the brown envelope she had brought from his apartment against his thigh.

The circular corridor binding the inside of the temple was empty and from an observation point they could see the hall, crammed with people, almost all of them middle-aged women, chatting animatedly in groups of five or six as they squatted on red cushions. On his throne, under theatrical floodlights, Morozumi was receiving his queue of believers, his inaudible words and ready, patronizing smile causing them to prostrate their bodies before him. Mariko grimaced. 'I'm glad I never knew what went on here,' she murmured.

Ohya, the man who seemed to be the confidant of Morozumi on Araki's other two visits, gave Mariko a few solemn words of condolence and recognized the paid investigator. They exchanged greetings with Araki, whose bow was deep and uncharacteristically prolonged. Mariko watched him, bemused. His face forced itself into a smile of embarrassment and a brief sucking of air broke his sentences into sharp, distinct segments.

'Izumi-san's mother found comfort within these walls, and for that I express my thanks to you and your esteemed leader.' Mariko cringed, but Ohya's low, reciprocal bow prevented him from seeing her look of distaste.

Araki continued, 'It was Mrs Izumi's wish that the arrangements she had agreed with your master should be fulfilled. I'm referring to the Kamakura temple naturally.' Ohya's face broke into a vacuous smile. 'Her wishes will be respected.'

Araki had broken through and pressed his advantage. His hand made a fist which he tapped against the tip of his nose and his face lined with anguish. 'Mrs Izumi made regular cash contributions to the temple.'

Ohya nodded.

'Her family does not want to neglect these obligations which they are sure were intended to continue beyond her mortal life.'

Ohya smiled gratefully, but a hint of suspicion was clear in his drawn out, meaningless mutterings of reply.

'For her family's sake, Ohya-san, would you tell us what Mrs Izumi would normally offer the temple when she came here?'

Ohya sucked in air. It was not a difficult question but he wanted a moment to think.

'It depended on the occasion,' he said. 'She was such a regular visitor, what with her senior counselling role, that a few thousand yen would suffice.'

'But I understand,' Araki said forcefully, 'that her contributions were often much higher.'

'There were special occasions,' Ohya said. 'An anniversary, a fortuitous astrological day, an initiation day.'

'What would she give then?' Araki asked, toying with a cigarette. The signs would not allow him to smoke.

'A million yen. Perhaps less.'

Ohya seemed embarrassed by the amounts, several months' salary for an average salaryman.

Araki moved closer to Mariko. He sensed her terrible longing to cry out, to denounce those who had milked her mother's generosity. Araki simply nodded, another piece of the puzzle falling reluctantly into place. He turned and put his hand on the balcony. Below him on the stage two huge banners were being unfurled, one bearing the Chinese character for humility, the other for generosity. It was a call for the believers to gather and listen to their leader's sermon.

Araki spoke low into Mariko's ear. 'Walk quietly away, as if you're going to the toilet or something. Go back to the car and get it ready to leave.' He silenced a question with a fingertip to her lips and pressed the car keys into her hand. 'Downstairs, near the lifts,' Araki said loudly as Mariko departed.

Araki felt his anger welling deep inside him. People

269

were now kneeling towards the throne, some of them bowing with sharp, stabbing movements of the neck. Morozumi raised his arms majestically. The lip of the envelope crumpled under Araki's white knuckles. Ohya saw the visitor's change and looked around for assistance but before he could act, or Morozumi speak, Araki had found the nerve to make his own theatrical intervention. 'Generosity,' he bellowed. 'The ultimate gesture is here.' He held up the contents of the envelope and waved it at the startled faces. Two men appeared behind him, along with Ohya, but were unsure of what to do. Araki sensed the threat and as hands reached out to grab him he tossed the folded surveyors' plans into the air. 'Your temple and your fortune,' he shouted, as the plans for Morozumi's monument and the luxury villas, to be built on land he had already started clearing but did not own, tumbled down towards the crowded auditorium. Araki knew that the dead woman had the seal when she left home on her last day alive and was on her way to the Honshinkyo temple to place that tiny circle of red ink on to documents which would give away title to her land in Kamakura for ever.

'You'll never get it now,' he shouted ineffectively towards Morozumi, who was consulting earnestly with his aides. Three men marched Araki by the shoulders to a side door. He turned to curse his aggressors, his body off-balance, his reflexes unprepared for their final gesture. A fist flew from one of the arms. It hit Araki below his right eye, slamming against the hard cartilage of his nose. He staggered backwards, his arms flaying about as they sought a support, the flood of pain postponed by the shock his body was trying to absorb. He fell shoulder first on to a pathway, his scalp grazing the sharp gravel stones, and the image of a slamming door flashing across his eyes.

The car had left its bay and was pointing towards the gate. The engine was running but Mariko was not there. Clutching the side of his face Araki staggered to the driver's side and eased himself into the seat. He rested his chest over the steering wheel and accidentally pressed the horn. Mariko came running from a row of azaleas and mature, deep-green bushes bordering the parking lot. She pressed a hand to her mouth when she saw the blood oozing through Araki's fingers. 'They hit me. It's nothing,' he whined. He made to move but she motioned him back.

'I can't drive a manual,' she pleaded. 'I only just managed to get it out of the bay.'

'Where were you?' Araki blubbered.

Mariko slid beside him and produced a soft, white handkerchief which she eased through his hand and held it against his nose.

'The man, the one on the motor-bike. You thought you'd lost him. He was watching from the drinks machine across the road. I was trying to get near him, through the grove over there. His motor-cycle's in a layby.'

'We've got to get out of this hideous place,' Araki said nasally. The handkerchief was soaked and drops of blood had fallen on Mariko's pink shirt and vest. She looked alarmed as he rammed the car into gear and swung it into the road which bordered the northern side of Ueno Park and was all but deserted.

'That's the bike,' Mariko said, pointing to the powerful shape of a blue and white seven hundred and fifty Kawasaki. The car slowed, fifty metres from the bike.

'The belt, put the belt on. Hold on.'

Mariko screamed, 'What are you doing?' Then speechless, she reached for the seat belt. In his mirror Araki saw a leather-clad figure running along the pavement. He braked hard, the old, run-down car shuddering in pain, and then jammed it into first again. He pressed the accelerator violently. The tyres screamed and the Toyota bolted forward like a jet with the throttle released. The bumper hit the motorbike below the gasoline tank, smashing the web of cables and destroying the piston head, and hooking the frame so that the bike was dragged

271

with the car before becoming detached, losing parts and spinning away like a broken toy. The bumper of Araki's car had embedded itself in the bodywork. There was a smell of petrol. Araki hoped it came from the bike.

He drove carelessly, his head concussed and his left hand flashing between the gear lever and Mariko's bloody handkerchief which had stuck against his nose. 'Do you still want to go to the Kana tonight?' she said with concern.

A muttered grunt emerged from Araki's throat.

Mariko said, 'Let's go to your place and clean up first.'

Araki shook his head.

'Impossible,' he uttered painfully, gesturing backwards with his thumb.

'The biker has been with us since your father's factory. He must have waited while you went into my flat and followed us here.'

'Who is he?'

Araki shrugged.

'Might be one of Morozumi's men. He needs the seal badly and thinks I can lead him to it.'

'You don't have to lie,' Mariko said, touching his arm. 'It's the yakuza, isn't it?'

In a rare gesture of displeasure for Tokyo traffic, a car hooted at the meandering Toyota.

'It has to be. They want the seal more badly than Morozumi.'

'I know where we can go,' Mariko said decisively. She pointed ahead at the sign stretched across the road.

'Don't get on the expressway. Take the outer moat road towards Yotsuya and then head for Harajuku.'

'What's there?'

'You'll see.'

They were in the rush hour, and the four kilometres along the moat, with its cherry trees on both sides, now denuded of blossoms, took thirty minutes. It was almost six when Araki turned from Aoyama-dori into Omote-sando, the broad downhill sweep flanked with

272

boutiques and restaurants which led to the solemn gates of the shrine to Emperor Meiji.

'Not too fast,' Mariko said. 'Turn left at the wedding hall and then right into the underground parking lot.'

The flow of blood had stopped and Araki had two hands to negotiate the right turns as commanded.

'I've never been in here,' Araki said, indicating the ten-storey building which looked like a stack of unevenly laid blocks all made of opaque blue glass.

'We've three floors,' Mariko said after they had left the car in the basement and taken the lift. 'We have the top three. They give us the light all round.'

People, mostly under thirty, were astounded to see Mariko. They approached her reverentially, some of the younger women crying as they expressed their condolences.

'It's my first time in the office since they found my mother,' Mariko explained.

'Are you, er, in charge?' Araki said, as she ushered him through an open area where young men in black trouser suits sat at drawing boards and tall Japanese and Eurasian models practised their swirls under the critical guidance of the photographers and designers. One of these young women dashed across to Mariko. She had the high cheekbones, narrow face and full pouting lips of her mother's race and the long legs, narrow waist and trim torso from her foreign father. Her hair at first sight was black but under the lights it was a mellow, auburn colour with a soft, waving texture. The two women held each other's forearms.

'Thank you Emma,' Mariko said, and after a brief exchange asked her to bring the medicine box to her office. 'And ask everyone to leave. They've worked very hard,' she added.

Araki felt weak, irresistibly so, his body drained of energy. A few hours of disturbed sleep following his confrontation with Mariko, the tense encounter with her father, the fear of the unknown as the police surrounded

273

his apartment and finally the eruption of anger and energy as he denounced the shaman Morozumi and his greed before his astonished congregation. It was almost a relief when one of Morozumi's men hit him, leaving him momentarily in an unreal world of multi-coloured oblivion.

Araki lay on the soft, patent-leather sofa in Mariko's bright high-tech office with a view over the flat concrete blocks of fashionable Harajuku and through a side window to the designing and office space.

'Yes, it's mine.' And before Araki could query her she added, 'My mother put up the capital. I'm the joint managing director.' She told him the brand name the fashion house used but it meant nothing to him. She sat against him on the sofa and dabbed the swelling below his eye with a swab soaked in the contents of one of the bottles from the medicine box. Araki flinched.

'I forgot to ask,' he said. 'Was there anyone on my answering machine?'

Mariko had made hurried notes on the front of the envelope she collected in Araki's apartment. She turned away from him and looked for inspiration. 'The first's an insurance salesman. Let's forget him,' she said, seeing Araki's expression of disapproval. 'Chris called.'

Araki's thin eyebrows rose.

'I couldn't really understand him. Not just his English. He was excited. Maybe scared.'

'Scared?'

Mariko tried to remember the Englishman's message. '"The usual place. I'll see you in the usual place."'

Araki sank on to the cushion.

'What does it mean?' Mariko asked.

'I understand. Any other messages?'

Mariko rolled her eyes around the room.

'Mr Kondo wants to see you urgently at the . . . Roman?'

Araki nodded. 'Yes, the Roman. It's a bar in Shinjuku.'

'And someone called Bando called.'

'Bando?'

control. 'I have no intention of mentioning our conversation to the police.'

'I sincerely trust you,' Bando confided, and launched into his confession. 'My late manager called me in to talk about Mrs Izumi on the day she disappeared.'

Araki interrupted.

'Was this before or after she left the bank?'

'It was before she arrived. There were confidential matters Nakata-san said which had to be resolved during her visit and she wished to leave the bank anonymously, without my usual courtesy to her. If you recall, I told you I used to find her a taxi.'

'Yes, go on.'

'I'm afraid I lied to you. I did see her leave. I was so sad I was not allowed to help her but I watched from inside the bank.'

'And so.'

'A car pulled up and she went straight over to it.'

'What colour was it?' Araki asked urgently.

Bando was probably shaking his head at the other end of the line.

'I'm sorry I don't remember. I'm not young any more. Colours mean nothing to me. But I saw the driver.'

Araki had two hands on the telephone.

'How could you? Your bank's on the left-hand side of the road and the driver would be behind the wheel, on the right side of the car.'

'She got out to help Mrs Izumi.'

'She? It was a woman?'

'Of course,' as if Araki's question had been stupid. 'She came round and helped Mrs Izumi into the car. Her kimono made it a bit awkward to move. And it was a small compact.'

Araki braced for the answer to his next question.

'Did you recognize the woman?'

'No, absolutely not.'

Araki was bitterly disappointed. 'Was she young, old, ugly?'

Infuriatingly, Bando hissed negatively into the mouth-piece.

'Would you know her again?' he said hopefully.

'Saaa,' Bando mused. 'I might.'

'Where are you now?'

'I'm at home. In Mitaka.'

'That's the Chuo-line,' Araki said, grateful that the nearest station was only a forty-five-minute train-ride from central Tokyo. 'I will reimburse your expenses,' he said, insinuating a reward along with the modest train fare, 'if you will meet me as soon as possible. I'd like to show you a photograph.' He waited for the reply. He was asking a sixty-five-year-old man to leave the comfort of his tiny apartment, and the pleasure of a hot bath and a televised baseball game, to return to the metropolis and the gaudy, base delights of the Kabuki-cho floating world.

'A short while,' Bando said. 'It might not be safe for me to be out late at night.' While Araki was explaining in excruciating detail the location of the Roman in the heart of the Shinjuku pleasure district Mariko returned to the room. His voice trailed off.

'I'll see you there in an hour.' And he hung up.

Araki's voice had faded because his attention had wandered across the broadsheet to the opposite page and a cut-away photograph of Chris Bingham. It was the picture taken outside the Kawaguchi Town police-station following their interrogation by Inspector Sasaki and the Five Lakes Police after their discovery of the corpse of Mrs Izumi. Araki had been cut away in the Asahi photograph, leaving the face and upper body of his blond English companion. Below the picture was a request from the police for the public to assist in finding Chris in connection with a murder late the previous evening or during the night in Nakano. Chris had been seen in close company with the victim for four days previously and was seen in the vicinity of the killing by a member of the public. Araki was staring at the article when Mariko returned. He quickly folded the newspaper.

278

Mariko had found a coral pink one-piece dress rounded at the neck. It was loose, but not enough to hide the lines of her thighs when she crossed her legs or the swell of her breasts. The sleeves ended in a flare above her wrists, leaving visible the entwined loops of her gold bracelets. She stroked one side of her hair, exposing an ear and a tear-drop cluster of tiny pearls bunched on her lobe. Her lipstick matched the colour of her dress.

'Will this be suitable?' she teased. 'I looked for something between a high-class bar girl and low-class mistress.' There was a trace of sadness as her voice weakened.

'Perfect,' he admitted sincerely. 'Is it one of yours?'

Mariko smiled. 'I designed it myself. Of course it's for export. It's far too risqué and colourful for Japan, apart from the floating world. Are you going to change?'

The open spaces and the offices were deserted and dark except for a considerate patch of inlaid lights leading to the door. Mariko showed him to a changing room where he showered and dressed in slacks and thin cotton, dark-grey jacket, slightly frayed around the sleeve ends. Mariko carried a light, navy-blue jacket across an arm and made for the door.

'You look smart,' she said honestly, but her flattery was lost. Araki was staring at the wall in the brightly lit recess in the reception area. Mariko had found security in Araki's confidence and when it was apparent he was unnerved she felt threatened and reached for his reassurance.

'It's nothing,' he said, sensing her fear. 'It's something you said this morning, in the car on the way from your father's office. You asked me if I had a diary. With a calendar. There's one over there, on the wall.'

There were scenic photographs for each month and inevitably the picture for April depicted cherry trees, this one showing the grey fir-tree shape of Himeji castle through a cluster of the rich, pinky-white blossoms. Mariko stood for a moment scouring the depths of her memory for the recollection. Silently and slowly she

279

approached the calendar, lifted it off its hook and flipped the pages. The previous months had been kept, and she turned them back to February. Then to March. Araki was loth to interrupt. He sat in the receptionist's chair and lit a cigarette. He flinched as the smoke stung the graze around his nose. Mariko's eyes were transfixed, one moment on the silky, colourful pages, the next looking upwards, her mind deep in thought.

'What is it?' Araki said when Mariko joined him, perching on the edge of the desk, the calendar resting on the top of a word processor. She was still silent. There were strands of hair across her lips and her soft body fragrance spread around, unnerving Araki who struggled to force his interest away from the mesh of her stockings and the rise and fall of her tight dress.

'When my mother didn't return home on 28 February, we all gathered at the house. Father, my brother, Shinobu, someone from the Honshinkyo, a procession of neighbours. Everyone was trying to be helpful.'

'So?'

Mariko turned the calendar to March, and its picture of snow country in the Japan Alps. She was motionless. Finally, she turned to Araki.

'Reiko wasn't there.'

Somewhere in the vast office area a telephone rang. They ignored it.

'Was that important?' Araki said gently.

'Important?' Mariko stammered, rising to her feet and standing over Araki.

'You told me my mother posted the family seal in desperation from Kawaguchi. You said it would have reached the house during the first two or three days in March and Reiko would have received it and paid the postage.'

'That's right,' Araki said calmly. 'It could only have been Reiko.'

Mariko slammed the calendar on to the desk.

'That's a mistake!' she screamed, jolting her companion.

280

'Reiko wasn't there. She was visiting her family in the Kansai for the whole first week in March. She couldn't have picked up the mail that week.'

Araki thumped his forehead. 'Are you sure?'

'Positive.'

'So who was there?' Araki asked tremulously, horrified at his mistake, the implications and the chain of events he had initiated in the wretched gay bars of Shinjuku and the danger he had submitted his friend Chris to – Chris, who was now on the run on suspicion of murdering a transvestite.

'There's only one person. Old auntie. Shimazaki. Our housekeeper.'

It was early in the cool, sunny afternoon when the bus left Kondo where the road curved reluctantly and bridged an effervescent stream which cut through steep, terraced hillsides whose patches of thick foliage hid all but the roofs of the two-tiered village houses. It took a ninety-minute train ride from Tokyo to Chichibu City and then a crowded bus had taken him to the virgin woodlands and dark, uninviting valleys of the Oku-Chichibu mountains and their ghostly, sharp peaks which rose two and a half thousand metres above sea level. The mountain sides, with their coat of thick, brackish trees, saw little of the sun and the houses in the isolated hamlets were built on stilts, as if striving to rise above the gloom. In thirty years of journalism, Kondo's network of relationships was deep and wide and there were favours he had yet to return and equally obligations owing to him. He had cashed in some of the latter and the information given to him may have balanced the account, such was the time it had taken his police contacts to carry their delving to an era before microfilm and the floppy disc.

A school girl with prominent canine teeth which stretched her mouth when she spoke, pointed to a dauntingly steep lane which met the main road between compact fields of mulberry trees. It rose quickly, and

Kondo's tired legs ached in protest. The house was separated and hidden by plum, cherry and young cedars and the natural curves and dips of the mountain. Like its neighbours, it was raised on short, stout wooden piles but it was newer. The wood had not yet lost its clear tan and the damp earth around the feet of the wooden supports was free of weeds and moss. There was no name-plate on the post-box at the foot of the winding gravel path leading to the house, or attached to the frame of its box porch. Kondo's repeated knocking and polite calls of greeting went unanswered. He felt chilled, the unwelcoming house and the stack of dark clouds on the peaks behind filling him with foreboding. He rubbed the stiffness from his knees and in the stillness heard a shuffling noise inside the house. Excusing himself dutifully he twisted the knob and eased the door open. An old man, mid-seventies Kondo guessed, his back straight and rigid, sat in the centre of an expanse of tatami matting, the rear rain windows of the room opening on to a rock garden. A smell of incense suggested a Buddhist altar honouring the dead but Kondo could not see it from the lowered entrance where he was removing his shoes. The man had thin, silver hair over a scalp pocked with livery patches and an emaciated, almost skeletal face from which sunken, darting eyes swept the visitor and sent appropriate messages to an alert brain.

'Is it Yamada-san?' Kondo asked tentatively.

The old man had a bony frame beneath his loose, dark-brown kimono. Kondo assumed there was an electric heater in the pit below the table where his legs dangled. The images on a television screen flickered silently, as if telling the visitor that he had interrupted the watcher and to judge the length of his stay accordingly. The man's neck twisted and the face looked bewildered as if the question was being processed in slow motion. There was a nod.

Police records in the early post-war years were inaccessible without a barricade of authorizations requiring a column of bureaucratic seals. Kondo bypassed all of them through a chain of approvals which began with a nod from a twenty-year-old friendship with a personnel officer in the Tokyo Metropolitan Police Headquarters.

The records were lengthy and well-preserved, some with snatches of translation for the benefit of the occupation forces. The files were stored in a labyrinth of corridors below what was the military prison in Fuchu in western Tokyo and Kondo had coughed painfully as the cold and damp permeated his body during the long hours he sat flipping through the packed wads of fading turquoise, hand-written pages. Instructed by Kondo's friend, the custodian had directed him to the arrest and detention records covering the violent left-wing uprisings of 1949 and continuing into 1951. There were dozens of Yamadas among the endless list of detainees; apart from Suzuki, Kondo could think of no names less common than this, and it was largely luck in a lucid moment that threw the name of Izumi Denki Seisakusho across his tired eyes. According to the records there were violent demonstrations in January 1949 when outside agitators allegedly inspired a shutdown of the fledgling electric component company, physically abusing the president, Daigoro Izumi and locking senior management in the head office building. A character called Asato Yamada was arrested but later released without charge. Kondo had, days before, perused the company records of Izumi, and been directed constantly to the name of Asato Yamada. He had told Araki that he suspected a Masao Yamada as the man who had suppressed the communist-led conflict and gone on to marry the president's daughter and become the head of the company, but the name disappears from personnel records after 1953. He found no Asato Yamada among the personnel of Izumi since the war but he was mentioned specifically as the leader in police records relating to the trouble at Izumi Electric. Kondo had no other leads and a tedious trace along the rigorous population control system the Japanese police developed in the following years of stability led him to this isolated mountain hamlet. He came in the certainty that Asato Yamada had fought the workers but was this old man him and if so who was looking after him?

A walking stick, a piece of shiny, knotted pine with a straight grip, lay on the mats, attesting to an infirmity. There were distant sounds, like a muffled loose floorboard or a television, which implied the presence of another. A rain door had not been fully drawn and lodged within the wall cavity, and it rattled when sudden gusts of turbulent mountain air blew across the compound.

'Sit down,' the old man commanded, as if talking to an errant child.

Kondo squatted, then slid his legs under the blanket and into the pit where they were warmed by an electric heater.

Kondo saw a direct approach might confuse a slow, suspicious mind. He claimed an interest in the history of the region, the famous peasant revolt at the end of the last century and the collapse of the mulberry silkworm industry on which the livelihood of the people depended. As a professor, Kondo lied, the living records of history were invaluable.

'Are you from these parts?' he asked ingenuously.

The old man had few, if any, teeth and this and his age made it difficult for him to articulate. He motioned dismissively with his hand and pointed out of the window, presumably across the mountains to the north-west.

'Yamanashi,' he spluttered.

'You haven't been here long then?' Kondo said, alluding to the newness of the house.

'Two years in this one. The other collapsed in a landslide. Hurt my leg,' he chuckled, tapping the walking stick.

Kondo said, 'Are you alone?'

The deep, sallow eyes registered a first trace of suspicion. Kondo read them and hurried to reassure his host.

284

'I myself live alone in Tokyo. A widower. It's frightening when you get ill, no one to turn to when you can't get up.' Kondo was sincere, and the older man nodded in sympathy. He did not mention the headaches which racked him mercilessly, ever more frequently, and left him cowering under his blankets. He put it down to the loneliness which had tortured him since his wife had died two years earlier, leaving him a childless old man approaching the winter of his life. Araki was his only comfort and he could never tell him that, without his friendship and odd jobs, he would have willingly joined his wife in the after-world.

'Family,' Yamada said, jubilantly opening his palms outwards. 'They make sure I have help to clean the house. They visit me.' His voice told Kondo they did not come to his isolated retreat very often. 'They built this house when the other one collapsed.'

'You have good luck,' Kondo said, using a word which implied destiny, something not bestowed on himself.

'I'm a poor host,' Yamada said, feeling comfortable with his new company. 'Let's have some tea.'

'I'll make it,' Kondo offered generously.

'Absolutely not,' Yamada said, pushing himself backwards and rising painfully to his feet. Kondo followed, handing him his stick.

Yamada was uncomfortable with the gas range in his kitchen. Kondo made no move to help him. He had seen another room, a small six-mat room, shuttered and in darkness but furnished with bookcases and photographs and drawings tacked to the sand-plastered wall.

'Can I use the toilet?' Kondo asked. 'It's through here, isn't it?'

'Please, please,' the old man said, finally igniting the gas ring and pondering the location of a second cup.

Kondo went straight to the darkened room, the light flickering to life under his touch. The photographs were all taken between 1930 and the early Fifties, Kondo guessed from the fashions. He recognized Yamada in

285

most of them. He was much stockier, wore a confident scowl and appeared as the central figure among Sumo wrestlers, family portraits and groups of men pictured in matching kimonos, no doubt on visits to hot-spring resorts. The stern faces of Shinto priests stared from the largest of the pictures. Traditional wedding records. The bride and groom were dressed in traditional clothes, holding the good luck trappings of the ceremony in front of the offertory of the shrine. Guests in military uniform dated the wedding to pre- or the early war years. Kondo pressed his face close to the images but recognized none of the characters. In the kitchen Yamada's water had boiled and he had thrown the dregs of an earlier brew away. New, hard fragments of tea gave off a rich, earthy aroma and he was pleased with the result. He had forgotten his guest for the moment. Kondo had moved to the final photographs, simple portraits of Yamada with unsmiling companions. He raised a finger to the image of a woman wearing a spinster's full-sleeved kimono. Even that long ago she wore her hair in a bun, although in the photograph it shone with youth and promise. The matting absorbed the footsteps and the tread of the stick and Kondo did not see Yamada, watching him from the doorway.

'Tea's ready,' he said. 'Would you help me carry it through?'

Kondo spun, expecting an admonition, but received none.

'I'm sorry,' he said. 'I was rude enough to notice your excellent photographs. They are a beautiful record.'

The old man just nodded, flattered, but confused. He ambled up to Kondo and stared at the photographs.

'I like this one,' Kondo said carefully. 'Is she a relative? She is very attractive.'

Yamada chuckled. 'An old maid. I arranged lots of men for her but they kept getting killed.' His shoulders shuddered at the thought. 'Are you interested? She's a lot older now though.'

'She's alive?'

286

'Yoshi's just about alive,' Yamada babbled.

'Yoshi?' Kondo said, desperately trying to urge him on.

'Yes. My first cousin Yoshiko.'

Kondo took a final look at the fading photograph as his host turned away. He was staring at the face of Yoshiko Shimazaki, cousin of the convicted strike breaker and now housekeeper to the Izumi family of Tokyo.

Chris would not recall the walk, half-running return to his rooms above the Korean restaurant. It had consumed the dead of night, ninety minutes of escapes, of carefully restrained movements as he met the rare pedestrian when he crossed a main road, and minutes of relentless tension as he raced along a dark, residential lane, distracted only by the barking of a dog which heard and smelled the fear in the stranger's passage. As he ran he tried to weigh the situation and rationalize his actions. The transvestite homosexual was clearly dead when Chris had rushed to the tryst and Chris was not the killer. His confused, frightened mind knew enough of the Japanese jury-free legal system to deduce that it would not be on his side. He did not relish police interrogation which brought enormous pressure on the arrested party to confess. The press would be informed and a consensus of guilt would be reached. They could not prove he had committed the murder but in Japan he knew he would have to prove that he hadn't. And he was a gaijin. It was not worth the mental strain, he concluded, no harm would be done to justice by leaving the body for later discovery.

It was after three before he dropped on to his futon, too tired even to contemplate the consequences of his actions, his mind simply trying to convince itself that he had strode anonymously through the lower side of a Tokyo night.

He woke up feeling as if he had never slept. He was alert and the reality of the killing in Nakano clung to him, but now with a clarity unobscured by drink. He made a mental recollection of his path the previous night, trying to convince himself that he had moved anonymously. No way! He flung the futon contemptuously aside and sat on the rim, his head in his hands. The features of a white westerner might be difficult for a Japanese to describe after a brief encounter but he had spent three nights flirting with the victim. Who would believe that the gaijin's overtures were really only pretence? The light in the room seemed to inspire hope. No-one would tie him in with Hayato's apartment: unless they had heard him making a date with the victim.

Looking through his window-door, into an alley with stacked crates of empty bottles and packed garbage bags, the sight of a kitchen worker in white overalls and a sweatband struck him a damning blow. It reminded him that he had asked a man for directions last night, only a few hundred metres from the murder site. Clamping the door frames together, he pulled on his clothes, and left a message on Araki's answerphone. He had to talk to him before the police, to explain what happened to a sympathetic ear first. He gathered money, tucked his chunky blond hair under a baseball cap and with a light raincoat over his arm went down uneasily into the street. The sky over Shinjuku had darkened, a fresh clean breeze below it. Chris hoped it would rain and give him the chance to buy a cheap umbrella and hide his face if not his height beneath it. The bars and pleasure dives were shuttered, no strollers or drunks emboldened enough to challenge the gaijin, and he walked unhindered between the garbage bags and the fortress-like wall protecting the overhead railway tracks. He had reached the bright ticket barriers below the tracks when he heard the siren. He showed his pass and hurried on to the southbound platform, not knowing where he would go. The whining screech grew closer. Chris pulled his cap a little lower and moved to the centre of the platform, feeling vulnerable and isolated among the sparse passengers awaiting the

288

Yamanote trains. He leaned on a pillar, giving himself a view of the upper half of the buildings on his narrow street. A northbound train arrived and some of those who boarded looked disappointed at not being there long enough to see how close the as yet unseen emergency vehicles came. As Chris watched, his own train was nosing into the station. Now he could see the flashes of the whirring blue lights but could not identify the vehicles slowing near the station in Okubo Road. The train slid silently to a halt in front of him, the monotonous recorded voice intoning its destination for the hundredth time that day. Chris eased through a clutch of uniformed primary school children to the opposite door. Below the parapet, blue lights had stopped in front of his building. From where he stood, moving slowly away, he glimpsed the black and white roofs of three police cars.

He stayed on the train while his mind raced to decide how to pass the five hours before he saw Araki again. He had to avoid walking, avoid passing the ubiquitous police-boxes where serious officers dispensed never-ending requests for directions while ensuring the peaceful movements of the people. The rare occurrence of a murder would be more than enough cause for extra vigilance but the involvement of a gaijin would give it increased tension and excitement. He stayed on the loop line for thirty minutes, alighting in Shimbashi and seeking refuge on the dark platforms of the old Ginza underground line. On impulse he changed at Ginza to the Hibiya-line and killed half an hour going to Hiroo, his goal a supermarket catering to the foreign community in an area known as the gaijin ghetto. The National Azabu is small by local standards, its aisles narrow between the imported products the bankers and diplomats craved. Chris wandered among the foreign wives and the wealthy Japanese who shared the Azabu area with their visitors. He bought the evening English language newspaper and sat in the adjoining coffee shop, the *Asahi* lying unread on his knees. When he had judged his stay overdue he crossed the road to the Aruisugawa Park, a former baron's garden which preserved the neat pathways and tendered trees, where tall cedars and maples provided a canopy for the shorter plums and cherry trees whose blooms had lately faded. He turned the pages, more to give the impression of activity than interest. There were a few strollers in the park, mostly western women with small children. Page three, with the local news, almost escaped him. His image, taken at the Kawaguchi Lake site where he and Araki had found Masako Izumi, stared at him in a blurred reproduced form. He smashed the pages together and looked around. A policeman stood a hundred metres away, seemingly admiring the varieties of moss in the shaded area on the slope leading to a dark green pond. A small blond boy approached him and asked him something with the sublime innocence of children. It caused the officer to remove his cap and scratch his scalp. Chris slipped away. Emerging from another hour on the underground, he found with enormous relief that darkness had fallen. Shinjuku shone under its nightly side-show but the strollers were not looking for foreign murder suspects and he trekked quickly and uninterrupted to the familiar staircase and the relief of friends.

When Araki entered the Roman the barman looked twice at the jacket and tie and then swept his head surreptitiously towards the rear of the bar. His eyes followed admiringly the slender woman who was half a head taller than her escort. In ten years he had never seen Araki with a woman in the Roman and could not imagine him with one as elegant as Mariko.

'Oi!' Kondo called out from a booth. Araki introduced him to Mariko and the older man's head almost touched the table as he proffered his condolences.

'You're very kind,' Mariko said, smiling instantly, recognizing his sincerity. The quieter of the serving girls brought a bottle of Suntory Gold. Mariko asked if they had 'sake'. Surprised, the girl thought they did. When she left, Kondo leaned forward, his elbows on the table, a sheaf of papers and photographs in front of him.

Araki raised a hand and begged to be excused and collecting a bottle of cold Kirin beer moved through the back of the drinking club to a storeroom opposite the pair of toilets. Chris sat on some unopened beer cases scribbling furiously on to sheets of paper torn from a school writing-pad. He looked tired and pale and there was already a purple cover of growth on his lower face, another feature which would characterize a foreigner, however elaborate the headgear or high the collar. Araki tapped his shoulder and offered him the beer in lieu of an apology.

'What are you doing?' the Japanese asked, finding himself a seat on a case. Chris drank from the bottle and without looking up continued writing.

'It's my statement. I want to get it right in English before the police give me one to sign in Japanese.' He reached the end of a paragraph. 'Have you seen the photograph? Was it in the Japanese press?'

'It was blurred. The Kawaguchi picture, with me taken out.'

'The police moved bloody quickly. They couldn't have found the body until this morning and twelve hours later my face is in the papers.'

'You made yourself well-known in the gay bar for three nights in a row. Didn't anyone recall seeing you in the papers a week earlier?'

Chris shook his head, not negatively but with resignation.

'Of course. One of the guys who tried to date me asked me if I was the one.'

'Didn't you deny it?'

'Of course I did. But you imagine talking to the police, trying to describe the gaijin. "He looked like the one in the paper. In the Izumi murder case."'

'A few calls, bringing Sasaki into it, and there's the suspect. Me.'

291

Chris tipped the bottle, but it was empty.

'Was there anything to tell who might have killed Hayato?' Araki asked.

'It was so deliberate. He was tied up, slashed and presumably asphyxiated.'

'Torture and a swift death.'

'Yakuza?'

'Obviously.' Araki tapped a cigarette from a packet but he had no matches.

'Now they have the seal,' Chris said dejectedly.

'I hate to have to tell you but your efforts were wasted. And so were the yakuza's. Reiko didn't have the seal to give him. It seems the old housekeeper reached the post first. She must have it.'

Chris leapt to his feet.

'You mean we set up that poor sod to get killed?'

Araki sought for an excuse. 'We had no intention of hurting him. I thought this was a family matter. It's got out of hand.'

Araki made for the door.

'We'll bring the police in,' he said, 'but first I want to confront that woman at the Kana, the one who shared Izumi senior's lap. By tomorrow we should have the last piece of the mosaic. I'd like you to lie low tonight.'

'Where?' Chris said desperately.

'Do you remember that short-time hotel near the Kabuki theatre in Tsukiji. We stayed there a few times after drinking in Ginza. The old crook who runs it owes me a favour or two.'

Chris nodded.

'Take a room there. We'll join you later.'

'We?' Chris asked surprised.

'Mariko Izumi is with me.'

There was a knock at the door. Both men flinched.

The voice of the barman came through.

'There's a visitor for you.'

Bando looked embarrassed by the place and the circumstances. He had never enjoyed the company-paid

292

pleasures of Shinjuku and while wishing to expunge the guilt he felt at withholding a vital piece of knowledge he was worried what punishment the unusual character called Araki might exact. He stiffened when Araki introduced him to Kondo, while the name of Izumi which followed presentation to Mariko provoked a ludicrously low bow. Araki led him to an empty table where fresh drinks were quickly served. Araki thanked him for his time and assured him that his name would not be prejudiced.

The old man had greased his hair, wiry black except for a rim of grey around his ears. He said, 'I need the comfort of knowing my information will assist the resolution of the crime. The police . . . '

Araki helped him.

'The police will have your information and you will not be involved. I can assure you.' From an envelope Araki extracted the upper half of the damning picture of Yasuo Izumi and the senior mama-san of his son's exclusive Ginza bar, leaving her naked form hidden. Bando drew Araki's hand closer to his dark, olive-coloured face. Although a Polaroid, the images were sharp, and Araki let him study the picture before asking, 'Is it the woman you saw driving off with Mrs Izumi?'

Bando raised his glass and sipped gratefully. He smacked his lips.

'It's her,' he said confidently.

Araki said, 'Why are you so sure?'

Bando sucked in air and when he spoke his voice had the precision of a man whose main occupation, if not his whole job, was observation.

'That foreign hair,' he said severely, with a trace of disapproval.

'Excuse me?'

'She had coloured hair. You know, like foreign women.'

Araki muttered his comprehension. He had also noted the auburn tinting in Mayumi Maeda's hair but it was not unusual in the women of the floating world and on television, but it was in Bando's. The bank guard's thumb nail was toying with the edge of the crude strip of paper stuck over the nude body of Mayumi Maeda.

'You've been very helpful,' Araki said, retrieving the photograph and handing over a folded five-thousand-yen note.

When Araki returned to the booth, Mariko had been in deep conversation with Kondo. They both looked up.

'Did he recognize her?' Kondo asked.

Araki nodded, but he had no intention of telling Mariko that her father's mistress was the last known person to see her mother alive. He led Kondo back to the seal.

'We're being hunted. We don't have much time,' he said firmly. 'Either by the yakuza or a pseudo-religious conman.'

'The yakuza, I can assure you,' Kondo said.

Mariko looked frightened: Araki was too preoccupied with his own statement and he missed his colleague's confidence.

'I made a crucial mistake,' he confessed, accepting a whisky-water and a light from Mariko. 'I assumed Reiko, the daughter-in-law, had opened the letter with the seal. Now I know she couldn't have,' he said, indicating Mariko as the source of the evidence. 'She was in Osaka at the time. If Mrs Izumi had posted the seal, the person around at delivery time on any of the four days after she was last seen alive was the housekeeper, Shimazaki-san.'

Kondo gasped, the image of the retainer alongside a retired yakuza godfather flooded back. Before he could describe his visit to the mountain retreat, Araki continued.

'It's true. Mrs Izumi could not remember addresses, and so in panic, to stop the seal being taken by her attackers, she sent it back to herself. And it was opened by someone who knew the sender would not be there herself to do it.'

Araki's anger was aimed at no-one but himself.

There was a sensible silence when Mariko was given

294

another pot of steaming sake and a plate of chewy, dried squid. Araki hit the table with his fist, a firm dull thump absorbed by a beer mat. His temple throbbed.

'She told me. The old hag actually told me.'

Mariko touched his arm, embarrassed for him.

'Told you what?' she asked gently.

'When I looked around your house in Todoroki, a couple of days after the dinner with your family, I asked Shimazaki where she thought your mother was.'

'And what did she say?' Mariko asked, strangely fascinated.

Araki looked sadly into her deep black eyes.

'She said your mother was dead.'

There was giggling in the bar, from an unseen corner where red-faced salarymen exchanged ribald stories and cursed their seniors.

Araki said, by way of summary, and in a voice pitched high in self-mockery, 'I thought it was just the semi-senile ramblings of a frail, fatalistic old housekeeper who had witnessed decades of wealth around and almost hoped her sentiments were true.'

Kondo placed his open palms on the table, a signal for him to interrupt.

'Your frail old housekeeper was not a confused old woman. I met today the man called Asato Yamada who was arrested in 1949 for helping suppress a workers' uprising in your grandfather, Daigoro Izumi's factories.' He had looked at Mariko when he spoke. Now, turning to Araki he continued, 'The house of this man, Asato Yamada, has been rebuilt in the last two years. It's owned by Inaba Financial Services, the consumer financing arm of Inaba Construction.'

Araki was excited and nodded knowingly.

When Mariko looked puzzled, he said, 'Many Japanese construction firms have their origins in the day-labour employment, palm-greasing of local and national politicians and territorial enforcement. Yuji Inaba, who's in his mid-seventies, was financed in the Fifties by the

295

Endo-gumi, a yakuza syndicate from urban Tokyo. They live off prostitution, pachinko, night-clubs and the supply of day labourers.'

Kondo took over. 'What we're saying is that the man Asato Yamada who served Izumi Electric in its difficult days, is being kept in his old age by a crime syndicate through its legitimate agent. The two men who intimidated Araki so unpleasantly in the Kana Club are yakuza from the same Endo-gumi syndicate.'

Kondo was dragging out his findings and hanging suppositions: Araki was becoming impatient, remembering a friend in trouble because of him and needing his help.

'We're aware of all that,' he said impatiently. 'What's new?'

'What's new,' the older man said, peeved. 'It is that there was a picture of Yamada's wall showing him with his cousin Yoshiko. It was your housekeeper, Yoshiko Shimazaki,' he said to Mariko with restrained emotion.

Kondo anticipated her question, which dumbfounded shock delayed.

'If Yamada is yakuza then Shimazaki-san's one too, simply by family association. She may not be active, may not even benefit from their earnings, but she is still a part of them.'

'But my father,' Mariko said aghast. 'He must have known.'

Kondo looked at Araki, who guessed there were unpleasant disclosures to come. He nodded for Kondo to continue.

'Your father was the seventh and last child of Goro Shimazaki from Yamanashi. He is three years older than your mother and he is your housekeeper's youngest brother.'

Kondo waited for a reaction but the last few minutes seemed to have inured Mariko to the emotional aftershocks.

'But all her brothers died in the war. She told me many times.' Her voice betrayed her hopeless desperation.

296

Kondo removed his notes from under a wet whisky glass.

'It appears the youngest, your father, survived, and he was contracted with his sister Yoshiko to the Izumi family.'

Mariko downed the sake and shook her head disbelievingly.

'I'm afraid it's true,' Kondo said sympathetically. 'Old Yamada was enjoying our conversation, a rare moment of relief it seems, and he corroborated the theory I had developed in the last two weeks. Your father was very intelligent and a brilliant businessman, and when he was selected to marry your mother he had no objections to losing Shimazaki and taking Izumi as his family name. The local authority records were duly changed and in the turmoil of war and the different priorities afterwards it never occurred to anyone to delve into his history. There was no reason why they should. He probably had nothing at all to do with the criminal side of his blood relations.'

'Until now,' Araki said cruelly, refilling Mariko's wafer-thin thimble with sake.

'But surely my father's not yakuza,' she said.

'We've got a lot to do tonight,' Araki said defensively. 'If his sister, your family housekeeper, is the blood cousin of a proud, old, retired yakuza, then so is he, although it doesn't mean he's been active. I don't think your father has been involved in Endo syndicate business since he became the chief executive of Izumi Electric. It's not an unusual situation, but I believe someone has been corrupted because of his or her origins and your family's wealth is the goal. It could be your brother. He introduced me to the two Endo-gumi thugs in the Kana and he might, or might not, be working with your father's sister, your housekeeper, who I now believe is in possession of your family seal.'

Mariko seemed suddenly ill at ease in the glamorous coral pink dress.

The mention of the Endo crime syndicate triggered

297

another circuit in Kondo's memory bank. He rummaged through a worn, soft-leather briefcase. He spread a sheaf of photographs on the table, drawing Mariko's recollection to the lobby of the Imperial Hotel and their surreptitious capture of the man who was putting pressure on her mother's elderly tenants, the Andos, to leave the last old house on the land his employers hoped to possess.

The image of the man with the narrow face, jutting jaw and surprised expression was of no legal value but Kondo had identified him through police sources without great difficulty by being able to isolate the man's business area. He had used his real name, Terashima, and a procession of telephone calls had found him at the Suwano Real Estate office in Toranomon.

Araki slapped his hands joyfully.

'That's where the dead banker Nakata went when Chris followed him from the Tekkei Bank.'

'Nakata went into the same building where the Suwano office is located,' Kondo corrected.

Araki was unrepentant. He said, 'It's not police evidence but it's enough of a coincidence for me. So who are Suwano?'

'I suppose we can call them all-purpose real-estate dealers on the fringe of respectability,' Kondo said authoritatively.

'More than the fringe,' Araki retorted. 'You didn't see what their men did to the front of that house in Nakameguro. That's jiage. Eviction with violence. Do you know who backs them?'

'The big banks don't normally touch them. They leave it to the smaller outfits like Tekkei, the savings and loan institutions, banks that borrow from their bigger brethren and on-lend at high margins to firms like Suwano who buy, sell and develop land.'

'Any interesting clients?'

'They do a lot of work for construction firms in the Tokyo fringe prefectures, mostly Saitama and Gumma.

The papers I've unearthed mention Kataoka Homes, Inaba Construction, Mizono Land Development . . . '

Araki seized the other's forearm.

'Say that again,' Araki demanded, his senses suddenly alerted. 'Those names. Suwano clients.'

'What were they?' Kondo said to himself, trying to reconstruct his thoughts, 'Mizono . . . Kataoka.'

'The other?' Araki said impatiently.

'Inaba. Inaba Construction. I'm sorry,' Kondo said, apologizing for not seeing the connection.

'The same as the people who built old Yamada's house,' he said to Mariko, 'from Saitama, specializing in putting up ten-storey office blocks where you wouldn't think it were possible. If there's a plot among some houses Yuji Inaba will organize a work gang to take in all the materials by hand.'

Mariko said, 'You obviously know him.'

Araki nodded.

'Construction's a favourite outlet for yakuza money. Nothing surreptitious. It's a well known fact. We're back to the Endo syndicate. They've also got a strong base in Saitama, the same as Inaba. I looked at them ten years ago when all the weekly magazines were having a superficial investigation of mob involvement in construction. Yuji Inaba was particularly interesting because of his clear connection with the old Endo godfather, Shimpei, I think his name was, or is. A former managing director of Inaba Construction is currently an Upper House member of the Diet, representing the governing party of course.'

They stared at their drinks in silence, Araki toying with a cigarette until Mariko took a book of matches from her handbag and lit it.

'I think it's time we went to the police with everything we know. This thing's getting too complicated,' he said.

Mariko's thinly covered arm was touching Araki's dark sports jacket and in the short, tense silence that followed his uncharacteristically despairing outburst he thought he sensed the muscles in her arm tense beneath the fabric.

She shook her head, but Araki did not know whether it was a response or simply to rearrange the trails of hair which had intruded across her cheeks. Finally, in a slightly reproving and disappointed tone, she said, 'Before we find out who is behind my mother's death?'

'It's not what I anticipated,' Araki answered, surprised at Mariko's sudden belligerency. 'The yakuza and some of their satellites are involved. They murdered the transvestite Chris led them to believe had your family seal, followed us around Tokyo assuming I've got the bloody thing or know where it is. Now we find your housekeeper is part of that very syndicate family that crushed the workers' uprising for your grandfather. They've now come to collect their reward.'

'After forty years?' Mariko said incredulously.

Araki's shoulders bobbed, leaving the explanation to Kondo.

'It goes back longer,' he said. 'Yoshiko Shimazaki was a teenager when she was given to your family to look after your mother. That was about eight years before the war. Your mother would have been about three. Word of the Izumi wealth probably passed from Shimazaki to her relatives and the knowledge stayed with them throughout the war until the opportunity arose to exploit. The labour problems at Izumi Electric gave the Endo syndicate the perfect chance to incur your family's obligation. They made the company operable, probably saving it from bankruptcy, and now they are claiming their prize. There's no time limit on your obligation. And to monitor their interests over the years they had a benign family member as housekeeper and have probably corrupted at least one member of yours.'

Mariko tapped the table helplessly.

'Look at Reiko, your sister-in-law,' Kondo continued. 'She's the slow-witted daughter of an Endo branch family whom your parents were persuaded to take as the bride for their eldest son.'

300

Araki said, 'And the big pay-off for them is your family seal on a pile of documents which would transfer buildings and land to the yakuza or their front agents.'

Mariko found the complicated plot too much to absorb and fought to comprehend the basic elements of the alleged conspiracy.

'Where does the money go?' she asked, hurt and shocked as the cruel facts and suppositions were laid before her. 'Surely we get something for the land you say we're selling.'

Araki said, 'If your family, or whoever is acting as your agent, is paid in cash it'll probably find its way back into syndicate hands through back-to-back deals. You might just be paid in promissory notes.' He looked at his watch.

'It's after nine. The Kana's in full swing.' By way of conclusion he said to Kondo, 'We're staying in Tsukiji tonight. It should be safe.'

As he steered Mariko towards his Toyota, Chris's words stayed with him. 'Why,' the Englishman had pleaded, 'if that housekeeper Shimazaki has the seal, why are the fucking yakuza still chasing us?'

One side of Araki's face ached as he strained to park his car between telegraph poles in a road of boutiques and clubs running parallel to the main Ginza thoroughfare. It was illegal, and the car's newly stoved-in front left side, with entrails of wire dangling from the crushed light socket, combined with its old and already battered state to give the impression of an abandoned wreck. Hostesses in colourful, exotic clothes hopped between assignments and knots of older, senior businessmen were reaching their bars after a meal with clients or colleagues. Ginza four-chome was not a playground for junior salarymen or Japan's wealthy young.

There was no flashing neon or crude sheet billboard. Only a barely visible plaque with two simply carved phonetic katakana characters. The dark, arched doorway gave anonymity to the politicians and company presidents who took their seats in the padded, soft, discreetly sheltered corners. Mariko had highlighted her cheekbones in soft orange and brushed her hair until it shone and lay in cascades across her shoulders, hiding the straps of her evening dress. She could have been the actress-companion of a company president, but the kimono-clad door attendant hid her opinion of her escort, with his scarred, swollen face and ill-fitting jacket with scuffed pockets, behind a vacuous mask of politeness as she accepted his name-card and request to see Mayumi Maeda. Araki wanted a clear view of the door and pre-empted the directions of the girl by occupying with Mariko a low sofa in a reception area by the entrance. Mariko again went to her purse for a match and cupped Araki's fingers as she lit his cigarette.

'Is this how they do it for you?' she said playfully.

He responded with a smile but it was shallow and brief and betrayed the growing fear for himself and the woman who had sought his help. The task of finding her mother completed, he should have presented the facts to the police, both those he knew for certain and those he speculated. And while part of his mind sought a way of bringing the killers and their conspirators into the hands of the police, a tiny sector of his brain was sending another message. Something was not in the pattern. He had to clear Chris of the killing he had provoked when he suspected Reiko Izumi of stealing the seal and giving it to her supplier so that he could sell it back to the family or the highest bidder as if he had found it in the street. To clear Chris, he had to bargain possession of the seal, or knowledge of its whereabouts, in return for a confession. A minor Endo-gumi trooper could be sacrificed at little cost and the chosen one would do so willingly knowing that his family would be cared for while he was in prison and a healthy payment and job awaited his release. But Chris was right. If the

302

housekeeper Shimazaki was part of the conspiracy, and she had retrieved the seal from the mail on that cold March morning, why wasn't it now in the hands of her yakuza relatives? The lure of the seal, and the fortune it controlled, transcended family loyalties. Araki drank from the complimentary glass of whisky and piled ice. Mariko was in profile, her sharp jaw raised, her lips curving downwards at the corners, her slight overbite exposing the tip of her teeth. She looked strong, in control and strangely aloof.

Mayumi Maeda wore an ankle-length silk gown which wrapped her body in sari-like bands and was moulded tightly to her slender, trim figure. Mariko turned her head slowly to the newcomer. Araki had not shown her the photograph of her father with Mayumi but she knew instinctively that this elegant woman in her late thirties was her father's mistress.

'You have your father's high nose,' Mayumi said disarmingly after they had been introduced. Her voice was also cold and distant. The two women talked with the polite distance of rivals. Araki remembered the level of intimacy he had witnessed between Mariko's brother Ken and Mayumi Maeda. The presence of the two yakuza, Yano and Sugishita, had bothered neither of them when Ken had brought him to the Kana. When Yano and his dangerous colleague had menaced him in the toilet that evening, they claimed to be representing the Izumi family. But which member? Araki mused. Ken, his father, both of them? Or Reiko with her lowlife connections? Which ruthless relative of the murdered woman coveted the wealth invested in possession of her registered seal? Whoever it was, Araki knew that the woman with the deeply dyed hair, the foreigner's colour, old Bando had called it, and the mature immaculately made-up face was the last person to be seen with the dead woman. Araki looked at his watch, more to check the passage of time than the hour. If this club was a meeting place for the conspirators, then a message to their harder side would not be far away. It came sooner than Araki had expected.

'Would you excuse me for a moment,' Mayumi Maeda said. 'I have to greet a guest.'

Araki raised a restraining hand.

'It won't take a moment,' he said, his voice falling a degree of politeness. 'I'd prefer you to stay.'

Mayumi had half-risen from her chair but fell back after she had assessed the threat.

Araki said, 'I have information that you met Masako Izumi outside the Tekkei Bank on her last known day alive and you drove away with her.'

Mayumi Maeda's face was impassive, her early solicitous smile now eradicated.

'That's a serious allegation,' she said lamely, after a pause.

'What you think doesn't bother me,' Araki said without faltering. 'Tomorrow the police will be told everything.'

Mayumi sipped at an orange-coloured drink through a plastic straw.

'Why not today?' she asked casually, shifting her weight nervously.

'Because I want to talk to your oyabun.' He used the underworld word which implied leader, as of a crime syndicate or group of conspirators. 'I want to exchange the Izumi family seal for the murderer of Masako Izumi.'

Araki sensed Mariko's puzzlement while his eyes stayed fixed on the woman opposite. A pair of elderly men were led past by a hostess, who stopped and lowered her mouth to Mayumi Maeda's ear. Mayumi nodded gently and then spoke back at the pale nape of the beautiful, young escort. Araki heard nothing, but suspected that the rapid exchange was more than talk about the new arrivals.

'There's a lot to discuss,' Maeda said after the hostess had left. 'Would you like another drink?'

Araki declined with a rueful smile.

'Do you know Tsukiji fish market?' he asked.

304

'Tsukiji? Of course. Higashi Ginza.' She looked puzzled.

'There's an auction pit at one end. Tell your principals that I'll be there at seven tomorrow morning. I suggest you come yourself as it's crowded and I don't want to waste time looking around. We can negotiate the future of the seal and the surrender of Masako Izumi's killer.'

The natural, built-in vagueness of Japanese, the absence of definite or even indefinite articles, worked to Araki's advantage as he floated the hint, the tantalizing suggestion, that he may or may not have the seal. He did not wait for an acknowledgement. None seemed necessary. He touched Mariko's elbow and steered her towards the door, and when she was far enough ahead of him, already on the carpeted stairs leading to the street, he turned abruptly and faced Mayumi Maeda. Reaching into his pocket he took out the buff envelope and removed the contents. 'This is yours,' he said, tossing the incriminating photograph of the Izumi patriarch and his naked companion on to the table. 'You have a very attractive body. It sure enslaved old man Izumi. You used the picture to entice his wife into your car. The second envelope, the one Chris found in the garbage at the villa, contained some money she hoped to pay you off with.'

'What did you say to her?' Mariko asked as they retraced their course, half-running, half-walking along the outrageously gaudy streets.

'Nothing. I wanted a book of matches.'

More than one stroller cast a second look at the couple. It looked as if Araki was dragging the beautiful woman in the tight, pink cocktail dress.

They had rounded a corner into the road where the car was left, when Araki pulled up and shoved Mariko roughly into a doorway.

Mariko gasped, clutching her light, open coat at the neck.

'What's the matter?'

'Policemen. Two of them looking into my car.' He looked cautiously around the window corner.

'Shit,' he said to himself. And then to Mariko, 'They're looking at the damage. One of them's talking on his radio.' He took her arm. 'Let's go.'

Sugishita was sharpening a straight flat knife which had only the slightest of angles between the tip and lower blade. Yano took the call and then bellowed across the room.

'They're in the Kana. Araki and the Izumi daughter Mariko.'

'Liar,' Sugishita said pleasantly, an eye closed as he examined the blade in the glare of a table lamp.

'They are,' Yano said urgently. 'Get ready. Now.'

A third man appeared at the door. Wearing a tight baseball warm-up jacket he was of even heavier build than Sugishita, with a round, boyish face below a head cropped to little more than a dark stain.

Yano emerged in jeans and training shoes and jacket. He was weighing a short, stubby revolver in a hand and wedged it into his belt when he reached the door. Sugishita joined the other two, sliding his short-sword tenderly into a leather scabbard sewn into his loose jacket.

Araki sought the anonymity of the evening revellers and the last, tired salarymen, dropping into the broad, low-ceilinged passages which dissect the area below Ginza. They walked from the Sony Building to where the underground routes diverged, one heading for Nihonbashi, the other to east Ginza. As they walked, they looked among the dark, uniform heads for the harder faces of the Endo-gumi foot soldiers Araki knew were close. Mariko stopped at the entrance to the Ginza-line subway, at the bank of red telephones next to the automatic ticket dispensers.

'I must call my sister. I haven't spoken to anyone in the family for two days. I don't want them to worry. You know. Like they did for my mother.' Araki smiled with compassion, but inside his heart raced. He was desperate

306

to reach the sanctuary of the hotel only a few hundred metres away and watched impatiently as Mariko turned her back to him and slipped a ten-yen coin into the red box. Conscious of the people around, Araki backtracked, alert for the pursuers he knew had been summoned by Mayumi Maeda. He wondered whether she had managed to get a message to them while he and Mariko were in the Kana. If she had, then Sugishita and his smoother, more dangerous partner were not far behind. He bought cigarettes and matches in a kiosk and watched idly as sombrely suited salarymen side-stepped the prostrate shape of a bearded, ragged vagrant. The passage to east Ginza continued beyond the four-chome crossing, heading for the bay and an area of exhibition centres, markets and warehouses and suddenly became free of the shoppers, drinkers and casual Ginza strollers.

'We'll go this way,' Araki said when Mariko had finished.

Hurriedly they walked to the second exit, and surfaced near the Kabuki theatre.

'How is Shinobu?' Araki asked, as he guided Mariko down a shopping street criss-crossed with red and yellow lanterns.

'Excuse me?' Mariko said surprised.

'Shinobu. Your sister. How is she coping with the stress from your mother's death?'

'Oh fine,' she said finally. 'It has been a relief for all of us but it will take time to heal the wound. Particularly for Shinobu. She's incredibly sensitive.'

The coloured lights and lanterns gave way to narrow streets of shops and intimate bars. They could hear the nearby hum of cars surfacing on the expressway as it cut through east Ginza. There were few short-time love-hotels in the area, most having moved to the suburban stations or inner city play districts in the north and west, but somehow the Swallow had survived amid the encroaching, tall, modern buildings. A steep-sided drainage canal with a lethargic shallow flow bordered one side of the road. The Swallow was three hundred metres from the main east Ginza road in a row of shops which included, Araki noted ironically to himself, a craftsman's shop selling seals. It was set back from the street just beyond the part where the hanging lighting ended, its entrance guarded by a pair of stone pillars with a squatting lion atop. A lantern illuminated a sign displaying the prices for a short and all-night stay and beckoned along a short path of raised, irregularly embedded stones.

Araki pushed a ten-thousand-yen note across the counter and in return fingers emerged sliding a key through the gap below an opaque, blackened screen which half-covered a hole in the wall of a dimly-lit, furniture-free lobby. Nobody waited in the lobby of the Swallow.

'Is the gaijin here?' Araki asked, bending low so that his breath warmed the screen.

'How should I know?' a squeaky, irreverent voice replied. 'This window guarantees my customers' discretion.'

'Crap,' Araki snapped. 'You can see through your side of the fucking window. It's me, Araki.'

'Gomen, gomen,' the condescending voice said in apology. 'He's in twenty-one.'

A new wing, a three-storey, ferro-concrete annexe had been added to the back of the old wooden structure which fronted the street and the canal. There were muted voices, chilling squeals and the sounds of recorded voices.

'Interesting,' Mariko said teasingly as they passed through a corridor to a brighter maze of apartments. 'Have you booked us for a quickie or the night?'

Araki ignored her, placing an ear to the door before opening room twenty-three.

'Leave the light off for a moment,' he said, peering gingerly around the edge of the window frame and, satisfied that there was no immediate threat from the drab offices in darkness opposite, drew the plain, dark-blue curtains.

308

Mariko bounced on the king-sized western-style bed and then looked around the room, commenting with childish glee at the ceiling mirrors, the television with its remote control and collection of films stacked on the video unit below the screen.

'You seem to be at home,' Mariko said, stretching on the bed, a knee rising slowly, rubbing the inside of her thigh before sliding back to the cover.

It was not distaste Araki detected in her voice, nor sarcasm or reproval, but he was suddenly sure that this was not the first love-hotel for Mariko. Even the people who lived alone, the office girls and the salarymen in company dormitory housing, enjoyed so little privacy from the paper-thin walls and back-to-back housing where knowing your neighbours personal habits was part of the social harmony process. The love-hotel was an institution, an outlet for lustful, natural release. But if she had lived since her return from Hawaii in the thick-shelled mansion block, she would never have had the need to steal a few hours in a purpose-built sex palace. Araki felt he should explain. 'I used to bed down here when I needed to be near a story in the Ginza.'

'When you worked for the *Tokyo Weekly*?' Mariko asked.

'That's right,' Araki said.

There was a dull knock on the door. Mariko sprang upwards.

Araki rose to calm her. 'I ordered some food,' he said, reaching for the telephone.

He called Chris, who arrived quickly, a hungry look on his tired face. He had bathed and shaved and wore the hotel's cheap cotton gown.

'You weren't followed?' the Englishman asked, his eyes passing from the steaming bowls on the lounge table to the body of Mariko Izumi whose usual modesty had succumbed to the carelessness of numbing tiredness. Mariko raised a hand in greeting and a brief embarrassed smile. The two men ate greedily from bowls of tempura-ed

309

shrimps on rice and talked in quiet voices, mixing English and Japanese in a manner Mariko could not follow. They nodded in a kind of final, knowing gesture when Mariko joined them and accepted a fat, yellow shrimp from Araki's chopsticks. Chris finished a glass of icy Sapporo Dry beer and left, a little reluctantly, Araki thought, persuaded that he should rest before the six-o'clock call he had requested from the hotel management.

'I'm so tired,' Mariko sighed when Chris had left.

Araki asked, 'Are you still hungry? I can get Kaneda to bring in some more food.'

Mariko's head moved languidly sideways.

'I'm too tired. I'll just take a bath.'

The bathroom was out of sight around a corner and when Mariko turned into it the light filtered through the wavy glass door and illuminated the alcove.

Araki lay in the depression made by Mariko on the vast bed. His body was drained of energy but it quickly relaxed and his confused mind wandered. He turned on his side, staring at the wisps of steam seeping into the room through the bottom edge of the hidden glass door and thinking of the woman cleansing herself a few metres away. His body stirred, and he turned on his side. As if to torment him, Mariko emerged from the bathroom, a towel folded around her, clutching a bundle of clothes. She giggled, apologizing for the embarrassment of the situation, and laid her underwear and dress over the back of a reclining chair. Araki returned the smile as she retreated, wondering whether she relished the danger of their situation and the possibility that the confrontation he had designed for the early morning might provoke a violent reaction from the impatient forces that were conspiring against her and were desperate to claim the fingerful of carved ivory that held the key to the Izumi fortune. He had slept for four hours in the last thirty-six and as his mind began to hallucinate he wondered where he would find the strength to protect her against the yakuza and somehow persuade her tormentors to offer one of them as a sacrifice to free Chris from the accusation of murder. His hand moved involuntarily to the chair, to the tiny heap of still warm underwear, and found a silky mass, actually Mariko's tights, running through his fingers. There was another involuntary stirring, a dulled rush of physical affection for the body of the person he was committed to help. His mind wandered, wondering what kind of men she took to her apartment. Were they foreigners, like Chris, with the kind talk and charm that so enchanted Japanese women who passed from puberty to adulthood under the influence of soft French and Italian films. Perhaps not, after Hawaii and the baby. But he could not imagine her with a Japanese salaryman. It would have to be someone from the fashion world or fringe professions like advertising or entertainment.

Craving a cigarette, he tugged a Hi-lite from his shirt pocket, groaned and then smiled as he saw his newly bought matches on the table among the empty food bowls. He felt separated from his legs when they did not respond to the signals he was sending. He looked the other way and saw Mariko's handbag within reach on the chair with her clothes, and remembered pleasantly that twice the Izumi daughter had lit his cigarette from matches she usefully kept in her bag. Clumsily, his arm reached out and found the strap of the plain, white bag and dragged it to the bed. His fingers found a clip and as he stared blearily upwards they rummaged in search of the book of matches Mariko had used to timely effect like a practised bar girl. He heard the click of make-up holders, perhaps lipsticks and eye-shadow, touching. He felt the soft texture of a packet of tissues or a handkerchief and then the sharp corner and loose cover of what he assumed was the book of matches. It was trapped loosely under a velvet-smooth box which slipped against his fingers. Both came out in his hand, the small, purple jewel-holder rolling across his chest when it fell from his hand. He lit the cigarette and looked down his chin in bored stupor

311

towards the tiny box. A ring? No, the box wasn't square. It was rectangular with a hooded, semi-circular lid. He assumed it was Mariko's personal seal, the one she would use to withdraw money from her bank account or testify to the receipt of a registered parcel, and it was little more than boredom that led his thumb to flip the lid and reveal the contents.

Araki's exhausted body stirred, his senses abruptly shaken. He lifted himself slowly from the stupor, his eyes focusing on the finger-sized object, and realized he had been mistaken about the personal seal. His fingers ran across the smooth surface. Then he froze. The crash of water on tiles had stopped. Araki's hand closed around the box. There was silence from the bathroom. Mariko had washed and slipped into the soothing water in the shoulder-high tub. Opening his hand slowly, tremulously, Araki saw that it was a seal, but not the slender, plain kind used for everyday authorizations. It was slightly longer, certainly broader and had a perfectly rounded tip. Araki lifted it from its velvet cocoon as if it would disintegrate. It was made of pure ivory, a rich, light tan in colour. Araki ran a finger over the single ideograph carved into the instrument's tip, and in the less than adequate light from the slim lamp above the bed examined the way the nine strokes had been personalized with delicate cuts and minute flourishes. It still bore traces of deep-red ink, evidence of an earlier, rare use. Izumi was a common name, and an everyday seal could be purchased at the neighbourhood shop, like the one next to their love-hotel. But the registered seal was unique, carved with precision and invested with frightening authority. Araki weighed it in his hand, the key to the Izumi land and fortune. His skin tingled with excitement before giving way to a swelling surge of anger and resentment. Then the muffled sound of splashing water disturbed him, and he rushed to return the registered seal, snapping shut its velvet container and replacing it in Mariko's handbag. A twist in the strap was still unravelling when Mariko emerged

312

from the bathroom, a sky-blue towel wrapped around her and tucked at the front. Her wet hair sparkled, her legs shone from the heat of the water and she exuded the fresh perfume of flowers.

'I topped up the water for you,' she said, tipping her head to one side and tapping it to dislodge some water from her ear. She mistook Araki's aloof, distracted look for simple weariness.

'Let me feel your shoulders,' she said, springing on to the bed. She began to knead his neck and back with the heels of her hands. Araki flinched.

'The muscles are tight. You're tired and very tense. Please take a hot bath. It has been a long day and a half.'

Araki took another look across the yard, searching in the dark recesses for a threat he knew was there somewhere but now was also working from within. The situation had changed and where he had started from a position of weakness he had moved to dominance and now, in a moment of furtive exploration, back to uncertainty.

'Please,' Mariko pleaded. 'You must relax.'

Sitting on a plastic stool, he shampooed his thinning hair and washed himself thoroughly, dousing himself with ladles of hot water from the tub before again dragging the cloth angrily across his shoulders and back. He felt a passionate urge to scour himself, to purge himself by inflicting punishment on his body for the failures of his mind. Cleansed of the long day's grime he stepped into the steaming bath. It was deep and long, designed to be shared according to the special needs of the love-hotel's clients. The flowery scent of Mariko hung in the hazy steam and, where before it would have suggested her lithe model's body, it now seemed to mock him and recall her deception, the calculated web of lies and diversions she had conjured up to hide from him the fact that all the time she had the seal. But to what end? How could she turn assets

313

the seal controlled into hers? Angrily, he turned on the hot-water tap, relishing in the near-boiling flow as it spread through the bath and spilled over the rim on to the patterned tiles. His tired mind was clouded. He had sought the seal, chased the wrong person and probably caused a death and been deceived by the one member of the Izumi clan he believed to be honest and decent. And now, having manipulated him with the ease of a master of a slave, Mariko Izumi was in possession of the key to her family's wealth and was planning some last devilish, climactic act. Steam rose in bursts of thick, lazy clouds, filling the room in a sultry, misty half-light. Turning off the tap he leaned back, his neck resting on the rim, his legs buoyant in the deep water. His thoughts were drifting and he almost missed the light, metallic rasp as the sliding door of the bathroom was opened. He tensed, seeing nothing in the misted mirror until the ghostly human form emerged from the steam and knelt behind him. He was conscious of the stupidity of his position, and if it had a knife it could have cut his throat with ease and from the advantage point behind and above him could have forced him under the water until he choked and bled to death. He reached out and with both hands grasped the porcelain edges of the bath, his muscles stiffening as he prepared to force himself upwards. Hands closed around his neck, pressing inwards. He felt a tingle, and then a rush of tensile pressure which ran down his spine to his feet.

'Don't move yet,' she said. There are no words in Japanese to complete an endearment with 'beloved' or 'dearest' or in the extreme 'my love' but Mariko's mellow voice contained within the simple demand a depth of compassion which transcended the superficial western expressions and came close to what might pass as an expression of love in Japan. Her fingers dug into his shoulders and a cascade of damp hair fell across him as she reached forward to claw his pounding chest playfully.

314

Araki squirmed helplessly, his body responding to the delicate, perfumed assault his mind fought to resist. Her breath was cool on his neck and he felt first the hardness and then the spongy softness of her breasts on his skin. 'Let's rest,' she whispered. 'Before the final day.'

12

The telephone purred but Araki was already awake and stopped the call with one swift movement. Mariko stirred and her warm, naked buttocks touched his legs. She was on her side, hands crossed in front of her breasts which rose and fell with gentle, even swells. He wanted to twist and tug again the trails of silky hair and bite and tease the ripples of womanhood she had given to him before he had buried himself within her as they fought, concealing for ever the frightening truths of their passion at the final release. Araki slid from the bed. He looked across at the handbag and then at his own jacket, with the bulge in the cloth where it overhung the chair. He smiled. A last, desperately sad smile of futile affection.

The bonnet of the sleek, dark-mauve Mercedes rippled as it waited by the bloomless cherry trees along the outer palace moat where it met Aoyama-dori by the National Theatre. Behind it, a Toyota sedan held four men: the heavy Endo-gumi driver in the baseball cap; Goto, nervous, the choreographer of the morning's plan; and Yano and Sugishita, cynical killers who saw no difference and suffered no pangs of conscience at having murdered a defenceless woman and a pitiful transvestite who had no connection at all with the Izumi fortune. In the Mercedes, behind an impassive, uniformed driver and a narrow-faced, lithe bodyguard who was committed to die before his oya, sat Shimpei Endo, his thin figure draped in a thick overcoat, and Yoshio Suwano, Endo's boyhood friend and now director of the syndicate's real-estate arm.

Endo was nervous. He disliked the pre-dawn stillness, the chill, and the demand to appear in the vulnerable surroundings of Tokyo's enormous wholesale fish market. Suwano was relieved and a constant smile stretched the broad, purple lips on his angular face. He tapped the brief-case covering his lap and tried to reassure his friend.

'I have most of the documents we need to complete the transfer of the Nakameguro site and the land in Koto and Taito wards. Don't worry. We'll have the rest soon. Within the next two hours we'll have the seal.'

Endo stared ahead and sniffed through a cold nose.

'What about the Tekkei Bank papers? The back-to-back loan agreements.'

Suwano had already explained once, when they had met an hour earlier at five o'clock, when the air was cold enough to mist their breath.

'That fool Nakata's suicide has distracted the inspectors from the Finance Ministry. If we can get the seal to the bank today we're safe. It's been close, but we're going to be safe.'

Endo finally grinned and looked instinctively back-wards to the unlit car behind.

'Take the seal,' he said, 'and get our friend out of the area.' He looked at his watch. 'He's late. Get the documents legalized and call me tonight. Disappear quickly because Araki, and that fucking gaijin if he's with him, are going to study the fish more closely.'

A car flashed its lights at the deserted intersection. The driver checked the rear-view mirror of the rare, low-slung Jaguar, and drove in front of the lead car, stopped and extinguished the lights. Endo and Suwano left their vehicle to greet the passengers. The usual exchange of greetings was foregone. They were all tired, tense and saw the forthcoming exchange as the culmination of a year's planning which almost went awry because of a lapse of attention of the guards and the stubborn de-termination and self-control of an old woman who had despatched her treasure seal out of reach of her pursuers.

317

The newcomer's normal, full, tanned face looked drawn and fatigued in the unflattering light inside the car. Mayumi Maeda sat next to him, hunched inside a heavy coat, staring silently over the driver's shoulder.

Suwano's face peered in like an eager child looking for his present. 'Did you get the documents?' he said, reading the younger man's smile and breaking into a broad grin.

'They're all here,' the man with trim, permed hair said, indicating a slim, leather briefcase. 'The original deeds to the properties we are selling or lodging as collateral.' He looked towards the two cars, his face now anxious. 'Did you gather the cash?'

'It's not easy to raise a hundred million in cash after the banks close.'

The driver of the Jaguar's jaw dropped.

'But we found it.' Suwano, a finger loosely picking out one of the sedans inside which were two briefcases, the size of chart bags carried by airline pilots and packed with ten-thousand-yen notes.

The syndicate chief, Shimpei Endo, clutched his padded arms in protest at the chill April dawn and said gruffly, 'Let's get to the market. We've enough money here to buy all the fucking fish in the place.'

'Don't forget your handbag,' Araki said warily as they prepared to leave the room.

Chris joined them in the sparse lobby, looking refreshed but nervous, a camera over his shoulder, the baseball cap set firmly on his head. Araki tapped on the shaded window and heard a grunt of acknowledgement. 'It's only a kilometre but I'm not taking the chance of being picked up by the police at this stage,' he said as they waited in the doorway for the Honda hatchback, their shoulders huddled against the chillness.

'The old man will take us. He says it will make us quits.'

Standing in the darkness in the entrance to a love-hotel, the trio formed a curious portrait to the casual few

318

who passed by, probably on their way to the wholesale markets. A tall man, possibly a gaijin, in a baseball cap and sneakers; another man, a Japanese, tieless but wearing a creased suit, with a rough, harassed, furtive look; and an attractive woman in a bright evening dress and a light jacket inappropriate against the crisp breeze whipping off the Sumida River, unseen four blocks away. A pornographic photo session, one rider concluded to his satisfaction, noting the expensive Nikon on the gaijin's shoulder.

In the short ride to the market they discussed the flimsy plan and the roles each would play. How Araki would look for Mayumi Maeda, and meet through her the person who had conceived the entire vile, flawed plot and had come into the open only because he needed the tiny piece of carved ivory in order to appropriate the immense fortune which had been under the control of the murdered woman. And Araki would only disclose what he knew in return for the murderer. Chris would drift through the market like a foreign tourist, of which there would be the odd group, snapping pictures of the criminals where he could. Mariko would stay out of sight, possibly on the gangways from where the auctioneers had been selling the produce to the buyers in the pit, and try to identify the players from the other team. But Araki knew it was a lie, just like the affection he felt in the warmth from Mariko's body as they sat cramped in the back of the car. The Izumi seal was not possessed by an elderly housekeeper looking for a buyer: it was a brief hand motion away, in the handbag clutched tightly by his beautiful companion. How would Mayumi Maeda's murderous companions react when they saw he had nothing to offer? What was Mariko's plan, having encouraged his suicidal confrontation? Why did she insist on accompanying him? She already had the seal. What else did she want?

'You're cold,' Mariko said, as they crossed Harumi-dori, already busy with utility vans and refrigerated lorries.

319

He wanted to touch her, to stare into those dark, intelligent eyes and tell her he didn't care what plan she had as long as he could be part of it. But he gazed ahead, directing the driver towards the rumble of engines and the cacophony of men and women at work before the first light of dawn.

Araki knew the central wholesale market well. The early hours following an all-night drinking session in the Ginza would find him in the cheap eateries on the edge of the market, snacking on sushi and rousing himself with a pot or two of hot sake. Ignoring the fruit and vegetable section, he would watch the fish auctions at half past five, marvel at the motions of hands and fingers which decided the destination of the lots among the fifteen hundred middlemen, representatives from retail chains and food processors, and the hundreds of wholesalers who carried their goods a few metres to their stalls where, between seven and eleven in the morning, they sold to the smaller fishmongers and restaurant owners. There would be several thousand people in the market today, giving Araki, Chris and their dangerous friend some comfort by numbers. Almost all the fresh and frozen produce arrives by lorry but the market is bordered on three sides by water: the Sumida River, and two docks dug to receive the fishing boats and coasters and still laid with the now rusting tracks for the trains which also supplied the market. The group left the hole-in-the-wall cafés, with the tired market workers, identified by the rubber boots and aprons, still sucking from the bowls of steaming noodles, and edged between the rows of restaurant vans and the refrigerated delivery trucks which packed the concourses leading to the auction pits and the row upon row of wholesaler's stalls.

They walked in a broken line between tubs of red and orange octopus, writhing eels, displays of striped bonito and stalls selling twenty varieties of bright red, white and pink shellfish, freshly scraped from their covers, and prawns and shrimps, cooked, shelled or still wriggling in

320

a sawdust bed. Sushi shop owners, wrapped against the early morning chill, compared cuts of turbot, yellowtail and jackfish, or selected a live specimen and let the fishmonger despatch it with a heavy blade and wrap it with speed and skill. At the narrow crossings an orderly chaos prevailed. Motorized carts and hand-pulled trolleys followed some unwritten traffic code which the workers on foot respected and the casual visitor, often foreign, quickly learned. Everywhere the air was chilled by the constant running water and stacks of ice, and reeked of the diesel fumes from the ubiquitous carts with their unique barrel-shaped engine and steering unit. Buffeted, and gruffly scolded by the uncompromising, strong-backed workers, the group reached a wider path which led to the docks and bordered a series of circular areas, deserted now except for clusters of market officials tallying up their records. There was still a clutch of gutted frozen tuna carcases in the auction pit Araki chose. Stripped of head and tail-fin the heavy, bloated pods, some the length of a man, awaited removal to the specialists with their mechanical, high-speed saws, their hooks and their cleavers, where they would be cut and packaged in marketable sizes for the shops and restaurants.

Chris split off, mingling with the workers and observers near the carcase of a three-metre shark and a large ray, while Araki led Mariko up the worn, wooden stairs from where the auctioneers had dominated the packed proceedings until minutes earlier. They withdrew into a recess, giving them a broad view of the area while largely concealed themselves. Stacks of polystyrene boxes, brimming with fish and seafood packed on crushed ice, rattled past on trolleys or the noxious, barrel-driven carts. Araki looked at his watch. There were still fifteen minutes before the appointed hour of seven. He knew the message he had given Mayumi Maeda would be delivered: he could only wonder who would appear.

321

*   *   *

The Mercedes and the Toyota pulled on to a forecourt off the dual carriageway which led to East Shimbashi. The Jaguar stayed on the main road, its driver sitting impassively behind the steering wheel while Mayumi Maeda, the collar of a thick jacket pulled over her hair, led her tall, stocky companion, a slim briefcase hanging from each hand. Ahead of them, the four Endo-gumi troopers marshalled by Goto, were stripping off their shoes and replacing them with rubber boots from the boot of their car. Sugishita wrapped a flannel sweatband around his scalp. With their loose, waterproof jackets and short brushy haircuts they could have been market workers, which indeed was the intention. Another man emerged from between two fish trucks and handed Sugishita a short stick with a curved, steel-tipped pick which the real workers used to drag the frozen carcasses of the tuna.

The disguises were complete. Suwano seemed reluctant to release the broad chart case but he did, in return for the two cases of documents. Endo joined them and spoke to a man from the Jaguar.

'Araki wants our men in return for the seal.'

The other joined him in an enthusiastic burst of laughter. 'As you know,' Endo continued, 'the situation has changed. My men will have a different response. It's better you are not aware of it,' he said to the taciturn man in the black overcoat. 'Please leave the area once you have met the other parties.'

Sugishita strode purposefully into the fringes of the market, his fingers opening and closing around the shaft of his weapon-tool.

'Araki's mine,' he said to the others, in case there was any doubt.

Dawn announced itself as a dim greyness in the gap between the market's corrugated roof and the edge of the dock.

322

'Where do you think the police are?' Mariko murmured, her body close to Araki's. 'They're here,' Araki said confidently. 'You got through to Sasaki?' Araki asked easily, his attention on two men who carried the tools of the market worker but seemed to have no apparent task.

'Of course, you asked me to. When you went to take your bath.' She clutched his arm. 'It took some time before I convinced the duty officer to track him down. I got him at home.'

Araki looked at his companion. Her hands played nervously with the straps of her bag and she seemed to be trying to avoid Araki's eyes. He was about to tell her she was a liar, that he had checked with the love-hotel's owner and found no-one had telephoned from his room, when she seized his arm, pointing to a crowded pavement near a stack of fish crates.

'There's the man who was in my apartment. The fat one.'

'Sugishita,' Araki added. 'And over there, by that pile of tuna heads.'

He pointed over the railings, his concentration on the man with the black overcoat and familiar permed hair. They shrank involuntarily further into the recess. He would not remember the moment he realized Mariko was not at his side. There were the usual market noises and then a flash from a camera in the corner, and in an instant the figure of Mariko dashing across the auction pit and down a cobbled path leading to the maze of stalls towards a man dressed more for the Marunouchi financial district than the free-for-all fish market. Araki cursed, his hand grasping instinctively at the tiny package in the pocket of his suit jacket, and jumped the unsteady stairs in pairs. Men looked up and around, their six-day week a hard, hectic routine rarely disturbed by the antics of outsiders. They saw a woman, slim, tall and as attractive as a film actress, struggle for a foothold on the damp cobbles and then a small group of their colleagues rushing towards the

323

man who stood lost beside the frosty pod of a frozen tuna carcase.

'This way!' Chris shouted in English, the only way he could attract Araki's attention amid the din of echoing voices and rumbling motorized carts. The two men dodged a trolley.

'Mariko went off with some guy,' the Englishman gasped. 'They've got her.'

'No they haven't,' Araki said calmly, his mind trying to focus, to interpret the implications of the last few, momentous seconds. 'She's just met her own brother.'

'Jesus!'

Araki's arm chopped the air as he tried to package the events into a logical sequence.

'So Ken Izumi, not his father the widower, planned the expropriation of his mother's authority and probably unwittingly her death. Or let's say he was manipulated by the heirs of those who saved his company from extinction and now demanded their reward. He enticed his father into the honey trap of Mayumi Maeda, neutralized him, along with his sister Shinobu and his addict wife Reiko. And thought he had enough on his sister to ensure her compliance and silence.'

'But she fought back,' Chris said.

'Fought back and went on the attack,' Araki retorted drily.

He looked around, suddenly frightened by the crowded, intimidating market.

'She fought them because she has the seal, and instead of waving it around, showing her family and the police that her mother had made a last gesture to save her fortune, she kept it and has just trekked off with it and her mother's killers.'

A commotion interrupted them. Brandishing the steel-tipped stave Sugishita was trying to push his way between the stallholders and their clients. He shoved a woman and knocked over a tub of live eels. Yano peeled away from his colleague, his eyes on Chris. There were shouts of protest from market people, mild at first, as if the speakers expected an apology after a routine occurrence, but rising when the traders realized an unusual incident was in progress.

Araki screamed in English, 'Break!' and they separated, the Englishman moving towards the light which indicated the edge of the indoor market, Araki sidestepping a stack of cases packed with mackerel.

Araki lacked the ruthlessness and determination of his pursuer, who elbowed unfortunate bystanders aside and when he saw Araki stumbling apologetically among the cartons he raised the pick menacingly. Market men in waterproof aprons gathered their women and hustled them inside the booths at the back of stalls. Araki's heart raced as his mind fought to disengage the fantasy from the reality. He had anticipated a verbal confrontation of some kind, perhaps with abuse, even some ill-tempered shoving, and that was why he had chosen the most public of places for the final meeting. He had never expected an open attack by the demented killer of his client's mother. Sugishita was near enough for Araki to hear the big man's demands for him to stop and fight. He turned in his panic into a narrower alley where the stalls encroached so close he had to sidle between them, bumping the stacks of crates. Not realizing what was happening, the storeholders grunted their disapproval. Sugishita was closing in and at one point his enthusiasm caused him to misjudge the distance to his foe, and a naked bulb hanging from a low beam shattered as he swung his vicious club recklessly. There was a wall at the end of the alley, one side of the old market; the alley spur Araki had chosen ended there. He stopped, then staggered involuntarily, falling helplessly on to a low stack of fish boxes, spilling their slippery contents. He was soaked with icy water but hardly noticed. There were screams and curses around him, but they seemed disembodied, as if he and Sugishita were alone in a still-life tabloid which could only have one ending. The

325

killer gangster charged through the polystyrene boxes, his hooked weapon flaying and scattering piles of fish, his prey only metres away. Araki was on his knees, but soon found his feet again. He broke into a cabin at the rear of the stall, scattering bills and other bits of paper and stumbled through a canvas curtain into the rear of the stall on the other side. Startled faces turned on him. Four men, not hearing the pandemonium above the fierce whine of the long, slim vertical blade, were moving the frozen tuna carcasses from carts to a cutting slab. They bellowed ferocious warnings, pointing at the shimmering blade. Araki was off-balance and he fell into a paunchy worker with a stained head-band and cracked yellow teeth. A second later there was a wrenching sound and a flash of steel as the pick tore through the canvas sheet. Sugishita's reddened face shone with sweat and was creased with rage and hatred. His passage was momentarily stymied as he stooped to unhook his weapon. Seeing the danger from the saw, he side-stepped the cutting table and launched himself at Araki, overturning a rack of cleavers, long-staved hooks and other implements. Men scattered, slipping on the cobbled ground now strewn with ice. Women shrieked in their panic. Araki heard nothing, sensed only an instant of dream sequence where his legs were immobile and his screams for help unheard as his pursuer approached. He was on his knees again, victim to the treacherous surface, and as he tried to scramble away he felt the first blow and the stab of pain as his flesh was punctured. But Sugishita was also struggling to keep his feet and was off-balance when he swung the lethal hook.

Araki slithered out of reach, avoiding by an arm's length a backhand swipe. As he rose awkwardly and painfully, and feeling for the wound beneath the growing patch of crimson on his calf, his hand found a long-handled cleaver used for breaking through bone and cartilage. He faced his adversary, who stopped to assess the situation which had suddenly turned against

326

him. Sugishita's scowl returned, his confidence renewed. Araki swung the heavy weapon in a demented gesture of fierce anger. He was alone, frightened to death and within him only his instincts for survival remained, not fear of the consequences. Sugishita grinned, changed his pick to his left hand and withdrew his short knife from the scabbard inside his jacket. He took another step towards Araki, jabbing the air with his weapons, grunting provocative noises and then inviting his frightened prey to approach. Araki swung again, forcing Sugishita to reach backwards, his guard dropping. The broad cleaver sliced a box of squid, spraying ice and inky particles, and its momentum pulled Araki off-balance, the handle breaking out of his right-hand grip. In his rage he sank his hand into a squirming heap and hurled a handful of flesh and tentacles at the advancing Sugishita, who recoiled as the mess hit him on the side of his head. Araki gripped the blade and charged forward, though when the opportunity to strike arose, his courage failed and the final swing was feeble, the blow landing with the flat of the blade. Sugishita bellowed with pain and rage, dropping the hook and struggling to keep his balance on the treacherous floor. His anger had unnerved him, wrecking his already ragged reflexes and, when the moment called for a final, supreme effort of control, the gangster was unable to respond. The cobblestones were as ice, Sugishita's shoes skimmed off them and he lurched backwards, startled.

Araki would be exonerated by the witnesses who had tentatively regrouped within sight of the incident. One of them said he saw Sugishita stumble without control at least four paces backwards before his legs gave way and he collapsed against the whirring teeth of the vertical saw. The force thrust him upright before his body settled on the vicious razor which cut into his skull and shoulders with ludicrous ease. Blood, brain tissue and bits of clothing showered the area and Araki thought he saw a look of bemused indifference on the face of the Endo-gumi murderer whose own moment of reckoning had arrived.

*   *   *

Stunned at seeing her brother in the company of the men
Araki claimed had killed their mother, Mariko allowed
herself to be hustled away. She looked back, too shocked
and harried to protest, and was soon pressing through
the knots of tradesmen and restauranteurs loading their
utility vans, her brother's hand gripping her arm painfully. They crossed a bridge over a drainage canal and
hurried past the packed cafés and shops already open
to serve the market. The taxi-driver hired to wait at
the main Harumi-dori intersection saw them approach
and released the rear door in acknowledgement. It was
quieter on the fringe of the market and the police-sirens
had a distinct, clear resonance in the fresh, dawn air.
Ken Izumi looked up once and then bustled his sister
into the taxi, followed by the black briefcase which
he lifted with two hands on to the seat beside her.

'The seal,' he growled, the sirens now shrill and close.

Mariko's shaking hand fumbled with the clip of her bag.

'Quickly,' her brother barked urgently. Once the velvet
box was in his hand, he thought for an instant of opening
it and looking at the priceless tool but the wailing of the
sirens was drawn out and loud. The police were near
the market. The taxi-door slammed and Mariko was
gone. Ken Izumi pulled up the collar of his coat and
hurried to his car.

In the principal forecourt, where the workers had
stopped as word reached them that there was an incident
in the market, the rear doors of a large van, painted
with the trademark of a well-known sea-food wholesaler,
open and grey-uniformed police officers poured out. Four
hundred metres away a cordon of policemen approached
the market, their goal to seal the exits. They were late.
The detectives in the market, suitably disguised, had
misread the way the situation would develop: they had
been advised to expect a routine rounding up of suspects
and were slow to give the order to move in when the
suspects separated.

Chris found himself on the disused wharf, suddenly free from the congested, claustrophobic, odorous fish market. Across the dock he could see a sparkling of security lights in the garden of the Hama detached palace. Then he heard voices behind him, ordering him to stop with fierce, guttural shrieks. Silhouetted in the light from the strings of naked bulbs Chris saw two men who broke into a trot when they saw they had his attention. He set off himself, running along the edge of the dock whose oily, still water shimmered beneath him in the pale, dawn light. At a point where there was an access route back to the covered market and the safety he craved, Chris shuddered to a halt. He did not remember hearing the crack from Yano's pistol or feeling the entry of the bullet, but he was conscious of his inability to move, in spite of a desire. His right leg was numb and when he looked down he saw the hole in his trousers, just below the buttock. As a dark cloud of red began to spread, a spasm of pain engulfed him. There were more shots which he did not hear. He fell to his knees, his hands searching for the source of the pain and he rolled uncontrollably over the edge of the wharf into the vile, stagnant water of the dock.

Epilogue

Araki skimmed a popular weekly magazine without much interest, his coffee untouched for twenty minutes. It had been five days before the call he knew would come finally rang on his answering machine. The voice was calm, precise and uncompromising. 'The Hakozaki Air Terminal. Third floor departure lounge. Twenty-sixth of April. Two o'clock.'

Ken Izumi was taken into custody two hours after returning home, the seal still in his possession. The charges would be conspiracy to murder amongst others. The godfather, Shimpei Endo, and his real-estate manipulator friend, Yoshio Suwano, were caught as they returned to their car, unable to explain why they were in possession of property deeds belonging to the Izumi family. Their solitary bodyguard, Goto, drew a short-sword but his boss ordered him to surrender as the phalanx of police officers swarmed around the Mercedes and their support car. Yano was shot twice by the two police officers who had seen him chase and shoot the Englishman. He died later in hospital. His colleague in the baseball cap surrendered when his colleague fell. The murderers of Masako Izumi and the transvestite Hayato were dead, their masters charged with conspiracy to murder, intimidation, bribery of local authority functionaries and ten other charges.

Araki's individual pursuit was condemned by the police authorities in the form of Inspector Sasaki, who expressed outrage at the mayhem and bloodshed which brought discredit to his force in the eyes of the public. In the end, privately, he congratulated Araki's tenacity and trusted

330

he would prosper from the experience. The magazine article he was reading in the cafeteria of the departure lounge gave lurid and graphic details of the incident the previous week and listed the arrests. They included the head of the Honshinkyo religious order, who was indicted for unauthorized building activities and falsifying authorizations and permits. Araki did not pursue a charge of assault. Under interrogation, he had assured the police that Mariko had helped him unreservedly and at some personal danger. They were separated in the market but she had managed to escape her brother and the Endo mobsters, unlike Chris and himself.

She wore a grey two-piece suit, with culottes and loose, long-sleeved jacket, its two buttons undone to show a black plain blouse. Comfortable clothing, as Araki thought, for a long aeroplane journey. Her hair had been trimmed severely and a pair of sunglasses hid the dark, intelligent eyes Araki had often longed to see again. Mariko sat demurely, hands in her lap, and by the chair a traveller's collapsible hand-trolley holding a small bag and a larger, sharp-cornered black briefcase. A Japan Air Lines baggage identification tag hung limply from the travel bag.

'How's Chris?' Mariko asked, as if they were discussing a friend suffering from a cold.

'He'll be fine. He managed to hang on to an old mooring ring. He was only in the water a couple of minutes. He sends his regards.'

She ordered coffee but left it untouched, with Araki's.

'Are you all right?' she asked with sadness.

Araki nodded. 'A bit bruised. I haven't touched fish for a while.'

They both smiled, but Mariko's faded quickly.

'Thank you for not implicating me,' she said weakly, but sincerely.

'There's nothing to thank me for. You weren't involved in your mother's death or your brother's plan to take over

331

her assets and sell them to the Endo-gumi once he had the seal. Their bad luck began when your mother escaped and despatched the seal before Sugishita caught her. Anyone could have received it. As fate had it, you were the only person at home when the envelope arrived.'

'When did you start to suspect me?'

Araki tapped his cigarette on the ashtray.

'It was Chris really,' he said. 'He kept asking why you happened to turn up at the Kawaguchi chalet like you did. It was an unfortunate coincidence wasn't it? But you hid your surprise at finding us there very well. I assume you were looking for the photograph and any other evidence your brother was using to control you and ensure you were not interested in pursuing a claim to the seal. You didn't want the story of your illegitimate son to embarrass either you or the reputation of your family.'

Mariko nodded, her eyes watching him with intensity.

'Chris also asked why, if the housekeeper was related to the crime syndicates who rescued your grandfather's company after the war, why, if she had the seal, didn't she hand it over to her relatives in the Endo-gumi. It should have been obvious. She didn't have it. Your father, as Shimazaki-san's brother, was of course also connected to the syndicate by background, but I know that neither of them had been influenced by the yakuza since the war. Shimpei Endo and his network chose to collect their debt by corrupting Ken Izumi, your brother. They made Mayumi Maeda your father's mistress in order to manipulate him and used the Kawaguchi villa for most of their plotting.'

Araki lifted her cup. He said, 'It's cold. Would you like another one?'

'No thank you,' she said, checking her watch. 'I'm on the three o'clock bus to the airport.'

'Hawaii?'

Mariko nodded, a sad smile creasing her face.

'Is that why you kept the seal so long?'

Again Mariko nodded. 'I saw the chance to find my son again. The seal could liberate me, give me enough money, if I used it properly, to set me up in business in Hawaii and start again. I needed the month to get the necessary visa and other permissions which would allow me to stay on the islands.'

'So you waited until I found out who was behind the plot against the family property and contacted them, offering them the seal in return for cash or perhaps the seal on some of the deeds they held.'

Mariko looked surprised.

'How did you know that?'

'After we left the Kana, in the underground passage beneath Ginza, you stopped to call your sister Shinobu. You didn't call her, did you? You rang the Kana and spoke to Mayumi Maeda again. You had the number because I saw you take a book of matches on the way out. You told her you had the seal and wished to do a private deal with the other side and so you devised another plan for the market. And Chris called your sister from the hotel, and asked her, amongst other things, whether she had heard from you lately. "Not for three days," Shinobu said.

'That call to Mayumi Maeda was almost mine and Chris's death sentence,' he said without bitterness.

'I'm sorry,' she murmured, and after a pause, 'When did you switch the seals?'

Araki gave an ironic chuckle.

'Kondo had a phony seal made up ten days ago in case we needed to show people how different it was from your common all-purpose chop. We had no idea how Izumi was carved on your registered seal but it was made large enough and with a fairly distinct Chinese character which might buy us a few hours if needed. Fortunately your brother didn't have time to verify it when you gave him the one I switched in the bedroom while you were in the bathroom at the hotel before we left for the market. The police have given the real registered seal to your father. He sends his thanks for

333

keeping it safe and asks you to contact him when you are settled.'

Mariko gave him a fleeting smile that fell short of admiration. She said, 'Did you find the seal in my purse before we . . . '

'Yes. Before.' Araki conceded in muted undertones.

For the first time she laughed aloud, a girlish, unfettered outburst which jogged the sunglasses off her nose. Behind the opaque lenses Mariko's eyes were pink around the rims and the light dab of make-up stained with moist trails. 'That's why you were a little cool towards me at first,' she said, replacing the glasses.

'Will your son be at the airport to meet you?'

'Of course,' she said, her expression brightening.

'In that case,' Araki said, reaching across to an empty chair. 'This is for him.' He handed her a package in a well-known book-store's wrapping. Mariko held it as if it would break.

'What is it?'

Araki was almost embarrassed. 'I asked my son what an eight-year-old Japanese boy would want. He said a book on baseball. I'm afraid it's in Japanese.'

'That's all right,' Mariko said hurriedly. 'He's going to learn our language properly.'

A voice on an unseen loudspeaker echoed around the concourse, calling for passengers for the three-o'clock limousine bus to Narita.

Mariko tapped her knees.

'That's me,' she said, avoiding his eyes.

'Let me help you to the gate,' Araki's voice caught in his throat. He seized the heavy trolley.

'Take the black bag off,' Mariko ordered. 'That's for you.'

He unclipped the elastic straps and lifted the heavy chart case off the frame.

'Just a second,' he said, 'I have to pay.' He hurried to the cashier on the other side of a pillar with his bill and tossed some coins on to a tray. When he returned Mariko

334

was already at the first check-in point, at the foot of an escalator, unburdened now from the bulky bag. He looked at the chart case and rushed to the ticket gate. An arm restrained him. 'Passengers only beyond this point,' a woman admonished.

He watched the monotonous empty escalator for a minute and when he knew it was hopeless he carried the heavy bag to a red payphone.

The telephone was answered immediately and after a pause Inspector Sasaki's firm voice greeted him.

'I never realized how much a hundred million yen weighs,' Araki said, forcing a laugh.